APOSTLES OF MERCY

APOSTLES

OF MERCY

LINDSAY
ELLIS

ST. MARTIN'S PRESS

NEW YORK

First published in the United States by St. Martin's Press, an imprint of St. Martin's Publishing Group

APOSTLES OF MERCY. Copyright © 2024 by Lindsay Ellis. All rights reserved. Printed in the United States of America. For information, address St. Martin's Publishing Group, 120 Broadway, New York, NY 10271.

www.stmartins.com

The Library of Congress Cataloging-in-Publication Data is available upon request.

ISBN 978-1-250-27456-4 (hardcover)
ISBN 978-1-250-27457-1 (ebook)

Our books may be purchased in bulk for promotional, educational, or business use. Please contact your local bookseller or the Macmillan Corporate and Premium Sales Department at 1-800-221-7945, extension 5442, or by email at MacmillanSpecialMarkets@macmillan.com.

First Edition: 2024

10 9 8 7 6 5 4 3 2 1

For Christopher

APOSTLES OF MERCY

Lorenzo nearly tripped and fell into the mud as he tore out of his friend Jojo's front door and into the wet street. The rain had come early this year, not that he would have stopped to grab his poncho even if he had brought it with him. He just ran, scarcely able to see in the darkness, flailing toward his house as fast as his legs would carry him. The rain was heavy, and warm, and washed his friends' blood off him.

Philomena, he thought, feeling his pocket to make sure his rosary was still there. Lorenzo was of an age where the only reason he ever had his rosary on him was because his *lola* would be disappointed if he didn't, but at this moment, it felt like the sole thread tethering him to this world. A demon had killed his friends. Now, it was coming for him. Prayer was the only thing that would save him.

"Philomena!" he cried as he ran. She was his mother's favorite saint, and the one she prayed to most often, but that didn't feel right. A distant bolt of lightning illuminated the street in front of him, and for an instant, it was as bright as day, showing him a clear and unobstructed path to his house. He sped toward it, not thinking about what it might mean to lead the monster right to his parents, to his *lola*, to his sister. But what else could he do? Had he not actually seen his friends effectively get dismembered? It all happened so quickly—before they had even known it was in the room with them, it grabbed Jojo, then Lito. He had moved to grab Jojo's baseball bat to fend the demon back, but before he could grab it, the demon had brought Jojo's neck to its mouth and—

Lorenzo nearly stumbled at the memory, still not truly accepting that his friends were dead. The demon only had two hands, and there had been three boys in the room; therefore, Lorenzo had gotten away, saved by virtue of not being as close to the window as his friends had been when the creature came inside, silent as a snake. It seemed almost impossible that something so big could be so quiet, that it could be on top of them the instant they even realized it was there.

Lorenzo made it to his house, slamming into his front door—*locked!* "*Nanay, Tatay!*" he cried to his parents. Why locked? They usually never locked their door, but they had heard of things, evil spirits in the woods, and started locking the door to calm his little sister's fears. *Of course—his parents didn't know he was out. Hopeless!* This was hopeless, and that's why Saint Philomena felt wrong; she wasn't who to pray to when things were hopeless. It hadn't occurred to him because he had never truly experienced hopelessness in his young life. When he didn't hear an answer from his parents, he cried to the heavens, "*San Judas, San Tadeo, San Tadeo, tulong! Sagipin mo ago!*" *Save me, Saint Jude, save me.*

He banged on the door, screaming and crying and turning his head every which way to scan for the demon. He didn't immediately see it, and when the door didn't open, he ran for the tree by the house that his father had nailed a couple of boards to for easier climbing. He stumbled onto the tree, climbed one step, then another. He turned around just in time to see the demon on the other side of the road, illuminated by a flash of lightning, blood still dripping from its maw.

This demon seemed more armored than the smaller one had been, which itself he and his friends had initially mistaken for a crocodile. If the bigger demon could be compared to a crocodile, it would be a saltwater one from Australia or some long-extinct giant species, nothing like the little ones found in the rivers nearby. Both of them had that grayish-black skin that looked like a wet suit, but where the smaller one had eyes that were black and empty, this one had yellow eyes that lit up like bulbs in the light of the storm.

The thing moved with supernatural speed and had traversed the distance between his neighbors' house and his position on the tree in an instant. When he felt it grab his leg, he lost his grip, and it was only his rib cage getting stuck in the V between two strong branches that prevented him from being torn from the tree altogether. He scrambled to hold on to the tree, and again, he felt a tug, more violent this time, then he heard a howl as the creature let him go.

Out of the corner of his eye, he saw that someone had attacked the demon with a baseball bat, his *father* had attacked it with a baseball bat. Lorenzo grabbed once more on to the bark of the tree, focusing on that as he climbed out of arm's reach of the demon, repeating to himself, "*San Tadeo, San Tadeo, sagipin mo ago, sagipin mo ago!*"

The branches of the tree were slick, like climbing a giant wet noodle, and he nearly slipped a couple of times before he chanced a look at the ground. In those few seconds, half a dozen of his neighbors had come into the street, wielding whatever they had close by to take the monster down—baseball bats, axes, machetes, and even a couple of rifles. A dozen more neighbors were either getting their bearings or were on their way, flashing torches wildly into the storm, but none of them knew what they were dealing with. Lorenzo yelled at them to run, to get away, but his voice was drowned out by the rain and thunder and shouting below.

One man lunged at the creature, only to be caught in midair and thrown into a tree, his back making a horrible thud on impact. Another, whom he recognized as Jojo's father, hacked madly at the creature. He got a few hits in, slicing into the thing like slabs of old meat before the monster grabbed him by the neck, hurled him to the ground, and tackled him, opening its jaws and taking one large, loud bite so hard Lorenzo could hear the crunching even up in the tree.

More and more men from the village attacked, which gave the monster only more and more fodder to burn through. Even a tiger the same size would have fallen several times over after the pummeling it had taken, but not this thing. It had nearly a dozen people lying at its feet, injured, dead or dying, before it finally showed some sign of slowing. Then one of the men on the ground saw an opportunity, and using his machete almost like a javelin, he skewered the monster right through its neck. It failed to grab the man as blood spurted out of the wound, illuminating the mud with red when another flash of lightning passed overhead. The man raised the machete and brought it down on the demon's neck like an executioner—once, twice, and the third time brought it down for good.

Lorenzo wanted to stay put, away where no one could see, where no one could ask what he had done to bring this horror down on their village. His six-year-old sister, Clarinda, knew what he and his friends had done, but would she tell? Lorenzo scanned the small crowd forming a semicircle around the demon, but he didn't see his father. He fell out of the tree, stumbling toward his neighbor, who was still hacking away at the demon's neck. Another flash of lightning revealed how much blood the man was covered in—not his but the demon's, and in the back of his mind, Lorenzo couldn't help but wonder, *What kind of demon bleeds like we do?*

He saw his mother, too shocked at the situation to begin to take stock of the carnage on the road in front of their house. Others were trickling out into the rain, realizing that their family and neighbors were lying in the road, victims of the same demon that had come for him and his friends.

Then he heard his mother's voice crying, "*Rodrigo, Rodrigo!*" with a level of despair that could mean only one thing. He ran toward her, hoping that perhaps this was an overreaction, that she was mistaken, that this wasn't his father lying dead in the mud by the side of the road.

But it was. His father's face was partially illuminated by the light coming out of their front door just a few yards away, as was the wound to his neck. The muscles in his face were slack, his eyes unfocused, and what the demon had done to his neck no person could survive.

Lorenzo wanted to say something, do something, pray for this to be undone, but he was rooted in place, still as stone and just as numb. This had to be a nightmare, because if it wasn't, it was divine punishment, and now his father had paid the ultimate price for his sins. His, and his friends', who had tried to fight demons. And now . . .

"*Kasalanan namin ito,*" he muttered as he watched his mother hunch over his father's body, her back heaving with sobs. *We did this.*

We did this. He thought it over and over, like a prayer. *We did this.*

PART 1

. . . .

SHE'S NOT A GIRL
WHO MISSES MUCH

September 23, 2009

And before we judge of them too harshly we must remember what ruthless and utter destruction our own species has wrought, not only upon animals, such as the vanished bison and the dodo, but upon its inferior races. The Tasmanians, in spite of their human likeness, were entirely swept out of existence in a war of extermination waged by European immigrants, in the space of fifty years. Are we such apostles of mercy as to complain if the Martians warred in the same spirit?

—H. G. Wells, *The War of the Worlds*

The Guardian

Kaveh Mazandarani, Political Lightning Rod and Brilliant Mind, Dead at 35

BY IJEOMA OKERE

April 20, 2008

T he Iranian American journalist Kaveh Mazandarani was well known for much of his adult life – certainly to anyone following the increasingly invasive methods of U.S. intelligence gathering and the treatment of its immigrant populations in the years following 9/11. But the terrible circumstances of his death brought him instant notoriety, positioning him either as a martyr or a traitor to the human race, depending on one's politics.

Mazandarani spent much of his career critical both of his native country and his adopted one. However, he always insisted that he did not see himself as a dissident but as a patriot – both Iranian and American.

Born in Tehran, Mazandarani fled his home with his family in 1979 when he was only five years old. "Kaveh used to talk about how the theocracy in Iran couldn't last, because that kind of oppressive regime just isn't sustainable in the long run," an American friend recalled. "He often longed to return home, like any exile."

Mazandarani studied journalism at the University of California, Berkeley, before receiving a Rhodes Scholarship to pursue his graduate studies in political science at Oxford. His collaboration with Nils Ortega exposing secret CIA black sites in the Middle East and Asia and uncovering mass human rights abuses earned him international acclaim and helped influence sweeping reforms in U.S. intelligence gathering. Like Ortega, Mazandarani was a lifelong advocate for increased government transparency, although the two drifted apart later in their careers as Ortega's methods became more controversial and radical.

The final chapter of Mazandarani's life began a few months before his death with a chance meeting with Cora Sabino, the eldest daughter of Mazandarani's former collaborator, Nils Ortega. Only Sabino, the sole surviving human witness, knows exactly what happened in those seconds surrounding Mazandarani's death, but this is what the public at large knows based on video and forensic evidence: Mazandarani and Sabino were alone in the San Bernardino County desert with two amygdaline ETIs, known to us by their "human" names, Jude Atheatos and Nikola Sassanian, who appeared to be somehow incapacitated, where they were followed by four gunmen driving two trucks. At 7:24 P.M., the two trucks suffered an electrical shortage roughly two hundred meters from Mazandarani, Sabino, and the two ETIs. What caused the shortage is still unknown, but given the circumstances (as well as the fact that the shortage occurred in the two vehicles simultaneously, an astronomically improbable occurrence), we can assume that the shortage was caused by an alien electromagnetic pulse, perhaps to stop the gunmen from advancing farther.

The gunmen, however, did not stop when their trucks did. They continued on foot and, between 7:25 P.M. and 7:27 P.M., unleashed 128 bullets between the four of them. Recently released footage taken by a U.S. Air Force helicopter shows Mazandarani trying to rouse Nikola Sassanian, the larger of the two ETIs, when one of those 128 bullets struck Mazandarani in the back of the head, killing him instantly.

Immediately after his death, there was a push for disinformation, that Sassanian acted aggressively before Mazandarani was killed or even that it was Sassanian who killed Mazandarani; it wasn't. I illustrate this moment-by-moment recap of events first to dispel the notion that it was some sort of shoot-out, rather than the one-sided attack that it was. It is true that one or both of the amygdaline ETIs killed the gunman, but only after Mazandarani was shot and killed, and the instruments they used were, perhaps poetically, the gunmen's own bullets.

In his brilliant final essay, published posthumously in *The New Yorker*, "A Fiction Agreed Upon," Mazandarani makes a passionate plea for recognizing the personhood of ETIs while chronicling his fascinating relationship with Sassanian as his case study, arguing that humanity's refusal to do so would only serve as the greater reason why our civilization may not survive in the long term, first contact or no.

Mazandarani lost his life because of his connection to an ETI, but his death was not at their hands; it was at our own.

· 1 ·

Paris Wells looked at her watch for the third time in the last minute, her 2:00 P.M. now almost twenty minutes late. She'd made over a dozen inquiries to Cora Sabino, Cora Sabino's people, and Cora Sabino's people's people before the girl finally relented and agreed to meet with her at a bar in the financial district. Not an interview, just a meeting, a conversation, a testing of the waters, but by now, she was having serious doubts Cora would show up. After all, she'd successfully avoided Paris for more than a year. Why stop now?

A no-show would almost be a relief, to be honest; Paris didn't know if she'd be able to conceal her many and complicated feelings about Cora Sabino in the interest of unbiased journalism. When Kaveh had given Paris his essay wrapped in a neat manila package, he had told her to make sure it got delivered to his editors at *The New Yorker* "if anything happens." She'd known then that whatever was in that manila folder could get him deported, imprisoned, or worse, but the danger as she understood it stemmed from the weight of his words, not the possibility that his head would take up the wrong square foot of space at the wrong instant. She never entertained the idea that "anything" could mean his death.

And now the last person who had seen him alive had agreed to meet with her. The selfish witness to a government cover-up who had a habit of fleeing when doing otherwise might reflect poorly on her. The careless accessory to murder, the reason Kaveh was dead. After all, he had abandoned his plans to skip the country for her. Because, as a ten-foot-tall space monster had told Kaveh the night before he died, she needed him.

"*You who love her so dearly,*" Nikola had said. "*Who take care of her needs so well.*"

She glanced out of the window and was surprised to see her—source? Interviewee?—her 2:00 P.M. arrive nineteen minutes late, scanning the faces inside the bar with unmasked dread. Paris stood up to make herself easier to spot—she wasn't the only Black woman her age inside this bar, after all, and Cora may not even know what she looked like.

"Nice to finally meet you," she said as Cora approached her, looking the part of a sleep-deprived college student played by a noticeably older actress. She shook Paris's hand limply, took off her wool jacket and knitted red beret-looking thing, and sat in the booth.

"Can I get you a drink?" asked Paris, not taking her seat.

"Sure," she said, eyes to the window as if she were expecting a brick to fly through it.

"What's your poison?"

"Um, you can choose."

"Okay—beer, wine, cocktail, tequila shots?"

"Cocktail."

Paris ordered an IPA for herself and a whiskey sour for her 2:00 P.M.—the fancy kind made with egg whites instead of sour mix—while her guest continued holding herself like an abused circus animal relocated to a sanctuary that wasn't itself a huge improvement. A couple of minutes later, Paris returned with their drinks, pushing the sour in front of Cora.

"You've been difficult to get ahold of."

"I know," said Cora tersely.

"So what changed your mind?"

Cora looked at the sour. "I suppose there aren't a huge number of people in this world who deserve an explanation."

Paris straightened. "You feel like you owe me an explanation?"

"I'm not saying I, personally, owe you anything. I don't know you. But you deserve one, and I'm the only person who can give you one. So here I am."

"Thank you," said Paris, relaxing her shoulders and taking a long swig of her IPA.

"I know I cannot legally compel you to make anything we say off the record, but I would ask that you keep this conversation off the record."

"Of course." Paris felt herself softening. Bleeding heart that she was, she couldn't help but wonder what this girl had been through since Kaveh's death to make her like this. "I had no intention of putting anything on the record."

"So you're working on a story for *The New Yorker*?"

"I hope so."

"I thought you were an associate editor there."

"Not at the moment. Indefinite hiatus." Paris was unable to keep the bitterness out of that last word.

"What happened?"

"Well, sort of a one-two punch. Kaveh's death alone I probably could have pushed through, but my dad died not two months later."

"I'm so sorry."

"Yeah. Kaveh left me some of his assets, thinking he was going into exile, not that he was going to die. But I had money, so I said screw it, I have to have some time to heal from all this before I'm able to write again."

Cora looked at the whiskey sour she had not touched. "Who are you with?"

"Freelance Enterprises Inc.," said Paris, pointing two finger guns at herself. "Congratulations, by the way."

"For what?"

"For Columbia. I was on the basketball team for a minute at NYU, although as you know, Columbia is our historical enemy."

"NYU has a basketball team?"

Paris chuckled. "The Columbia team's taunt for us was, 'Safety school!'"

Cora didn't even begin to crack a smile. "It was what Kaveh wanted," she said mechanically, like she'd used this phrase so often it had lost all meaning.

"I hope they aren't cutting you with tuition," said Paris.

"I have a trust that pays my tuition."

"Oh . . . does that mean—"

"My lawyers say I can't disclose any details."

Paris didn't know how much of this was just natural churlishness, but her nonanswer confirmed Paris's suspicion that the "trust" had likely been set up by Kaveh before he died. "I have to ask . . . I understand why you—*they*—chose Japan to seek asylum in, but . . . did you know doing that would effectively kill the Third Option?"

"No," said Cora, almost cutting her off. Eighteen months ago, it was a practical inevitability that Congressman Jano Miranda's Third Option, a bill that would have created a separate subcategory for "personhood" under which extraterrestrial intelligence would be classified, would become the law of the land. Kaveh's *New Yorker* essay froze it in its tracks, but Japan's refusal to extradite any ETIs to a country that did not legally consider them "people" killed it. After all, you can't try a nonperson for murder.

"It was purely about survival," said Cora. "It had nothing to do with affecting policy. I just . . . they . . . Jude . . . neither of them were . . . they were both sick. I couldn't take care of them by myself. I needed help."

"And Japan helped?"

"A few of their eccentric billionaires did. Money can't cure all ills, but . . ."

"And Jude has been doing better since—"

"Just tell me—" Cora cut her off, collected herself, and continued. "Just tell me what you want from me."

"Well, if I'm being honest, it's not you who I want," said Paris coolly as she pulled out Kaveh's journal. "Do you recognize this?"

"Yes." Cora looked at it, seeming to be running through some interior Rolodex of what humiliatingly intimate details he might have written about her.

Paris slid the book across the table, and Cora looked at her like she'd just slid her the *Necronomicon*. "Aren't you curious?"

"You said it didn't have anything to do with me," said Cora.

"I said it wasn't you who I'm after. I wouldn't be talking to you if it didn't have anything to do with you." Paris opened the journal to the page she had bookmarked, and Cora hesitated before looking at it. "Did you ever see this?"

"N . . . no," she said. "They were his private journals. I never asked to see them."

Paris held her gaze for a moment, and Cora quavered slightly before looking down at the pages. "It looks like a to-do list."

"*Two* lists. Is there anything about this second one that you find interesting?"

"It's just a repetition," said Cora. "He always wrote his notes in a weird code in case they got confiscated, but he never showed me what his code was."

"I know that," said Paris gently. "This second list is identical, but it doesn't have the strokes of a ballpoint. It's almost like it came from a printer instead of a pen." She tapped her index finger on the duplicate list. "I think Nikola wrote this."

"Maybe. So?"

"Kaveh had this journal with him every time he was with Nikola at Los Alamitos, but he wrote his notes in his own feral-child language. It's completely indecipherable. There's only one person in the world who knows what these notes mean or at least what was happening when they were written."

Cora looked at her like she'd just proposed opening a restaurant that served human flesh. "He's hospitalized four people."

"You mean besides the people he killed?"

"Yes," said Cora, growing irritated. "The people he killed were killed, not hospitalized."

"At least he hasn't killed anyone else."

"You want to push your luck?"

Paris leaned back against the booth and took a long draft of her beer, scrutinizing Cora, who sipped her whiskey sour like she thought it might be roofied. She was just so . . . sad. Not sad in a "boo-hoo" kind of way but sad in a "this is how eighteen months of international attention hailing you as a hero slash damning you as a traitor to the human race chips away at one's psyche" kind of way. It was one thing to know that this cruel, uninvited sort of fame must wreak havoc on a body, but it was quite another to see it.

"Why did Jude turn Nikola over to the feds after Japan extradited them? They're . . . space aliens. Why play by our rules?"

"Nikola killed four people. And I needed help—food, shelter, the bottom rung of Maslow's Hierarchy of Needs—I just couldn't get those things off the grid with Jude in the condition he was in."

"So they changed the law to extradite for a trial that didn't even end up happening," said Paris, chuckling dryly. It had cost the DA his job, and it was one of the most controversial decisions to come out of the whole mess. But there was footage of the killings taken by a military helicopter that showed exactly the order that the events had happened—at least one of those aliens surely had killed those men, but only *after* those men popped off over a hundred rounds. *After* they killed Kaveh. The DA knew that a trial would be a complete waste of time with such concrete evidence of self-defense, even if that self-defense had been alien telekinesis so advanced it may as well be magic. A team of lawyers had taken a plea deal on Nikola's behalf, and he had been tucked away into a custom-made mental institution ever since.

"We didn't know that would happen. It's just, someone had to look after Nikola while Jude . . . worked on his own issues. Bella Terra takes better care of Nikola than we could. And either way, it's a better setup for Nikola to be in an institution. Jude can't look after him, he . . ." She stopped herself. "It's good that Nikola has a facility that looks after him. Even if he's a danger to anyone who enters it."

"I'm not asking to help in his rehabilitation," said Paris. "But he's still the only person left alive who knows what was happening when these journal entries were written."

"Okay, but . . . so what? In the extremely unlikely event that Nikola cooperates and tells you whatever he and Kaveh talked about—and believe me, he won't—what good would that do?"

Paris finished her beer in two long gulps and placed it on the table in front of her, just short of a slam. "Julian hasn't even been president for a year, and he's already asking for a year-over-year budget increase in defense spending of 9.5 percent—that's a bigger increase than after 9/11, a bigger increase than almost any year on record since World War II. And all this during the biggest depression since the Great One."

She placed her elbows on the table and leaned forward, causing Cora to stiffen. "We are living in a country where everyone is just taking it as a given that increasing our firepower will protect us in the decades to come from a hostile alien civilization, and you and I both know that's not true. Right?"

It took several awkward seconds for Cora to give a stiff, forced nod in the affirmative.

"Kaveh wrote about a civilization that will strike first and ask questions later if they perceive a threat," Paris continued. "But that threat may not be completely imaginary or hypothetical—if the amygdalines show up and we come out guns a-blazing, they have every right to assume the worst. Right?"

"How will talking to Nikola change any of that?"

"People are afraid to push back against what Julian is doing because they can't offer any viable alternatives, because they don't understand the existential threat we are facing. But Nikola does. Firepower won't save us. I don't know what will, but firepower ain't it. We have nothing to lose by trying to push a more nuanced narrative. Worst-case scenario—the world burns in slightly less ignorance."

Cora looked at the journal like she might be sick and closed it. "I imagine it would also be incredibly lucrative."

"I imagine it would be," said Paris, taking the journal off the table and stuffing it into her bag. "If I were planning on selling this as a book. For now, all I want is an essay, same as Kaveh did. I want to continue what he started. I think this is what he would want."

"Well, there is no 'what he wants,' because he's dead," said Cora. Paris half expected her to walk that back, cringe, and withdraw into awkwardness, but she had turned to ice. "Any 'what he would want' that you decide on is just a construct you made up, because what he wants doesn't exist anymore."

"Actually, what he wants—what he *would* want—very much does matter," said Paris, a plume of anger flaring at what she could only read as disrespect. "You just told me that the sole reason you decided to go to Columbia was because it was what Kaveh wanted. So how is this any different? Do you think we just go about our lives completely irrespective of everything that came before us? When people die, are they just forgotten?"

A glassy red film spreading over Cora's eyes doused that plume of anger, and Paris reminded herself that even if her world had been demolished by Kaveh's death, at least she hadn't had to watch him die.

"There is some catharsis in honoring the wishes of the dead," said Paris gently. "You're right that we can't know what those wishes would be for sure. We can only make our best guess. But we do it in good faith . . . because we loved them."

Cora sat stone-still, as if any movement might unleash the wall of emotion she was holding back. Then the iPhone on the table buzzed, and her hand flew to it like a cobra. Paris didn't catch who the message was from, but she did get a glimpse of the message itself:

> Dear one, I want you to come to me.

The two looked at each other, and Paris caught more than a hint of shame. Either Cora had some new Ivy League paramour who spoke in a stilted manner that bordered on Victorian, or Jude Atheatos was feeling . . . *better.*

"I have to go," said Cora, dabbing her eyes with the cuff of her sleeve. "I can't help you. Sorry. You're right about firepower doing more harm than good, but I don't think there's anything that can be done about it. It's just what we do. It's what we always do." She stood up, putting on her jacket. "Best of luck to you."

"Wait," said Paris, pulling out one of her business cards she always had at the ready. Cora took it and then froze as their skin made contact, and Paris couldn't help but wonder how long it had been since she'd been touched by another *human.* "If you change your mind," she said in the most compassionate tone she could muster.

Cora swallowed and nodded the nod of someone who had no intent of doing so. She put the card in her pocket and continued toward the door.

"Hey . . . ," said Paris.

Cora stopped but didn't turn.

"It wasn't your fault."

Cora's head tilted, not quite a turn, and then she left without another word.

2

Cora closed her eyes at 2:30 P.M. in New York and opened them at 3:15 A.M. on the other side of the world. Ampersand never left the lights on in this upper portion of his house because he never used it, but sometimes she wished he'd leave the light on for her when he knew she was coming. When he'd *asked* her to come.

She sat up as the last of her semiautonomous plating slid back into the implant that hovered over her spine between her shoulder blades, unnoticeable to anyone who wasn't looking for it. One of Ampersand's conditions for letting her spend most of her time on the other side of the planet was a built-in system of transportation like his, which she carried with her in the form of a surgical implant. As with all her implants, it was operated by an ocular overlay controlled by her eye movements and which itself had taken months of trial and error (and many, many up-grades) before it became second nature, and even now, like everything he'd implanted in her, it was still effectively a prototype.

She felt at the incision where the billions upon billions of micro-scopic drones that looked like liquid metal had disappeared to—she couldn't feel it at all. She stretched out her wings, trying to shake off the "jet lag." The journey took about forty-five minutes, but even the ones that only took five made her feel hungover. Sometimes she had to enter Japan legally, but unless she had to deal with any humans (which wasn't often these days), she usually came straight "home."

Home, for now, she reminded herself. They had to leave Earth even-tually. That hadn't changed. Eighteen months ago, the two agreed that there was no saving this civilization and began to formulate a plan to save themselves in a galaxy far, far away. A major variable had been Ampersand's "disease" (his word for his precarious mental health), as they could never leave Earth with him in such poor condition, but he had improved considerably since Nikola had nearly murdered him— enough that he was now starting to make coherent plans. They had not yet agreed to specifics, such as when and where or, most stressful to Cora, whether their plan would feature human repopulation efforts, but in the abstract, this was and always would be the plan. Japan was "home," but only for now.

"Where are you?" she asked the house, which was dark and verging on uncomfortably warm, as per the amygdaline preference. "Are you downstairs?"

Everything upstairs looked like a normal man-made house because it was—their main angel investor, rock star Japanese billionaire Kentaro Matsuda, had gifted one of his many properties in the mountains of Fukushima Prefecture and put it in the name of a trust known only to him and his team of lawyers, but even they didn't know about every- thing belowground, where Ampersand spent most of his time.

"Behind you, dear one."

She turned and rose to her feet to greet him, lit only by the stars and the moon filtering through the giant windows of the house. Even now, he was still an intimidating presence, standing at around eight and a half feet tall and looking like a giant praying mantis wearing a mech- anoid dragon costume as imagined by Steve Jobs. But it was the small details that made him intimidating: the odd placement of his shoul- ders, the strange joints at every junction of his limbs that screamed of wildly different evolution that arrived at some similarities of the human form—a bilaterally symmetrical creature with two arms, two legs, and a head with two eyes. She reached her hands around his neck, pulling him down toward her into an awkward embrace. Realizing what she was trying to do, he lowered his nearly nine-foot stature to her height, placing his hands on her back like a cowl.

"Are you well, my dearest?"

"I'll live," she said, closing her eyes and holding him tightly. "Did you message me to get me out of that interview?"

"No, I had some improvements I wanted to administer to your im- plants."

"Oh . . ." She slackened her grip.

Ampersand pulled out of the embrace and regarded her. "*But these upgrades are not so pressing that I cannot attend to your needs first.*"

He guided her into the first-floor bedroom, and it took her a moment to see what he was getting at—no poking and prodding quite yet—they were going to have a moment to decompress. This was good. He was learning.

The "human" portion of the house was both extremely high end and extremely minimalist, consisting only of a kitchen, a living/entertaining space, a large master bedroom that opened onto its own balcony overlooking the mountains, and a smaller, presently empty office space. She'd insisted on there being an outwardly human layout to the main space because she'd assumed there would be human visitors, although by this point, only Kentaro's people and her aunt Luciana had actually been inside it, and that had been months ago. Cora preferred the upstairs bedroom, as it felt, far less claustrophobic than his underground sleeping space that she had come to think of as the Lair. If the upstairs projected "humans live here, human human human," everything underground projected the opposite.

Cora sat on the side of the bed, which was far bigger and lower to the ground than her twin-sized dormitory bed in New York. He placed one spiderlike finger under her chin, tilting her head up to look at him.

"*Have you eaten?*"

"Not tod—"

She didn't even get the word out before he turned to leave to get whatever amount of calories he deemed necessary. Yes, he did effectively have a thermonuclear perpetual motion machine inside his torso that gave him his powers, but that power was ultimately finite. While sometimes it seemed like it would be more practical for him to use his telekinesis, most times when he needed a physical object, he got it the old-fashioned way.

Within seconds, he returned with a prepackaged protein smoothie, which she took, smiling in concession. Though her food aversion wasn't as bad as it once was, it had never really gone away, and she usually just let him tell her when and what to eat than to stress about it herself.

As she forced the smoothie down, Ampersand positioned himself next to her, roosting in the deerlike way with his limbs tucked under him. He used to be so uncomfortable watching her eat, but now he would often stare at her as though making sure the process was going along smoothly. It was as disconcerting as it would be if a human did it, only instead of human eyes, his were almost the size of footballs and seemed to glow amber with the light reflected in them; instead of human skin comprised of cells, his was an iridescent silvery white comprised of billions of nanites; instead of stubby human fingers, his were the length and size of the legs of those Japanese spider crabs at the aquarium.

It had taken some getting used to for both of them.

"What improvements are you working on?"

"*An upgrade to protect your internal systems from energy pulses.*"

He'd spent more time and energy on developing fail-safes against electromagnetic pulses than nearly any other project—not unreasonable given that it was his only major physical weakness. "Still worried about that?"

"*While the upgrades I've added to myself should be approximately 98 percent effective against man-made electromagnetic pulses and 87 percent effective against amygdaline-made energy pulses, I need to ensure that the same fail-safes will apply to the systems I have installed into you.*"

"Is this the last improvement?"

"*Nikola could engineer better ones, if he were willing. I am a biologist, not an engineer.*"

There that name was again—Nikola—and just as when Paris Wells had said it barely an hour ago, it sent a thrill of fear through her. Nikola, Enola, it didn't matter what they called him—he was a problem and would be an even bigger one once they left Earth. Nikola couldn't come with them, not as a free companion, anyway, but he could not stay here.

"*I can sense you're upset. How might I ameliorate it?*"

She looked at him, impressed. It wasn't often he put words to her emotional state before she did. "It's just . . . it makes me sad, sometimes. Thinking that we have to leave."

"*Leaving one's home civilization is a pain that few have truly experienced, but I am one of those few. The fear is valid because the pain is deep and never goes away.*"

"It's more than that, but I'm having a hard time articulating."

"*We are not yet advanced to a point in our communications where we are able to share consciousness. Regrettably, in order for me to understand what is causing you pain, you must communicate it verbally."*

She took a few deep breaths, trying to beat back the well of emotion that accompanied thoughts of Kaveh, at unhealed wounds that had been poked and prodded by talking with Paris Wells. Every waking moment the first six months after his death was a struggle to keep her head above water with Ampersand acting as a four-hundred-pound brick. Every day, a new scenario she had no idea how to navigate, and always something Kaveh would have known how to handle. "I knew talking with her would only make me confront how much I miss him, but . . . I really miss him."

"You speak of your dead lover."

"He had a name, Ampersand." It was a linguistic quirk that amygdalines tended to address subjects by their relationship to the speaker rather than given names, but it did sometimes feel dehumanizing (for lack of a better word).

"Kaveh Mazandarani. You rarely speak of him."

"It's just . . ." Heart ripped out at the mere mention of his name? Screaming agony medically known as survivor's guilt? "I don't want to bother you with it."

"I understand why you still think of your grief as a burden to me. So many times in the past, I have failed you. I cannot promise you I will take the correct approach in addressing it, but I do empathize with your loss, and my desire to do for you what you have done for me is strong."

She smiled; it wasn't that him trying to comfort her was rare at this point, but expressing *gratitude*? Even tiptoeing up to an *apology*? A breakthrough.

"You are my protector and my advocate, and I am your caretaker. For now, we must make do with the limitations of human language, but soon, we will surpass those limitations. Soon, I am confident I will be able to exist inside your consciousness, and neither of us will be burdened with the need to explain ourselves through the medium of spoken language."

She stiffened, now realizing what he was getting at. "You have another . . . run-through you want to do?"

"I am ready to try again, when you consent."

He'd been frustrated by the limits of spoken language since they'd met, as he considered amygdaline "high language" far superior. At first, she had taken it for granted that their neural wiring was just too mutually alien for such a form of communication. But soon, he admitted that he thought it could be possible. Stranger still, he *desired* to do it with her.

She'd been terrified of the idea at first, but eventually volunteered to be his guinea pig. He'd been working at it for more than a year by now—creating digital maps of both of their neural networks, opening her up, operating on her, filling her with implants the function of which she only understood a small fraction. High-language attempts were always draining and at best left her feeling sluggish, at worst with a splitting headache. The last attempt, three weeks earlier, had been the worst one so far. She'd spent about an hour under the shower afterward crying from the pain while he seemed totally oblivious, treating what to her felt like nothing but if a migraine and a tsunami had a baby as some big success. His "successes" felt like being hit with a bigger and bigger truck each time, never like two consciousnesses melding and becoming one.

And this would be attempt number eight.

"*You are anxious.*"

She sighed, drawing her hands around his slender neck. *The things we do for love*, she thought. "It's okay. I'll be ready in the morning."

She looked out the window into the night sky; the ground floor of the house was full of massive windows that took up much of the walls, out into the mountains that the nouveaux riches both of Japan and abroad paid top dollar to enjoy. The stars were especially clear through those massive windows, but tonight they felt cold. They used to evoke a sense of awe, but now she saw an icy, empty future.

But an inevitable future because there was no saving this civilization.

· · · · ·

"Well, it sure is bigger."

Ampersand had built what was effectively a sensory-deprivation chamber, theorizing that the first several attempts failed because she was still too attuned to her own senses. The first try was a shallow pool of warm water the size of a large closet and was only big enough for her body. But in the following weeks, he'd scooped out more of the earth with whatever nuclear hellfire he used when she wasn't there, creating a giant obsidian womb from the earth. The dim reddish lights he used down here made it feel like a darkroom.

"I'm curious why you made it big enough for both of us."

"*So I can be in it with you.*"

"I can see that."

She took off her robe and lay down in the water, exactly the temperature of the human body. It took a minute for the water to settle completely, and then for her breath to slow enough to where she didn't really hear anything. She'd done one of the human-made sensory-deprivation chambers a couple of times for therapy, but unlike those, this silence was near total, and the first time they'd tried it, she was surprised she didn't experience more from Ampersand than the usual splitting headache. And it was for the splitting headache that she braced as he turned off the lights.

She opens her eyes to a thin, gray fog, like it's early morning in nineteenth-century London. Only this fog isn't in a city, or the country, or anything familiar. She can't see more than a few feet in any direction.

The fog begins to dissipate. The whiteness of the plane dims as the thing on the other side of the fog comes into view. It is the size of a house, now a skyscraper, now a mountain. It is looking for her, and every cell in her body electrifies with the instinct to get away from it.

She tries to run, but a tadpole could more easily outrun a speedboat. It is as if the ocean has risen from its bed to stand, only these aren't the cool blue waters of the Pacific but a roiling, cold blackness, a strange nether region between oil and smoke, and it is reaching for her.

No, no! Help me, help me!

She tries to get away. She knows that if it touches her, even if it gets too close, it will crush her, obliterate her. This is a cold, black void that sucks the life from any and everything it touches, and it is reaching for her, close, too close, soon it will—

She sucked in a deep breath as her limbs flailed about in the shallow, salty water. A red light came on, and she backed away from him until she slammed into the slick, black wall of the chamber, staring at the alien inside of it with her. This nine-foot grotesque that more resembled an insect than a human.

"Was that you?" she said, looking at the alien shell that stared back at her with its fiery, cold eyes. She saw not a person but a creature, a beast, something so unfathomably foreign it may as well not be made out of the matter of this universe. It had no expression, no skin, no heartbeat, no *heart*—it was the body of a machine that only aped the movement of a living thing. For the life of her, she couldn't remember how she had ever anthropomorphized this thing.

"Is that what you are?" she asked. "Is that what you *really* are?"

THE PHILIPPINE
STAR

Questions Remain After Palawan Bar Fracas Leaves 6 Dead, Injures 12

MANILA
APRIL 2, 2005

BY HAMMITHA HULSE

The sleepy fishing town of Bahura was turned upside down last month by a bar brawl that left 6 people dead and 12 injured. But given the paucity of details and relative lack of media coverage, some question if there might be more to the story.

Romeo Chavez, a journalist with *Palawan Daily*, first became intrigued by the fracas when he noticed that the families had not submitted any obituaries for the deceased. Last week, Chavez was denied access to the scene by local authorities. "I've made inquiries to all of the bereaved families, but none have responded for comment," Chavez claims.

"Six dead at any sports-related riot would be a cause for national shame, but for it to happen in such a small, rural town is unprecedented. Why is so little light being shed on such a tragedy?

"The brawl represents the greatest loss of life at any sports-related riot in the history of the western Philippines, and yet we've seen hardly any national coverage," said Chavez.

The bar at which the brawl reportedly happened is registered as having a security system in place, including security cameras, but police have not released the footage.

Local police have not responded to requests for comment.

· 3 ·

Cora sat on the edge of her bed in her dorm room, staring at her phone.

> Dear one, I want you to come to
> me next weekend.

She hadn't even been back in New York for fifteen minutes, hadn't even had time to get her bearings, and he was already looking to schedule round two. Yes, she had left with a haste she had never displayed with him; historically, it was *he* running away while she begged him not to, but today, it had been she leaving the eldritch horror that had just invaded her mind alone and confused in his fallout shelter.

Not confused, she thought. *Humans feel confused. Maybe you project confusion, but "confusion" is not what's going on in that alien shell.*

> I need some time.

> I do not understand your meaning.

She huffed, dragged her palm across her face, then responded:

> I need some time to process what
> happened.

> What happened was a success.

She threw her head back against the wall. Her upset was far too visceral for him to miss even without the empathic bond, so clearly, he just didn't care. Which, of course he didn't, because *he was not fucking human.*

The entire time she'd known him, people cautioned her against anthropomorphizing, which she ignored because she had always known more than they had, had a literal metaphysical bond with him. Yes, she had had it explained to her by both Ampersand and Nikola that what she felt through their metaphysical wall wasn't what he was *actually* feeling but rather her brain's interpretation of whatever alien energies Ampersand was projecting. She had known that, but she hadn't really *understood* it. All this time, she'd been imagining that on the other side of those amber eyes was a consciousness that was strange, perhaps, but ultimately comprehensible, not the Call of Cthulhu she'd just experienced.

> You are frightened. I can sense it. But you have nothing to fear. We are making great progress.

> I just need some time to get used to this.

> It will take some time to become accustomed to. Perhaps a very long time. But I am pleased with our success.

Was *that* what "pleased" felt like to him, that incomprehensible mass that consumed all, the abyss personified?

Less than a second later, another message:

> Your fear is understandable, because it is both unnatural and alien. Our high language is the most ambitious experiment that has ever been attempted.

"Just talk to me through the earbud," she said aloud.

"If it pleases you, dear one."

She nearly growled. *"My dearest," "dear one," "my love," you don't even know what any of that means.* "Did you know this would happen?"

"*I anticipated that there would be some challenges.*"

"Why didn't you tell me?"

"*I did tell you that I expected any early success to be difficult.*"

"*Difficult?*" This time, a growl did escape. "That wasn't difficult, that was—"

"*I had no means of anticipating degrees of difficulty.*"

"Okay, then on a scale of one to ten, with one being the easiest you would have expected and ten the most difficult, where would you place that?"

"*I cannot reduce something so complex to a simple one-to-ten measurement.*"

"Sure you can. You simplify complex topics for me all the time."

"*There are far too many variables in this experiment to accurately rank it by the scale you're asking.*"

"Do it anyway."

"*Six.*"

"Six?" she nearly shrieked, clapping a hand to her forehead. "You call that a *six*?"

"*I have always warned you that this would be a difficult process.*"

"But you never told me that I'd be the one bearing the burden of the difficulty!"

There was a pause, one uncharacteristically long enough to make Cora think that something might have happened to his encrypted line. Then, "*That is not how I interpret our dynamic.*"

"Well, if you are bearing the burden of 'difficulty' on the level of what I just experienced, you should have told me."

Again, a pause. "*I do not think my difficulties are comparable to yours.*"

She resisted the urge to push, to get angry, to tell him that whatever "difficulties" he had endured without her knowledge, he should have told her. Perhaps it was obvious that he wouldn't have known what would happen in an experiment that had never been tried before, but didn't that make it all the more dangerous? If he hadn't anticipated what the *difficulties* would be for her, what else was he overlooking?

"You know what my 'difficulties' are, and you just go full steam ahead because you don't have to live with those difficulties?"

"*I don't understand your meaning.*"

"I know you don't understand. You don't understand all I've gone through—"

"*You don't know the specifics of my past before we met,*" he cut her off. "*And even if you did, you have no right to be the arbiter to which of us has the claim to the greater personal trauma. Yours are no greater than mine.*"

She stopped herself from spewing some defensive diatribe she did not mean and would inevitably regret. Even if he was a nightmare hell-spawn from another world, he was still a sentient social creature, just as capable of sustaining damage to the psyche as she was. There had been times over the past eighteen months when, while he never divulged anything, he alluded to incidents in his past, wounds that had never healed. They were never more than allusions in his darkest moments, and even then only in fragments.

They made me watch.

"You're right," she said, sitting back down on the bed. "I'm sorry. It's not a competition. I just—"

The ring of her phone cut her off—not her secret encrypted line but her *actual* phone. "I have another call. I have to go," she said, picking up her iPhone. "Hello?"

"Hello." It was her sister, Olive.

"Hey . . ." She stopped just sort of calling her own sister, "Hey . . . you," and winced. To think there had been a time not so long ago when she called her "butternut" every night; now Cora treated her with almost the same formality she treated Kentaro Matsuda.

"Mom wants to know if you ordered Monster Truck's medications."

"Oh, sh—I'm sorry, I forgot." Monster Truck had always had ear problems, and they had only learned last month that she was nearly deaf. The fact that Cora was now the person in the family with expendable income (and the fact that Monster Truck was still, on technicality, her dog) meant that she had to pay for all of Monster Truck's prescription ear medications that might slow the rapidly onsetting deafness (or at least clear out the frequent infections). "I'll get on that right away. It's . . . been a rough week. How's Thor doing?"

"Same as ever." Good old Thor. Monster Truck the purebred with all her health issues, but no worries about Thor, dog of indeterminate age and breed, just as healthy as ever. "I was going to call you earlier, but I got put in detention."

"For what?"

"I got into a fight."

"Why?"

"Simi Parquette said some stuff again," she said with a scoff. "Her dad says we're a whole family of traitors."

"What, because of Nils?"

"Mostly because of you."

Ah, the brusqueness of youth. "You know, you really shouldn't make a habit out of this."

"Why not? Someone's got to stand up for you."

What few brittle heartstrings Cora had left were thoroughly tugged. *Why* did Olive still bother standing up for her? *I hated Nils for abandoning us, and here I am plotting to do the same thing to you. Hell, I've already done the same thing to you.* "Yeah, but that doesn't mean you should be engaging in fisticuffs."

"It isn't your fault, what those gunmen did. Nikola killed those guys in self-defense, and that isn't against the law. They're just acting like this because they're aliens."

"Well, thanks for sticking up for me, but please try to limit that sort of thing to verbal defense."

"Simi *really* sucks."

"Please?"

A sigh hissed through the phone. "Okay, unless she starts it."

Cora tried to breathe out the hurricane of guilt inside her. "You planning anything fun for your birthday?"

"Sleepover with Siobhan and Kitty."

"That sounds fun." She paused. "Are they pro- or anti-Jude?"

"Pro!" she said without hesitation. "I wouldn't have xenophobic friends."

"Okay, good."

"Will you come?"

Uggghhhh. She'd hoped Olive wouldn't come out and ask, because that put her in the position of either coming up with an excuse not to or making promises she didn't know she could keep. "I might be able to swing it . . ."

"And meet Siobhan and Kitty?" she asked with the tone that implied that she might have promised Cora (and by extension, Ampersand) stopping by as a possibility to Siobhan and Kitty.

"Sure."

"Yeah!" A pause. "Miss you," she added, sneaking it in like doing so was breaking a rule.

"I miss you, too."

They hung up, and Cora slumped back down on her bed. It was one thing to feel hideous, horrible guilt about her inadequacy as a sister who'd effectively become a surrogate parent when her bleak decision to leave seemed obvious, but *now*? Now when the last thing she wanted to do was ever look at Ampersand again? Now when her sister, who was creeping up on adolescence, who was getting into fights at school because of *her*, needed her most?

No one knew about the high-language experiment. No one knew she had cybernetic implants. No one knew she was planning on leaving Earth. No one knew there was a tentative plan for her to be neo-Eve, that there was a possibility of a second attempt at human civilization billions of light-years away.

She wished she could tell Luciana.

She wished Kaveh were still alive.

She wished . . .

They made me watch.

A year ago, things had been dire. They had been in Japan for a month, and Ampersand's condition had not improved. But although she had intended to take care of him by herself, she soon realized it was not feasible and called her aunt Luciana for help. They'd parted on terms bad enough that Cora half expected them never to speak again, but to her surprise, Luciana was on the next flight to Japan, and within a few weeks, to her even greater surprise, they had the entirety of the Japanese government at their back, refusing to extradite two aliens (one comatose, and one functionally comatose) to the U.S.

They had been kept in austere government compounds for a couple of weeks—that is, until the wealthy started getting involved. It was Kentaro who paid to move them to a *ryokan* he had bought out entirely and indefinitely, a tiny old-fashioned Japanese boutique hotel in the mountains full of creature comforts that a still near-catatonic Ampersand did not appreciate (and would not have even in the best of circumstances). Kentaro had made his fortune in aerospace and pharmaceuticals, and gladly threw more money at Ampersand than was needed. An "investment," in his own words—in Kentaro's industries, a technocrat alien xenobiologist *might* be very useful one day.

Luciana had to go back to the U.S. for visa-related reasons, leaving Cora alone in the *ryokan* with Ampersand for weeks. She kept him hidden away from the bureaucrats and government types as best she could, and waited. By this point, it was late summer, and she felt like she had done everything in her power to help him, but hardly even got a word in response for her efforts. One night, she went into the bedroom, knelt next to Ampersand, and asked, "Are you asleep?"

A slight twinge of fear from the other side of the wall. It was rare that she felt anything from him at all these days, but when she did, it was a relief. Fear was good. Only a creature that does not want to die feels fear.

"What is it?" she asked. "Are you still afraid of me, after all this?"

"*Instinctively, yes. But I understand and accept that you do not intend to eat me.*"

This had been a running theme since they'd met, a fear he knew to be irrational but still wallowed in, anyway. "Why are you so . . . hung up on cannibalism? You're . . . post-natural. There's nothing to *eat*."

"*You know I have organic parts.*"

She sensed that he was offended, as if to say, *How could you ask something so insensitive?* She resisted the urge to give him a comforting pat on the arm or back; he did not respond well to that sort of thing. "You never told me what happened to you."

"*I have seen it,*" he said.

"Not by humans?"

"*Not humans.*"

Of course it hadn't been humans. When could it have been a human? There were probably a few weirdos out there dying to know what alien tasted like, but what human would even know how to crack open a post-natural amygdaline to find the "living" bits, let alone have the opportunity to do so?

He must be referring to their sister species.

She knew little about the amygdalines' sister species, called *physeterine* by the people at ROSA. Ampersand called them *transients*, which felt almost like a pejorative when he said it. She knew little about them, save that they were nomadic, that they traveled in "pods," and that unlike amygdalines, they did not inhabit cybernetic bodies but ones made of meat and bone. She was unclear when the two sister species had declared forever war on each other, or why, but at this point, it didn't really matter. Both sides decided that one could not thrive while the other survived.

"You've seen . . . physeterines cannibalize . . . amygdalines?" she asked.

"*They made me watch.*"

"What are you talking about?"

"*They made me watch. They made me watch,*" he said, over and over. "*They made me watch.*"

To this day, he had not told her any more than that.

Back then, she had feared that the end of the conservatorship that fall would be where he gave up on life, but by that point, he was a legal person in most countries. By that point, Nikola had been committed into Bella Terra. By that point, he had both unlimited funds and one of Kentaro's spare houses in a beautiful mountain village in Fukushima Prefecture. By that point, he had the safety and freedom to pursue the high-language experiment. She never pushed, because even though he had not moved on from it, he wanted to believe that he had.

And now, a year later, what was she doing if not the same damn thing? She was aping him in his tendencies to keep his pain buried, first with her physical trauma with Obelus (Ampersand's *other* shitty symphyle who had *also* almost killed her), and now with her grief over Kaveh. The harder she tried to put him out of her mind, the more insistently his ghost claimed squatter's rights. She remembered something he had told her once after he talked her down from a panic attack:

"Deep down, I think you understand that you can't just wish that shit away. That if you try to keep it down, the pressure builds, and it explodes."

She felt something in her jacket pocket and pulled out Paris Wells's business card, wondering why contacting her felt like a good idea now where yesterday she had never wanted to see this woman again. Yes, they were going to leave Earth and everyone on it, from Japanese billionaires to her own errant sister, but she still felt an obligation to postpone the crumbling of civilization; after all, even if she wasn't going to stay in it, people she cared about were. She didn't know if Paris really had the pull or talent to make the world better, but she certainly couldn't make it worse.

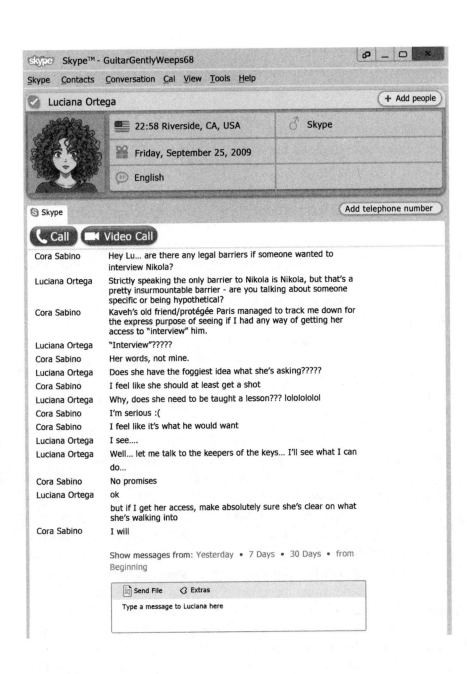

Skype™ - GuitarGentlyWeeps68

Skype   Contacts   Conversation   Cal   View   Tools   Help

+ Add people

Luciana Ortega

	22:58 Riverside, CA, USA	♂ Skype
	Friday, September 25, 2009	
	English	

Ⓢ Skype   Add telephone number

📞 Call   📹 Video Call

Cora Sabino	Hey Lu... are there any legal barriers if someone wanted to interview Nikola?
Luciana Ortega	Strictly speaking the only barrier to Nikola is Nikola, but that's a pretty insurmountable barrier - are you talking about someone specific or being hypothetical?
Cora Sabino	Kaveh's old friend/protégée Paris managed to track me down for the express purpose of seeing if I had any way of getting her access to "interview" him.
Luciana Ortega	"Interview"?????
Cora Sabino	Her words, not mine.
Luciana Ortega	Does she have the foggiest idea what she's asking?????
Cora Sabino	I feel like she should at least get a shot
Luciana Ortega	Why, does she need to be taught a lesson??? lolololol
Cora Sabino	I'm serious :(
Cora Sabino	I feel like it's what he would want
Luciana Ortega	I see....
Luciana Ortega	Well... let me talk to the keepers of the keys... I'll see what I can do...
Cora Sabino	No promises
Luciana Ortega	ok
	but if I get her access, make absolutely sure she's clear on what she's walking into
Cora Sabino	I will

Show messages from: Yesterday • 7 Days • 30 Days • from Beginning

📄 Send File   ⟨⟩ Extras

Type a message to Luciana here

· 4 ·

Cora dreaded seeing Paris in the way that one dreads going to the dentist, and she hesitated a solid two minutes in front of the high school in Harlem where they were scheduled to meet. Strings had been pulled, things had fallen into place quickly, and Paris was scheduled to leave for California on the morrow. Cora could have just left her to the fates, but Paris needed *some* guidance, for all the good it would do.

It was late in the afternoon, and the building was mostly empty. Cora found classroom 110 easily enough, peeked inside, and saw about ten teenagers at the front of the room, most seated at desks and a couple kneeling on the floor, with Paris and another woman standing over them. One of the girls had her fingers interlaced on top of the chest of a mannequin—a CPR training course, and Paris was teaching it.

"You want to do it firmer and faster," said Paris. "You're trying to get their heart kick-started, not give them a massage."

The girl, a teenager with hair that was a faded, dyed-weeks-ago pink, started pushing harder, but still too slow. She'd noticed Cora, and her eyes lingered for a moment, the expression of near recognition that Cora had gotten very familiar with over the last year and a half.

"Okay, so you're going for a rate of 100–120 compressions per minute, so think of it like your heart rate after you've been jogging." When the girl continued going too slow, Paris amended. "Okay, you know the song 'Stayin' Alive'? Do it to that—ha, ha, ha, ha, stayin' alive, stayin' alive, one, two, three. Come on, Tucker's got a wife and two-point-five kids who depend on him. Think of Tucker's children, Blaeleigh and Grayson. One, two, three . . ."

Paris shot her a "glad to see you!" look before returning to her lesson. Cora was struck that even in this informal environment of instructing a tween to pump a plastic torso Paris presented a casual professionalism that felt both effortless and cultivated. She was wearing a white vest that hugged her little waist so perfectly it looked tailored, and her natural, tightly curled hair, held back by a matching white headband, framed her heart-shaped face like a Christmas wreath.

Cora took the opportunity to use her ocular overlay to scan the room for bugs; her system for detecting electromagnetic activity was nowhere near as sensitive as Ampersand's, but it did give her the ability to suss out live wires where there weren't supposed to be any. It wasn't that she didn't trust Paris; at this point, it was just force of habit.

A few minutes later, the clock struck 4:00 and the gaggle of teenagers shuffled to their feet. "Next week is when it really gets real," said Paris as they filtered out. "We're going to learn some methods to stop bleeding in the field."

The self-conscious CPR girl shuddered so hard she practically spasmed. "I can't with blood," she said with a thick Bronx accent.

"If you want to be an EMT, you're going to have to deal with blood."

"I hope I don't ever have to . . ." She full-body spasmed again. "Nope!"

The girl moved to leave, lingering on the possibility of some awkward "you look familiar" variant before thinking better of it and leaving Cora alone with Paris and the other woman.

"I appreciate you coming down here," said Paris warmly.

"It's no problem. It's just a short walk from campus."

"Renée, this is Cora," Paris said to the other woman. "Cora, this is my sister, Renée. She runs an after-school enrichment program, and today we are teaching CPR."

Renée looked Cora up and down skeptically, as if she expected Cora to start evangelizing about how the aliens were here to bring salvation and enlightenment to all. "Nice to meet you."

"Likewise. Are you a first aid instructor?"

"I'm a teacher," said Renée, nodding to Paris. "That one's the amateur field surgeon."

"I was an EMT when I was in grad school," said Paris. "During my last year's journey of self-discovery, I renewed my EMT certification and started volunteering for the Red Cross, so I give first aid certification classes here a few times a semester."

"That's really cool," said Cora earnestly.

"I have an event tomorrow," said Paris, picking up Tucker the Mannequin and putting it on a desk. "Then I'm going to California to meet our *friend*. Exciting!"

The whites of Renée's eyes flashed as if Paris had just mentioned she was taking up BASE jumping. Cora looked at Renée, then at Paris again, hoping she'd take the hint, that this was a conversation they should have *alone*, but Paris was wearing a polite but transparent expression of "whatever you have to say in front of me you can say in front of my sister."

"Realistically, that is probably true," said Cora. "Nikola doesn't really . . . 'communicate' as such. At least, not with words."

"What do you mean?"

"Well, that was one thing I wanted to tell you about was . . . the precedent. They set up an apparatus that translates Pequod-phonemic—that is, their spoken language—into English. Like, if he were to speak, the translation would appear on a flat-screen TV near his, um . . . cell." She almost said the word *enclosure*, because the one time she had seen it, that's what it looked like. "But he doesn't use it."

"Ever?"

"Well . . ." The phrase *only in hostage situations* felt a little bit dramatic. "Not really."

"Interesting. Maybe I can talk him into it."

Cora's heart dipped, and going on Renée's reaction, she felt the same. Her expression alone told Cora that she thought this was a terrible idea and had already made her piece known and was not about to trouble herself any further.

"I'm guessing you have some feedback," said Paris.

"Nikola . . . tends to respond poorly to people who try to appeal to his better angels," said Cora.

"Hospitalized four people, huh?" said Renée, her eyes darting to one side in a "hoo-boy." "How?"

"Well, bear in mind this doesn't include incidents that didn't end up in hospitalization."

Renée coughed.

"Go on," said Paris.

"Well, you know the invisibility cloak from *Harry Potter*?"

"Yeah."

"Well, Nikola basically has a built-in one of those. One time, he cloaked himself *and* found a way to fool the infrared scanner. A nurse entered the enclosure thinking he was safely sealed off on the other half and—"

"Girl," said Renée, addressing Paris, "if that thing does anything to you, Abuela is gonna kill *me*."

"Also, Nikola can sense weaknesses in structures," Cora continued. "If he creates enough micro-fissures in the acrylic wall, it'll create a weakness that the staff isn't even aware of until it's too late. He's done that . . . four times?"

"*Four* times?" exclaimed Renée.

"That I know of. But only two of them hit their target."

"What do you mean, 'hit their target'?" asked Paris, now becoming alarmed.

"One time, he used vibrations to weaken a rafter outside of his cell to fall through the ceiling, and beaned a night janitor in the head. That guy ended up in a coma for two weeks. The next one was on one of the nurses; it was just a light fixture, but, you know, *glass*. She sued Bella Terra, and they settled out of court for . . . I don't know how much, but it was not nothing."

Renée's eyes went wide again, her lips puckering in an expression that almost looked vindicated, like she'd *told* Paris this would get her killed! And think of what Abuela would do to her *then*! "Who the hell is paying for all this?" she asked.

"Some of it comes from Kentaro Matsuda, since he's footing the bill for Jude's expenses already, and they are, well, 'family,' but most of it comes from American industrialists." And, yes, some from the government, but they didn't need to know that.

"That is so much to unpack," said Paris, mostly to herself.

"Riri," said Renée, "I don't want to be putting words in anybody's mouth, but I think she's trying to talk you out of it."

"I'm not," said Cora. "But I do want you to understand what you're getting into. Just because Nikola is confined doesn't mean he's not dangerous."

"He killed four people!" exclaimed Renée.

Paris took a deep breath. "Even if he doesn't do exactly what I'm asking . . . as long as he does *something*, it'll be more than I have now."

"This ain't ours. I gotta go return it," said Renée, picking up Tucker the Mannequin. She looked at Paris pointedly. "You gonna help me return these rentals?"

"Yeah, I'll be down in a few," said Paris. Renée left the room, shaking her head, Tucker under her arm.

"I do wish there was more I could do to help besides being sooth-sayer of doom," said Cora.

"Well, I appreciate that you're here at all. You didn't have to come down."

"No, I did. You need to know what you're getting into. Even as horri-fying as he is to be in the same room with physically, no one's prepared for how . . . *mean* he is."

"'Mean'?"

"Mean and spiteful."

"He didn't strike me as either of those things."

"What do you mean?"

Paris moved toward her purse on the desk at the front of the room. "I didn't tell you how I plan to communicate with him. I wasn't going to rely on a flat-screen."

Paris opened her purse and pulled out a small jewelry box that looked like it would house an engagement ring. She returned to Cora and opened the box. "Do you recognize this?"

There was indeed something ringlike in there, a device that looked like a tiny daddy longlegs hugging an invisible straw—an aural com-municator, the same earbud as the one Ampersand used to talk to her.

"I've met Nikola before," said Paris.

"When?" said Cora, gobsmacked. She'd just been sitting on this for eighteen months?

"It was the night before Kaveh died," Paris said, growing somber. "I was hanging out at Kaveh's apartment while he was packing to skip the country. I was actually looking for information on you, trying to find if there were any credible leads on where you were."

"For me?" she asked, a splinter of guilt biting her at the memory of her disappearance after her Senate testimony last year. Bad enough to think of how worried Kaveh and her family had been, it was even worse to think the shrapnel had hit people she'd not yet even met.

Paris nodded. "And then I feel this shadow over me, and I look up and . . . there he is! And I'm racking my brain like, *Did I get blazed this morning and just forget? This has to be a hallucination.* But no, Nikola was there in Kaveh's living room, and Kaveh came back in and was all, 'Oh, Nik, my friend the giant spider-lizard monster, I've been so worried about you!'" She laughed shakily.

"That sounds like Kaveh," said Cora, voice barely above a whisper.

"I told Nikola to please protect Kaveh, and he said he would. I said that I wish we'd had the chance to talk more, under different circumstances."

"Nikola gave you this?"

"No, Kaveh did. He still had his earbuds from when Nikola had been speaking to him months earlier, and since he had two of them, he gave me one so I could hear Nikola."

"I see . . . ," said Cora. "Did Nikola say anything to you?"

"Yes, the last thing he said before they left was that we would meet again."

Cora blinked. "What, really?"

"I apologized for being afraid of him when he first showed up, and said that I wished we'd met under different circumstances. He said to me, and I quote, '*Dear gentle creature, we will meet again.*'"

Cora looked at her in slight wonderment. "A hypocorism."

"A what?"

"It's like . . . a name. He gave you a name. Their language is . . . pretty complicated with how they address one another; some of those quirks filter into ours." Cora looked down at the earbud, identical to hers. "Yeah, this is . . . very much uncharted territory. He all but gave you instruction."

"I don't really think my charm offensive is going to be what makes or breaks this," said Paris. "This is my real trump card."

"He doesn't have that power core that gave him his telekinesis, but even defanged, he's still extremely dangerous. Ancient Japanese proverb: 'Cut off a wolf's head and it still has the power to bite.'"

"Ancient Japanese," said Paris with a smile. "The ancient era of 1997?"

Cora brightened. She hadn't expected Paris to catch a quote from *Princess Mononoke*. "That's the one."

"I love that movie."

"Me, too! I've gotten to know the Japanese film industry very well in the last year, so . . ."

"Really?"

Cora shrugged. "Lot of downtime, and it's a good way to help learn Japanese." One of the first things Ampersand had programed into her ocular overlay was a feature that translated spoken Pequod-phonemic to written English; she had initially refused the feature that would do the same for human languages, as she wanted to learn Japanese and didn't want it as a crutch, but it wasn't long before she had to concede that it would make life much easier. "My grasp on the language is still . . . halting."

"Well, it's one of my deep, dark secrets that I am of the weeb tribe. Maybe one of these days, we can hang out in a 'watching anime' context and not a 'homicidal aliens' context."

It had been so long since Cora had felt this sensation, it took a moment for her to place it—*butterflies*. "I . . . actually have to go to California this week, too," said Cora, speaking on pure impulse. "It's my sister's birthday."

"Oh, word, I may need more help along the way." She cocked an eyebrow. "Did you ever consider going into journalism?"

"I . . . hadn't thought that far ahead."

"Something to consider."

It really isn't, she thought. She closed her eyes and sighed. Why wasn't it, though? It wasn't like the plan was to leave Earth tomorrow. Was she really so nihilistic as to think there was no greater good to work toward? If that were the case, why bother helping Paris at all?

Paris clearly noticed the shift in her demeanor, and Cora added, "But please be careful. Nikola, the person that Kaveh wrote about, he died when Kaveh did."

Paris crossed her arms and smiled. Her dark skin was so smooth and perfect and in such contrast to that white top. She didn't want to admit it to herself, but perhaps Paris's writing acumen hadn't been the only reason she wanted to reach out to her. "We'll see," said Paris, looking at her phone at an incoming text. "Duty calls. You good?"

"Yeah, I can see myself out," she said. Paris nodded and went on her way. For want of any couch to flop down on, Cora took a seat at one of the student desks and buried her head in her hands.

Paris was warm and intuitive, the human equivalent of a comfy couch after months of nothing but a cold, stainless steel barstool. It was bad enough, the mere thought of any relationship with another human having the specter of leaving Earth looming over it, but that it was her dead boyfriend's best friend who caused the butterflies? Ugh, weird. Weird weird weird. What would Paris think if she knew?

"Excuse me."

Cora looked up, and there was Paris's student from a few minutes ago, the pink-haired Asian girl who'd shuddered at the thought of blood. Her look of recognition had gone from tentative to definite. "It took me a minute to realize—you're her!"

Oh, goddamn it.

"My name's Marisol Martinez," the girl continued. "I was born here, but my family is from the western Philippines."

In any other situation, she'd leave without a word, but this was Paris's student, and she didn't want to come off as mean. "I'd love to chat," Cora cut her off, improvising a very poor bullshit excuse, "but Paris and I, we have an agreement, I can't really talk—"

"I just have one question—"

"It's a legal thing. I can't—"

"Have you ever heard of 'physeterines'?"

She felt as though the oxygen had been suddenly sucked out of the building. "How do you know that word?"

"From the internet!" said Marisol, contrite. "Four years ago, my uncle was killed. When we went for the funeral, which happened almost three *months* later, they denied us entry."

"Entry to what?" asked Cora, rising to her feet.

"To . . . the country," said Marisol. "To the Philippines. They said there was something wrong with our visas, and they made us go back. They've denied us entry ever since."

"How did he die?"

"I'm still not entirely sure. Our family there weren't allowed to say. Then a year passed, and my grandmother made a Skype call to us from the city. She said it was . . ." Her eyes shifted around as if she suspected a CIA mole to pop out from behind the whiteboard. "She called it a 'demon.'"

They made me watch.

"When did this happen?"

"In 2005," said Marisol. "My grandmother said that the people of the village did kill the 'demon,' but it killed several people before it went down. And that was how my uncle died, trying to kill it."

They made me watch.

"Who made them keep this a secret?"

"The Filipino government told them that they couldn't tell anyone or they'd go to jail, that they'd get to the bottom of it, but they never did."

"The *Filipino* government?" repeated Cora.

"Yes, the government never gave any closure or explanation. We had no clue what it could have been until . . ."

"The Fremda Memo?" asked Cora softly.

Marisol nodded. "Before the Fremda Memo leaked, everyone assumed it had to be a demon from hell, or a science experiment gone wrong or something, but then came the Fremda Memo and we thought, *Of course, this must be it.* The 'demon' was actually an alien. Maybe the same thing the U.S. government had in custody was what killed my uncle. But then the photos of you from Pershing Square came out, and . . . it—you—*they* didn't look like what they had described to me at all. The only thing I can find was on DeceptiNation.com—a drawing someone in America made that sort of matched the description of the demon from someone in Puerto Rico in 1989, and they called it a name that they said came directly from ROSA—*physeterine.* And that's the only lead I have. And I thought you might know—is 'physeterine' a real thing?"

They made me watch.

"Yes," breathed Cora. "It's a real thing."

PART 2

YOU'VE GOT TO HIDE
YOUR LOVE AWAY

October 5, 2009

Gradually, the truth dawned on me: that Man had not remained one species, but had differentiated into two distinct animals: that my graceful
children of the Upper-world were not the sole descendants of our generation, but that this bleached, obscene, nocturnal Thing, which had flashed
before me, was also heir to all the ages.

—H. G. Wells, *The Time Machine*

*Transcript of televised debate between Nils Ortega, founder of
The Broken Seal, and* Los Angeles Times *columnist Andrew Szucs
on the topic of the president's proposed defense bill*

SZUCS: The president claims that a large portion of this proposed increase in defense spending will go to developing technologies that may in the future help protect us from the Pequod Superorganism, but we have absolutely no guarantee that's where this money will go or what these technologies even are.

ORTEGA: Have we already forgotten what we learned from the April 16, 2008, Senate hearing? Four CIA agents dead—

SZUCS: Mr. Ortega—

ORTEGA: *Dr.* Ortega.

SZUCS: [Pause] Dr. Ortega—

ORTEGA: Four CIA agents dead at the hands, so to speak, of one of the ETIs using a method so advanced and powerful it didn't even leave a corpse. Human bodies disintegrated in an instant.

SZUCS: Therefore, we are obligated to support a year-over-year increase in defense spending bigger than the total annual budget of the Department of Homeland Security, the Department of Education, and the Department of Energy *combined*?

ORTEGA: Defense spending is a solution to an unknown problem, and in the absence of knowledge, the only thing we *can* do is bolster all possible defenses.

SZUCS: But at what cost? We are staring down the barrel of the greatest depression in living memory, and *this* is where our money is going?

MACK: Gentlemen—

ORTEGA: I'm not here to argue in support of any policy, but knowing what little we do know—

SZUCS: When we *should* be removing our troops from Iraq and Afghan—

ORTEGA: Knowing what little we *do* know, again, to cite my earlier point about the ETI code-named Obelus and their ability to—

SZUCS: It sounds to me like you are implicitly if not outright in support of the president's defense proposal, *Dr.* Ortega.

ORTEGA: I'm in support of any government official brave enough to bring harsh truths to light, and President Julian was the individual who made the truth about the gruesome deaths of these CIA agents public. What is your suggested alternative?

MACK: Gentlemen—

SZUCS: I think government spending should be aiding the millions upon millions of Americans in crisis, not being funneled sight unseen into the military. We have millions out of work and an economy in free fall. Six major banks have failed. I think it is the height of hubris to dump money into developing military technology when we don't even have the foggiest idea what we are up against.

ORTEGA: Well, if there's anything we learned from the last time this happened to our great country, nothing fixes a depression like a war.

SZUCS: A war against *what*, *Dr.* Ortega?

MACK: Gentlemen, thank you. We need to go to break. We'll be right back with more *Hot Seat*.

· 5 ·

"'Monster,' huh?" said Luciana Ortega, her back rigid as she talked to Paris from the other side of her office desk. This building was neither new enough to be modern nor old enough to be classy, and from the outside, it looked like an industrial park. Luciana was lucky in that her office had a window, but it was a pretty small space, made smaller by the fact that what she did have in here was only partly unpacked, like she'd just moved in. "Well, as one of Nikola's counselors, I'm not supposed to use language like that, but . . ."

"Do you consider him dangerous?" asked Paris.

Luciana sighed deeply. "I asked to work here for the purpose of his rehabilitation, and I was hired on the spot because there are not many people on this earth with direct experience with amygdalines, but the reality is, most of what I do is damage control."

Paris looked at her recorder to make sure the light was still red, and then down at the May 2008 issue of *The New Yorker* in her lap. Luciana hadn't mentioned anything about communication methods with Nikola, and she didn't intend to share her one major asset. Even if this facility wasn't government run, she didn't want to risk the possibility that anyone might try to confiscate her earbud.

"I suppose, in a way, there's something incredibly . . . human about becoming so devastated by someone's death you just shut down."

"But there's something alien to it as well," said Luciana. "They don't just die when their time runs out; they choose when they die, and Nikola would like to *choose* to do it right now. He sees it as a violation of his 'human' rights, so to speak, that we aren't letting him."

"Can you tell me why Jude isn't involved in his treatment? From what I can tell, the two haven't interacted at all since he arrived at Bella Terra in . . ."

"November of last year." Luciana leaned back, the mask of someone trying to phrase delicate information in a way that wasn't damning. "Nikola's refusal to accept treatment has made it potentially harmful for him to interact with Jude at all."

"Harmful to Jude."

Luciana nodded. "Jude has cooperated with us a few times, but only with Nikola sedated."

"So if he isn't accepting any treatment," said Paris, "what is your job exactly?"

Luciana smiled humorlessly. "To keep trying."

Paris nodded and believed her. Given that she was Nils Ortega's sister, Paris had assumed that this woman must be at least a little opportunistic, but she didn't strike Paris that way at all; it was as if all of the opportunism in the family had gotten sucked up by Nils.

"Interactions with Nikola have resulted in the hospitalization of at least four people," said Paris. "How is that possible?"

"Well, that's another topic I can't speak to due to ongoing litigation, but . . ." She bit her lip. "It isn't only that Nikola is intelligent in ways we can't quite fathom or that he is able to cause harm in ways we don't anticipate; he has retained some of his post-natural capabilities that Jude was unable to remove without putting him in another body entirely. Even in a cage, even without that power core that gave him those incredible telekinetic abilities, he is still extremely dangerous." She licked her lips and nodded slightly, more to herself than to Paris. "So bear that in mind when you're in there."

. . . . .

"The few times he has communicated through spoken Pequod-phonemic, it was during a hostage situation," said Luciana as the elevator door opened to the basement where Nikola was kept. The higher levels of the building looked more like regular medical offices; down here, it was giving her Area 51 vibes. Luciana put her lanyard up to a key card reader, and a thick transparent glass door slid open. Inside was an orderly sitting in front of a large spread of security feeds.

"Barney, this is Paris," said Luciana as the orderly stood up to take Paris's hand. He was a large Black man in his thirties with the build of a security guard and a baby face that looked like it belonged to the host of a children's show about the importance of reading.

"Nice to meet you," said Barney. Paris shook his hand, still keeping the issue of *The New Yorker* close to her chest like a shield. "Have you been given the safety spiel?"

"I think so."

"So, I know you're here for a few days," said Luciana, "but the likeliest scenario is that you won't see him at all today."

"He's off the grid right now," said Barney.

"If he's able to give your infrared sensors the slip, how do you know he's in there at all?" asked Paris.

"Air movement," said Barney. "He can give us the slip if he moves very slowly, like a python, but he gives up his position when he moves at a normal pace. He can't help showing a bit of body heat then, and our sensors detect the air circulation."

"Plus, staying cloaked takes some energy," said Luciana. "He doesn't sleep often, but he has to sleep eventually, so even when he goes for stretches of days cloaked, eventually he'll collapse into exhaustion. The cloak slips off him then."

"Trying to keep himself awake seemed to be one of his suicide strategies for a while." Barney's brow furrowed sadly, and Paris got the impression that he actually saw Nikola as a patient on the level with any human, and he was saddened that his patient had not only shown no improvement but had possibly regressed. "Jude had to install a number of fail-safes in his body to keep him from harming himself. Every time Nikola figures out a new trick to try to weasel his way out of this earthly coil, his body shuts down entirely until Jude can arrive to fix the problem."

"We think he does it to lure Jude here," said Luciana, "but he's never been able to . . . mount an attack against Jude, if that's what he intended to do."

"Jesus," said Paris, clutching the magazine to her chest.

"Is that the issue of *The New Yorker* that Kaveh's essay appeared in?" asked Barney.

"Yes," said Paris. "Has he seen it?"

Luciana and Barney looked at each other.

"I don't know, has he?" asked Luciana.

"I don't know," said Barney. "He hasn't seen it since he arrived here, as far as I know."

The door to the room housing Nikola's cell reminded Paris of the door to a commercial-grade refrigerator that doubled as a gate to hell. Luciana put her lanyard to the key card pad, and the door slid open. "Good luck," she said. "Don't touch the 'glass.'"

"I've left a chair for you," added Barney.

The door opened to the room that housed Nikola's transparent enclosure. She moved inside, and it felt like the air pressure almost changed a little as the door slid shut behind her. She took a breath and moved forward.

Nikola's "cell" was more of a giant glass cube about thirty feet by thirty feet, freely standing in the center of a much larger concrete space that felt like an empty warehouse. The entire floor of the cell was covered with a foam pad, which in a pristine state might reveal where Nikola was standing, except he had mottled it all over to hide his whereabouts.

Paris stopped about ten feet from the side of the glass, observing the mechanical devices that hung above the ceiling of the cell. They almost looked like guns, and she figured in some regard they were. They were pointed downward in a way that spoke to something that could be deployed in an instant if Nikola needed to be subdued. She wondered how often that happened.

"Nikola," she said gently, hugging the magazine to her chest. "Do you remember me? You told me that we'd meet again."

Nothing.

Paris figured she may as well take advantage of that chair, and she took a seat. "I don't know if you got a chance to look at the article Kaveh wrote about you."

Still nothing.

She pulled out one of the journals, holding it with the *New Yorker* issue. "I'm here because I'm working on a project. I have questions about your relationship with Kaveh. I want to know what was going on when he wrote these notes. Some of it's in code, but not all of it. This has some of his drafts, too, that he wrote in longhand after you and Jude left the Los Alamitos base."

She approached the wall of the cell, now less than a foot from it, mindful of the instruction not to touch the "glass," looking at the thousands of indentations on the foam, on which somewhere stood Nikola. She recalled his size and shuddered; Kaveh's loft in Tribeca had had twelve-foot ceilings, and even then it had felt like Nikola had taken up the entire room.

"I'd like to read you one of them. He wrote this while you and Jude were missing. Before the Senate hearing."

She swallowed as she fumbled to open to the correct page of Kaveh's journal. "'I've never been religious,'" she read, slowly beginning to walk the length of the cell wall. "'And I think the idea that the revelation of the existence of aliens will result in a spiritual crisis is overblown, even in fundamentalist countries, but I can't deny that it does have me asking questions that I haven't thought about in years. One would expect that an advanced alien civilization would have all the answers, but the thing that surprised me the most was when Nikola told me how much his civilization still didn't yet understand about the universe, that every question answered only created a dozen more.'"

Once she reached the corner of the cell, she turned and slowly made her way back to the other side, looking up periodically to see if she could spy any movement on that foam floor. "'Perhaps this wasn't the line of thought Nikola would have wanted me to take, but the most surprising thing I've learned from him is that what they know about the makeup of reality leaves room for the possibility of souls, and *that*, more than the discovery of their existence, is what gives me a spiritual crisis. If the physics of the universe allow for the existence of souls, if we have some tether to what he calls 'noumenal' dimensions that we cannot perceive but are an inextricable component of our being, does that mean that souls have natures? Are kindness, cruelty, altruism, greed, et cetera, possibly rooted in some extra-dimensional essence we can only guess at, and not just our upbringing, our genetics, our brain chemistry?'"

She reached the opposite wall of the cell, and took another lap.

"'And it's a sentimental thought, childish even, but I feel that if there is such a thing as true personhood, then its definition must go deeper than what is and is not anthropocentric. The strange thing about Nikola is that the words that come to mind, even after all this, when I think of him are *gentle soul*, because if souls exist, then that is what I think he is.

"'The other strange thing is that I don't have any doubt that I'll see him again. Perhaps that's just as irrational as the idea that the biggest thing that binds us together is the possible existence of a soul, but—'"

Paris felt the blow before she heard it, a large blunt object crashing into her shins and sending her face careening into the acrylic wall. She felt the crunch of cartilage being pushed into her skull, the feeling of blood on the back of her throat as she bounced onto the floor. Before her body even hit, something grabbed her legs and pulled her into the cell through the new hole in the acrylic wall. The next thing Paris saw was a monster standing over her.

"ARE YOU HERE TO DEMONSTRATE YOUR COMPASSION?"

The voice hissed at her into her earpiece, cold, cruel, and mechanical. She was too stunned to scream as he used one giant hand to pin her arms to her chest and wrap the other around her neck, pinning her head to the floor and choking her so she couldn't even make a noise if she tried. Nikola's eyes were wild like two stars on the verge of collapse, the crest on the back of his head flared out like the fur of an angry wolf.

"YOUR COMPASSION IS WASTED, AS EVERYTHING YOU DO IS WASTED," said Nikola, moving his face close to hers. Distantly, she was aware that those gun-looking things on the roof had dropped into the cell, and were taking aim. "YOUR COMPASSION IS JUST ANOTHER MALADAPTIVE QUIRK AND WILL LEAD TO YOUR UNDOING JUST AS QUICKLY AS YOUR HUBRIS. DON'T COME TO ME WITH YOUR COMPASSION; YOUR COMPASSION WILL NOT SAVE YOU!"

The grip on her throat slackened as the guns went off, and the giant heft of the monster almost fell on top of her. Nikola collapsed headfirst, landing on her stomach while the rest of him fell on her legs, and in a panic, she tried to push herself out from under him. She pulled in a gulp of air, nearly choking on the blood from her nose, which she was pretty sure was broken. She heard people shouting as she pulled herself out from under the creature.

"Are you okay?" yelled Barney as the door to the cell opened. Several men with guns trained on Nikola came in before him, and he made a beeline for Paris, scooping her up as she gulped hungrily for air. Within seconds, he had her out of the room with the door closed behind them.

"Are you okay?" Barney repeated, putting her down on her feet, but she nearly stumbled, her legs like Jell-O, her throat still trying to find its natural shape and her lungs still demanding oxygen.

"That is a new one," said Luciana, looking at the little hole at the bottom of the cell.

Paris turned and saw the new hole in the acrylic wall, about the size of a pillow, shaped like the outline of a mountain in a Bob Ross painting.

"He must have been working on that one for a while," said Barney. "We didn't even notice any structural abnormalities in that section of the wall."

"Probably because it's so close to the floor," said Luciana.

"We should get her to a hospital," said Barney.

Paris couldn't help but laugh in quiet incredulity as she recalled the first thing Cora had told her when she had pitched her this project: *He's hospitalized four people.*

Now, he was up to five.

· 6 ·

> I would confer with you, my
> dearest.

Cora lit up when she heard the *ding!* she'd been waiting for, only to deflate when she saw who it was from. Yearning for a text from the person on your mind practically guaranteed that the next text you got would be from the person you wanted to hear from the least.

Olive's birthday had been her excuse to be in California, so she made an appearance at the sleepover, although given how excited Olive had been at the prospect, the three girls were far more interested in learning the dance moves from the new Lady Gaga video than they were in Cora. Now she sat on her mother's cold concrete front stoop, the lilting sounds of a trio of eight-year-olds singing, "I want to take a ride on your disco stick," floating through the window, staring mournfully at the text.

After her initial disappointment that it had been from Ampersand and not Paris, her overriding emotion was guilt. She hadn't spoken to him in over a week until two nights ago when she'd delivered what she'd learned from Marisol to him, but even that had been difficult in a way it had never been before. Talking to him at all brought her back to the shrieking alien void that existed on the other side of those amber eyes, and every atom in her body pulled to get away from it.

"Yeah, I'm here. Shoot."

"*I've begun an investigation into the incident in the Philippines. There is very little record of it from 2005, noteworthy in its sparseness, even for such a remote rural region.*"

"What's the official line on what happened?"

"*The cause of death reported to the press was that of a bar brawl that grew violent after a national-level basketball game, which shows a questionable lack of contemporary corroborating evidence. Moreover, two of the six dead were children.*"

"Kind of weird for kids to be collateral in a bar fight."

"*Indeed. This detail in particular prompts me to investigate further.*"

"Can't you just hack into the Filipino mainframe, like Obelus did?"

"*It is not so simple. I would need to know what terms to search for, and Filipino intelligence will use different terminology from American intelligence. And regardless, I am nowhere near as talented at navigating alien systems as Obelus was.*"

When she'd first met Ampersand, she'd assumed that there was nothing he couldn't do, but the longer she knew him, the more she learned how far that was from the truth. Just as Nikola couldn't begin to approach his skill in biology, Ampersand couldn't begin to compete with Nikola's skill in engineering, nor with Obelus's skill in navigating computer systems.

"So what's your plan?"

"*I will investigate myself in person, when the situation allows.*"

"You won't want me to go with you."

"*Not yet. Japanese authorities can't know.*"

"If this is legit, if it really was a physeterine that killed those people . . . what if they're still here?"

"*You needn't concern yourself with that now.*"

She started to push, but stopped herself. "Okay."

"*Will you come to me, dear one?*"

She winced, trying to tamp down the memory of that cold morass coming to engulf her. "What, right now?"

"*You have no other obligations in the United States until Monday.*"

"Paris thinks I'm still in LA. I should debrief with her once she's done failing at Nikola."

"*You could speak to her over the phone.*"

"Yeah, but she thinks I'm in LA."

"*She also resides in New York.*"

"Yeah, but I told her I'd debrief with her once she was done today; she doesn't know how many times they'll let her try talking to him."

"*You are infatuated.*"

Cora sat up like she'd been shocked by a Taser. "What? No, I'm not."

"*We share an empathic bond. You are infatuated.*"

She laughed quietly. Dense as he sometimes was, there were literally things she couldn't hide from him. "Maybe a little. Are you jealous?"

"*I don't experience jealousy like primates do.*"

"Why are you calling me a primate?"

"*You are a primate, my dearest, and jealousy is a distinct trait to all primates, not just humans. I would not deny you anything or anyone that brings you comfort or happiness, but be careful of forming attachments you may not be able to maintain.*"

It was only now that she had momentarily stopped obsessing over it that she got another *ding!*, and this time, it was from Paris.

> Saw Nikola. Huge bust. Heading back to NY tomorrow. You did warn me. I appreciate everything you've done for me. Hope we can chat soon.

"Uh-oh."

"*I fear she may have been the victim of Nikola's ire.*"

"I need to go to her."

"*If you feel it best, my dearest.*"

As the memory of the eldritch horror receded, she recalled that there were plenty of reasons she had fought so hard to keep him within this mortal coil. "Not this weekend, but I'll come visit soon." She paused. "I miss you."

As she said it, it felt true, but also she wondered what it was she missed—did she miss him, or did she miss the anthropomorphized, inaccurate image of him she'd constructed in her mind, one that she now knew had never even existed?

• • • • •

"Hello?" Cora knocked on the hotel room door again. "It's me."

She checked to make sure that she'd gotten the room number right. Paris had told her where she was staying at the Holiday Inn in San Bernardino, a two-hour drive without traffic but only a few minutes via semiautonomous plating. It was only as she stood there, timidly knocking a second time, that she realized Paris would assume the former, and that looked like A Bit Much.

The door opened, but the chain remained in place. "How did you get all the way out here?"

Cora shrank away from the door. Okay, yeah, on its face A Bit Much. "I just borrowed my mom's . . . Civic."

"I'm . . . not really decent."

"Why not?" Cora laughed nervously. "Did you end up in the hospital?"

Silence from the other side of the door. A silence that might read to some as guilty.

"I was joking. Please tell me you didn't end up in the hospital."

The door closed, the chain unhooked, and then Paris opened it. She stood tall with an air of embarrassed defiance and a big white square on the middle of her face. "It was only for a couple of hours."

"Oh my God. What did he do to you?"

Paris gestured for her to come inside. "Let's just say I should have been paying more attention when you talked about his ability to weaken the acrylic walls of his cell when nobody's looking."

"Good God, between the hospitalizations and the murders, he's closing in on double digits."

"Jesus," said Paris, putting a hand to the bridge of her nose, apparently having forgotten she'd just broken it. "Ow!"

"Maybe call this one a wash, I . . ." Cora sighed and sat down on the end of one of the two beds. "He's killed humans before, and without Kaveh around, there's no reason he wouldn't do it again if he was feeling spiteful enough."

Paris nodded, sitting down on the other bed. "I just have so many questions that only Nikola can answer. Like *why* does he think we're so very doomed? What goes on in their political world that makes *ending* us the obvious play?"

"There is precedent," said Cora without thinking.

Paris looked at her. "Precedent?"

Cora bit the inside of her cheek; the *correct* thing to do would be to walk it back, because this information was above top secret. But also, the existence of physeterines might become a matter of public interest very soon if Ampersand's investigation in the Philippines turned up anything. She got up and unhooked the phone and the TV—those were the quick-and-dirty ways the feds usually eavesdropped on people in hotel rooms.

"What are you doing?" asked Paris.

"Checking for bugs," she said, shifting her viewfinder to look for electromagnetic activity, scanning the walls for wires. Seeing none, she shifted her vision back to normal and looked at Paris. "I'm going to tell you some stuff that—*for now*—must remain off the record, like you can't tell *anyone*."

"If this is skip-the-country levels of secrecy, you sure you want to be telling me?"

"There's a good chance it won't stay a secret for long." She sat down on the bed opposite to Paris, took a breath, and said, "There are more than just amygdalines out there."

"How many more?"

"Just one that's relevant. Their sister species. Jude calls them *transients*, but *physeterine* is the official name at ROSA. They share a common ancestor, but aside from some similar physicality, they're nothing alike, from what I've heard."

"You've never seen one?"

Cora shook her head. "Some people claim to have seen aliens that match their description, but it's all testimonies from the 'I was abducted and anal probed' crowd, so not the most legitimate."

"What does that have to do with why Nikola thinks the earth is doomed?"

Cora sat up, steepling her fingers in front of her. "Once upon a time, x hundreds of years ago—so not that long, by amygdaline standards—we are already centuries deep into this forever war between amygdalines and physeterines. The Pequod Superorganism discovers that a large population of physeterines, hundreds of millions of them, have colonized a planet a few dozen light-years away from their locus—the people at ROSA named it Erythra. To my knowledge, the physeterine colonists on Erythra had not done any harm to the Pequod Superorganism, but their sheer numbers, the perceived *potential* for harm based on past conflicts, prompted the Superorganism to make a . . . preemptive strike of sorts."

"Against what?"

"Against . . . the entire planet."

Paris stared at her blankly. "They just . . . blew it up?"

"The word Jude uses is *sterilize*, but . . . the effect isn't too dissimilar. The planet is still there . . . just not what you'd call 'life-supporting.'"

Paris looked like she half expected Ashton Kutcher to bust through the door and announce that she'd been punk'd. "Nikola thinks they'd do that to us?"

"Maybe not that exactly . . . but my point is, there is precedent for the Superorganism to eliminate what they perceive as a potential threat before it has the opportunity to *become* a threat. And that fear doesn't come from nothing—even the witness testimonies we have of physeterines on Earth, most of them describe violent encounters."

"Why?"

Cora shrugged. "That's just kind of the way they are."

"'The way they are'? Intelligent enough for space travel yet indiscriminately violent?" Paris stood up, slowly pacing toward the door and back a couple of times. "The only source you have for information on them are unverified witness testimonies, and Jude?"

"And Nikola."

Paris rested her chin in her hands, taking a couple of laps around the room as she processed. "This only creates more questions, questions only *they* can answer." She returned to the bed, sitting so close Cora could feel the heat of her skin. "I don't suppose—"

"No," Cora cut her off apologetically. "No, Jude would never talk to the press, not even if I asked nicely. Sorry."

"And Nikola has already made his piece known." With the giant white square in the middle of her face, it wasn't immediately obvious that she was trying to hold back tears. "Why did I think I could just walk in there and he'd treat me differently than he did everyone else?"

"Because Kaveh did."

Paris pressed her lips together tightly. "Was it really as simple as that?"

"Honestly, yes. He just walked up to him and said, 'Hey, we're friends now.' And Nikola was like, 'Okay, sounds good.'"

Paris laughed sadly, a shine on her cheeks from recently spilled tears. "I thought I was going to march in there like I was fucking Oprah and he was just going to show me the respect he hasn't shown anyone since . . ." Another sheet of tears rolled down her face, and she looked down at her arm at one of her tattoos, a word in Arabic script. "He was so fearless."

Cora clenched her teeth, remembering how Kaveh spent days alone with Nikola, just talking to him, learning his wants, his needs, his fears. Somehow he'd turned himself into the only being in the world Nikola might actually listen to. He *was* fearless. It was what made him great. It was what made him unique.

And it was what killed him.

"I need to stop comparing myself to him," Paris continued. "But he was just everything I wish I was and I'm not. He was so fucking fearless."

Cora opened her mouth to speak, her throat now sore from trying to hold back tears, and it took a few tries before she got out, "Sometimes I miss him so much it hurts."

Paris wiped her eyes through a sad chuckle. "We should all endeavor to obliterate so many other people's lives by dying."

"It is genuinely impressive how many lives he ruined," said Cora, also laugh-crying.

"I wish there were something left of him that could tell me what to do. Some journal entry somewhere that I just haven't found yet that would tell me what to do."

Cora squeezed her hands together so tightly it bordered on painful, gripped both by the desire that Paris might reach out and comfort her and terrified of that very possibility. "Well, maybe Jude won't talk to you, but, you know, you've got me."

"I've got you?" Paris wiped her tears and smiled at her. "How've I got you?" she asked, leaning in toward Cora ever so slightly.

"I, you know, in any way you want?" She felt like she might be growing more legs just so she'd have more feet to put in her mouth. Okay, fine, so she was infatuated, but that didn't mean this wasn't deeply weird. "I mean, in any way I can help."

"You always this flustered when talking to the press?"

Okay, the borderline-teasing way she said that told Cora that she was fully aware of her "infatuation" and might even be humoring it. "Only when it's you."

Paris looked her up and down as if taking stock of her body language, and Cora noticed just how close she had leaned. Close enough that it would take only the least of efforts for their lips to touch. Just as she had this thought, Paris's phone went off, and the spell was broken.

"This is Paris," she answered, and her expression quickly grew serious. "I see. Are you sure?" A pause as she got an answer. "Yes, yes, of course. I made sure I had plenty of time. Yes, I understand. Thank you. I'll see you tomorrow." She hung up the phone, her expression dazed in a way that would befit either someone who'd won the lottery or had just learned that their entire family died in a plane crash.

"Who was it?" asked Cora.

"Luciana," said Paris. "She asked if I could come back."

· 7 ·

"That's all he said?" Paris asked, looking into Barney's security feed and resisting the urge to touch her still-healing nose for the eighteenth time in the last five minutes. It wasn't *broken*-broken, and the doctor told her the swelling should go down in a day or two, but she still had to wear the evidence of her dumbfuckery *right* smack in the middle of her face. At least being near LA, people might mistake the white gauze for a nose job and not evidence of her own dumb ass getting too close to an alien cyborg with a body count.

"That's all he said," said Barney. "'I will speak.' We can only assume he meant you. If he didn't, maybe he'll correct us."

Paris nodded and again resisted the urge to touch her nose. She really didn't want that to become a habit, especially in front of Nikola.

"The flat-screen should still work, though I doubt you'll be needing it."

Paris nodded. She'd had to disclose the earbud to Barney and Luciana in order to tell them that Nikola had communicated with her and what he'd said.

"He's already being a little more cooperative," Barney continued, pointing to the main security feed. Nikola was visible this time, lying flat on his stomach like a crocodile. He was mostly in shadow, his eyes peering out of the darkness like uncut diamonds. She started to entertain the thought that maybe Cora was right, maybe the Nikola Kaveh had known was just gone, and in his place was a being that was just as demonic as he looked.

"Well," said Luciana, giving that wide-eyed "ooookay" look and holding her lanyard to the key reader. "Good luck."

The hydraulic door opened, and Paris entered, holding Kaveh's journal to her chest like a talisman. She kept her gait steady as she approached, and much as she had hoped it wouldn't be the case, she was even more frightened this time around. She took a seat in the acrylic chair Barney had left out, placing the journal on her lap like it was a schoolbook. "Thank you for giving me the chance to talk to you again."

Nikola didn't move, save for a slight flash in his eyes that made her shiver.

"They told me you said you'd speak. Did you mean with me?"

Nikola didn't answer, and Paris racked her brain for how to get him to open up. One of the first things Kaveh taught her about interviews, especially the difficult ones, was to always be thinking about the subject's WIIFM—"What's In It For Me?" Interviews weren't fundamentally too different from hostage negotiations; at its core, success came through building a connection, and getting your subject to trust you, and to get them to believe that they might get something they wanted by opening up. Thing was, she didn't have much to offer him, no cold quid pro quo, so her first order of business was to find out what Nikola *wanted*.

"Have you read the *New Yorker* piece Kaveh wrote about you?"

At last, Nikola moved, slowly raising his head up above his body like a swan. "Hubris will be our end."

So that was a yes.

"I'm the only person who has access to Kaveh's journals. He left me these." She patted the books on her lap. "You were present for a lot of these entries."

Nikola cocked his head slightly, like an intrigued dog in slow motion. There was an androgyny to the computerized voice he used to speak, like a woman's voice slowed down by half into an unnatural-sounding depth. "You will show me the documents."

Her fingers stiff and shaking like she was one hundred years old, she fumbled to the correct page and held it up for him. He stood up slowly, approached the acrylic wall, and stopped in the middle of the cell, now halfway into the light.

"You will need to come closer."

She stood up and took a step toward the cell.

"Closer, dear gentle creature."

She shivered; he'd called her that once when they'd first met, but it took on a decidedly sinister timbre here. She took one step forward.

"CLOSER."

"That's close enough," said Barney from a speaker.

Nikola glided toward her, now only a few feet from the acrylic wall.

"CLOSER."

She took another step, until she was standing less than a foot from her side of the acrylic wall, and Nikola less than a foot from his, now at his full height of nearly nine feet. She wondered if she could have been more frightened than if the wall weren't there at all.

Nikola regarded her for a moment, then lowered his head, first to her eye level, then to the level of the journal she was holding at waist height. As he did so, he placed the tips of his long, spiderlike fingers against the wall as if daintily using them to steady himself, balancing on the acrylic like black widows resting in their webs.

"Does this look familiar to you?" she asked.

He slowly lifted his head until he was about halfway between her full height and his, fingers still delicately perched on the acrylic. She eyed those fingertips, wondering if he was drilling some microscopic flaws in the acrylic that would go undetected for weeks until he bashed another hole in the wall. Nikola backed away and settled down in the center of his cell. "IT DOES."

"Were you there when he wrote this?"

He tucked his hands under him, sitting up in that prim and proper way Kaveh had described, level on his center, head upright and hind legs pulled up to his sides, like a deer dipped in ink. "I WAS."

Paris backed away from the wall, sitting back down in the chair about fifteen feet away. "Something that struck me about this entry . . ." She fumbled back to the page with two identical lists and tapped her finger on the second one. "This looks like a reproduction of Kaveh's handwriting using the same pen. I think you wrote this."

"HOW VERY PERCEPTIVE YOU ARE, DEAR GENTLE CREATURE."

She reminded herself to breathe. "I was hoping you could tell me what those conversations were, if you remember."

"WITH REGARD TO THIS LIST, IT WAS REQUESTED OF ME THAT I REPLICATE HIS HANDWRITING, TO SEE IF I WAS CAPABLE."

"Under what context?"

"Your mentor's curiosity. We were being made to wait for our military escort, which was delayed."

He must be referring to one of the "appeasement" trips into nature the government had taken him and Kaveh on at Nikola's request. "Where was the military escorting you?"

"What is your intent, dear gentle creature?"

She hesitated, figuring that saying something to the effect of *I'm trying to undermine the political movement that will inevitably hasten the downfall of our civilization, and I want to use your relationship with Kaveh to educate the masses and inspire some goddamn hope* might be met with some hostility. "I want to better understand how two beings so incredibly different from each other could become friends."

"This word, friend, implies peerage, and our dear departed was not my peer. You are animals, dear gentle creature. Natural animals that exist through no engineering or intent but only through the whims of evolution."

Her nose flared in response to his light eugenicist sympathies, and she reminded herself, *You are talking to a space alien.* "He considered you a friend, even if you don't feel the same. I want a better picture of how your relationship evolved."

"To what end, dear gentle creature? You know that your civilization is not long for this world."

"But it's still here now. And while it's here, I want to write this."

"I do not think you grasp the severity of what is in store for your civilization, even without the looming threat from the Pequod Superorganism. The laws of thermodynamics cannot be changed. Soon, inhabited parts of your Earth will become uninhabitable. Water will run dry. Low-lying cities will flood. Refugees will appeal to wealthier countries, and they will be refused entry. Militarists will gain power with the promise of protecting their people from these refugees, and they will use their weapons to fight one another. And your militarists have engineered some remarkably powerful weapons.

"And this is only the short term; the rise in greenhouse gases will create a runaway greenhouse effect, releasing methane and carbon dioxide trapped in the Earth itself. The

VERY PLANT LIFE THAT COULD HAVE SAVED YOU WILL BEGIN TO POI-
SON YOU. THE HEAT OF THE OCEANS WILL KILL NEARLY ALL MARINE
LIFE. IT WILL HAPPEN, AND SOON."

Paris sat up straight and reopened the journal. "Perhaps your ancestors have some lessons they could teach us. Did something similar
happen to your ancestral world?"

"IT WAS A COOLING SUN THAT MADE OUR ANCESTORS FLEE
THEIR WORLD, BUT THEY HAD TEN THOUSAND YEARS BETWEEN THE
DISCOVERY OF THAT HARSH REALITY AND THE PLANET BECOMING
UNINHABITABLE. EVEN WITH SO MUCH TIME, ONLY TWO DISTINCT
POST-NATURAL GROUPS ARE EXTANT. YOU DO NOT HAVE SO MUCH
TIME. AND YOUR ONE ADVANTAGE, YOUR CLEVERNESS THAT MIGHT
OTHERWISE BE YOUR SALVATION, WILL PROVE YOUR DOWNFALL. IF
ANY WERE TO SUCCESSFULLY ESCAPE THE DYING PLANET, IT WOULD
ONLY CONFIRM THAT YOUR ADVANCEMENT IS PROGRESSING FAR TOO
QUICKLY, THAT AT THIS RATE, YOU WOULD SURPASS OUR OWN TECH-
NOLOGICAL ADVANCEMENT WITHIN THE SPAN OF A FEW GENERA-
TIONS. AND THEY CANNOT ALLOW THAT TO HAPPEN. THERE WILL BE
NO ONE LEFT TO READ YOUR RECORD."

"Things sound pretty dire," said Paris. Maybe his intent was to wear
her down, but mostly she was getting annoyed. She didn't know how
accurate his science was, but honestly, "everything will end eventually
and that's why there's no point in doing anything"? Yes, he may be an
unfathomable extraterrestrial intelligence that was hundreds of years
old, but that didn't mean he wasn't the type that might wear his people's
equivalent of a T-shirt that read YOU LAUGH AT ME BECAUSE I'M DIFFER-
ENT; I LAUGH AT YOU BECAUSE YOU'RE ALL THE SAME.

"I don't care if it'll be lost to the sands of time. The same is true of
everything, eventually. It has value here right now."

"YOU ARE TRYING TO PREVENT THE INEVITABLE, SAME AS YOUR
MENTOR DID WITH HIS PROPAGANDA. AND I AM TELLING YOU THAT
IT IS IMPOSSIBLE."

"Does Jude agree?"

"I HAVE NO WAY OF KNOWING WHAT HE THINKS."

"Would you like to know what he thinks?"

"WHEN YOU HAVE COMMITTED ACTS AGAINST YOUR LOVED ONES

so unspeakably terrible as I have, such connections are permanently severed."

"Permanently," Paris repeated. Then it occurred to her what his
WIIFM was, and it was so obvious she felt silly she hadn't thought of
it sooner. Kaveh had spelled it right out in his article: *Amygdalines are
much more long-lived than humans, and as such, they decide on their
life spans, and choose when they die centuries in advance. Nikola has not
come to Earth to live but rather to die, specifically to die with his last remaining "next of kin," Jude Atheatos.*

"I know Bella Terra won't even begin to have end-of-life conversations with you. I agree that is cruel. It's us imposing our cultural norms
onto you. I think you should have the right to exercise your own customs. A part of that is you deciding when and where you die, correct?"

"Correct, dear gentle creature."

She closed the journal, placing it squarely on her lap. "Because if you
don't get to choose when you die, then you just keep on going until your
body runs out of energy or breaks down entirely, and you have no way
of knowing how long that will take."

"Correct, dear gentle creature."

"And the main thing in your way is our laws, but I don't see any
reason why we couldn't bend them with the right incentive. You being
violent and lashing out isn't going to get you any closer to your goal. That
just shows them that you're not of sound mind, and frankly, if you aren't
of sound mind, you shouldn't be allowed to make that decision anyway."
She pulled out her own notebook, placed it on top of Kaveh's, and clicked
her ballpoint pen into action. "But if you cooperate with me, if you give
them a greater understanding of your culture, your biology, and if you
can show us that you *are* of sound mind, then they might consider giving
you what you're asking."

Nikola didn't move, but his eyes grew a hair wider and even seemed
to brighten. "You believe my compliance with you would provide them with an incentive to allow me to end my life?"

"I believe it would provide them with some sympathy and understanding. Your relationship with Kaveh, the way he wrote about you, is
the reason you have legal personhood at all. So the next step should be
for them to better understand you. And if they better understand you, if

they become sympathetic to what you're asking for, then they might be willing to meet your needs."

Nikola continued to watch her, still as a statue. Even the light in his eyes seemed frozen.

"Does my reasoning make sense?"

"SHOW ME YOUR JOURNAL ENTRY."

Thur, Oct 1, 2009 at 3:21 PM
From: T. Julian <TJ13591951@aol.com>
To: Alejandro Miranda Vasquez <JanoMirandaV@gmail.com>
Subject: Re: Defense bill talking points

Re: your inquiries on the AG-ETI sister species, have
requested CIA records but nothing in the witness testimonies
is reliable. No physical evidence, etc.

* * * * *

Thur, Oct 1, 2009 at 4:11 PM
From: Alejandro Miranda Vasquez <JanoMirandaV@gmail
.com>
To: T. Julian <TJ13591951@aol.com>
Subject: Re: Defense bill talking points

Can we be sure they exist? That this isn't just woo-woo hippies
giving testimony that coincides with how AG-ETI describes
AG-PHY?

* * * * *

Thur, Oct 1, 2009 at 4:14 PM
From: T. Julian <TJ13591951@aol.com>
To: Alejandro Miranda Vasquez <JanoMirandaV@gmail.com>
Subject: Re: Defense bill talking points

The images that have leaked out of Russia infer a crime no
greater than trespassing. Nothing that helps with the bill. I've
attached the images for reference.

* * * * *

Thur, Oct 1, 2009 at 4:19 PM
From: Alejandro Miranda Vasquez <JanoMirandaV@gmail
.com>
To: T. Julian <TJ13591951@aol.com>
Subject: Re: Defense bill talking points

Looking at them—nothing we can use for direct propaganda,
but they might be useful through back channels.

* * * * *

Thur, Oct 1, 2009 at 5:21 PM
From: T. Julian <TJ13591951@aol.com>
To: Alejandro Miranda Vasquez <JanoMirandaV@gmail.com>
Subject: Re: Defense bill talking points

What kind of back channels were you thinking?

* * * * *

Thur, Oct 1, 2009 at 5:25 PM
From: Alejandro Miranda Vasquez <JanoMirandaV@gmail
.com>
To: T. Julian <TJ13591951@aol.com>
Subject: Re: Defense bill talking points

How about Ortega? You still got him on a short leash?

* * * * *

Thur, Oct 1, 2009 at 6:24 PM
From: T. Julian <TJ13591951@aol.com>
To: Alejandro Miranda Vasquez <JanoMirandaV@gmail.com>
Subject: Re: Defense bill talking points

Shorter than he'd ever admit—he's allowed to stay in his cushy
little Upper East Side apartment by my grace alone, and he
knows it. Ortega might be a good play. Slip him the Russian
documents. See what he does with them.

· 8 ·

"This is . . . ," said Portia Black, Paris's once (and hopefully future) editor at *The New Yorker*. Paris had gotten her interview with Nikola, but an interview did not an essay make. Now, she needed a publisher. Portia pushed the rim of her reading glasses, touching the bone of her nose as if she were the one who'd gotten it crushed in. "Harrowing. I'm . . . impressed that you went in a second time."

"I'm still a little surprised I did it myself," said Paris. Cora sat next to her for . . . help? Reassurance? Encouragement? Well, she smiled at her, and Cora smiled back. When Paris set up this meeting, at a midtown restaurant called Almond frequented by the business lunch set, Portia had implied that she was interested in meeting Cora as well, and when Paris relayed that to Cora, she'd volunteered to come along. "It's rare I get the opportunity to help someone rather than be helped," she said. "If my showing up as a warm body helps you get them to commit to publish, then that's more good than I've done someone else in a long time."

"So the reason for the duplicate list is . . . they were bored?" asked Portia.

"Yeah," said Paris. "That's not how Nikola described it, obviously, but it was just two dudes messing around one afternoon while they were waiting for the military to take them on some excursion, and Kaveh was jotting down a to-do list. Apparently, there were these CIA guys watching them and being really obvious about it, and Kaveh realized he could ask Nikola to do the same to them, and he started jotting down what he was hearing. Then the subject changed when Kaveh wondered aloud what Nikola's handwriting might look like."

"Hence the second list," said Portia, taking a sip of her chardonnay. A consummate drinker of expensive fermented grapes, she was on her third glass but was showing no sign of it.

"I don't get the impression that Nikola understood what Kaveh was asking him to do," said Paris, taking a sip from her second glass of wine. She could not keep up with Portia.

Portia took off her glasses. "So you may have gotten a confession of espionage?"

"I'm not sure about that," said Paris, suddenly nervous.

"But she did get him talking," said Cora. "That's impressive in its own right; he doesn't talk to anybody."

"The exclusive of the century," said Portia, putting Paris's transcript to the side. "So, what's your narrative?"

"Well, it hasn't really changed—frame an honest picture of how Nikola's relationship with Kaveh developed. But to be honest, I feel like I haven't really tapped the potential of talking to him. I think if I made another inquiry, he might talk to me again. But . . . there is a complication."

"That is . . . ?"

"Nikola is being moved to a new facility soon—Bella Terra doesn't want to deal with the liability anymore. The fact that his current location is publicly known creates a huge safety concern, so the location of his new facility won't be made public."

"My aunt Luciana is going to work with him at the new facility," Cora added. "But she has a lot more sway at Bella Terra."

"Nikola's new facility doesn't want you talking to him?" deduced Portia.

"The new facility is being a lot more bearish about my presence, but with certain commitments as well as certain assurances that certain information will remain off the record, they might be willing to continue to let me have access. They might even let me go along during his transfer."

"If . . ."

"Well, they won't even consider it unless I'm officially working for a publication; they won't abide by 'freelance, but has a lot of interest.'"

"But what's your angle?" asked Portia. "What do you intend to communicate with this portrait?"

"That meaningful connection between us and them is possible," said Paris. "Conflict is not inevitable. And that is important, because the trend is a world gearing up to fight the invaders. And that is going to mean the end of everything if nothing else does."

Portia looked at Cora. "I'm going to guess that you know more about this topic than just about anybody. Does a new arms race to defend ourselves against their civilization really make a difference to them?"

"Yes, absolutely," said Cora, sitting up straight. "I'll put it bluntly—if humanity presents a threat to them, our demise is not a matter of if, it's a matter of when."

"People are talking like war is inevitable," said Paris. "Not just because that's how they are, but that's how *we* are. If we're told that these aliens might want to kill us all, of course people are going to want to arm up, because that's all we've ever done as a species. But we have to be able to imagine what an alternative looks like."

"Why is that?" asked Portia.

Paris didn't respond immediately, worrying she might be getting too up in her head about her narrative. Instead, Cora jumped in. "You have to understand that we can't outfight them, right?"

Portia leaned back, starting to look a little concerned.

"Maybe if we had a few hundred years to catch up, but we don't have a few hundred years. Any amount of armament is futile."

"What about the electromagnetic pulses?" asked Portia. "Don't those take them out?"

"See, that's the problem. You're thinking like a militarist," said Cora. "Yes, an EMP will take out an individual, some of the time, not an entire fleet at great distance from Earth. And even against EMPs, the amygdalines here have already built fail-safes against those. An arms race is a waste of time."

"So you're hoping Nikola might give us an alternative?"

"I don't think Nikola can give us an alternative," said Paris, "but maybe just learning more about him could inspire people—*human* people—to dream one up."

"So you want to inspire the masses to turn away from an arms race we are doomed to lose regardless and imagine alternatives?" Portia chuckled. "Nothing if not ambitious. People of my generation *hated* hippies during the Vietnam War—not because they were hurting anybody but because they believed that you don't *have* to hurt anybody. But the average American was offended at the mere idea that war wasn't a necessary component of civilization. I remember how angry people got at John Lennon when he started advocating for peace. War *must* be a necessary evil, or else all of this pain and suffering we inflict on one another is meaningless. What a difficult truism to let go of—even I struggle with it."

"And there isn't any clear alternative," said Cora. "War is easy. Restructuring society around peace has never been done before. Like . . . Lennon's 'Imagine' doesn't provide anything actionable; it doesn't say, 'Here is how we're going to achieve world peace,' it just says to 'imagine' it. *Imagine* nothing to kill or die for. Presents it like a challenge: 'I wonder if you can.'" Cora looked at Paris. "It's like we're in the thick of the Vietnam War, but no one is saying, 'Give peace a chance.'"

Paris nodded, feeling emboldened, and looked at Portia. "I'm just not of a disposition to sit idly by while pigheaded men destroy the world. Even if the odds are 99.9999 percent on the side of failure, that 0.0001 percent chance of success is worth working toward, because the alternative . . ." She shook her head. "If I can paint a picture of how one of them can come to care about one of us, maybe that could inspire some hope. Incentivize people to"—she shot Cora a knowing smile—"'give peace a chance,' you might say.'"

"Mmm," said Portia. "Beautifully said. I'll run it by the publisher, but we can work out an advance to help fund your research. If you can deliver something half as compelling as your pitch, it'll be a cover."

Every muscle in Paris's face grew slack. "Really?" A cover? *Li'l ol' me?*

"It's a real possibility," said Portia, standing up. "You two make a good team."

Paris coughed, still light-headed, and she caught Cora blushing out of the corner of her eye. She regained her composure and rose to her feet. "I think so, too."

The three exited the restaurant, and once clear of the revolving doors and back into the bright midday sunlight, Portia turned to Cora. "I have a thought," she said. "The Atlantic Press Awards are coming up next month, and there's going to be a memorial segment for Kaveh Mazandarani."

Cora's confidence wavered. It was no Pulitzer, but it was a prestigious enough award that she'd clearly heard of it. "Oh . . ."

"I don't know how practiced you are at public speaking, but considering that you haven't said anything publicly about Kaveh, perhaps that might be a good opportunity?"

"Public speaking? Like . . . a eulogy?"

"Something like a eulogy."

She looked at Paris as if for guidance, then back at Portia. "Um . . . I don't exactly . . ."

"You don't need to answer right now. But if you're open, can I put you in contact with the director of the awards?"

"Um, yeah, sure. I mean, if you think I could do him justice."

"If your pitch here is any indication, I think you could. It was good to meet you." She gave Paris a very pointed "don't let me down" look. "We'll be in touch," she said, and she turned back toward the *New Yorker* building.

Paris let out a long breath and looked at Cora. "We make a good team, huh?"

Cora shook her head, snapping out of it. "Well, you know, like I said, if anyone deserves an explanation or anything in that vein—"

"Well, well. Fancy seeing you here."

Cora's eyes widened, and Paris turned to see what had her dumbstruck.

"I was just on my way to the office," he said, sauntering up to them with the casualness of a neighbor they'd bumped into while walking the dog. Paris could not mask her surprise.

It was Nils Ortega.

Nils seemed to be experimenting with new styles nowadays, no longer wearing the black turtleneck but instead a peach button-up under a tailored navy-blue blazer. His jet-black hair was no longer slicked back and flat as it had been two years ago when he'd shot to worldwide fame. It was still sculpted and geometric, but it read as more approachable. He seemed completely relaxed, looking at both of them as he would any work colleagues.

Cora just looked at him, nonplussed, like she wasn't particularly surprised to see him. Nils smiled, and it occurred to Paris that she had no idea what their relationship even was. She hadn't thought to ask.

"It's been a while," Paris said genially, saving Cora from having to respond.

"Indeed it has," he said to Paris. "Two years ago, wasn't it? Was it the London Press Club?"

"The European Press Prize, actually. Amsterdam."

Nils gave a forced self-effacing eye roll. Then he acknowledged Cora. "How's school going?"

"Um . . . it's going."

"Good. Declared a major? Going to stick with linguistics?"

"I haven't decided yet."

"I guess you've got a bit of time. Fun to be at the old stomping grounds?"

"Yeah," said Cora. "A little surreal."

"Fancy that I should run into you both, actually. I have come into some information that I think might be interesting for you to look at, you being in the know and all."

"Oh?" said Paris. "Is it of the variety that's going to leave me wondering why you haven't published it?"

"Well, to be honest, we aren't sure if it's legitimate," said Nils. "While the source itself seems like it probably is, it does not, shall we say, comport with what we already know about the Pequod civilization."

Paris looked at Cora for some direction on how to steer this conversation but saw only a blank wall. "Interesting," she said. "Maybe we'll have to have a chat later."

"Indeed," said Nils. "Well, I need to get to the office before everyone leaves for the day. You two seem busy. I'll leave you to it. Talk soon?" This, he directed at Cora.

"Sure."

Nils gave a polite, professional nod before heading on his way, following in Portia's tracks toward the *New Yorker* building.

"What'd he mean by 'stomping grounds'?" asked Paris.

"He used to be a professor at Columbia. Was actually a point in my favor during admissions as I understand it."

"Is he always like that?"

"Always?"

"I mean, when he sees you, is he always so . . . formal?"

"I don't know how to answer that," said Cora, staring at nothing. "That was the first time we've spoken in seven years."

"Holy shit." Paris looked in the direction he'd gone, but he was already out of sight. She cased their immediate surroundings for options and saw that a bar a few doors down had just opened and was completely empty.

"Let me buy you a drink," she said, holding out her hand, which Cora took catatonically.

They sat down at the far end of the bar away from doors or windows, Cora maintaining a strange, detached calm. "I don't think his running into us was a coincidence," said Paris.

"No," said Cora. "He knew. Someone at *The New Yorker* must have told him we were meeting Portia, or maybe he hacked into someone's email. Who knows? But he knew."

"Excuse me," said Paris, signaling the bartender. "I'll get a Jameson, neat, and . . ." She looked at Cora, who did not seem like she was eager to make any decisions at the moment. "A whiskey sour."

The be-bow-tied bartender nodded and got to work. *Why do I always default to buying drinks? I should do something besides order her a drink*, she thought, but Cora's body language told her that right now, she was closed for business. This, of course, only made Paris want to reach out for her even more, because she just loved a project, apparently. That she might be attracted to one of Kaveh's girls shouldn't have surprised her, as Kaveh's type hadn't been far off from her own. Paris had once goaded Kaveh about their shared penchant for waifish, fragile, emotionally unavailable white women, once the sting of the breakup that had sent him to rehab had eased enough that they could joke about it.

"Do you hug?" she asked.

"Not as often as I'd like to."

Paris brought her in as close as barstools would allow, and Cora melted into her, and perhaps it was the two-glasses-of-wine thinking, but she found herself wanting to indulge Cora's obvious little crush and take it a step further.

No, she thought, mentally smacking herself. *No, don't even think it. She's your . . .*

Her what?

They didn't have a formal working relationship. This wasn't like hooking up with a coworker or a subordinate, Cora wasn't going to co-write the piece, she wasn't even a source; she'd just put her in touch with people who could help her. At most, she was an uncredited research assistant. There would be no ethical violation here; it would just be . . . *weird*.

They pulled back from each other, and Cora looked up at her, her gray pupils encircled with a corona the color of rust, the whites of her eyes reddening, and she smiled sadly. "I'll never be free of him."

Paris placed a hand on Cora's neck and used her other hand to brush her hair past her ear before she realized she'd done it. It was so simple yet intimate and could go either way very, very quickly. It wasn't the memory of Kaveh that gave her pause or the no-no of inter-colleague hookups; there was something behind that melancholy that felt like a flag as red as the cute dress she was wearing, like she always had one foot out the door.

But Paris didn't have two seconds to really contemplate her next move, because Cora made it for her, going in for a kiss, quick and desperate. She pulled back almost as fast, looking at Paris like she couldn't believe she'd done that. "I'm sorry, I—"

"It's okay," Paris whispered. Relieved of the burden of having to make the first move, she cupped Cora's face and brought her in, slower this time, a gift instead of petty theft.

When they pulled apart, Cora was still giving her that sad, desperate look as if to say, *What next? Do you want to make out in a bar? Neither of us are drunk enough to make out in a bar, especially an empty bar at 2:00* P.M.

"Let's skip the drinks," said Paris.

"And . . . ?"

Paris smiled playfully. "Let me take you home."

9

Within a week, Cora was contriving reasons to see Paris every night.

At first, it was somewhat credible contrivances—*Oh, I remembered this thing Nikola did; we should meet up and talk about it. Oh, I need help writing this paper. Oh, I found this thing online that might be a legit physeterine sighting where someone* didn't *die*. But within a few days, she dropped the pretenses and was spending every night at Paris's house.

In his will, Kaveh had left Paris his Tribeca apartment, but she quickly decided to sell it, as it was the last place she had seen him alive and she couldn't bear to be inside it, let alone live in it. She used that money to buy a brownstone in Bed-Stuy, which became one of Cora's main contrivances; it needed *lots* of work, and Paris needed all the help she could get—painting the walls, testing the integrity of the kitchen counter when a body was rapturously thrust upon it in the throes of passion—all sorts of projects.

One week passed, then another, then another, and it was around this point that Cora realized that this was the longest she had gone without seeing Ampersand in the entire time she'd known him. *Well, except for that one time he abandoned me for three months without a word*, she rationalized, and it wasn't like they never *talked*. They talked every day. And besides, Japan was really far away. Even if it took her half the time to get to Japan via autonomous plating than it did to get to Paris's house via the subway, the trip was still a hassle. Why make the trip if she didn't *need* to? There were still several more kitchen counters to test.

This day was one of those perfect, crisp autumn days, and the fall colors of Brooklyn had just hit their peak, still shining vibrant reds and yellows in the brisk fall air. Cora was a couple of blocks from Paris's brownstone when the sound of Jay-Z's "Empire State of Mind" floated out of a nearby bar, and she stopped short, overcome with emotion. It wasn't just the excitement of a budding relationship or the beauty of the reds and golds of the trees contrasting with the clear blue sky, but at infatuation with the city in general. The city *did* make her feel brand-new, the big lights *did* inspire her. She had only just begun to tick off the long list of things that Paris, who had lived here her whole life, planned on sharing with her in New York—next weekend a tentative trip to the Brooklyn Botanic Garden and the Brooklyn Public Library, and later in the year the Christmas market in Union Square. That was to say nothing of all the bars, local haunts, speakeasies, and oyster bars she'd told her she was "totally going to drag her" to. She had a feeling she'd never had before—that this was *home*. That she could stay here forever.

And then a computerized voice intruded in her ear: "*Will you come to me this weekend, dear one?*"

Cora started walking again, the magical moment gone. Tears in the rain. "I can't. I have plans."

"*I have made some discoveries of concern with regard to the incident in the Philippines.*"

She put her phone to her ear so passersby wouldn't think she was a crazy person talking to the voices in her head. "What's going on?"

"*Filipino intelligence has recovered some physical evidence from the altercation in a village called Bahura, but I was unable to ascertain where the evidence is being stored or what it even is.*"

Cora slowed to a stop, now having made it to Paris's front stoop. "It . . . seems noteworthy that Filipino intelligence got involved."

"*Precisely. I did locate the security footage that Filipino intelligence has withheld from the public record, but there's nothing unusual aside from a small crowd to watch a basketball game, and certainly no evidence of a fight. I could attempt to locate the evidence on my own, but I can't guarantee a complete survey of what happened, and moreover, I would alert the authorities to my presence in their systems. I don't believe there is an efficient means of going forward with our investigation without the cooperation of the Filipino and American governments.*"

"Why the American government?" she asked, slowly ascending the brownstone's stoop.

"*Because they are the only other body that we know of with evidence of physeterines on Earth, and it would be more fruitful for us to gain access to intelligence from both of these agencies, rather than one or the other.*"

"Okay." She stopped just shy of the front door to the brownstone. Luciana and her friend Stevie Odissu no longer worked for ROSA, and she had a visceral distaste for anyone and anything CIA-related, so the least objectionable person she knew to reach out to in government land was Dr. Sevak Ghasabian, who was still the director of ROSA despite the Department of Defense's hostile takeover of the agency last year. He was kind of a space case that Cora had never quite figured out, but she considered him harmless. Mostly harmless.

"I'll tell Dr. Sev about what Marisol told me, and we'll take it from there."

"*Will you come to me soon, dear one?*"

Paris's door swung open, causing Cora to yip in surprise before she could respond.

"You gonna just stand out here?" asked Paris, crossing her arms with a smirk and leaning on the doorframe. She was wearing a tight white tank top over skinny jeans, and her hair had been braided into dozens of tiny spirals that faded from her natural black to a deep burgundy at her waist.

"Paris says hi," said Cora, chest flooding with butterflies.

"*Will you come?*"

Cora put a hand to her face and shook her head. "*Yes*, I will come."

"*I will see you soon, dear one.*"

Cora pulled the phone away from her ear as if it had actually been the source of his voice.

"*Jūdo-san?*" asked Paris.

Cora's shoulders fell as she walked past her host into the house, waiting for Paris to shut the door before letting herself fall into Paris's embrace. The two shared a deep kiss.

"I like your new hair," said Cora dreamily after they'd pulled apart.

"Thanks," said Paris, tossing it like she was in a Pantene commercial. "It only took about ten hours, including a lunch break. So, uh . . . bad news from amygdaland?"

Cora forced a smile and was immediately annoyed that she had to force it. This was still the honeymoon phase, goddamn it. She was supposed to be having fun, not having to deal with the looming threat of flesh-eating aliens or, worse, possibly having to *explain* dynamic fusion bonding to her new . . . well . . . whatever this was. "I'm just . . . going to have to go back to Asia soon."

"Guess we have traveling for aliens in common," said Paris, heading up her staircase. "'I'm going-going back-back to Cali-Cali.'"

"Nikola agreed?" Cora asked, following her.

"Yup. I still have a few entries in Kaveh's journals to go through with him."

The two entered the spare bedroom Paris was using to store a small forest of unpacked boxes. She didn't have much furniture yet, but she had plenty of ephemera to put on the furniture, albeit not the sort of thing that would impress the New York journalism intelligentsia. Cora opened the box labeled "Nerd Shit." *Akira* poster, full DVD box set of *Neon Genesis Evangelion*. "More evidence of weebery," she observed with a smile.

"Tasteful weebery," said Paris. "I have to figure out how to incorporate it into my décor, lest I chance being seen as less of a serious journalist by the Portia Blacks of the world." She side-eyed Cora. "When are you leaving for Japan?"

"Not sure. Have you ever been to Japan?" she asked, trying to steer this conversation away from Ampersand.

"No, not yet."

"Would you like to?"

"Of course I would! I'm dying to go to the Studio Ghibli museum, and I've always wanted to go to one of those *onsen* towns. I had some friends who did a *ryokan*—you're trying to change the subject, aren't you?"

"No!" Cora yipped. "I just . . . You *do* like your Japan."

"It's interesting, Kaveh was careful never to write about you or him . . . or should I say you *and* him."

Cora's stomach took a swan dive onto a rock. "What do you mean?"

"Well . . ." Paris waggled her index finger between them. "Since you and I are . . ."

Paris looked at her like she expected Cora to finish her sentence. You and I are *what*? Enmeshed? Entwined? Intended? Affianced? Was Paris

about to suggest renting a U-Haul? Her mind was racing with hypotheticals so fast that her expression had turned to one of deer-in-headlights,
which clearly made Paris uncomfortable.

"I mean," Paris amended, "I suppose I have a degree of separation to
this alien fellow that's pretty significant *to me . . .*"

Cora blinked. What did she mean by *that*? Did she mean the degree
as in the concept of having an in with an alien was significant or that the
person who was the degree was significant?

"And I don't really know anything about him," said Paris. "What your
liaising entails, how often you see him, how he treats you . . ."

"He treats me fine!" said Cora, *way* too eagerly. "Fine. Really! Sorry.
It's just I've spent the last two years building up walls to defend him
against people; volunteering information doesn't come naturally. He's
fine. We're fine!"

Now it was Paris wearing the mask of the deer staring down the on-
coming truck. "You can see where that isn't very convincing."

Cora felt like she was getting hives. This sort of prying would inevitably lead to a disclosure not only of dynamic fusion bonding and all
that entailed but also that she'd had her brain wired for amygdaline high
language, to say nothing of her nascent terror of the consciousness she
had spent the last year prepping to mind-meld with!

"I'm not . . . I mean, I'm not trying to *hide* anything from you." Welp,
there was her first official lie to Paris. "I'm sure you'll meet him one day."

"In Japan?" asked Paris skeptically.

"Yeah, in Japan! I can take you."

Paris's expression shifted to an almost childlike eagerness. "Really?"

"Yeah! He actually lives in one of those mountain *onsen* villages in
Fukushima Prefecture. Not that he uses any of the facilities there, but I
do. It's super cute. I could take you there one day!"

Again, Paris's expression melted back into skepticism. "So why are
you so . . . on edge?"

Fuck fuck fuck what do? What say? Paris was intimating that she
might feel that Cora was a *significant* presence in her life while at the
same time prying for information on the very alien reason why their
relationship was doomed—if not for Paris's inevitable horror and disgust at the whole situation, then for the fact that he was still planning to

abscond with her to Planet Xethorp in the Gnar Galaxy eventually. She had to respond. *Think fast, think fast!*

"It's just the reason I'm going to Asia isn't fun. Literally, the thing he called me to tell me—you remember that sister species I told you about?"

"Yeah . . ."

"He's found some evidence that there might have been an 'incident' with them and some rural villagers a few years ago and the Filipino government covered it up. So when I say, 'Asia,' I don't mean Japan this time."

"Oh," said Paris, the tension in her body dissipating. "So shit's getting really real."

"I guess it is," said Cora, relieved that Paris had accepted that very real and very valid explanation that, in a sane world, would have her far more freaked out than what her new . . . *special friend* might think of her relationship with her nonhuman *special friend*.

"Wonder if there's anything Nikola could tell me?" Paris wondered aloud.

Cora shook her head. "There's nothing Nikola knows that Jude doesn't."

Paris's eyes popped like a light bulb just went off. "You know, I've been thinking, maybe I should reach out to Nils. Remember what he said about having some intel that didn't 'comport' with what we know about Pequod?"

Cora's heart sank at the mere sound of his name. "You think his 'evidence' might be of physeterine activity?"

"Couldn't hurt to ask."

"No, it very much could. Nils is a snake."

"When do you depart?"

"I'm not sure. I have to . . . talk to some government bureaucrats first."

"Shit, I leave the day after tomorrow. I don't know if I can get in touch with him before I go."

Cora sighed. "I'll do it."

Paris stepped over a box and placed her hands on Cora's shoulders. "You don't have to interact with that man."

The protective way she said it was a warm breeze on Cora's cold heart, and she allowed herself to fold into Paris's embrace. She did not want those warm embraces to end.

"I think I do," she said. "He doesn't just want to disclose information—he's been trying to get to me for years. He can't ruin my life more than he already has."

"That's the thing," said Paris, pulling back and putting a gentle finger under Cora's chin. "I'm afraid he might take that as a challenge."

He would, Cora knew. This was a trap, but all the same, there still might be something to be gained. "He will. But in fairness, I am my father's daughter."

"What does *that* mean?"

Cora shrugged and smiled slyly. "I can't help but take it as a challenge, too."

Date: November 2, 2009
From: Director Nicholas Mallari
To: Deputy Director Macallan
Subject: NICA Specimen

Director of ROSA Sevak Ghasabian has relayed to us a key
piece of intelligence supplied by AG-ETI-46 liaison/interpreter
and former ROSA contractor Cora Sabino, regarding a possible
ETI encounter in the western Philippines that left several
people dead in 2005. Evidence purportedly comes directly from
AG-46. We have had several correspondences with NICA to
facilitate rendezvous with AG-46, and while they are willing
to allow one of our agents to observe and report, they have
no interest in talking to us—only to AG-46 and its interpreter,
Sabino.

The Japanese have agreed to covertly act as intermediary
between the CIA and NICA and their Department of Science
and Technology, which now admits to having recovered a
specimen from the 2005 incident.

* * * * *

Date: November 2, 2009
From: Deputy Director Macallan
To: Director Nicholas Mallari
Subject: NICA Specimen

Field agent will rendezvous with Cora Sabino at JFK airport to
escort her to Japan. Filipino military will take over escort from
Haneda. Field Agent will accompany Sabino and AG-ETI-46 as
guest of NICA and the Filipino govt. Field agent understands
that they are on assignment only to observe and report.

* * * * *

Date: November 2, 2009
From: Director Nicholas Mallari
To: Deputy Director Macallan
Subject: Re: re: re: NICA Specimen

The president has requested that field agent pay special attention to any information regarding the 2005 incident that can be utilized in advocating for his defense bill.

* * * * *

Date: November 2, 2009
From: Deputy Director Macallan
To: Director Nicholas Mallari
Subject: Re: re: re: NICA Specimen

Understood.

· 10 ·

Nils had suggested a coffee place in SoHo that served drinks with names like Beanwich Village and Upper Roast Side. Cora reached the designated meeting spot at 1:58 P.M. If he showed up even a minute late, she'd know. She'd reached out to Dr. Sev less than two days ago, but the ROSA-to-active-investigation pipeline had worked quickly; her flight out of JFK was in only a few hours, so she'd scheduled this meeting to Nils right before she had to go to the airport to give her a quick out, as well as an excuse to put a hemisphere between them after it was over.

Seven years.

Neither of Cora's parents were particularly warm people, but Nils had always had a bad case of "cool dad." He was more interested in being liked than being an authority, which no doubt played a factor in her brother, Felix, now a teenager, defecting to his father's custody the second Nils set foot back on American soil. She'd felt outrage on principle at the idea of being abandoned by a parent when she was a teenager, but looking back, had she really been abandoned by a *parent*? She'd had a "sire," as Ampersand would put it. A legal guardian, for a time. But she'd never had a father.

She sat in the corner by the entrance to the café, hugged by the glass of the window on one side and exposed brick on the other, when he arrived at 2:00 on the dot, his face popping into a polite smile when he saw her. His worn leather jacket was strangely blue-collar for him, almost rustic, and he was wearing a pair of stonewashed jeans. Even his black hair, normally perfectly sculpted back in a wave, was deliberately un-styled, a strained interpretation of natural.

Seeing him again was like running into a celebrity you'd developed strong opinions about, someone you had seen on television a million times but never expected to see in the flesh. For years, she'd been imagining this moment, and in those imagined moments, she was always dressing him down, perfectly articulating all the wrongs he'd done to her and her family so quickly and concisely that he couldn't get a word in edgewise. But now that the moment was here, she didn't have anything like that begging to get out at all. This was a stranger.

"Glad to hear from you," he said in a warm yet professional tone, hands in his pockets.

"Thanks for seeing me," she said formally. "How's Felix?"

"Good," he said, and then gave her a look as if to say, *And that is all there is to say about that.* "Shall we patronize the establishment before we take up their precious floor space?"

Cora ordered a macchiato and Nils a Red Eye, which was a cup of coffee with a shot of espresso dumped in it. When the barista served up their drinks, Cora reached for her wallet.

"I got this," said Nils in a jovial tone, like they were friends just catching up. She shot a nervous glance at the barista, who didn't seem to find either of them remarkable. She refrained from scanning the place for bugs with her ocular overlay, as the process required unnatural eye movements that Nils would surely notice.

"So," he said as they returned to her table in the corner by the window. "How's it feel to be on the student side at Columbia?"

"Surreal," she said, accepting her coffee from him. "Some of the student groups have been a lot more welcoming to me than I expected, but it's still sort of odd. It's not at all like Irvine, where I was just one of the crowd." She looked down at her coffee and saw the name he'd given to the barista, which he'd written in Sharpie on her coffee cup—"Beano."

"Are . . ." She stopped herself before she added, "You kidding me?"

Nils said nothing, chuckling good-naturedly as he took a sip of his Red Eye. Cora took an uncomfortable sip of her bitter espresso and foam, unsure what using her childhood nickname, from when farts were the very pinnacle of comedy, was meant to communicate. An acknowledgment that they were, in fact, related? That they had a history that began earlier than a few weeks ago?

"So, are you going to tell me what it is you have?" she asked.

"I can do you one better. I can show you."

Nils pulled a five-by-eight-inch envelope out of a pocket inside his jacket and slid it across the table. Cora opened the envelope, removed the contents, and froze before she'd even fully removed the photographs inside. There were three figures in the first printout, perhaps twenty feet from the camera and seemingly unaware of its existence. The image of that forward-leaning center of gravity, the arms and tails like a velociraptor's, the amygdaline-like head, the crab-leg fingers that almost looked skeletal—it was unmistakable.

Nils had come into possession of photographs of live physeterines.

The family resemblance was there—they had similar postures, head crests, and proportions to amygdalines, but there were some differences that made it hard to mistake one for the other—these creatures were stockier, their fingers shorter and thicker relative to their arms. The night vision of the security camera made their eyes glow like tiny nuclear explosions. Most distinct were their tails, as long as their torsos and heads put together. They were thick like any limb meant to act as counterbalance, but mimicked the free-flowing nature of an octopus's tentacle rather than the rigidity of a vertebrate tail. Going by the Cyrillic script on the bottom of the frame, this was not from the Philippines. Next to the Cyrillic script was a time stamp—02:04:15 A.M. 05/04/2008.

This was from last year.

"H . . . how . . ." She swallowed. "How did you get this?"

His mouth formed into a smirk that bordered on victorious. "Same way I always do. 'Anonymous whistleblower.'"

"And the dates . . . Are the dates from when the photos were taken?"

"These are stills from a security camera; the dates would have been burned onto the frame as it was captured."

She continued flipping through them, dread swelling in her chest like a balloon. All the photos were taken at night, and the figures were anywhere from fifty to two hundred feet from the camera. The dates ranged from May to July of 2008, meaning that this pod had been sticking around whatever former Soviet nation this was for a while.

"The look on your face tells me that these photos were probably not doctored, either."

Shit shit shit. "I haven't . . . seen anything like this before."

"And yet something about this seems plausible?"

She looked up at him, realizing that she didn't *need* to tell him anything; he may have just wanted to gauge her reaction, and he sure had gotten it. He took the photos back, flipping through them and glancing over his shoulder to make sure the barista wasn't telegraphing info to the CIA. "I have to admit, I had my doubts at first. These things look more like a human-imagined space monster, you know?"

"What makes you think these aren't CGI?"

"I had my security camera expert look at them," he said, sliding the pictures back to her with a different photo on top—this one only had two physeterines, but at a similar distance and on a different date. "Word on the Russian street is that this is not the same species, but they might be related—they resemble amygdalines way too much for it to be a coincidence." He raised a carefully manicured eyebrow. "Do you know anything about that?"

"No. He doesn't tell me anything."

Nils chuckled. "You never were a good liar."

Cora glared at him, but he just kept smiling calmly. Then he took the photos from her and flipped to a couple he had marked. "The Russians code-named them Semipalatinsk. I wonder what our boys code-named them."

"Sloop John B." She closed her eyes. *Why the fuck did I tell him that?*

He laughed like this was some joke he was in on, but she knew he could tell that there *was* some legitimacy to the code name Sloop John B.

"Where is this feed from?" she asked.

"We think it's somewhere in Ukraine or maybe Belarus. Needless to say, leaking this sort of thing near Russia is a much bigger occupational hazard than it is here, and it is a pretty fucking big occupational hazard here."

"Do you know what happened to the leaker?"

"As far as we can tell, they have been disappeared into the Russian abyss."

She looked back at the photos, her mind swimming. Four years ago, they'd been in the Philippines, and one year ago in Ukraine. *Jesus.* The dates meant this footage was taken not too long after Nikola very publicly revealed his existence to the world. All signs pointed to them having arrived on Earth before even Ampersand had.

"I can't tell you whether or not the CIA has this intel," she said. "I don't know, but I can tell you I haven't seen it. The international intelligence agencies aren't sharing what they know with one another, now less than ever. It's a patchwork of half evidence, so no one knows anything for sure."

"Perhaps if I knew a little bit more about what to look for, I could see if there's more where this came from," he said. "If this is legitimate, the people really should know."

Cora nearly rolled her eyes. *The people.* Gag. "You and I differ a bit in our opinions on when information should be made public, let alone how."

"You think this should be kept secret?"

"No, but I also know this would be very easy to weaponize, especially in the current political climate."

"Truth is truth; it can't be weaponized, it can only lead to consequences."

"No, it very much *can* be weaponized. There is no such thing as a universal objective truth because truth always comes in the context of a story. I'm not skeptical of the facts you're sharing. I'm asking, what story are you trying to tell?"

Nils opened his mouth to respond, but paused, considering. "I don't even know what it is that I have. But you're right, how and when the truth is released, and especially how it is framed, matters. That's why I'm sharing this with you and no one else."

She reminded herself that this was a stranger, a person she had not interacted with since she was a child. She had no idea how to navigate his mind games. "I think I'd believe your commitment to the truth if I didn't think you see yourself as the person who decides how and when to disseminate it."

He took another swig of coffee and set it down on the table between them, shaking his head and smiling softly. "I really don't know you."

"I know you don't."

"There's this part of me that wants to say the cliché that I'm proud of you, but to be proud implies a sort of ownership, like I had anything to do with the person you turned out to be, and we both know that's not true. You've made it very clear that you don't want me in your life, and I know I don't deserve it, anyway."

She nearly responded with the obvious—*Of course you don't deserve it.* But she refrained.

"So instead, I think it's more appropriate for me to just express my admiration as a colleague. It's obvious that this was a situation you were thrust into, but for you to hold yourself as you have, considering all you've survived, the fact that you are in a position that no human has ever been in before . . . honestly, it's incredible."

He shuffled the photographs back into the envelope and handed it to her. "These are for you."

"Why?" she asked, eyeing the photos as if they were laced with anthrax.

"I figure you know better than I do what to do with this, so I'm letting you decide."

Every inch of her felt covered in worms. She had to get out of here. She stood up and put the envelope into her satchel. "I have a flight to catch."

"Then go catch it," he said with a wistful tone that implied that he wouldn't mind coming along, too. "I'm not going to tell you I'm sorry for the choices I've made. We both know it's not true. And I'm not going to ask you for forgiveness, because frankly I don't deserve it."

He stood up, taking a last gulp of coffee. "No oath do I lay upon you, but I *hope* we might learn to be of service to each other."

. . . . .

According to Dr. Sev, once the Filipino NICA learned Ampersand was willing, even eager, to play ball with them and share information, they fessed up immediately to everything Marisol had accused them of—that indeed there had been an ETI-related incident that had led to several deaths, and there were witnesses, and the Filipino government had kept this hush-hush. They agreed to share all they had with American intelligence on one condition: that Jude Atheatos be present for everything. So, this was to be their first *official* trip abroad since Ampersand had settled in Japan.

Cora rarely traveled by plane, but if it was an international trip that involved her interacting with any human, especially in a government capacity, she had to. When entering Japan, she transported herself to the nearest U.S. port of departure, in Guam, as that meant it was only a four-hour flight, but she hadn't done an actual trans-hemispheric flight in over a year. Which would be fine but for the fact that the U.S. government was footing the bill, so she had to fly American Airlines. Woof.

At least she'd be flying business class.

She was among the first to board, and the stewardess welcomed Cora onto the plane, not even hesitating at having to say, "Ms. Sabino," as she showed her to her seat as if she were any business-class passenger. Perhaps she'd seen her share of (in)famous business class passengers. "Here you are," she said as she turned back to the entrance. "Enjoy your flight."

"Well, well," said the window-seat passenger. "What are the odds?"

Cora dropped her carry-on flat on the floor where she stood. Here, apparently, was the person she'd be spending the next week with. Her "intelligence liaison." He folded down his copy of *The Wall Street Journal* and looked up from the window seat smugly.

"Aren't you happy to see me?"

Sol Kaplan.

▪ 11 ▪

Less than twenty-four hours prior to boarding American Airlines flight 8402 nonstop to Tokyo, Special Agent Sol Kaplan stepped into one of the Flatiron Building's two (2) elevators that were actually in service on this crisp autumn morn to take him from the ninth floor to his superior's office on the fifteenth to receive his briefing. Sol did not know *why* this CIA subdivision had chosen the Flatiron Building as their new field office after their previous digs had been unceremoniously obliterated by a couple of Boeing 767s. Say what you want about the eyesore that had been the old World Trade Center, at least it had central air-conditioning. Not like this old jalopy of a building that had AC units of all make and measure hanging out half of the windows, including his own.

The only other occupant was a mousy, bookish young woman about a foot and a half shorter than him who'd backed herself into the corner when the elevator door closed them in together. Probably from one of the publishing houses, he figured. They tended to be skittish. She didn't know he was CIA—or if she did, it didn't register on any of her text or email correspondences—but like a Geiger counter picking up elevated radiation, she could sense that there was something about him to steer clear of.

The elevator dinged to signal that he had reached his destination, and he could feel his mousy companion relax when he exited. "You have that effect on women," his mother had once told him, ever disappointed at the grandchildren she'd never get. She'd never known that the slight joy he took in being a naturally intimidating presence was far, far from the most, shall we say, off-putting thing a woman might discover about him.

Hell, his mother didn't even know he was CIA.

His superior, Deputy Director Susan Macallan, had left her office door open for him, and he rapped his knuckles on the doorframe to announce his arrival.

"Kaplan," she said, shuffling some papers around and gesturing to the chair on the other side of her desk. "Have a seat."

As Kaplan sat down, Macallan leafed through the papers in front of her until she found the one she was looking for. The CONFIDENTIAL at the top he had expected, but then his eyes fell on the code name he'd thought he'd left behind: Sloop John B.

"Oh . . ."

"It seemed to me you were getting bored with office work," said Macallan, leaning back in her chair.

Sol blew a thin stream of air between his lips and caught his reflection in the part of the window that wasn't blocked by an air conditioner. His dark, wavy hair, still full as it ever had been, was becoming flecked with gray, another one of his mother's favorite talking points. Maybe the office work *was* making him old.

Being a field agent at ROSA wasn't exactly like being a field agent in counterterrorism; the day-to-day caretaking of the Fremda group had been the job of the DHHS pencil necks, so he had been effectively in charge of the Men in Black (minus the *in Black* part) investigating potential alien activity. It had been a fairly mundane couple of years, at least until Nils Ortega became the world's most famous Rogue for Truth when he released the Fremda Memo, revealing that yes, the conspiracy nuts were somewhat right (but mostly wrong) about a government cover-up of alien activity.

"Surely my skill set can be applied to *something* other than counterterrorism or aliens."

Macallan leaned forward, resting on her elbows. "Well, ignoring the fact that most of what we do revolves around counterterrorism or aliens, you're in an especially unique position. It's not often an operative gets their identity revealed *twice*."

Sol stayed placid, but inwardly prickled. He'd had to leave his old position as CIA liaison at ROSA last year after Nils Ortega had leaked his identity, *again*. The first time he'd done it had been during an exposé he had coauthored with Kaveh Mazandarani for *The New Yorker*, back in 2004 when Ortega was playacting at not being a total can of smashed ass-holes. The information that Mazandarani and Ortega had was obsolete by the time they published it, as Sol had already left counterterrorism by then, but his exposed identity had meant he would never have the option of going back. Then he'd managed to do it *again* about a year ago when he'd come into a bunch of documents detailing ROSA person-nel, including his own goddamn sister. Despite all this, Sol hadn't been shunted off alien duty entirely—now it was his job to hunt for other governments hiding the sort of thing he'd spent two years helping his own government to cover up.

"I thought being doubly exposed disqualified me from fieldwork," said Sol.

"Well, if that fieldwork isn't covert, then it doesn't really matter, does it? Maybe a non-covert form of intelligence gathering might be fun. And besides, you are one of our foremost experts on the Ortegas."

Sol skimmed the letter in front of him. "Nils?"

"Now that he's back stateside, we no longer have the privilege of spy-ing on him."

It took him a few milliseconds to see who she was getting at. It wouldn't be Luciana Ortega—they had their own set of people keeping an eye on her on the West Coast, and they weren't CIA anyhow. Demi and her other kid were nonentities at this point. Which left only . . .

"What have I done to offend you?" he asked, sighing the sigh of a parent who just discovered their newly painted wall covered in crayon scribbles.

"I thought you'd be happy," chuckled Macallan. "From what people tell me, Cora Sabino was the closest you came to getting along with any-one at ROSA since Agent Park died."

Sol didn't react. Maybe ten or fifteen years ago, it would have taken some conscious thought not to react to upsetting things—say, the gruesome, untimely death of your junior agent, which was ultimately turned into a political weapon by the current babyfascist president—but at his age, it was second nature. "You're speaking like you're expect-ing me to work *with* her."

"Well, I am. Sabino actually supplied us with a big piece of intelligence that our people missed. Four years ago, *something* happened in a village in the western Philippines that left six people dead, and not only did NICA bury it, they did not share it with us when our dirty secrets came to light."

"Gee, I wonder why."

"Now, as you know, NICA aren't the only ones playing this game. But until this intel came in, there wasn't any reason for us to suspect anything. This incident seems to be a one-off, if it happened at all."

"Thought NICA was one of the few agencies we were on good terms with." He'd never been to the Philippines, but he'd known a few CIA agents who had worked in collaboration with their Filipino equivalents. The Filipino agency had had a few costume changes over the years but for now went by the National Intelligence Coordinating Agency (these foreign intelligence service names were always so damn wordy).

"We thought so, too. The more you know."

Sol skimmed over the letter—*possible physeterine encounter, six dead.* "What makes you think this is legitimate?"

"Because NICA admitted to having more evidence than six dead *human* bodies with very little prying. This intel didn't *just* come from Sabino—she claims that it came directly from 46, and the Filipinos are very eager to talk to him."

"I see."

"The president is very interested in this case," Macallan added.

Sol looked up at her, concerned. No good could come from Julian being interested. "What, does he want more fodder to publicly flagellate Sabino with?"

"Julian doesn't have the votes to pass his defense bill. If we find some hard evidence of flesh-eating aliens with a trail of bodies behind them, that might get him the votes he needs."

"And you want to *encourage* this?"

"Obviously, your job is to supply unbiased intelligence—I'm just telling you what kind of unbiased intelligence they want."

"So you're asking me to go to the Philippines to find them some WMDs so they can have an excuse to invade Iraq. Didn't we just boot that administration?"

"Regrettably," said Macallan. "At least their enemies didn't have godlike superpowers. So what I want you to do is fly to Manila—"

"American Airlines?"

"Of course."

"This is sounding more and more like I'm being punished."

"You'll be traveling with Sabino and Dr. Ghasabian—"

"Fuck me. Him, too?" Sol had figured that leaving ROSA would mean he wouldn't have to work with "Dr. Sev" again, the weird creep.

"—and see what there is to see. The Filipinos will cooperate if we keep our involvement minimal—intelligence gathering only, *no* military. If what we are hearing is true, then they actually have a physeterine specimen on ice. Won't *that* be interesting?"

"Well, maybe I like it here. I get to see my mother all the time now."

"I'm very happy for you, but let's be honest, you don't exactly *excel* as a hacker. You're kind of a Luddite, and the computer world is changing fast. You're a field agent. We're so used to stealing intelligence, but sometimes it's more efficient to just ask."

"With Sabino."

"Not *just* Sabino. You'll be expected to cooperate with 46 as well."

"Oh, good. He loves me."

AG-ETI-046, the amygdaline ETI attached to the event code-named Ampersand, had taken a legal name that made him sound more human, a goofy one gifted to him by Sabino that was probably laden with some deep meaning or something. But no one in the agency had taken to using Jude Atheatos, or even his Esperanto code name, Scio, which had lasted all of three months, and just kept on calling him what they always had, AG-46, or more often just 46.

Sol gingerly placed the letter back on the desk and looked up at Macallan, who was studying him in a way that few people had the balls to do. "But before I send you out," she continued, "I'm going to ask you a very straightforward question, and I want you to be honest with me, Solomon."

"When have I ever been dishonest?"

"It's your job to be dishonest. That is what I want you not to do right now."

"Of course."

"Cora Sabino. Did you fuck her?"

He allowed not even the subtle twitch of a surprised eyebrow, but the question tinged his blood with just a soupçon of anger. Kaveh

Mazandarani had insinuated something similar not two hours before he started getting it in with Sabino, a classic psychological phenomenon known as *projection*. How was it that everyone thought he was as scummy as Mazandarani? "No, I did not."

"Did you try to?"

A slow smile spread over his features. "No, I did not. Mazandarani got to her first."

Macallan chuckled. "He really got under your skin, didn't he?"

"He certainly got under hers."

She leaned back in her office chair, which creaked slightly. "This is an opportunity for you to get back on your feet within the agency. Don't take this as an opportunity for some revenge by proxy."

"Now, Susan," he said smoothly, standing up from his chair, "why would you ever think such a thing of me?"

"You have a history of that very thing, Solomon," she said knowingly. "The cold, shriveled black raisin inside me that some call a heart has one request—the kid's been through enough. Don't put her through any more."

Sol shielded his eyes from the wind as the helicopter carrying Cora Sabino and 46 landed in the parking lot outside of a NICA black site. They didn't *call* it a black site, but Sol couldn't help but think of it as one; it wasn't on any map, it didn't exist officially, and it functioned like an oubliette for whatever the nation's intelligence service wanted to hold on to without disclosure—felt like a black site to him. Only thing missing were the torture chambers.

"If Luciana Ortega were here, we'd have the whole Scooby gang," said Sol.

"Scooby gang?" said Ghasabian, likewise shielding his eyes. He had also arrived early, as he'd had to fly coach with Sol and the other plebs.

"Didn't you ever watch *Scooby-Doo*?"

"No," chuckled Ghasabian as if Sol had asked him if he was familiar with the lost early short films of Sergei Eisenstein and not *Scooby-Fucking-Doo*. Ghasabian had been with ROSA during *Scooby-Doo*'s heyday, and he certainly moved through the world like a guy who'd spent the entire 1970s in a basement with aliens. "I'm a good bit older than you."

Sol just shook his head and watched as Sabino and 46 disembarked from the helicopter, greeted by their Filipino military entourage. It had taken thirty-six hours since he'd set out from New York to arrive at their destination, an austere government compound about thirty miles north of metro Manila that was remote enough not to attract attention but not so remote that it took too long to get to from the capital.

This was the first time Sol had seen 46 in the "flesh" in almost two years, wearing that outfit his Japanese stylists had designed to "human-ize" him. In a way, it was brilliant. The way the intent of his uniform had been described to Sol was for it to be easily recognizable as clothing of a sort, but nothing that might come off as too human. After all, it wouldn't do if it looked like it was wearing a T-shirt and a bow tie. The getup hung off him not unlike a space-gray horse blanket, the "coat" somewhere between a Sherlock Holmes–style outer jacket and Jedi robes that wrapped around the front, giving him two large sleeves that cradled his arms like slings and came together in the middle, hiding his horrible spider hands if he closed the two sleeves together.

The funny thing about it was how well it worked. On paper, it should have looked ridiculous, but seeing him "clothed" made Sol realize how naked they all seemed, incomplete to the human eye. The clothing didn't look anything like clothing a human would wear, but that was the intent—recognizably clothing, but distinctly alien. Even if it was com-pletely impractical, it was easier to see him as a person if he wore clothes.

Sabino approached them, seeming mildly pleased to see Ghasabian, because of course.

"How was the private jet?" asked Sol.

"Private," said Sabino tersely and probably hungover. She'd spent half the trip to Tokyo loading up on that free business-class wine, which, given that it was American Airlines wine, woof.

"Guess you're used to that sort of thing now, huh?"

"No," she said. "Usually we don't need them."

"La-di-da," he said, a little annoyed that she didn't even seem to appreciate that she'd gotten a private jet. *He'd* have appreciated the pri-vate jet.

Sol had parted ways with Sabino at Haneda to rendezvous with 46, who, with Sabino, got his very own private jet courtesy of the Fil-ipinos, while the lowly feds were forced to continue on their journey on commercial flights. There were purported security reasons for this, along with the fact that 46 was a "guest" of the Filipinos where CIA agents were very much not, but to Sol it just felt petty.

They stopped at the building's main entrance, and within a few sec-onds, a man in a white lab coat emerged, flanked by four other men in white lab coats. He looked to be Sol's age, maybe a little older, and had a practiced warmth that the science eggheads he worked with rarely had, especially the higher-ups.

"I am so sorry for the delay," he said, unsure whom among the humans to address. "We were told yesterday you wouldn't arrive until 10:00. I'm Dr. Estraton Catipay. I'm the director of science, technology, and weapons analytics for NICA."

"*Huge* pleasure to meet you," said Ghasabian with a forcefulness that Sol could not help but read as insincere. "Sevak Ghasabian, director of ROSA."

"He thanks you for speaking with us," said Sabino as she took her place directly in front of 46. Sol suspected that 46 had not, in fact, thanked anyone, as Sabino always paused to listen to him before speaking if he'd actually relayed an instruction.

"Forgive me. I wasn't briefed. Whom should I address?" asked Catipay.

"Address Jude if you're speaking to him," said Sabino. "Me if you're speaking to me, and I'll speak for both of us."

Catipay nodded and looked up at all nine-ish feet of the alien. It seemed to Sol like this man was using every fiber of personal restraint in his being to suppress his excitement. He then shot Sol a glance of, "And you are?"

"Sol Kaplan, C—"

"CIA, I know."

Sol bristled. Where did this guy get off being on a high horse when he was a stooge of his country's equivalent of the exact same agency working in more or less the exact same department?

"It's truly an honor to meet you," said Catipay to 46 as if he were some foreign dignitary. "Although I wish it could have been under different circumstances," he added with an eye toward the military entourage. "I would have found a way to share what we know with you sooner, but unfortunately, those decisions were out of my hands."

Sol looked at the two military goons, figuring they weren't there for the intent of intimidating their "guests" but for keeping people like Catipay in line. Catipay donned a professional smile. "Please, follow me."

· · · · ·

The corpse lay in a custom-made acrylic tube on its side like it was in a giant tanning bed. Even alive, the specimen (which the Filipinos had nicknamed Johnny) would have been a gruesome thing to behold, with its multi-jointed jaws and tail like an anaconda's, but the fact that it was floating there, all mangled in its embalming fluid, made it even worse. Its hands had the same six-fingered structure as the amygdalines': four on the top, two on the bottom, bilaterally symmetrical, more shaped for clamping like a jaw than grabbing like a human hand. Its skin gave the effect of a jaundiced albino, except for its extremities, where the color faded from off-white to a purple so dark it was almost black on its muzzle, head crest, the skin around its eyes, its fingers, toes, and the tip of its tail, giving it a color scheme almost like a Siamese cat's. Its mouthparts more like insect mandibles than jaws, and the closest point of comparison in Sol's mind was the Predator from, well, *Predator*.

"When it arrived, it was wearing clothing of a sort," said Catipay. "A dark skintight suit that covered its entire body."

Sol shot a glance at 46, whose gaze, unless he was in direct sunlight, was usually soft and on nothing in particular. Right now, it was laser pointed—fiery balls glowing inside his dark, football eyes, watching the corpse like he expected it to burst out of its acrylic coffin. The specimen was covered in wounds and slashes, and its head was nearly severed at the neck. Even as a reconstruction, Johnny felt bigger than 46, despite him having a good foot or so of height on this thing. Amygdalines, even the Similars, seemed latticed and lithe and delicate; this guy looked like one of those ridiculously muscled kangaroos.

"We've learned from this specimen that they are omnivorous," said Catipay, "and are capable of digesting Earth-based foods. We know they are nocturnal, as they have excellent night vision. Their eyes are almost primitive in that regard—they have no irises."

"How does that work?" asked Ghasabian.

"Our eyes are like a camera," said Catipay, making his hand into a circle around his eye and then closing it. "The iris acts as an aperture, letting in more light when it's dim and blocking light when it's bright. Physeterines never seemed to evolve this feature, which means they are probably very sensitive to the light of our sun. They also see vastly different colors than we do. They have incredible infrared vision, but anything higher on the color spectrum than green, they're blind to it. This tells us that they—all of you"—he nodded respectfully at 46 like he was a billionaire he was trying to get to pledge grant money—"evolved in the light of a K-type star, not an M-type like our sun."

"That's correct," said Sabino.

"Are amygdalines blind to greens and blues?" Ghasabian asked Sabino.

"Most of them, yeah," said Sabino. "Jude isn't, because he's in a Similar's body, but most of the ones back at Riverside are."

"It's almost sad, isn't it?" said Ghasabian, looking wistfully at the butchered creature in the tube. "They choose a green-and-blue planet, and they can't even see it."

Sol pursed his lips. It would be Ghasabian, of all people, who would look at this thing and immediately start thinking about writing its college recommendation letter.

"I'm sorry, 'a Similar'?" Catipay asked Sabino.

"It's a . . ." She paused for a moment, trying to gather her words to concisely describe such a complex topic. "Everything about their society and social structure operates on a strict caste system—from macropolitics to interpersonal relationships, everything. 'Similar' is the name Jude came up with for the caste that's sort of . . . let's say space travelers. Explorers."

Sol chuckled silently. *Big* lie of omission there. Even he knew that.

"Similars generally have very large bodies and are designed to exist on all kinds of alien worlds and are capable of . . ." Sabino shot a glance at their military escort, as if only just remembering what she might be divulging about 46. "Incredible power. Jude wasn't born into this caste, but he has the body of a Similar."

"And I take it Nikola Sassanian has one of these bodies as well, but the smaller refugees like Andronicus and Junia Odissu do not?"

Sabino opened her mouth to answer but was cut off by a pointed throat-clear from Sol. "I can't really go into that," she said.

"Of course, excuse me; that's not why we're here," said Catipay, shooting a micro-glare at Sol before returning to Johnny. "Is there anything else you can tell us about this cadaver?"

"It's an adult," said Sabino after a listening-pause. "A young adult, by their standards, probably younger than sixty."

"Can you tell anything about the sex?" asked Catipay.

"Physeterines are simultaneously hermaphroditic," said Sabino. "They engineered themselves that way. Then they can have twice as many off-spring with the same number of parents. They can both impregnate and be impregnated at the same time."

"Are amygdalines hermaphroditic?"

"No, they are not," said Sabino in a pointed way that said there was a *story* here.

"Can you speculate on why they are here?" asked Ghasabian.

"There are many reasons they might settle here temporarily," said Sabino. "They can mine resources, they don't have to waste energy on spacecrafts or on space stations, they don't have to artificially generate gravity. They're . . . hardier than we are, so they can withstand the natural atmosphere and pathogens of alien worlds—with some caveats."

"So no *War of the Worlds* scenarios on the table where they're taken down by the common cold," said Ghasabian.

Sabino nodded. "The biggest issue with Earth is our atmosphere; the amount of nitrogen in the air is toxic to them in the way that too much CO_2 would be toxic to us. But that's an easy fix—they'd just wear filters around their airholes." She pointed to her neck—amygdalines both breathed and spoke out of two holes on the side of their necks that almost mimicked blowholes. So, too, it seemed, did their cousins.

"Why are they 'transient,' then?" asked Catipay. "Why not live on planets, create settlements here or elsewhere?"

"There's an extremely finite number of life-sustaining planets in the Milky Way," said Sabino. "Any long-term colonies they might establish would get found by the Pequod Superorganism eventually; they found that out the hard way."

Sol saw the look on Catipay's face that everyone displayed sooner or later when they truly began to grasp just how vindictive and powerful the amygdalines were; it was one thing to have a vague concept that there was an alien civilization out there that not only didn't have much experience dealing with lesser civilizations but was likely to be extremely put off by humanity; it was another thing to learn they already had a genocidal track record.

Sabino looked at 46, and her eyebrows popped like he'd just told her a dirty joke that wasn't particularly funny. "Can you tell us if there was anything in the stomach?"

"Some digested material," said Catipay. "Some that was definitely cellulose, some proteins that look like they may have been animal-based, owing to the cell structure."

"It wasn't . . . human?"

The man paused, considered, and said, "They weren't." When no one jumped right in, he continued, "Does this confirm that these creatures do eat human flesh?"

"Well, as you said, they're very adaptable," said Sabino. "They *could* eat anything, in the way that we *could* eat anything, but there's all measure of reasons why it's a bad idea; obviously, we're at the top of the food chain ourselves. Unlike a deer or something, humans actually fight back."

"But you want us to confirm that there was no human flesh in the contents of the stomach . . ."

"Yes."

"We can confirm that."

"Would you care to enlighten us as to why human-eating even enters the picture as a possibility?" Sol asked Sabino.

"He's . . . seen them do it before," Sabino said quietly, as if this was a very sensitive subject.

"To humans?" asked Sol.

"No, to them," said Sabino, gesturing her head to 46.

"He's seen physeterines . . . cannibalize amygdalines?" asked Ghasabian. Even he seemed skeptical.

"That's right."

"So if there are no human remains in the stomach, that rules out that he did this to feed?" asked Catipay.

"That wouldn't have been the sole reason regardless," said Sabino. "There are all sorts of subcultures within the wider species, and some have their own version of alien machismo. It's possible this was a hunt gone awry."

"If that's true," said Catipay, "wouldn't there be other incidents like this?"

"We don't know that there aren't," said Sol. "Given your government's reluctance to share this information with the international community—no offense—"

"None taken," said Catipay coolly.

"It's possible this has happened dozens of times and we'd have no way of knowing. We have witness testimony that it has happened at least twice in the United States, though no physical evidence. And we have some intelligence saying it may have happened in other countries, as well."

"Which countries?" asked Catipay in a way Sol didn't like, like he might know something.

"That, I'm afraid I can't share."

"And you wonder why the international intelligence community is so fractured," said Catipay.

Sabino approached the tube, her eyes unfocused as she listened to 46. "He's hesitant to speculate on why this happened. It doesn't make sense that a physeterine would just attack random human civilians. Like imagine being an astronaut on an alien world and attacking the natives, knowing that it'll get you hurt or killed. This is . . ." She shook her head. "It doesn't make sense. Jude says they're perfectly capable of violence, even relish it, but they aren't mindless monsters."

Sabino looked at Catipay. "Unambiguously, this was not a provoked attack?"

"Every living witness says it was unprovoked. The thing just started attacking children—"

"*Children?*" repeated Ghasabian.

Dr. Catipay's lips drew into a tight pucker, and he nodded. "Children."

Sabino shook her head, like she had already known that little detail. "He can't draw any meaningful conclusions here. We'll have to talk to the witnesses. Can it be arranged that we go to the village where this happened?"

"We've already made arrangements," said Catipay. "We will take you to your accommodations when we're done here and then escort you to the village tomorrow."

"Do they know we're coming?" asked Sol.

Catipay looked at him as if he were surprised a man of his station would ask such a stupid question. "There's no way to brief an entire village without it getting back to the press before we even arrive."

Sol side-eyed 46, the cybernetic gargoyle who was so tall he grazed the ceiling with the tips of his head fronds. They were about to go into a backwoods fishing village, already traumatized from an attack by another alien monstrosity that had been suppressed by their government for years, to interrogate the victims, with *that*.

This was going to be fun.

· 13 ·

"I first saw it there. After it had already killed Danilo and Joriz."

A resident of Bahura was giving Cora (well, really Ampersand, but he was addressing Cora) a very nervous account of the massacre that had happened five years ago like she was some medieval judge and he was on trial for witchcraft. Dr. Catipay, to whom the role of translator had unofficially fallen, translated the man's Tagalog to English, but she ignored him in favor of her own ocular overlay translations. Catipay was clearly displeased with how this was going but was doing better than she was at maintaining his composure. Cora was almost shaking with fury.

When they arrived via helicopter at around 9:00 A.M., the few dozen witnesses had already been corralled to the scene of the crime and cowered at the sight of the helicopter as if it contained Johnny back from the dead to finish them off. She soon learned that the witnesses had been dragged out of their beds at 5:00 that morning, herded to the scene of the crime, and told to wait with no indication what they were waiting for. Given the way they had already been treated by their government, many had assumed the worst.

Stupefied awe at the sight of Ampersand she was used to, but open weeping in terror was a reaction he had never received before. Moreover, these people were so shaken from their treatment that none of them could get it together enough to tell him anything coherent. It took almost twenty minutes before someone finally volunteered to give an account of what had happened, a fisherman named Mikey, who had lost a brother and a nephew in the attack. Dr. Sev stood nearby, and Sol hung back in the shadows, arms crossed; he was like Gaston about to agitate the local villagers into an angry mob.

"*Calm yourself, my love,*" said Ampersand, standing up a bit straighter and causing half the crowd of witnesses, still on edge, to jump out of their skin. People unfamiliar with him tended to startle whenever he moved, as if they thought they were in the presence of a statue and not a cyborg. With most of his body obscured by heavy fabric, he looked like an animatronic if he stayed still long enough.

"I'm fine."

"*Your agitation is affecting me. Please, calm yourself.*"

She took a long, deep breath in, trying to think happy thoughts. This would be a few days at most, then she could go back to New York and be with Paris again. They could bar the doors and shut themselves in with all the anime the island nation of Japan had ever produced, and then, one day, she would take Paris to Japan. Finally, she would have someone to enjoy an *onsen* with. She released the breath and nodded at Mikey.

"First, it attacked the boys, here," he said. He pointed to a house on the right side of the road with a yard rimmed with a bamboo fence, then his finger drew to the blue house on the opposite side of the dirt road, both of them about half the size of her family's house in Torrance (itself quite small by California standards). "Then it followed Lorenzo out here." Mikey pointed a trembling index finger at a spot in the road bordering the blue house's yard.

"*Ask him to describe the physicality of the creature.*"

Cora relayed the request to Dr. Catipay, who relayed it to Mikey. "It was darker-skinned, but I couldn't see what color; it was too dark. It had a long tail, but not like a tail I've seen on an animal before. It moved like a snake coiling."

"*Ask about any differences between the creature he saw and amygdaline physiology.*"

Cora relayed the request, and Mikey responded again, giving a fairly accurate account of what Johnny looked like. "I'll never forget its mouth. It had two fang-like appendages." He held up his index fingers like two candy canes, turning them toward each other at the corners of his mouth. "They looked like the fangs of a tarantula, tucked inside the other mouthparts." Mikey then looked at Ampersand like he suspected him of hiding two sideways tarantula fangs in his own mouth. "Danilo came at it with a machete. It turned and grabbed Danilo first, holding him by the wrist so he couldn't use the machete. Then it opened its mouth and—" He formed his hand into a claw, slapped it to his neck, and jerked it away. "It bit into his jugular and ripped it right out. It did the same to his son, Jojo."

Cora felt a slight buzzing from the other side of the wall, a sense of recognition and fear. "How old was his son?"

"Nine years old," said Mikey.

Everyone within earshot was silent, having lived with this for years and only now being allowed to share it. She could sense that Ampersand was also disturbed, less by the boy's age so much as the manner in which he died.

"The monster killed Jojo's best friend, Lito, as well," continued Mikey. "He was eleven years old. It crawled through Lito's bedroom window when the boys were in his room, playing a game. First it gutted Lito." The man again formed his hand into a claw and moved as though he were disemboweling himself. "Then it killed Jojo in the same manner, and then . . ." Mikey paused before delivering this next part. "Ripped the boy open with its claws and fangs.

"One of the boys managed to escape," Mikey continued. "It chased him into the street. That's when we found it. We watched it kill Pacifico, Jejomar, and Rodrigo before the rest of us were finally able to take it down." The man's voice shook, and again he chanced to look at the police before continuing.

"The police came and told us they would take care of it, but in the meantime, we needed to keep it secret. They said they would find out what happened. They said they would help us. We were never given any compensation by the government as we were promised. Then we were told this never happened. They threatened us if we said we might go to the press. So the only thing that we have are rumors, but no one believes us."

A woman standing behind Mikey spoke, her tone at once indignant and bereaved. "The corpses were so mangled, we couldn't even have a proper wake for them," she said, alternately looking at Cora and Ampersand. "We had to keep the coffins closed, even for the boys, the poor boys."

Only the sounds of the buzzing of birds and insects filled the air.

Dr. Sev looked like a daytime talk show host for how concerned he looked for these people's plight, and Dr. Catipay looked like he was writing a strongly worded letter in his head. Sol just coughed.

"He says this is a terrible thing to hear, and he is very sorry for your loss," said Cora, and Catipay translated. This seemed to put them a little bit at ease, even if Ampersand hadn't actually said anything. Wouldn't hurt to make him *appear* a little sympathetic.

"It was as though the devil sent a monster that devours children," said the bereaved woman. "We had no way of knowing what it was. We never considered that it might be alien."

"*Where is the child who escaped?*"

Cora relayed the question, and a few members of the families parted to let the lone surviving child come through, and Cora had to stop herself from gasping. His cheekbones stood proud from his face, his eyes sat far back in dark sockets, the bones of his knees pushed out on the sides. He seemed lucid, his big, frightened eyes on Ampersand as a woman whom Cora assumed to be his mother helped him forward, but then he stumbled, as if hit with a wave of vertigo. The boy's mother looked at Ampersand for an uncomfortably long time, as if she were half convinced he bore some responsibility for the boy's condition, then encouraged him.

"Tell them what you saw, Lorenzo," she told the boy in Tagalog.

Lorenzo took a few labored breaths before speaking. "*Nagdasal ako . . .*"

"He says, 'I prayed,'" said Dr. Catipay.

"*Nanalangin ako kay San Tadeo—*"

"'I prayed to Saint Jude.'"

He barely got the last word out before his eyes lolled back into his head, he swayed, and then collapsed, his mother holding on to his shoulders as if she had fully expected this. Then his body started to convulse. His mother gently lowered him to the ground, looking at Cora and speaking with her hands as if there was some word that eluded her. Cora looked at Dr. Catipay for an explanation.

"Seizure," he said solemnly.

"He has seizure," said his mother apologetically in English. Her accent was thick, but understandable. "It's no disrespect, ma'am."

"That's okay," said Cora. "We can talk to him later."

The boy was an adolescent, but he was so emaciated that his mother was able to scoop him up and carry him back to the rest of their family easily.

"*Ask where the corpses are.*"

Cora shook her head. Of course he would be unfazed by that; he didn't care, and either way, he wanted to get this over with. She repeated his question, and Mikey answered, "They were taken by the government. They were given back to us after about three months. They are all buried in family plots."

"*The corpses will need to be exhumed.*"

Cora repeated him, and Dr. Catipay looked at her as though he had misheard. "Exhumed?"

"That's right."

Dr. Catipay looked at Mikey and the other bereaved families, then back at Cora. "Might I consult with you a moment?"

"Sure," said Cora. She followed Dr. Catipay in the opposite direction of Sol, hoping she wouldn't have to tell him to fuck off if he tried to follow her (he didn't). Dr. Catipay seemed surprised, even a little unnerved, that Ampersand followed them, too.

"Our spiritual cultures are very different from in the U.S. and Japan," whispered Dr. Catipay. "The people here are very religious and very superstitious. They still see the bodies as somewhat . . . not alive but still attached to the soul that once inhabited them. They suffered so much in death, to exhume them would be like asking them to suffer even more. And given all they've been put through by the military and the police . . ."

"*Attaching significance to corpses is irrational and should not act as an impediment if studying the corpses will give us more information.*"

Cora looked at him, lips thin.

"What did he say?" asked Dr. Catipay.

"Let's just say he's not exactly sympathetic."

"If you really think it necessary, we can exhume the bodies, and there will be nothing the families can do," said Dr. Catipay. "But it would be such an even greater trauma than they've already had to experience."

"*It's not our concern; the corpses must be exhumed. I can do so without their knowledge.*"

Cora had never done the lifelong Catholic rigmarole that so many of her relatives had; she had never gone to Catholic school, and she had never been confirmed, but even still, the spiritualism and rituals inherent to Catholicism felt somewhat encoded into her DNA. And though exhuming the corpses and examining them without the families ever knowing was the cold, logical thing to do, the thought of actually doing it turned her stomach. "Is there maybe some way we can frame this as, I don't know, 'We believe you, and we want to give you and your loved ones peace,' or something?"

"*I won't need to remove them from the graves.*"

"He says he won't need to disturb them too much; he can glean whatever he needs with—"

Cora realized that Ampersand's eyes were now focused on something behind her, and she turned to see a little girl who looked to be Olive's age with her neck craned up at him. Before anyone could stop her, the girl spoke.

"*Ang pangalan ko ay Clarinda.*"

"She says her name is Clarinda," said Dr. Catipay.

"*Kapatid ko si Lorenzo.*"

"She is Lorenzo's sister."

The girl looked straight up at Ampersand with terror and awe like he was a literal saint made of biomechanical flesh, one who could turn her to ash with a thought (which, strictly speaking, he could). She clasped her hands in front of her, fell to her knees, and cried in English, "My brother is sick!"

The crowd erupted in chatter. Clarinda continued speaking directly to Ampersand, in Tagalog. "It's an aggressive form of brain cancer," she said, near tears. "They say the tumor is inoperable. They say he only has a few more weeks to live. They say you're infinitely more intelligent than a human. Perhaps you know a way to save him. He prayed to Saint Jude, and you came. Please, could you save my brother?"

Oh, shit.

Ampersand stayed stone-still, looking down at this desperate creature small enough to fit snugly in his hand. Lorenzo's mother dashed to her daughter as if she meant to shield her from Ampersand. Not taking her eyes off him, she gently took Clarinda by the shoulders, coaxed her to her feet.

"She is only a child," said the woman in English, clearly frightened that this might mean some form of punishment, if not from Amper-sand, then from the massive police presence. "Beg your pardon, ma'am. She's only a child."

But he can *help*, Cora wanted to say. Of every amygdaline on Earth or possibly anywhere, Ampersand was the most adept at repairing liv-ing flesh. Operations that for humans would be impossible were child's play to him. But she said nothing.

Before long, the police escorted them back to their helicopter. Cora took Ampersand by the forearm as she always did when they were in public; maintaining physical contact with him always put people at ease. She turned to look at Clarinda, who was being consoled by her mother and grandmother. She could only imagine what they were telling her. *It's okay. It couldn't hurt to ask. You didn't do anything wrong. It's okay.*

"Prayer to Saint Jude," remarked Dr. Catipay.

"Is that what she's doing?"

Catipay nodded. "It's hard to imagine a more hopeless cause than a cancer like his. Who else but Saint Jude?" He looked at Ampersand, lingering on him a moment as if he suspected that he knew that this being could save the boy and was choosing not to. "I'll see about the exhumation," he said. "I'll encourage them to frame it as an attempt to bring peace to the dead. If the families cooperate, we can fast-track it to happen in the next few days."

As Catipay departed toward his own helicopter, Cora looked at the crowd of witnesses and the military escort who was now corralling them to some debrief, likely yet another flavor of "No, you can never speak about this to anyone or you'll go to jail forever." Again, Cora had to tamp down a well of fury at how they were being treated.

"You could help him, couldn't you?" she whispered, again taking Ampersand by the arm and continuing toward their helicopter like she were leading a blind man.

"*It is best for me to stay uninvolved.*"

"I know it might not be the best idea to start doing stealth super-heroics, but denying a dying child help when we can give it based on political hypotheticals just feels wrong to me."

"*That is not my concern.*"

"Then what is?"

"*I am.*"

"I don't understand."

"*Dear one, as you know, I am troubled by the knowledge that I could reduce human suffering in certain circumstances, but for many reasons, we have agreed that human affairs be left to humans. Our rationale was on the basis that it might create more problems than it solves, but it is also to protect myself.*"

"From what?"

"*The suffering of an amygdaline Oligarch's inferiors is their responsibility. Humans are unable to meaningfully imagine suffering on a large scale, but I am. I must turn a blind eye. If I expose myself to human suffering on a grand scale that I have the ability to lessen or even end, I will be compelled to act.*"

Cora was already deflating as she saw what he was getting at. Two years ago, Obelus had warned her that if Ampersand were to stay on this planet, he couldn't help but *desire* to control it. After all, there was so much that needed fixing, and these monkeys didn't know what was good for them. Ampersand's desire to protect his "inferiors" and his authoritarian tendencies were inextricably linked. Cora looked back to where the family had been, but they had already been ushered away.

"It's hard," said Sol, having appeared behind them without her noticing. "This sort of thing."

Cora looked at him, slightly incredulous.

"I mean, the more you step outside of your bubble, the more you're going to see stuff like this. I only spent three months in Afghanistan, and the stuff I saw there, it was enough to shave ten years off my life."

Cora resisted the urge to ask if he was referring to one of his torture tours. "What do you mean?"

"The child mortality rate there is insane. It's one thing to distantly know that as a statistic, but to see it up close . . ." He turned to look at the people who were still there. "Worse, to know that just one month of your salary could save several lives, but to be prohibited from giving anyone cash unless it was in direct service to buying off sources. But so many of those people that get roped into al-Qaeda and the Taliban, you can't even imagine the edge of the knife they live on. Who they accept help from isn't a choice between two warring ideologies, it's a question of which evil will give you the best chance of survival—the Taliban or the CIA?

"I saw several kids die of such tiny preventable things, things like cuts that turned to gangrene and colds that turned to pneumonia. Things that will haunt me to the day I die, especially knowing that the only thing that prevented someone like me from giving those kids the ten dollars that would get them the penicillin that would save their lives was that their parents didn't have any useful intelligence for us. And the orphans. *So* many orphans. Some fell into terrorism, some killed by the Taliban, some killed by us. But most of those kids just die in the street."

Sol looked back toward the crime scene as the helicopter blades revved. "At least that kid will die surrounded by loved ones."

"So what are you saying?"

Sol looked at Ampersand and then back at her. "It's not your place to fix the world."

She looked at the ground, feeling even more rotten. He was right; it wasn't her place to fix the world. How could it be?

She was planning to abandon it.

· 14 ·

"Good to see you again," said Paris, taking a seat in the acrylic chair Barney had put out for her. Nikola was in an almost catlike pose, hind legs tucked up to his sides with his hands folded neatly in front of him, one wrist on top of the other. His crest was more splayed than usual, closer to a triceratops than an un-bloomed flower. Paris waited an awkward few seconds before smiling and patting the journals in her lap. "How have you been?"

"YOU HAVE A LARGE ADORNMENT IN THE LIKENESS OF AN INSECT."

"Come again?"

"ON YOUR CHEST."

Her fingers moved to the butterfly tattoo just below her collarbone. "It's a butterfly."

"IT IS VERY PROMINENT."

"It's to scale. It's a big butterfly."

"IT MUST BEAR SOME SIGNIFICANCE."

"All my tattoos do." This tattoo was not a place she had the emotional bandwidth to go right now. Time to swerve. "They tell me you'll be moving to a new facility soon. They gave me permission to come along for the ride to cover it."

"I WAS NOT AWARE."

"You weren't?"

"THEY WOULD OF COURSE WITHHOLD INFORMATION FROM ME TO PRECLUDE POSSIBILITIES FOR ME TO PLAN AN ESCAPE."

A slight tremor ran through her at the idea she might have told him something he wasn't supposed to know. But surely, it couldn't be a big deal that she had, could it? She hadn't been instructed *not* to tell him about it. "What would you do if you escaped?"

"WHEN I ESCAPE, DEAR GENTLE CREATURE. NOT IF. WHEN."

"Do you expect that your escape will involve some human casualties?"

"ALL MY ATTEMPTS THUS FAR HAVE. I IMAGINE SOME LOSS OF LIFE INEVITABLE FOR A SUCCESSFUL ATTEMPT."

While it was obvious he didn't have much respect for life, human or otherwise, she didn't believe him. He had refrained from taking human life several times already, including hers, and while he had caused harm to people, he hadn't actually killed anyone when it would have been all too easy to do so.

All the same, he did have a body count.

"I've sometimes wondered—the men that you killed, you didn't have to. You could have disarmed them without killing them."

"I WANTED TO KILL THEM."

"Yes, but you could have shown those men mercy."

Nikola's eyes widened, their nuclei brightening like he was drawing a map of every neuron in her body, watching the electricity flow through them. "YOU CONFUSE ME, DEAR GENTLE CREATURE. THEY KILLED THE VERY PERSON WHOM YOU PURPORT TO HONOR WITH YOUR PROJECT, AND YET YOU WOULD ASK FOR MERCY FOR HIS KILLERS."

"I didn't ask for mercy. I'm only pointing out that you could have shown it, but you chose not to."

"WOULD YOU HAVE SPARED THOSE MEN, HAD YOU BEEN IN MY POSITION?"

She looked down at Kaveh's journal, feeling the leather against her fingers. "I don't know."

"I DO NOT REGRET KILLING THEM. I ENJOYED KILLING THEM. I WOULD DO IT AGAIN."

"You talk about them like they're insects."

"HUMANS ARE NUMEROUS. SMALL. AN INVASIVE SPECIES. VERY EASY TO KILL. IN MANY REGARDS, THE INSECT ANALOGY IS APT."

She swallowed the small boulder that had formed in her throat. "Would you consider Kaveh an insect?"

"DO NOT SOME HUMANS KEEP INSECTS AS PETS?"

She laughed humorlessly. "Would that make me on the level of a 'pet' as well?"

"FOR NOW, DEAR GENTLE CREATURE. BUT YOU ARE AN INSECT, REGARDLESS. EASILY CRUSHED AND JUST AS EASILY FORGOTTEN. WHEN I GET BACK MY POWER CORE, THEN YOU WILL UNDERSTAND."

"Is that a threat?" she asked. "If you got your power core back, would you 'crush' me?"

"ONLY IF YOU ARE A NUISANCE."

"And what makes you think Jude will give you your power core back?"

"I DO NOT EXPECT ANYONE TO GIVE ME MY POWER CORE BACK. I EXPECT TO TAKE IT."

She swallowed another small boulder as she looked down at the journal again, opening it to a bookmarked page. "And if there's one thing you want me to take from our talks, it's that you consider me and everyone like me to be beneath consideration. Insignificant. That we understand each other in this 'insect' analogy."

Nikola cocked his head to the side like a puppy who'd just heard a funny noise. "IN OUR ANALOGY, WHAT ARE YOU? SOMETHING DELI-CATE AND BEAUTIFUL, LIKE THE INSECT ON YOUR SKIN?"

"I don't think this butterfly works in your analogy," she said. "It's extremely rare. A lot of people are working to save it."

"PERHAPS SOMETHING MORE APT WOULD BE AN INFESTATION, SOMETHING THAT CONSUMES ALL IT ENCOUNTERS. A COLONY OF ANTS? NO, I THINK NOT; THEY ARE FAR TOO COOPERATIVE WITH ONE ANOTHER TO BE AN APT ANALOGY. COCKROACHES, PERHAPS."

"Even Kaveh?" she said. "Not to say that your analogy is completely without merit; it's hard to argue that we aren't invasive and destructive as a species, but he really did love you."

The crest on the back of Nikola's head, up to this point relaxed like a half-bloomed tulip, bristled. "I THINK IT POSSIBLE THAT HUMANS ARE NO MORE CAPABLE OF LOVE THAN A COCKROACH."

"Obviously, humans are capable of love as we define it, but maybe not as you define it."

"HOW DO YOU DEFINE IT, DEAR GENTLE CREATURE?"

"Love is patient, love is kind," she said. "It does not envy, it does not boast. Love is . . . selfless." This bit she ad-libbed, as using the prayer spoken at the weddings of the most basic people to walk this earth felt a bit trite.

"Even the most ostensibly selfless act is done in the interest of inducing feelings of devotion in the other party. No act is truly selfless."

"Perhaps our particular strain of chemistry that makes us feel conditionally attached to other individuals in our lives wouldn't qualify as 'love' to you. Though I suppose there's not a way we could ever know for sure, is there?"

"Oh, but there is, dear gentle creature. But it is not an experience I believe you would ever want to undertake."

Paris looked up. "What do you mean?"

"You would have to ask my dear little cousin."

"Dear little cousin?"

"My Beloved's human liaison."

Paris closed her book. "You mean Cora?"

"Yes, it was his intent to engineer her to be post-natural, like us. So she volunteered to be his personal experiment, his plaything, and he does what he pleases with her body and mind."

Such a strange and horrible thing to say, laid out so bluntly, but all worries she'd always had in the back of her mind about Cora's relationship with Jude. *Humans are insects. She is his plaything.* And even if Nikola was wrong about that dynamic, Jude had done *something* to her body—her ability to traverse hemispheres in a few minutes, the way she was able to scan for bugs with her eyes as if she were able to look through walls—she didn't get that from the Ortega side of the family. "You're saying he's . . . implanted things in her body."

"Not only her body; the most complex apparatus would be for the brain. It was his intent to engineer a biomechanical system that would show whether it is possible to know his little 'dear one' as we are able to know one another. But if he builds this apparatus, he could only do it through great suffering on her part."

She swallowed. "Suffering?"

Nikola stayed still, his hands resting daintily on the foam mat like he was in charm school. "He has always considered her suffering

AN ACCEPTABLE COST REGARDLESS OF HIS ENDS. BUT SHE WILL EN-
DURE IT, SO GREAT IS HER DEVOTION. SHE WILL EVEN FOLLOW HIM
OFF-WORLD, WHEN THE TIME COMES."

"What time is that?"

"WHEN TIME RUNS OUT FOR YOU."

"What does that mean?"

"THEY KNOW WHAT I HAVE ALREADY TOLD YOU; THERE IS NOTH-
ING THEY CAN DO TO SAVE YOUR CIVILIZATION."

"She would just . . . let him take her off-world?"

"HE IS HER SUPERIOR. SHE DOES AS HE TELLS HER."

She thought back to the last time she saw Cora, her almost painful
reassurances that he treated her well, how forced and dishonest her "He's
fine, we're fine!" felt. Something was up. All was not fine. She knew Nikola couldn't be *right* . . . but at the same time, he couldn't be completely
wrong. And then there was the way he looked at her—like it was she who
was under the glass dome, an insect on display for his amusement. She
couldn't shake the feeling that he already had a plan for escape, and she
was somehow part of it.

"DID YOU HAVE ANOTHER JOURNAL ENTRY YOU WISHED TO DIS-
CUSS WITH ME, DEAR GENTLE CREATURE?"

The process for corpse exhumation had been fast-tracked so much it probably violated the law, even if the government had ordered it. Cora and Ampersand returned to Bahura two days later to look at the corpses and see if there was anything to be gleaned from them. Only four of the six dead were buried in the village, the other two moved to family plots elsewhere on the island. Ampersand decreed this sampling *"adequate,"* as it wasn't likely there was something he could learn from the other two corpses that he couldn't learn from these four, and so they arrived at the local cemetery. It was completely unlike any Cora had ever seen in her life.

Relative to the size of the village, it was huge.

The cemetery felt like a village unto itself overlooking the ocean, with tiny alleys running between each of the mausoleums, and, with the sky overcast as it was, it felt even more a city for the dead into which they were intruding. It was not a plot of land set apart from the community but was instead a part of it, with streets and homes wrapping around it on three of its four sides, with the fourth facing the ocean. There was no planning or consistency to the graves, the direct inverse of a planned community—some were the size of a couch, some were gated off and bigger than many of the nearby houses. Some were modest headstones in the earth, but most were mausoleums parked above the ground, perhaps a necessity due to the climate. A backhoe lifted the concrete mausoleum lids, then the process of coffin removal began with Marisol's uncle, Pacifico.

Ampersand hung back, tucked away between mausoleums where

most of the workers and families couldn't see him, which was probably for the best. She could sense he was ticked that he'd been committed to this wildly inefficient and time-consuming endeavor. He didn't appreciate how many concessions had been made by both the government and the bereaved families in order to get this done as quickly as possible; he resented that he had to go through this at all.

After the workers slid the concrete lid off Pacifico's mausoleum, they lifted the casket out using nylon straps, and once on solid ground, one of the morticians opened it. The smell of four years of decay was far riper than Cora had anticipated, and she stumbled backward without looking into the coffin. She had not known this man, so to her it would have otherwise just been a corpse, but they did things differently here in Bahura than they did in Torrance; many of the graves had banners hanging over them with pictures of the deceased, their birth and death dates, and some quote from the Bible. Above the source of the rancid smell, faded by four years of sun, was a six-foot banner with a picture of who this man had been in life. Next to his picture read:

Pacifico Martinez
April 3, 1980–May 18, 2005
"I have fought the good fight, I have finished the race,
I have kept the faith."—2 Timothy 4:7

Cora breathed through her mouth, hoping Ampersand would be quick about it. He was, not needing more than two minutes before relaying to her the instruction to rebury Pacifico so he could move on to the other graves. The next one belonged to one of the children, the following to his father, and then finally the man named Rodrigo. Half a dozen workers from the government-affiliated mortuary strapped up the concrete mausoleum cover, hauled it off, and pulled up the casket. Just as with Pacifico, a weathered banner featuring the photo of a young man hung over the grave, looking down at her.

Here lies Rodrigo Morales
October 16, 1976–May 18, 2005
"Precious in the sight of the Lord is the death of his
Saints."—Psalm 116:15

This time, she had the foresight to hold her breath before the smell hit her, but Rodrigo's family, who were standing about twenty feet from the coffin in the opposite direction, did not. She only connected that this must be Rodrigo's family when his widow covered her face in horror at the smell, as did her little girl. And then there was Lorenzo, sixty-five pounds soaking wet, even frailer than he had looked two days ago, barely able to stand and looking down into his father's grave like it was his own. He hadn't just watched his friends die in the attack, she realized; he'd also lost his father.

I prayed to Saint Jude.

Cora glanced at them just in time for Lorenzo's eyes to dart away; he hadn't been looking at her, she realized, but at Ampersand, who had reappeared to begrudgingly do his assignment. His frustration at having to involve humans in this was bad enough, but she sensed also he wasn't learning anything useful, because his mood was not improving. Rodrigo's widow broke down in tears and turned away. Cora withstood the display of emotion for a few seconds before she couldn't take it anymore and marched past Ampersand, the grave, and the workers toward Rodrigo's widow.

"You speak English?" she whispered.

The woman looked at her with the same frightened expression she had hitherto been reserving for the soldiers. "Some."

"What's your name?"

"Corazon."

Both Clarinda and Lorenzo were staring at Cora, Clarinda's eyes wide with fear and hope, Lorenzo's almost dark. Cora glanced at the soldiers to make sure they were out of earshot, and leaned in close to Corazon. "He can help."

The woman's eyes grew wide. "What . . ."

"He might be able to help Lorenzo. Human doctors may not be able to operate, but he can. Do you understand?"

It took a solid five seconds for the woman to nod a curt yes, and her eyes floated toward Ampersand in disbelief.

"Can we come visit you tonight at your house?"

At this, she looked at Cora, even more incredulous. "At our house?"

"Yes, we'll come to you. But you can't tell anyone about this, or he won't do it."

This time, it was Corazon who looked around to see if anyone had overheard, but everyone else was still watching him, despite the fact that Ampersand had hardly moved, big eyes still staring into the hole from which the smell of death was pouring. "He can . . . operate?"

"Maybe," Cora whispered. "He can try. Maybe. But you cannot tell *anyone*. No friends. No family. No one. Do you understand?"

She swallowed, nodding frantically. Cora didn't say another word, returning to Ampersand as he withdrew from the grave.

"He's done," she told the mortuary people. "We're ready to go."

As preparations were made for them to be helicoptered away from the village, Cora leaned into him urgently. "Please, save this kid."

"We agreed that it was impractical."

"I know it's impractical," she said, finding it difficult to maintain a whisper. "But he needs help, and we can give it. You could do it, can't you?"

"I know I could remove it, but it would take some time."

"How much time?"

"Perhaps an hour."

She swallowed the rock that was forming in her throat, blinking back her bemusement that *that*, of all things, was what he considered "some time."

"It would be dangerous to set this precedent. It would beg the question as to why I don't do this for every child so afflicted."

She looked around to make sure no one was in earshot and leaned in closer to him. "I understand that allowing yourself to really see the extent to which people are suffering all over the world all day every day would be unbearable for you, but I'm not asking you to do that."

"It could put the child in danger if this were to become widely known."

"Then we'll make them swear a vow of secrecy. And if they later claim you miraculously healed their son, we deny it ever happened. No one will believe them."

She looked back at the family, who all were making some effort to not look at Ampersand, all but Lorenzo, who just stared at him, either in wonder or terror she couldn't tell.

"We do it under cover of night after they return us to our island and they think I'm relaxing on the beach with a piña colada," she whispered, watching as Lorenzo's mother urged him to follow her. "Nobody has to know."

. . . . .

Lorenzo hadn't looked at Cora once the whole time they had been in his house, only at Ampersand as he looked right through the boy—literally. Corazon and Clarinda stood with their backs against the wall of their small main room, along with their *lola*, Rodrigo's mother. Corazon had been very apologetic that they couldn't keep it from Lola, who lived with them. The Morales family, owning about a quarter acre of farmland, wasn't so close to their neighbors as others in the village were, and their house was made of concrete instead of thatching, making them comparatively well-to-do. Even so, it was probably the smallest house she'd ever been in, and the alien took up an uncomfortably large fraction of it.

"He says it hasn't metastasized," said Cora, feeling that the tension in the room might give her a migraine. "But the tumor itself . . ."

"How big?" Corazon asked, cutting her off. She'd backed Clarinda as far as she could against the opposite wall, barely the distance of a midsize couch.

"*Approximately 43.68 cubic centimeters.*"

"You're going to have to give me an object to compare that to."

This took him a few seconds, as he was likely going through a list of objects with standard sizes that *accurately* conveyed what he was trying to communicate. Unlike Nikola, he was not very adept at loose metaphors. "*Approximately three cubic centimeters larger than the size of a standard golf ball.*"

Cora shuddered at the thought of a golf ball inside that head, squishing his brain into his skull. She raised her hands in front of her, which were now shaking slightly, and formed the mold of an invisible golf ball. Upon seeing what she was getting at, Corazon winced like she'd been cut by a knife.

"*It is direr than I had anticipated. The cancer is heavily embedded in the brain. I cannot guarantee complete removal.*"

Cora swallowed hard and looked at the family. "He may not be able to get it all without causing brain damage."

Corazon shook her head as if she were unable to find the right words in any language, let alone a mess like English. "The doctors say they can't operate. They won't even try," she said at last. "He can try?"

"He can try," affirmed Cora.

Clarinda then chimed in urgently in frightened Tagalog, speaking to Cora and Ampersand in turn.

"What's she saying?" asked Cora. Thanks to her ocular overlay translator, she did know what Clarinda was saying, but she didn't want to explain all that to Corazon.

"It's . . . the sin," said Corazon. "She thinks we are cursed. Our family is cursed. That's why Lorenzo is sick. That's why her father is killed."

"*Do they consent?*"

"Are you sure you want to go through with this?"

"If he . . . if Jude does nothing, Lorenzo will die," said Corazon, struggling with his name as if assigning the name of the venerated Saint Jude to this alien creature were sacrilege. "Weeks, maybe days." Corazon's throat constricted, and she struggled to get the next words out in English, and so said them in Tagalog instead: "We lost Rodrigo. We can't lose Lorenzo." At this, Lola struggled to hold back tears and did the sign of the cross.

"*Does the child consent?*"

"Can you ask Lorenzo if he's sure he wants to go through with this?"

Corazon asked him, and Lorenzo looked back up at Ampersand. The child was alert now, adrenaline and fear pumping some energy back into his dying body. His mouth hung open, but he stayed silent.

"*Tell the child he has nothing to fear from me.*"

It was rare that Ampersand said something that could be construed as comforting or sensitive, even to her. She got on her knees next to Lorenzo and looked at him. "He says he's a friend."

Corazon quietly translated to him from behind her. Lorenzo looked at Cora, then back up at Ampersand, before giving a barely perceptible nod.

"*I will need privacy,*" said Ampersand. "*From all of you.*"

Cora started to ask, *Even me?* Before realizing, *Of course even me.* She wasn't a doctor. She'd just be in the way. Cora nodded, stood up, and relayed the instruction. Corazon stood rooted in place, everything in her person screaming against the reality that the only chance to save her child's life meant leaving him alone with this *thing*, before slipping past a curtain acting as a room divider, and then out the front door.

But Ampersand, to her surprise, didn't seem upset or annoyed that he'd been tasked with this. This skinny little boy, glued to an old wooden chair and struggling to keep his head up, looked at him with equal parts wonder, fear, and hopelessness, but Ampersand looked down at him like he was in his element. As if realizing that his posture was intimidating, he lowered himself into a squat, his head now level with Lorenzo's. Cora slipped past the room divider, now out of sight of Lorenzo, and half expected an instruction, but none came. It was as if she were not even there.

Lorenzo swallowed loudly and opened his mouth to speak. It took a few tries before he finally managed in his native language, "Am I going to die?"

Ampersand was still for a moment, just looking at the child with that intense, seemingly bottomless gaze, then slowly shook his head.

"Are we cursed?" the boy whispered.

Ampersand's eyelids fell in a long, slow blink, and he tilted his head ever so slightly. Again, he shook his head. Then he looked down at the tips of two of his forefingers, which had shifted into a phial, which looked more like a man-made syringe than what he usually used. He then looked at the boy, holding the phial between them. Lorenzo took several deep breaths, and she could hear him almost choking on them on the verge of tears if he wasn't already crying. Then he nodded. Ampersand slid the phial into a vein in Lorenzo's neck, and his body went limp. Cora followed his family outside.

· · · · ·

Almost an hour had gone by of furtive waiting on the porch. Most of the village consisted of straw-thatched houses with fiberglass roofs in close quarters to one another, more like an apartment complex than houses. The Morales family home wasn't so on top of their neighbors as other homes in the village, but it was still difficult to keep this a secret or keep people out of one another's business. Cora had had to hide several times when someone walked by.

She had left Corazon, eyes closed in prayer, alone on the far end of the porch. Corazon's English was passable, but not good enough for more than surface-level small talk (which didn't feel appropriate, anyway), and Cora's built-in translator wasn't super useful to that effect, as it only worked one way. After a while, Corazon offered her a cigarette. Cora nearly refused on a basis of not being a smoker, then decided, *Fuck it.* At least it was something to do with her hands. She'd smoked before and in theory knew how to do it, but these were Marlboros, *bad* Marlboros, and it was all she could do to keep her lungs in her body from coughing.

Clarinda was praying on her rosary with Lola, who was keeping her calm by speaking it along with her. Hearing the rosary so many times over the last hour, and given that Tagalog used some Spanish vocabulary, Cora could more or less follow it by now even without the translation overlay. Eventually, Corazon stood up, approached Cora, and offered her yet another cigarette. Cora took it, more because it would be rude to refuse than because she wanted it, and she didn't know if this was one of those cultures where you were *supposed* to refuse on the first offer (like in equally Catholic Ireland). Ampersand would have *words* about these Marlboros.

"She's praying for forgiveness?" asked Cora between coughs, hoping Corazon wouldn't ask how she knew.

"She thinks we have sin," said Corazon. "Sin—that is why the 'demon' attack."

"We, as in the village?"

"Our family," said Corazon. "Lorenzo. She says Lorenzo is a sinner."

"What was his sin?"

"She won't tell," said Corazon.

Cora's brow furrowed, and she looked at Clarinda, knowing from experience that girls that age were terrible at keeping secrets. She wondered, had perhaps Lorenzo seen something, or *done* something, and sworn Clarinda to secrecy?

"The operation is complete."

Cora started in surprise at the sound of his voice, then released a sigh of relief. "Everything okay?"

"The cancer is removed."

Corazon looked at her urgently.

"It's okay," Cora said. "He says he removed the cancer."

Corazon clapped her hands to her face, and, barely holding it together, the family went back inside the tiny house.

Lorenzo was where she'd last seen him; he was groggy, but other than the fact that he was still restrained in a sitting position, his head propped up for easier operation, he looked almost as they'd left him. Ampersand hadn't even shaved his head. Clarinda stopped short upon seeing the tumor lying in a bowl, a hard and ugly growth like the roots of a mangrove.

"He says he got it all," said Cora, dictating what she was hearing. Corazon's nostrils flared as she put her hand to her heart, did the sign of the cross, and wept. "He'll probably still have seizures for another six months or so, and the dizziness won't go away for a few weeks," Cora continued, "but his appetite should begin to come back in a few days. He'll probably be really tired for a while."

"We need to tell them!" Clarinda blurted in Tagalog into her balled fists, looking at the bleary Lorenzo. Corazon pulled her close, trying to calm her. Lorenzo, barely conscious, looked at her and shook his head. Clarinda repeated her tearful declaration several times. "We need to tell them! We need to tell them!"

Clarinda looked at Cora, eyes wide with fear, and began spewing her confession while her mother looked on in stunned confusion. "We're the reason the demon came to the village," she said, tears now streaming down her face as if she knew Cora could understand her. "It's the reason we were cursed. It's in the woods. We buried it."

Cora's face grew slack as Corazon struggled to explain what she was saying, and Ampersand stood up as tall as the ceiling would allow, now very interested. She approached Clarinda, who backed away from her apprehensively.

"We're sorry," said Clarinda, addressing Ampersand. "Please, forgive us."

As calmly as she could, Cora looked at Clarinda in the eye and said, "Clarinda, you need to take us to the place in the woods. You need to show us what you buried out there."

. . . . .

The scene of the crime was a few hundred yards into the jungle behind the Morales family home. Corazon was initially torn between the impetus of her daughter admitting to some new unforeseen horror and staying with her son who might survive after all; in the end, she left Lorenzo with Lola and, along with Cora and Ampersand, followed the half-incoherent child into the woods.

"There," said Clarinda, clasping her rosary in front of her. "That's where they buried it."

"*Remove her from this patch of ground.*"

"Back up," said Cora, pushing Corazon and Clarinda back. She could barely see Corazon's face, but her flashlight shook as she tried to keep it focused on the patch of ground.

"Is there anything there?" asked Cora, prepared for anything ranging from a small nuke to the neighbor's cat to be buried there.

"*I'm unsure,*" said Ampersand. "*Stand back.*"

He spread his hands out, forming a triangle as he often did when using his telekinesis, and the air felt thicker as the patch of ground seemed to ripple, then come apart like the parting of the Red Sea. At first, it was only the topsoil a couple of inches deep, but he continued to dig, peeling the earth back in layers.

"*There is something here.*"

Another ripple in the dirt, and another layer of earth peeled away, revealing something solid. Something white and solid.

Something that looked an awful lot like bone.

Another layer of dirt peeled away, and Clarinda prayed on her rosary. The two adults stood transfixed—those were bones, all right, but they weren't human. *Please say it's the neighbor's cat*, she thought.

"Is that . . . physeterine?" she asked.

Ampersand relaxed his hands, tucking them back into his sleeves, and stood up. "*Yes,*" he said. "*A juvenile.*"

THE PHILIPPINE
STAR

ETI Jude Atheatos Visits Palawan to Investigate 2005 Incident That Left 6 Dead

MANILA
NOVEMBER 8, 2009

BY SARAH FESALBON

A visit from two of the most infamous public figures of the last two years may confirm what Palawan locals have long suspected: that a tragedy that left six dead in the sleepy fishing village of Bahura was not the result of a bar fight but of extraterrestrial activity.

The amygdaline ETI Jude Atheatos is in the Philippines with his interpreter, Cora Sabino, investigating the incident, officials say. According to officials, although Atheatos does believe that this incident may involve ETIs, he does not believe his own civilization was involved. If true, this incident is confirmation that Earth has been visited by more than one alien civilization out of an unknown number.

Atheatos's visit to the Philippines is his first trip outside of Japan since he was granted permanent residency in the country last year.

Officials with the National Intelligence Coordinating Agency concede that there is more about the 2005 tragedy that has not yet been made public, and promise that more information is forthcoming.

· 16 ·

"I'm with the . . ." Sol pinched the bridge of his nose as he appealed to the guy blocking his entrance, a NICA agent whose lanyard read GIANCARLO BALANGUE (which was probably not his real name, anyway). Sol had no idea where the Filipinos had stashed the Guests of Honor (probably a fabulous private island frequently used by celebrities), but since he was not a guest at all and was in fact here on Uncle Sam's dime, he'd had to content himself with the best accommodations available in the system: the Filipino equivalent of a Holiday Inn a solid forty-minute drive away (assuming it was 3:00 A.M. with no traffic, as was presently the case). "I'm with the . . . procession."

Balangue stared at him with the air of a mall cop who had a very serious job to do. Sol slammed the rest of his cup of coffee (truly the worst hotel coffee he had ever experienced), tossed it at the trash can by the entrance, and missed. "I'm with your *guest*."

Balangue watched the coffee cup rolling around on the ground, obviously taking it as a sign of disrespect. It wasn't intended as such, but Sol was not going to give the guy the satisfaction of picking it up. He'd gotten a message from his superiors back stateside that something big had gone down in Bahura, though fucked if he could get Ghasabian or Sabino to respond to him. After about fifteen minutes of trying, he gave up, brewed this abortion of a cup of coffee, and called a cab. And now here he was, trying to talk his way into the same building he'd been in and out of all week as if he'd gotten his clearance revoked and no one had the decency to tell him. "I'm with—"

"CIA," said Balangue. "I know."

Sol looked at him, like, *Okay. We are on the same page. Let me in?* But the guy didn't budge, still wearing that same bored expression of a bouncer high on his own power.

"Yes," said Sol, trying to retain a veneer of patience. "CIA."

"You have no authority here."

Sol looked at him coolly but inwardly was perplexed. Had he claimed that he did?

"Let him in," said the voice from inside, and Sol saw Estraton Catipay down the hall with a begrudging tone of someone forced to extend an invitation. "He's clear."

Sol followed him down the hall, back into the bowels where Johnny's remains were kept. When he entered, he saw Sabino, Ghasabian, 46, and several NICA officers standing over a pile of mud that it took him a moment to realize had a skeleton rising out of it. This appeared to be alien remains.

But they did not belong to Johnny.

"Busy night?" asked Sol, looking at Sabino. He had seen remains like this before, but they had not belonged to an alien. They looked like human remains that had been uncovered after years of being buried— almost all the soft tissue long since decomposed, leaving only bones, only these bones were a dull silvery-gray instead of white.

"We got a lead," she said in a suspiciously defensive tone. 46, for his part, stood right behind her / over her as usual, his eyes on the remains.

"Smaller than we expected, huh?"

Ghasabian looked at him tiredly. "Cora, will you please tell Agent Kaplan what you told us?"

"It's a juvenile," said Sabino. "This is the reason 'Johnny' attacked the villagers. Clarinda and Lorenzo Morales were the only ones left alive who knew where the juvenile had been buried. I guess they understood on some level that the one that killed their dad had something to do with this."

A long hiss of air escaped Ghasabian's lips. "Why was the juvenile even there in the first place?"

"He can't say for sure." Sabino's timbre was normally a few semitones lower when she spoke for 46, but today, she wasn't bothering. "Maybe the juvenile got lost and wandered too close to the village, and the boys went hunting for it. Maybe it was doing some sort of adolescent hazing ritual. Maybe it was just curious."

"How old was it?" asked Dr. Catipay.

"About the same age as the human boys," said Sabino. "Somewhere in the neighborhood of eight or nine years."

"Awful," breathed Ghasabian, his hand covering the lower half of his face like an octopus. "Just awful."

"So the adult killed the boys as an act of revenge," said Dr. Catipay.

"That's what it looks like."

"And then the boys' parents attacked the adult trying to protect their own," said Dr. Catipay, "the adult kills the parents until it gets killed by the villagers, on and on the cycle continues." He looked at Sabino. "Can you tell how it died?"

"It was certainly . . . killed," she said after a listening-pause. Sol got the impression that 46 had used a term more loaded than *killed*. "Jude thinks it looks like it was killed from blunt-force trauma, like it was beaten to death. From what I can gather, the boys thought the juvenile was some kind of monster and chased after it into the woods."

"No clothing, though," said Dr. Catipay. "No effects, no artifacts . . ."

"There is clothing there, of a sort," said Sabino, "in that there is bio-degraded clothing material. It would decompose way faster than human clothes would. Their clothes aren't really . . . manufactured, per se, but grown."

"Grown?" repeated Ghasabian.

"The ones in this pod are expert biosmiths," said Sabino. Sol couldn't help but notice that she wasn't taking any listening-pauses, as if she were recounting information she was privy to, but was only pretending like 46 was a part of this conversation. "Rather than taking raw materials and processing them like we do for most things, it's much more effi-cient to just engineer biomatter—in this case, plants and fungi would be the closest analogue—that are designed to function as whatever mate-rial they need—clothes in this case. Kind of like, I don't know . . ." She grasped for the right words; yup, she was not getting any help from 46 at all. "Like a genetically engineered tree bark that can form fit to your entire body and protect you from all the inherent dangers of an alien planet."

"Amazing," said Dr. Catipay. He looked at Sabino, then at 46. "And yet, no effort to communicate. If amygdalines were able to learn our languages, why haven't they?"

Sabino looked at 46, as if wondering if he'd deign to chime in, but he was still as a statue, eyes on that desiccated corpse. "It's one thing to learn a word or that the sequence of letters *C-A-T* represents a certain animal, but that isn't the same as learning a language. Do you follow?"

"Yes," said Dr. Catipay and Ghasabian, at the same moment Sol said, "No."

"Let me put it this way: We've been studying dolphins and whales for decades, and most scientists agree that they have a form of culture and communicate with a form of language, but outside of like, 'This click is the mating click,' and, 'This click is the "I found fish" click,' we haven't come close to cracking cetacean language, and we evolved on the same planet. Jude thinks it's highly unlikely they've had the time or resources to really create an algorithm for human language."

"Let's take for granted that they consider us dangerous natives of a dangerous planet," said Ghasabian. "Why on earth would they bring their children here?"

"If there are juveniles here, that means they were born here," said Sabino. "On Earth. Which means they've been breeding here."

"Why in God's name would they do that?" asked Sol in an incredulous tone, like she'd revealed they'd come to Earth to cook meth.

"Breeding planets are sometimes chosen hundreds of years in advance. Earth is optimal for that purpose—high gravity, generally pretty consistent climate, adequate oxygen in the atmosphere. This juvenile was probably around eight or nine years old when it died; this pod probably arrived here around fourteen years ago thinking it hosted a preindustrial primate species, same as it always has."

"Just what the Superorganism assumed," said Ghasabian.

"And they may not have had the time or resources to go find another planet, so they stuck to their original plan to breed a generation here. Physeterines always breed on planets."

"Why?" asked Ghasabian. "If they're always on the run, why not just stay in space where it's safer?"

"They need to raise juveniles on planets," said Sabino. "To gestate correctly, to get their bones to grow properly. There are ways to get around this, but they're incredibly resource heavy, especially for something you need to maintain long enough for a child to develop."

"Human scientists are well aware of this issue," said Dr. Catipay. "Without getting into the weeds of it, as of right now it wouldn't be possible to conceive in low or no gravity, let alone raise a child to adulthood. Even adults lose bone mass as soon as they're in zero g."

"Physeterines don't," Sabino added. "They've managed to engineer that bug out in adulthood, but they have to grow into their bones first. There's no way to do that without gravity."

"So that's why they planet-hop," said Ghasabian. "To breed."

"Sometimes," said Sabino. "Sometimes it's for resources, sometimes it's to breed, sometimes it's just to live. But the problem with staying in one place for a long time is that makes it more likely for the Superorganism to find them. So when they come to a planet to breed, they'll do it all at the same time so the juveniles will come of age at the same time, and they can leave at the same time. The whole process would take about thirty years."

"So to these juveniles," said Ghasabian, "Earth is the only home they've ever known."

"Thirty years?" repeated Sol pointedly.

Sabino swallowed. Loudly. "Yeah. He says this is pretty close to a worst-case scenario."

Ghasabian broke his staring contest with the corpse, releasing the death grip he'd formed on his cheekbones. "How so?"

"Do the math," said Sol snidely.

Ghasabian shot him a look like a mother whose child had mouthed off. "What math?"

"Nine-year-old juvie found four years ago," he said, gesturing to the remains, "but they can't leave the planet's gravity until the kids are pushing thirty or their bones will turn to Jell-O. Means they're still here." He popped a glance at Sabino. "Right?"

She looked like she might be sick, and her gaze floated down to the remains in front of them, small as that of a human child of roughly the same age would have been. "Yes. They wouldn't leave the planet unless there was an immediate existential danger."

"But why do we have to assume hostility on their part—or ours, for that matter?" asked Ghasabian.

"Do you know when a bear is at its most dangerous?" asked Sol.

"How big is a generation?" asked Dr. Catipay.

"Depends on how big the pod is," said Sabino. "Could be a few hundred, could be a few thousand. You can expect that the number of juveniles will be roughly equal to the number of adults, since they're all capable of bearing young. Unlikely it's a few thousand. Even with their stealth, that number would be hard to go unnoticed for years."

"We're lucky it wasn't worse than it was," said Ghasabian. "That this was the only major incident."

"That we know of," added Sol. "There are any number of strange occurrences or disappearances that might be related to this. We only know about this one through a random grapevine. And our reputation isn't great at the moment, so it's not like other intelligence agencies are knocking down the door to tell us what they know."

"You make it sound like other countries are beholden to us," said Ghasabian.

Sol had to refrain from asking him just whose side he was on. There were a couple of NICA agents looking at him with barely concealed disdain, as if he alone made intelligence officers the world over look bad. "Don't you think we are beholden to one another, as brothers in humanity?" asked Sol, trying despite himself to sound sincere.

Catipay snorted, clearly a gesture he did not intend to make, but once it was out there, it was out there.

"Doctor?" asked Sol.

"I think we would all love to be 'brothers in humanity,' Agent Kaplan," said Catipay.

Sol waited for a *but*, but none came. "So you agree, offering intelligence sharing is imperative."

"I think it doesn't matter what we offer; if you want to take it, you will."

Sol supressed the urge to roll his eyes. It wasn't even that Catipay's assumption wasn't true, it was the naivety of it all, the assumption that CIA overreach was the *real* evil here and not, you know, the flesh-eating aliens. All the same, Catipay was right about one thing: if intelligence was not shared, then it had to be taken. And Macallan had been pushing him to get back into fieldwork, had she not? What better opportunity than this?

"Cora?" asked Ghasabian, ostensibly remembering she was still there.

For her part, she had almost zoned out, as if 46's trance was contagious. She shook her head and focused. "Yes?"

"What does Ampersand think?"

This brought her down to reality. "Jude?"

He didn't budge.

"Ampersand?"

Finally, he blinked, the focus in his eyes shifting as if he were only just remembering there was a real world one could focus on. Sabino's eyes widened at whatever 46 was telling her.

"We need to get back to Japan," she said. "Now."

17

"These guys are . . ." Paris shuffled through the copies of Nils's photos that Cora had left for her on the other side of the Skype call. "Well, when you said, 'Combo of Alien and Predator,' I didn't think you meant literally."

"I didn't think it would be so literal, either," said Cora, looking around and wondering where Ampersand had gone. Ampersand was stoic during the return trip to Japan, not in his normal way of one who was not terribly interested in the goings-on of the human world but as one who had retreated inside a protective shell. By the time they made it back to Haneda, that stoicism was beginning to feel to Cora less like preoccupation and more like a state of shock. When they got back to the house in Fukushima, the tension seemed to have eased a bit, as it often did when Ampersand was no longer among a group of humans. He'd even resumed his normal "*You need sustenance*" routine, but then he disappeared into his lair.

"Any reason you think the Russians call them Semipalatinsk? Think that's where they were discovered?"

"Doubtful. Our CIA code names were themed but didn't really mean anything."

"Themed after what?"

"They were all fictional ships; that's where *Pequod* came from."

"So amygdalines were coded Pequod, and physeterines?"

"Sloop John B."

"The folk song?"

"No, the Beach Boys song."

Paris laughed. "That's a Caribbean folk song. You know all your favorite sixties bands stole half their stuff from Black folks, right?"

"I was more of a Beatles person, anyway."

"Yeah, they *never* stole from Black folks," Paris chuckled.

"They gave credit where credit was due! Most of the time . . ."

Paris put the photos aside. "Well, I can't wait to get a full debrief when you get back," she said, adding, "Can't wait to discuss . . . some of the things I learned from Nikola."

Cora's stomach took a backflip. Oh, God, what had he told her? "Did he talk?"

"Mmm-hmm." Paris fell silent, watching the screen with the expression of someone who'd been hoping for some reciprocity for a while. At length, she added, "I miss you."

"Yeah, um . . ." *I. Miss. You. Too. Simple. To the point. Honest. Say it.* "I . . ." *MISS. YOU. SAY. THE. WORDS. YOU. DOOR. KNOB.* "I'll see you soon," she practically mumbled. "Bye!"

"Bye."

Cora slammed the computer shut and grabbed fistfuls of hair as she dropped her head onto her laptop. Sooner or later, she was going to have to tell Paris the truth—*I am not long for this world. Literally.* Was this what people with terminal illnesses felt like, before they disclosed their status to new friends, new acquaintances, new lovers? Knowing eventually they'd have to have the Conversation with anyone they meet? No, of course they don't feel that way. Terminally ill people don't *choose* to be terminally ill.

She sensed Ampersand's presence in the living room before she saw him. "I'm going to head back," she said. "I have class on Monday, so I'm going to try to get on East Coast time before—"

"*You cannot go to class anymore.*"

"What?"

"*You cannot be on the Columbia campus anymore. It isn't safe. You must stay here.*"

"What . . . How? You said there was no way they'd have figured out our language."

He approached her slowly, like she was a bomb that needed defusing. "*They will have decoded radio waves, they will have learned how to transcode binary computer data. They will have certainly seen the photo of us in Pershing Square. They will have seen multiple images of you and me together."*

"But if they don't understand human language—"

"They do not need to understand human language to recognize patterns. They could easily deduce that the sequence of letters that comprise your name appear in conjunctions of pictures of both of us quite often. They could also connect that the letter sequence that comprises your name often comes in conjunction with the letter sequence that comprises Columbia University. *They don't need to understand English to do that. The campus is small; if they were to make that connection, all they would need to do would be to surveil the campus and wait."*

It was only here that she noticed he was no longer perfectly still, but there was a slight sway back and forth, like a skyscraper in heavy wind. *"It is not safe. We are fortunate they have not made that connection yet as it is."*

"Ampersand, please." The wall was somewhat thick at the moment, so whatever was happening inside him wasn't careening into her as it sometimes did, but she could definitely sense that he was having a minor breakdown.

"You haven't seen what they are capable of—I have. I won't have it done to you. I won't let them near you."

She grabbed him by his long fingers. "Ampersand, you're spiraling. It's okay; you're safe."

"We are not safe. We are never safe."

"Sit down!" she said, pulling him toward the floor. She encountered only slight resistance as she guided him down into a roosting position. His eyes were wide and glowing *way* too brightly, as though he were trying to take in the whole world from right here in their living room. Then they dimmed and found focus.

"You never told me what they did to you," she said.

His eyes continued to dim as the focus finally found her face. He blinked in that languid way he did, long and slow, the blink of a creature that only blinks every few minutes. She put her hand on the area under his head where the jaw might be if he had one. "What did they make you watch?"

"Seven."

"Seven?"

"*I had seven.*" He closed his eyes. "*You were the Eighth. I never thought I would have an Eighth. Obelus was my first. Nikola was my Seventh. I did not intend to have more than seven.*"

"Symphyles, you mean," she said.

"*I had seven. Now I have three, including you.*"

"What happened to them?" she whispered.

"*Approximately eight weeks, by your time measurements, before the purge began, Obelus disappeared. Nikola understood what was happening. He told me we needed to leave the Superorganism altogether. He begged me to leave with him. But I couldn't imagine what leaving would even look like. Where would we go? To what end? Then he was gone. I never saw or heard from him again, until he came here.*

"*Then Čefo approached me, telling me that he intended to smuggle out Esperas and a small group of lower-caste support. I told him I would not leave without my symphyles, and Čefo would not wait for me.*"

His gaze became blurry, his focus dimming as he looked up into nothing. "*We don't have a term for what happened to my Second in modern Pequod-phonemic. It is archaic, it doesn't occur in the Superorganism, but you do have a word in English—assassination. I didn't understand what was happening at first, when I sensed it.*"

The thing he sensed, she knew, was his symphyle's death, but she'd never considered how he would know that's what it was if he'd never experienced the like before. If he was never *meant* to experience the death of a symphyle.

"*I was taken with several other Fremdan Oligarchs, including two of my other symphyles. We were compliant, of course; as Oligarchs, we did not humor the idea that our lives were in danger. Most of the Fremda were euthanized immediately, but two of my symphyles and I were sent off with a detachment of Similars. They removed us from the locus of the Superorganism and took us to a nearby outpost, and it was during this move that I sensed the death of my Third. I never learned how my Third was killed.*"

She rested her hands on his curled-up fingers, resisting the urge to move closer to him, to physically comfort him, which was just about the last thing he would want when he was like this.

"*When the Similars moved us again, they separated my Fourth from my Fifth and me. They killed my Fourth the same day. Then I saw Obelus again, one last time. By this point, he had assumed a new identity in his new Similar body. Obelus had known the Fremdan genetic purge was going to happen, perhaps had even helped orchestrate it.*

"*My Fifth and I were kept alive at Obelus's request. He told the detachment of Similars holding us in custody that our skills as xenobiologists had not yet outlived their usefulness, but as dissidents, we could not be allowed near the locus of the Superorganism. This detachment of Similars did not consist of explorers or scientists, as Fremdan Similars usually were, but militarists. Their missions were mostly ferreting out physeterine populations and exterminating them. That group of six Similars was responsible for the death of no fewer than twenty physeterine pods over those decades, although I don't know exactly how many. The Similars did employ our skills as xenobiologists from time to time, but not for science. Only for militarism. Only for killing.*

"*My Fifth and I spent long portions of our lives in near–light speed travel as they moved us from outpost to outpost. It was during one of these stretches of near–light speed travel that I felt the death of my Sixth. I never learned how my Sixth died, either, or how they survived for so long.*

"*My Fifth, who was with me the whole time, was a technocrat who specialized in genetics, amygdaline and physeterine. This was the reason given as to why they'd been kept alive, but that wasn't true; Obelus kept my Fifth alive as insurance to keep me silent about his identity.*"

Cora swallowed the bile that had formed in her throat. "And it worked."

"*I did anything they asked. I wanted to secure for myself and my Fifth whatever arrangement Obelus had bargained for himself. I would have done anything. Yes, even being complicit in a genocidal regime, if it meant saving myself and my Fifth, and perhaps even Nikola, whom I knew to be alive somewhere. Had our detachment not been incapacitated by a physeterine pod, perhaps I might have even gotten my wish.*

"*In subjective time, I had been away from the Superorganism for seventeen years, but in relativistic space-time, nearly two hundred years had passed, and in those two hundred years, several pods of physeterines had pooled their knowledge and found that Similars were vulnerable to certain frequencies of electromagnetic pulse at close range. It was exceedingly rare for physeterines to find a Similar before a Similar found them. But physeterines had one advantage; their bodies were fully not post-natural in the* same manner as ours. When one physeterine pod found the opportunity to disable our detachment, they took it."

"Ampersand . . ."

His eyes were brightening again in that hypervigilant way. "*They are cannibals. I have told you, they are cannibals.*"

The intensity of his gaze hit her like a hard shove, and once again, she felt not that she was in the presence of her friend but a biosynthetic body that housed the consciousness of an unfathomable terror, something fundamentally inhuman.

"*They took the Similars first, ripping their carapaces open while they were still alive. One by one, they split them down the back, opened them like clamshells, ensuring the others could see. They sent feeds of their actions to other pods, rival and ally, as a boast. It was exceedingly rare to capture Similars, and they wanted others to know what they had done. They made me watch everything.*"

"Including your Fifth."

"*They made me watch,*" he said, his eyes dimming back to a more neutral state. "*They made me watch.*"

Cora sat up, putting her arms around his neck and leaning her cheek on the space between his eyes. This wasn't for his comfort so much as hers. "Why were you spared?"

"*One of this physeterine pod understood enough Pequod-phonemic to learn that I was a high-ranking Oligarch and thought they might be able to use me as some form of ransom. They did not know about the Fremdan genetic purge, but in time, they learned that I was useless. Another pod convinced them to trade me to them rather than have me share the same fate as the rest of the Similar detachment and my Fifth. This pod took me, as well as the body of one of the dead Similars, for study. And it was with that pod I stayed until they intercepted the message from Čefo, giving his location here on Earth. They intended to follow Čefo's call for help, and I deemed this unacceptable.*"

"And you killed them," said Cora, sitting up to look at him. "That entire pod."

"*I did not kill them, but I did for all intents and purposes leave them for dead. I thought it possible that some of their own might find them where I left them, but Obelus found them first.*"

"That's how you got this body," she said, pulling herself away from his skin like it had grown hot. He looked at her, and she connected some haunted thing she'd always sensed but never known; he wasn't looking at her with his own eyes. Those were the eyes of a Similar who had died before Cora was even born, a "militarist" who had held him captive for years, forced him to do terrible things, and then died a gruesome death. "Oh my God."

She gently placed her hands under his giant head, cupping it, and then leaned her own head into it. Maybe that revulsion she'd been feeling post–high language wasn't irrational. This body had done innumerable terrible things. Could *still* do them, if he willed it.

"Are we just going to stay in hiding for the rest of our time on Earth?" she whispered.

"*This is an eventuality I had hoped would not come to pass, but as long as there are rogue physeterines on this planet, it is not safe for either of us.*"

He took a forefinger under her chin and lifted it until her gaze met his, grazing the skin of her cheek, sending a chill through her body like a wave. "*I am sorry, dear one.*"

She remembered Paris's expression on the other side of that Skype chat, one of resignation like she already knew. Now she'd have to tell Paris, and why would she waste her precious time or feelings on Cora then? "I thought I'd have more time," she whispered.

"*One way or another, my departure was inevitable. If not this, then eventually the Superorganism. This was inevitable.*"

"What about Nikola?" she asked. "What are you going to do with him?"

"*His letter sequence is associated with Bella Terra. The move will sever any means they have to find him and will suffice as a short-term solution. But if that location is compromised, I must take him into custody myself.*"

She swallowed. "And then?"

"*And then we must depart.*"

18

Paris looked between Kaveh's old journal and her own, marveling at the organized chaos on his pages. Her note-taking style was nothing like his, and she couldn't help but think that if anyone was ever left with the task of decoding what her journals had meant after her untimely demise, they'd have a much less difficult time of it than she'd had with Kaveh's. She circled the word at the top of the page:

Blackmail

Nikola's recollections were often scattered and broken, but through it all, she had made the connection—*jannaham* in Kaveh's journal meant hell. In this journal entry, on this day, he'd relayed some intense feelings of guilt to Nikola, confessing to him that he had been blackmailed into giving "my little cousin's sire" some sensitive information. What that information was, Nikola either didn't know or wouldn't say; Kaveh had been privy to a ton of highly sensitive information, far more than Paris even knew. But the real sticky thing was less the mystery of what the information was and more who the blackmailer was, and "my little cousin's sire" could only be one person.

Nils Ortega.

Cora was on her way to Paris's house at that very moment. She had been distant ever since she'd gotten to the Philippines, which at first Paris had chalked up to having met up with Nils, but after what Nikola had told her, she didn't know what to think. She *hoped* Cora's affectionless curtness was rooted in whatever they'd discovered in the Philippines and not the creeping sense that she was about to cut and run, because that tended to happen where Paris's woeful taste in women was concerned. As the philosopher Dr. Andre Young once said, "Bitches ain't shit."

The knock at her door was so soft, she almost didn't hear it, and when she opened it, there was Cora, expression vacant like a Stepford wife. Cora came inside as Paris shut the door behind her, shoulders all hunched up and hands grabbing her elbows in the way that she did when she was signaling, "I desperately need a hug."

"Hey," said Paris, drawing her close, and Cora released the grip she had on her elbows, wrapping her arms around Paris as if they hadn't seen each other in months. "Have a rough trip?"

"I'm just glad to see you," she said, and Paris felt her breathing in her scent.

Okay, so she wasn't fully a pod person yet. Good. But what to say after all the nonsense Nikola had put in her head? "Everything . . . okay?"

Cora released a sigh, a sigh that in Paris's experience tended to precede, "We can't see each other anymore," and the moment that possibility entered her mind, it suddenly became the most obvious possibility. The only possibility.

No, she told herself. *No, no, no. There is no reason to hop to that. Stop assuming the worst.* "So what happened?"

Cora looked at her, still wearing that vacant expression. "Amp . . . Jude . . . thinks I should drop out of school."

"*What?*" Again, she feared that Nikola's raving might have more credence to it than she wanted to believe. "Why?"

"He thinks it's not safe."

"Does this have to do with the physeterines?"

Cora's face twisted like she'd bitten into a rotten lemon. "I . . . I don't know . . . what I'm allowed—"

"Cora, you *owe* me the truth."

Cora finally snapped out of it. "We found a body. It was a juvenile."

"What does that mean?"

"That means they're still here." Cora then explained what they'd learned—how they'd figured that based on the age of the body and the way that physeterines reproduced, it meant the pod that birthed and raised the juvenile was probably still on Earth.

"Is there no way they can be reasoned with?" asked Paris. "That you could find a way to communicate with them, show them that we don't mean them any harm? That Jude doesn't mean them any harm?"

Cora looked ill, and if possible, the circles under her eyes darkened a little.

"Jude *does* mean them no harm, right?"

"Let's just say if he had the ability to piss, he wouldn't do it on them if they were on fire."

"Jesus." She wrapped an arm around Cora, and Cora softened a little, nestling into her shoulder. "We have to figure out some way to communicate with them. You can't just hide for the rest of your life or for the next two decades or whatever—" She stopped, as Cora's expression told her she hadn't even begun to tell her the tip of the bad news. "Or can you?"

Cora looked at her, an irrational mix of hurt and offense like Paris had accused her of stealing.

"What is your plan after you drop out?" Paris continued. "Is it literally going into hiding? Am I not going to see you anymore?"

"Th-that isn't what I want," she stammered. "But . . . I . . . we . . . he can't stay."

"What do you mean? Can't stay where?"

"He can't stay on Earth. One way or the other, he can't stay on Earth. He . . . We were going to leave when we knew an arm of the Superorganism was close, but—"

"What do you mean, 'we'?" said Paris, cutting her off as her heart plummeted into her feet. There was no way Nikola had fully been telling her the truth. There was just no fucking way.

"I mean, I guess ever since Kaveh—" Then her expression changed, no longer frightened or even resigned, but cold. "I knew there was no saving this."

"What do you mean, 'this'?"

"There's no saving this civilization," said Cora, looking at her seriously. "Maybe we can save humans as a species from extinction, if he and I leave, and we take enough genetic material—"

"Genetic material?" Paris said, feeling the heat in her neck rising up to her face. "What, is he going to be both God and Adam and you're . . . Eve?"

"I don't know! We don't have a plan, but it's a possibility—"

"You're just going to let him do whatever he wants to your body—"

"It isn't like that! He isn't going to *make* me do anything, but there's nothing we can do to save this, not in the time that we—"

"So everyone has to die?" Paris cut her off again. "Every person on Earth, no matter who they are or where they're from or what they believe, is doomed because of a few aspiring dictators?"

"I didn't say it was fair! But that is how amygdalines see things; they are incredibly hierarchical, and so whatever the powers that be want is what the civilization as a whole wants, no matter how much dissent from the underclass there is."

Paris stood up, shaking her head, trying to get a sense of perspective, but all she could think was, *Goddamn, Kaveh really knew how to pick 'em. I really know how to pick 'em.* "Why did you bother with Columbia at all?"

"I—it's what Kaveh wanted." She seemed to choke on his name. "The odds of us succeeding are infinitesimal, but if that infinitesimal chance succeeds, I wanted to—"

"What, have a well-rounded liberal arts education for when you land on Planet X to repopulate humanity?"

"I know I can't do anything to help here," said Cora, trying to de-escalate, but Paris's defenses were at one hundred. "I don't have that kind of influence, but we have a chance—"

"I get it," said Paris. "If I had the option knowing that the world is about to burn and I didn't have to watch, I'd fuck off into space, too."

Cora looked at her like she'd slapped her. "It isn't like that—"

"You have an escape hatch no one else has, so you're taking it. I get it." Paris's conscience, faint though it was, tugged at her, telling her, *This isn't helping. You need to back off.* But she was still too angry, angry at herself that she hadn't listened to her instincts, that she'd let herself get attached to this woman, this *child*, at all. "If I were in your position, I'd probably do the same thing. Why even bother helping me at all? Why all this John Lennon 'imagine' bullshit?" Her jaw trembled in anger, and she lowered her voice. "Why string me along when you were always just planning to leave?"

Cora's eyes grew glassy, and she stood there in a brief stupor. Then she turned to leave. It was only here that Paris's anger broke. "Cora . . ."

Cora moved like a robot, grabbing what few items she had—her jacket, her backpack—then barreled toward the door.

"Cora, listen—"

Cora did not listen; without a second of hesitation, she moved to the door, opened it, and ran outside. She didn't slam the door behind her, nor did she look back.

Paris took a moment, equal parts rage and regret, before she moved to the door, looking outside and finding that Cora had vanished. Her head fell against the frame of the door, and she closed her eyes.

Why the hell did I do that?

Date: Fri, Nov 19, 2009 at 4:54 PM
From: Julieta Lozano-Ramsay <JLozanoRamsey@bellaterra
.org>
To: Luciana Ortega <lortega@bellaterra.org>
Subject: Paris Wells

Luciana,
Nikola Sassanian is not an inmate, and I do not have the
authority to override you, his doctors, or his nurse practitioners,
so I do not have the authority to stop you from allowing Paris
Wells to cover his move to the Sacramento facility; however,
I do wish to record my objection to her presence on that
airplane. It isn't even that you are inviting the press into a
situation in which many unforeseen things could go sideways,
it is also out of concern for Ms. Wells. I appreciate that she
has signed liability waivers, but she still does not seem to
appreciate the danger she is unnecessarily putting herself in
and, frankly, neither do you. The whole purpose of surrendering
Sassanian to the Sacramento facility is to rid ourselves of
the near-constant danger and the bottomless legal costs
attendant—the fewer bodies on that plane, the better.
Please do not mistake this for me thinking the same of you.
Although we have had our disagreements, in some ways you
were a godsend, and even though it would not make sense for
you to stay with us, we are sad to see you go. We wish you the
best of luck with Nikola in Sacramento. Sincerely, I hope that I
am wrong and that the trip goes smoothly.

Best,
Julieta Lozano-Ramsay, Director of Bella Terra

19

Kern County, California, was sweltering in the fall, and the afternoon sun beat down on Paris. The armored car carrying Nikola had arrived almost half an hour ago, but they sure were taking their sweet time unloading him. All they needed to do was wheel him out of the armored car and into the 737 on the other end of the tarmac, and then he would be off, and she would be off with him. She had not told Renée that Luciana Ortega had secured her permission to actually follow and report on this—then she would have woken up handcuffed to her bedside table until the possibility of Paris boarding this flight had passed, and Renée would have been right to have done so. What the hell was she thinking?

Luciana had only given her about thirty-six hours' notice before they moved Nikola, so she had to get on a flight to California right away. It had been nearly three days since her fight with Cora. Their first fight. Probably their only fight. She'd sent a message to Cora saying as much:

> Nov 16 2009 2:08 PM
>
> Hey, hope you're doing okay. They're moving Nikola tomorrow and I have to go cover it. Talk when we get back?

No response.

Apologize, she thought. *Now is the time.*

She pulled out her BlackBerry and imagined herself expending that energy apologizing only for Cora to fuck off into space the very next day. She put her phone away.

Apologizing was certainly the *kind* thing to do, and she wanted to be kind, but she also wanted Cora to take it back. She wanted to mend the rift and all that came with it, but mending the rift while leaving the underlying issue in place? But then again, this wasn't just an arbitrary "I'm taking a gap year" decision for Cora. It wasn't like she was fucking off to some Disney resort in the sky; she was fucking off into the cold void of space, where she would likely die alone. Alone with a space alien who, according to the one who knew him best, was her puppet master, who, outside of the comforts of being coddled by a Japanese billionaire, was just as cold as that void. No more humans. No more Earth. His broodmare. His "plaything." Even in the best of circumstances, even if they found some habitable planet to repopulate, what a horrible prospect to even think about, let alone seriously consider. No wonder Cora had look so hurt.

"Paris."

She turned and smiled, relieved to see a friendly face. "Hey, Barney."

This was the first time she'd seen Barney in his civvies, so to speak, and her face lit up at the sight of his shirt—Jay-Z, *The Black Album*. "Oh no," she said, and he smiled knowingly. "You coast traitor."

"Hey now, I'm from Camden. I always kept it real."

"He's been one of us this whole time." She glanced at the old 737 that had been contracted for the move. It had long passed its tenure as a passenger jet and had the word CARGO emblazoned on it in big green letters. "So you're not making the move with him?"

"No, much as I'll miss his shenanigans. I got a family to look after; daughter about to start kindergarten and another baby on the way. I'm staying here. I'm lucky I escaped unscathed."

"Maybe he likes you."

Paris looked at the plane again and saw Luciana was at the bottom of the cargo ramp at the back of the plane, doing a bunch of paperwork while a couple of guys, perhaps the pilots, looked on. "She's really deep in this, huh?" she said. "Following Nikola upstate."

"This is her life," said Barney. "She doesn't have any family worth staying for. I'm not sure if she has any friends besides the ones she plays online games with, and they don't even know who she really is."

"Surprised they're moving Nikola without any amygdaline help," Paris observed.

"No, Jude's here."

"He's here?" said Paris, a sting of hurt following the logical conclusion—if Jude was here, so was Cora.

"He had to be," said Barney, mistaking her hurt for journalistic curiosity. "There's no way we could chance moving him without another one of them making sure there wasn't anything that could go wrong. Besides, Jude won't let no one else medicate him."

"No other human?"

"No one else, period. There are other options available."

Nikola and Jude had taken up so much real estate in the public consciousness, it was easy to forget they weren't the only amygdalines on Earth, that there were still a couple of dozen in government custody. Paris started to ask if Barney had seen Cora, but refrained; he was a perceptive guy, and she didn't want him to hear any desperation in her voice. And besides that, Paris was on the clock, and if Cora was here, then so was she. Now wasn't the time.

"Speak of the devil," said Barney.

Paris turned, and there was the sedated Nikola finally being unloaded from that armored car. As his keepers wheeled him across the tarmac to the plane, she shuddered at the realization that he was out in the open, that there were no walls of acrylic between them anymore. He was strapped to a heavily modified gurney designed to move very heavy (human) patients. When all of his limbs were folded up either under him or to his side, he came out to about the length of a large man. But the most striking thing about him wasn't how compact he was but the methods they'd used to restrain him, ranging from zip ties to handcuffs to Velcro to literal chains like he was Jacob Marley's ghost.

"When Jude took his telekinesis, he also took his superstrength, right?" said Paris, transfixed.

"From what we can tell, that wasn't exactly a power that *could* be taken from them. He has about the amount of strength you'd expect something that looks like that to have."

A little worm of nausea wriggled up into Paris's throat at the memory of Nikola's promise—not *if* he escaped, but *when*. And here she was about to board a pressurized metal tube made to hurtle through the atmosphere at thirty-six thousand feet with this thing? *Voluntarily?*

"Jude took care of his sedation. Jude okayed the restraints," said

Barney, likewise not taking his eyes off the black dragon being wheeled into the back of the 737. "He told us to move him ASAP so as not to risk the sister species finding him at Bella Terra, so here we are. We did the best we could do. Rest is in God's hands."

Paris turned to look at Barney and held out her hand. "Go and dust your shoulders off."

"Ladies is pimps, too," said Barney with a wink as he shook her hand. He turned to head back toward the hangar, then added, "Can't wait to read your story."

Paris nodded, steeled herself, and then headed in the opposite direction.

After about half an hour, the paperwork had been signed, and Paris got on the plane. There were two guys acting as security and one orderly keeping an eye on Nikola's "vitals," so to speak. He looked even more nervous than she felt.

She looked down at Nikola, now only a couple of feet away. Even though he was more compact with his head strapped down, eyes closed, crest of his head flattened by straps, and limbs tucked up under his body, somehow that only heightened how big he really was, bigger than the biggest Bengal tiger. She resisted the urge to run her fingers over his skin; even making conscious effort to see him as a person, it was tempting to engage in tiny dehumanizing (for lack of a better word) behaviors like that.

This plane had a few fold-down chairs like the ones flight attendants used on passenger jets, so she took a seat on one a few feet away from Nikola and looked out the window. At first, the tarmac seemed empty until she saw some movement over by one of the hangars—there was Cora a few hundred feet away, looking up at Jude.

This was the first time she'd ever actually seen him in the flesh, so to speak, wearing the space-gray clothes that he wore in the rare moments he was seen in public. She flipped out her phone, wanting to say *something*, even if that something was just, "I'm here." She held it open as she watched them; it was impossible to read emotion from Jude, but Cora was very expressive. At first, Paris thought it might be an argument of some sort, but then Jude lowered his head to meet Cora's, and she placed her hands under his "chin" (or rather, the place where a chin would be if he had one), speaking something to him with intense sincerity. Then she closed her eyes and guided his muzzle to meet her forehead.

There was something unmooring about actually seeing them together, especially when they thought no one was looking. More than a complicating factor, she had always known but had never really admitted to herself; no matter if Cora stayed or if she went, it would never be just the two of them in their relationship.

"Okay!" Paris heard a voice from behind her and turned to see a frazzled Luciana. "I guess this is as secure as it's going to get."

"Is Jude not coming?"

"Jude won't go near him any more than he absolutely has to."

Paris spared a glance back out onto the tarmac again, but both Jude and Cora were gone.

As the plane took off, Paris did the thing where she looked outside, quietly shitting bricks while everyone else sat secure in the knowledge of the safety of aviation. About twenty minutes into the flight, the pilot gave permission for them to move about the cabin, and Paris remembered the thing she had not brought up to Cora when she had the chance was also highly relevant to her current travel companion. Hell, maybe she had some insights as to what it was Kaveh had said to Nils that constituted "blackmail."

Luciana had unbuckled the second she'd gotten permission to do so and was kneeling next to Nikola, scrutinizing every restraint on his body.

"So," said Paris, approaching Nikola's gurney, "I know I'm supposed to be interviewing you, but I'd like to go off the record for a moment."

"Shoot," said Luciana, not looking away.

"It's about something Nikola said to me about one of Kaveh's journal entries. I suppose when you're hearing about someone from the point of view of an alien, you're bound to get some insights you wouldn't have gotten from a human."

"Like what?"

"Apparently, Kaveh told Nils something he regretted telling him and told Nikola about it later. Like a cyborg confessional."

"He told Nils lots of things back when they worked together."

"No, I mean something he'd told Nils like *that day*. The same day he spent with Nikola in Sequoia."

Luciana stood up, now very interested. "Really?"

Paris nodded, shielding her eyes from the afternoon sun piercing through the windows. "Apparently, Kaveh had a guilty conscience about—"

"REMOVE MY RESTRAINTS!"

Paris nearly shrieked at the sound of Nikola's voice in her ear, clasping her hand to her heart. His eyes were wide open, bright, their focus roving all over the place.

"REMOVE MY RESTRAINTS!"

"Stan!" yelled Luciana, turning toward the cockpit. "Nikola's awake!" She looked at Paris. "What's going on?"

"THE PLANE IS BEING INFILTRATED," said Nikola, bucking against the restraints as much as he was able. "WE ARE BEING ATTACKED. REMOVE MY RESTRAINTS!"

"He's telling me to remove his restraints. He says we're being attacked."

Without hesitating, Luciana ran to the front of the plane and tore the door open to the cockpit. Paris heard her informing the pilot and copilot what had happened and asking them if they saw anything on radar.

"REMOVE MY RESTRAINTS!"

Paris's hands almost reached toward Nikola of their own volition, and she jerked them back. This was an obvious ploy. One of many escape attempts that he had *told* her he planned to make, and somehow he'd figured out how to trick Jude into thinking he'd stay unconscious for the duration of the flight.

"We'd prepared for a ton of eventualities," said Luciana, trotting back to Paris's side. "Him just asking to be let go wasn't among them."

"Is there a possibility he knows something we don't?" asked Paris.

"PHYSETERINE. TRANSIENTS. ON THE HULL OF THE PLANE. REMOVE MY RESTRAINTS!"

"He says there are physeterines on the hull of the plane."

Luciana froze, staring at Nikola like he was a time bomb that had just started counting down, highly skeptical but, like Paris, not entirely convinced he was lying.

"REMOVE MY RESTRAINTS!"

It wasn't that last instruction that moved Paris to action, it was a clinking sound on the hull of the plane. It was possible the sound had been Nikola's doing. It was possibly a coincidence.

It was also possibly exactly what he said it was.

Paris unbuckled one of the restraints holding down his fingers, then another that held down his wrist before one of the security guys grabbed her.

"What are you doing?" yelled Luciana. "Stop it!"

Paris didn't know if Luciana was yelling at her or the security guy, but his grip on her loosened at the sound of a sharp, loud *creeeeeak*. It couldn't have lasted more than one second, even though it felt like ten, but it was enough for Paris to pull free of the man's grip and unbuckle one more fastener before the back of the plane exploded.

Sunlight poured into the cabin as the air was ripped out of Paris's lungs, and the rear of the plane disintegrated. Then she was falling, but she was only conscious of her predicament for about five seconds before she blacked out.

20

"If we are really going to do this," said Cora, holding Ampersand's arm like it was 1890 and the two were on their Sunday promenade. They were still on the tarmac outside of security where they weren't supposed to be, but she wasn't ready to deal with other humans again quite yet. "If we are *really* going to do this, and . . . *he's* going to come with us, how is that going to work?"

"*Assuming no physeterine interference, we have time to develop a strategy for how to survive off-world while also handling Nikola.*"

Cora looked eastward, to the life she had hastily been instructed to abandon. "You're asking me to give up what little life I have left because we *are* assuming physeterine interference."

"*It is a precaution, my love.*"

Cora looked up at him, but as always, he didn't look back. He rarely did in conversation. "Bad enough I've already lost Paris, now I have to lose all my friends, too."

"*A romantic entanglement was always going to be temporary, if you choose to come with me.*" He always made sure to sneak in caveats that it was her *choice* to leave when he did, that he never would force her to do this.

"I know," she sighed. "She should know the deal, and now she does, and she doesn't want to be with someone who's going to 'fuck off into space' when things down here get difficult."

"*I believe that is an uncharitable interpretation of our intentions.*"

"It's what it feels like to her."

A light went off behind her eyes, and then every light in the airport went out. It was hard to be sure at first—the sun had only just begun to set, and electric lights weren't yet the main light source, but what confirmed it to her was Ampersand, who froze right where he was. She moved to prop him up, anticipating that he would collapse. It had been over eighteen months since she'd felt this, seen this in action, but her sense memory was practically tuned to it at this point.

This was an energy pulse.

"Ampersand?"

He was nonverbal and swaying slightly, but he hadn't collapsed—whatever fail-safes he had developed within the last couple of years to prevent him being debilitated by an EMP were doing their job; it was the one thing he had prioritized over the high-language experiment.

"Ampersand!"

Okay, they were doing their job, but only somewhat. He hadn't collapsed, but he wasn't at 100 percent. She wasn't even sure he was at 20 percent.

For those few seconds, as she was making sure he was stable, her eyes instinctively darting around to search for the silvery sheen of the body of a Similar, her mind went to the rationalization of how Similars used the weapon—they used it from a very great distance. They'd had to, as they were just as affected by EMPs as their targets and had to stay out of range while the weapon was deployed, only moving in after it was safe to do so, assuming their target had been incapacitated.

But utilizing energy pulses against Similars was not a weapon or strategy that had been developed by Similars but by physeterines, and they did not inhabit biosynthetic cybernetic bodies but bodies of flesh and blood. They were unaffected by EMPs.

They were probably already on the base.

"We have to get out of here!" She shook Ampersand, but he didn't budge, didn't give any indication that he was listening to her at all. She closed her eyes, tried to sense what was going on; her own fear was so overwhelming that she hardly got anything, but he seemed to be in shock.

"Hey!"

She turned to see Sol running toward her. "What's going on?" he cried.

"We have to hide!" she said. "Is there like a fallout shelter? Blast shelter?"

Sol didn't hesitate or ask questions. "Come on," he said, and turned back in the direction he had come.

Cora pulled on Ampersand's wrist, trying to guide him, and mercy of mercies, he followed her, stumbling as if he had gone blind. Sol led her into the nearest building, running toward someone holding a flashlight.

"Fallout shelter!" said Sol. "Where's the entrance to the fallout shelter?"

"What's going on?" said the marine, and he nearly fell down in fear when he saw Ampersand rounding the corner.

"There are alien hostiles on the base! We need to hide him!" Cora spoke so quickly her words stumbled over one another.

"There's what?" said the marine.

"You're taking us to the fucking fallout shelter!" demanded Sol, actually whipping out his CIA badge and shoving it in the marine's face. To Cora's utter shock, it worked.

"This way," said the marine, pulling out a walkie-talkie.

"That won't work," said Cora. The man ignored her, vainly trying to contact his superiors as he ran.

"Physeterine?" said Sol.

"I think so," said Cora. "They're the ones who developed this technology in the first place, but—"

An explosion rocked the building behind them, nearly throwing Cora off her feet. Ampersand, for his part, stopped where he was.

"Come on!" she cried. "We have to go!"

It took him almost ten agonizing seconds before he moved again, and she ushered him as quickly as she could down the hall, listening to Sol and the marine yelling, "*Everybody to the fallout shelter!*"

The entrance was a large, rusted metal door with one small transparent window looking into the hallway, and a few other personnel, taking Ampersand's lead, had already run inside. There was an old metal staircase that led to the level below, a long, dark concrete hallway with cables and pipes running along its length. She worried that Ampersand might not be able to make the stairs, but he glided down to the shelter below like it was nothing, then crouched in a corner.

They made it inside, and Sol closed the door behind them, the marine who'd let them there still vainly shouting, "Breaker, breaker, do you copy?" into his dead walkie. Ampersand just crouched where he was, focused on nothing.

There were ten other air force personnel already inside the shelter, all trying to mask their fear of being in the same room as Ampersand, but they were terrified, almost as terrified as he was. She could sense he was now oscillating between shock and terror, backing away from the humans in the room, into the corner, where he collapsed into a haphazard roost, half on his side, his legs under him and his arms pulled up under his garb.

Then there was knocking on the other side of the door. *Human* knocking.

"What do we do?" asked the marine who'd led them here, looking at Sol.

"Let them in!" said a woman who looked like she worked in accounting. She started to spring back up the metal staircase, but Sol stopped her.

"Wait," he said, and everyone froze. There was silence and absolute darkness through that small window that looked into the hallway. The one marine with a working flashlight shined it into the window, but in seconds, it shorted and sparked into darkness. Another EMP. Now they were in pitch-blackness, and even the battle-hardened marines couldn't help but gasp in fear.

"Take out the batteries, flip them around," said Cora to the marine. "If it's a cheap, shitty flashlight, it might turn back on again."

"There should be more flashlights in here," said the marine.

Another flashlight turned on. "This one works," said the holder of the flashlight.

"That's because it wasn't on when the second EMP hit," said Cora. "Keep it off just in case."

If they were deploying an EMP at such close range, that meant any of the physeterine equipment that ran off electricity was down, too. There was a possibility that this was a calculated risk. That they were willing to sacrifice any defensive capabilities that weren't purely physical to make sure that Ampersand went completely down. Cora knelt beside him and felt that the air around him was thick, almost magnetic. Cora grabbed the marine by the jacket. "Is there another entrance to this shelter?"

"Yeah, it lets out on the eastern end of the complex, but—"

"Let me out. I'm going to try to distract them long enough for Ampersand to recuperate—"

"Now is not the time to be playing hero," said Sol. "Guns aren't affected by EMPs, and the military escort is going to figure out—"

A *bang* hit the door, and half the people in the room screamed, including Cora. The marine turned the flashlight off, and everyone held still. Then another *bang* on the door and the scream of a male human voice. Then silence once more.

The marine turned on the flashlight and shined it at the window. Nothing. Everyone looked at Ampersand, but Ampersand was as still as a statue.

"Listen," Cora said, grabbing Sol by the shoulder, "I am equipped with alien tech that I can operate independent of him. Trust me when I say I can do this, you can't."

"*No*, you don't know—wait!"

The marine acted like Sol wasn't even there, jogging away from the group as he led her to the other entrance to the shelter. He led her down one long hallway and then an even longer one, so long that they were both winded by the time they reached the other metal staircase.

"Up there," he said, and she grabbed the flashlight without asking, turned it off—it wasn't going to help him, anyway—and climbed up into the darkness outside.

The door to the fallout shelter was heavy and old, and it practically roared as she forced it open. As she closed it behind her, it clanged in the dark, empty hallway like it was the closing of a cell door, so loud it would be heard in the next county over, to say nothing of her breathing, which she tried to rein in as she pulled up her viewfinder. It gave her some triangulating ability based on whatever structure she was in, but it couldn't tell her where any bodies were, human or otherwise. She picked a location several hallways away and kept her transport plate ready to deploy. Ampersand had designed it to cover her in less than a second just in case of emergencies such as this, but it had never been tested in the field before.

She heard another distant *thud*, perhaps from them trying to beat down the other entrance to the fallout shelter, but then she heard a much closer voice, the moan of a human. She turned, feeling along the base of the wall before she rounded the corner and found a human foot.

"Hey," she said, but got no response. She felt up the body, which was still warm, but had to refrain from gasping when she felt hot wetness in the torso. This person was wearing a belt—perhaps he worked as security, as the belt held a gun and a flashlight. She took both, feeling around the edges of the handgun.

In the grand scheme of guns, Cora knew precious little, but owing to a weeklong fascination with handguns at the height of Nils's popularity, she had learned how safeties worked on basic handguns like this, had even gone to a range to practice once. She also knew that it probably didn't have more than six rounds in it, and even if she did have another magazine, she didn't know how to reload it.

Then she heard a sound like an animal barking, followed by a string of chirps and clicks that reminded her of a dolphin—animalistic, yet too complex to be anything but a language. She rounded the corner, and not even bothering to aim, she fired the gun at the sound of the alien noises.

The recoil was more shocking and painful than she was prepared for, and she nearly dropped the gun. Everything happened so quickly, the plating had half enveloped her when she could *feel* the beast on her, the wake of the air as it moved in absolute darkness. It tried to grab her, perhaps it did, but whatever electromagnetic power Ampersand had imbued this device with was stronger, and she opened her eyes seconds later, exactly where she'd programmed it to take her on the other side of the complex.

Adrenaline still pumping, she couldn't help but be a little impressed by the fact that she was keeping it together. She could faintly hear them speaking to one another from dozens of meters away and considered the wisdom of going back to try again—they would want to mitigate the threat that she now posed, sure, but she wasn't what they were there for; Ampersand was.

She triangulated another location in the complex, which she could only *hope* wouldn't be occupied, and shined the flashlight in the direction she'd come from as a lure. They weren't stupid; if they were coming for her, that meant they had some way to take her out before she took them out. She fired off another shot, hoping that that would give them the false impression that she planned for a shoot-out. She backed herself into a corner, keeping the flashlight shining down one hallway.

She didn't bother trying to quiet her terrified breathing. What was the point? They knew where she was.

And find her they did. Before they had the chance to turn the corner and do to her whatever they had done to that marine, she activated the plate, closed her eyes, and disappeared again.

When she opened her eyes, she clicked on the flashlight, and there stood one of them, nightmare made flesh, not more than fifty feet away, its entire body covered in greenish-black like sealskin. She screamed reflexively, and suddenly, the sharpness she'd possessed up until this point scrambled, and she panicked, pointing the gun and firing all four remaining shots.

The creature fell back but didn't stumble; maybe the bullets had shocked it, but it didn't look hurt. It took a moment to get its bearings and then pulled out a device of its own. Cora frantically tried to triangulate, but in her panic couldn't get the software to cooperate, couldn't find a place that felt safe; they were everywhere, each dark hallway a new terror.

Then the piercing sound of gunshots ripped through the hallway, and this time the creature did stumble. More voices, men's voices, and the air rang out with the sound of gunfire from automatic weapons, deafening in these enclosed spaces. Cora covered her ears and curled herself into a ball, letting the flashlight fall to her feet. There didn't seem to be much strategy behind the gunmen; they just plowed through the hallway like it was a first-person shooter, and it was just as likely as anything that she'd get caught in the cross fire.

She glanced up and saw that the creature was gone, and another flashlight was pointing at her, one that was mounted on top of one of those automatic weapons. She had barely opened her eyes when another explosion rocked the building, and then Cora leaped to her feet.

She managed to pull herself back from the panic just enough to triangulate where the second entrance to the fallout shelter was; she didn't try to program her plate to take her there, just ran, ran knowing there was a good chance one of these soldiers would think her a monster in a video game and shoot her.

They may well have, for all she knew, as the complex was now ringing with the sound of bullets like hundreds of deadly little bells. She threw herself on the door to the fallout shelter, but the marine was already there on the other side helping her to open it. She barreled right past him, down the metal staircase, and then ran through the several hallways back to where she'd left Ampersand.

The small group had barely moved save to consolidate away from Ampersand, where only Sol stood anywhere remotely near him.

"What happened?" asked Sol.

"I don't know. The cavalry showed up," she said, shoving the flashlight to the first person she slammed into and dropping the gun on the floor. It seemed that they had found a couple of lanterns that had been stored in the shelter for just such an occasion, as it was now actually somewhat illuminated. "I saw a bunch of marines shooting at them. They might have chased them off."

"We heard an explosion."

Cora fell to her knees next to Ampersand but did not yet touch him. He was still in "safe mode," and his shield felt even thicker than it had before she left. "I don't know. Might be a grenade. Maybe they just needed an escape route."

"You really think they're going to beat alien tech back with guns?" asked Sol.

"The physeterines deployed an EMP at close range; their equipment is affected by it, too. Their defensive capabilities will be limited at the moment."

"Are you *sure* it was physeterine?"

Cora turned to look at Sol, the mental image of the creature she'd seen flashing in her head—not a post-natural biomechanical body but a living thing of muscle and bone with jet-black eyes and a mouth like an insect. It had even had a smell, like a stagnant pond. "It's definitely them."

She switched gears, modulating her voice to something gentler as she leaned in toward Ampersand. "Hey."

"What's wrong with him?" asked the woman she'd shoved the flashlight at.

"I don't know," Cora lied. The shield was so thick she could hardly get her fingers to his skin, like the air itself was solidifying.

A loud knock came at the door at the top of the staircase, and on the other side of it, muffled human voices. Sol looked at her.

"I think it's safe," she said.

One of the marines opened the door, and with them stood three more marines, illuminating the hall with the flashlights mounted to their guns. "Everyone out," said one of them. Everyone in the room eagerly obeyed, except Cora.

"Sol, please help me," she said. "I need to be alone with him."

Sol nodded and didn't even look irritated as he climbed the staircase to negotiate on her behalf. She saw him flip out his badge, heard him say, "Sol Kaplan, CIA," before he explained that there was a very important alien in this fallout shelter, and he needed a minute.

"It's just me now," she said. "They're gone."

She tried to center herself; the adrenaline was only just starting to ebb, and she knew the crash was coming, but for now, she had to control it. "Come on. Let me in. It's okay."

She made herself small, getting on the floor next to him. Within a couple of minutes, she felt the shield begin to thin, and slid next to him as it enveloped her. She put her back to his front, draping one of his arms over her. The wall between them had thinned while she was upstairs, and she could sense that his shock had morphed into a sort of chaos—it wasn't all that dissimilar to what she'd felt from him at Pershing Square when he was immobile and a man was pointing a gun at both of them, but this was much, much deeper. The resurfacing of his longtime tormentors had shut him down.

They made me watch.

"It's okay. They're gone."

There was a light knock at the door. She opened her eyes and saw Sol peeking in. "Can I come in?"

"Yeah," she said, staying still where she was in the fetal position next to the inert Ampersand. "But close the door. And stay up there. Don't come any closer."

Sol nodded, putting his hands in his pockets and staying where he was at the top of the staircase.

"The security guard I took the gun from," she said. "I think he's dead."

"Miraculously, he is not," said Sol. "Whatever they used to slice him up cauterized the wounds. He's in rough shape, but he might pull through. There was another security guard that wasn't as lucky." He cocked his head to the side. "I'm guessing there's a sort of ritual going on here."

"He's in shock," said Cora. "And he doesn't appreciate the petting and soothing sort of reassurance; he considers that to be like . . . a dominance position."

"And dominance is bad?"

"Depends on your position on the caste ladder, and everyone on Earth is beneath him. So yes."

Sol chuckled. "So instead of petting and shushing, it works better if you're the little spoon."

"I'd appreciate it if you didn't tell anyone about this."

She started at the sudden movement from behind her as Ampersand lifted up his head, the focus of his eyes suddenly sharp. Cora let out a sigh of relief. "The military chased them off," she said. "But we need to get you out of here before they can—"

Ampersand shot to his feet. "*I don't believe they were here for me.*"

Cora rose to her feet. "Then what—"

"*This was a diversion.*" He had barely finished the sentence before his liquid metal plating slid out of him, covering him garb and all, and he disappeared.

21

Of the one hundred and fifty-seven seconds Paris Wells had left to live, owing to the shock of the explosive decompression and the thin upper atmosphere, she had been unconscious for about thirty-two of them. She had had this dream many times before, and usually in those dreams she would realize that she was dreaming before the terror became too much to bear, reassure herself that it wasn't real, that it was just a dream, and wake up. That period of denial lasted all of fifteen seconds before she accepted that this wasn't a dream; she had been sucked out of a plane at thirty-six thousand feet, and she was falling to her death.

Her hands were numb. She tasted blood. She tried to clench her fists, but it was as though they had already frozen solid. The sky was pink with the light of the setting sun, and beneath her was a craggy mountain range growing closer by the second. Then a new brief phase of denial; this couldn't be real. This was a thing that only happened in fiction, an extreme anomaly in the real world. She spread her limbs out to slow the fall as best she could, turning upside down to spare her eyes the brightness of the sky, and it was the sight of the ground, now close enough that she could start making out the details of the terrain, that made it hit home. This was it. There was no surviving this. So she did the only thing she could do—pray.

Prayer was something she was not practiced at, having lost interest in Jesus around the same time she'd lost interest in Kris Kross. She prayed that her sister would be okay, that Abuela would be taken care of, that someone would pick up where she left off and tell Kaveh's story. Maybe even tell *her* story. She prayed that Cora wouldn't blame herself for what had happened to her. It was around this point that something that felt like an invisible sedan T-boned her in the ribs.

She was too stunned to scream, her limbs flailing around the object like a rag doll as what felt like two giant spiders wrapped their legs around her entire body. She thought at first that this might be the delusion of a doomed woman. Her face was to the sky now, which was a mercy; she wouldn't see it when she hit. She tried to move her leaden hands around the thing that had grabbed her, felt a coarse, slender neck, a large oblong head with a crest at the top.

Then came the impact.

The whiplash from it forced her into Nikola's body so hard her rib cage bowed with the pressure, and the force nearly crushed her windpipe into the side of his arm. She gasped for air as there was another hit, and then another in rapid succession like gunfire. Not the ground but trees. He blew through four or five of them at an angle, wood splintering behind them like they had been blasted with a cannon, losing momentum with each destroyed tree. Then, not two seconds after that first hit, he stopped.

Paris opened her eyes and took in a loud, ragged breath (or tried to). For a moment, she wondered if her windpipe had been flattened altogether, if she'd survived the fall only to suffocate. They were still in a tree, perhaps fifteen feet in the air. Within two seconds, they were on the ground, and then he was whisking her through the woods, her head bobbing about on his shoulder, her body clasped to his like Ann Darrow being spirited away by King Kong. He was so fast and she was so disoriented, she could hardly see the dozens of spires of tall, tall trees whizzing past as he ran. He was still invisible, which might have made for a rather amusing picture to outside eyes under different circumstances.

Then she was in darkness again, and she half wondered if she'd gone blind. It was all she could do to lift her arms up, pull them over the back of the monster that had plucked her out of the sky. She was in darkness for almost a minute before the sound of running water echoing off of smooth rock walls told her where she was—a cave. Nikola wasn't moving anywhere near as fast now that he didn't have open terrain, but he had already gone so deep into this cave that the darkness was total. It was only when he stopped that she got a grasp on the situation, allowed emotion again. Fear, for instance.

"Nikola?" she said, and coughed at the effort, her windpipe still sore. "Is that you?"

She swallowed, and the pain of that effort made her cough again, and she nearly jumped at the feeling of being set down on the floor of the cave. She strained to sit up and was hit by an even greater peal of fear at the realization that the monster that had brought her here had left her alone in total darkness. "I can't see!"

"THAT IS BECAUSE THERE IS NO LIGHT."

That didn't stop her from trying to look, opening her eyes as wide as she could and turning around wildly, but her movement was limited by the pain of her bruised ribs, which felt like they were grinding together. "What happened?"

"TRANSIENTS TRIED TO CAPTURE ME. THEY DESTROYED THE AIR-PLANE."

"This is a cave," she said, stopping just short of asking *why* they were in a cave. Then a soft red light bloomed in the air a few feet in front of her, a glowing tiny fireball hanging in the air like a firefly. She didn't see Nikola until he moved, but when she saw him, she jerked back, crying out in terror. She couldn't help it.

The room of this cave was perhaps ten feet high, and Nikola's massive body took up most of it, illuminated from below by that soft red light. Those eyes looked down at her, and every neuron in her fired off some demand to fight or flee. But she was helpless, and she had nowhere to run. She opened her mouth, perhaps to beg for mercy, but only violent coughing came out.

"BE SILENT."

She coughed again and tasted blood. Breathing was near agony, but if any of her ribs were bruised or broken, she couldn't tell.

Nikola's eyes fell on her. "BE SILENT."

It was possible that she had never in her adult life been so frightened, and the part of her that was a hostage who knew that she should do what her captor said was being overridden by the animal part of her that was panicking and incoherent. A housefly caught on flypaper, immobile and at the mercy of unfathomably more powerful beings, unable to comprehend that it was already dead.

You are an insect, he had told her. *Easily crushed and just as easily forgotten.*

"No," she said as if speaking to the memory, and then coughed again.

"Be silent."

Nikola's gaze sharpened, and it only took a couple of steps for him to be standing over her. She tried to back away from him, but there was nothing behind her but smooth, eroded rock.

Would you crush me?

Only if you are a nuisance.

"Nik, please, no, please." She tried to whisper, but she didn't have control over modulation. He reached out to her, and she cringed, closing her eyes and pulling herself into a fetal position. "I'm not an insect. You don't have to do this. I won't be a nuisance. You can just let me go. Please . . . please don't . . ."

When she opened her eyes, the light was still there, but Nikola was gone. The fear that had been propping her up degraded, and her neck throbbed, her ribs throbbed, her lungs ached. Her fingers were numb, her skin felt coated in ice, and her blood felt as cold as the water running through this cave. As her eyes adjusted, she took in how big the chamber was, like a small church, curtains of stalactites the size of pillars dropping down at periodic intervals.

Nikola returned a few minutes later, still more focused on the walls of the cave than he was on Paris. That fight-or-flight response tried to kick-start again but was burned out. She felt like she might faint.

"Nik," she said. "I'm so cold."

Once again, he was standing over her, still the very image of Lovecraftian horror, but her fear reserves were now run dry. This time when he reached out for her, opened those hands that looked like two dog-size black widows, she didn't have the energy to shrink away. Gently, like he was swaddling a newborn, he wrapped those hands around her body and pulled her close, radiating warmth. He moved her deeper into the cave, the light now so dim she could hardly see anything. Soon, he stopped, crouching near the floor of the cave, resting her body on the ground, still cradled in his warm hands.

"They are here."

What little light he had summoned was gone, and they were again bathed in complete darkness. Some part of her still capable of reason realized that he'd plucked her out of the sky. *Why?* "Nik—"

"YOU MUST BE SILENT, DEAR GENTLE CREATURE. BOTH OUR LIVES DEPEND ON IT."

She stilled, unable to hear anything beyond the distant, soothing trickle of the water running through the cave. The darkness was so complete she was beginning to see kaleidoscopes in front of her eyes, and hesitantly, she reached up to feel the giant body she was pressed up against. She could still feel the place where his neck met his torso, mere inches from her face. His head was tilted at a sharp angle, facing the direction they had come from. She tilted her head in that direction ever so slightly and nearly gasped when she saw light coming toward them.

On first glance, it looked like it came from a man-made flashlight—people were looking for them, she thought. That must be why he had saved her; he needed a hostage. But within seconds, she saw that the light was not man-made, and neither were the noises that accompanied it. She could hear clicking and hissing, sounds that could be mistaken for amygdaline Pequod-phonemic to the unfamiliar. Then she saw them.

There were at least two of them, their shadows illuminating the cave walls like someone had taken H. R. Giger's alien and welded its head to the body of a velociraptor. They had the same arachnoid six-fingered hands as the amygdalines, but thicker, stronger-looking, more tarantula than black widow. Also unlike amygdalines, these things had tails, long tails that acted as counterbalance to their forward-leaning center of gravity. Her still-leaden fingers grasped at Nikola, urging him to do something. She could almost see the owner behind the light, as unlike human flashlights theirs weren't so bright that they blocked out what was behind them. They exchanged more of their hissing, crocodilian language. Then she felt a jolt run through Nikola's body, heard a *snikt* echo through the cave, and then a curtain of stalactites fell on the physeterines.

Even before the stalactites hit the ground, Nikola was on the move again, keeping Paris's body glued to his with her head held fast to prevent any whiplash. Nikola was almost silent in his movements, but over her own terrified breathing, she could hear commotion in the back of the cave. The light had gone out, but the voices hadn't. Yelling, practically screeching. Once again, the darkness was total, and Paris nearly cried out when she realized she could see light in the cave again—not unnatural, red alien light but *sunlight*.

No sooner did she have that realization than Nikola released his death grip on her, and she was being shoved through the tiny mouth of the cave toward the light of the already-set sun. Now alert with terror, she desperately scrambled toward the light, hoping against hope that the hole wouldn't become too small for her to pass through. Her shoulders got stuck, but she pulled back, reassessed the angle, and squeezed through. She had just made it out when she realized that she had made it out alone.

She turned back and reflexively screamed at the sight of Nikola's fingers reaching out through the hole she had just squeezed through, like a funnel web spider jumping out at its prey. Her instincts demanded that she keep moving, but another part of her thought that there must be something she could do for him. Then, as if they were being sucked out through a vacuum tube, Nikola's hand disappeared back into the darkness, and the hole to the cave was silent.

Paris didn't move, listening for the sound of commotion, for the sound of that staccato alien language. And suddenly, one of them lunged claws out of the hole, coming within millimeters of Paris's foot. She screamed, crab walking away into the open forest as the thing tried one more time to grab her, but it, too, was stuck, only its head and a sinewy gray-green arm poking through the opening.

She shook out of her horrified stupor and stood up to run. She had emerged out on the side of a mountain, the terrain beneath her rocky and steep and forcing her to move slowly and carefully. Perhaps hiding was the move—running would only draw attention. She slid beside a big tree, huge enough that it had a big, black carbonized scar large enough for her to fit inside. Just as she made it into the shelter at the bottom of the tree, one of them was already there waiting for her.

It was all she could do to stay standing at the sight of it; in the dim twilight, it blended in so well with the trees that it was almost camouflaged. Most of its body was covered in that gray-green film that looked like a wet suit, except for the tips of its fingers and its head. It stood at nearly seven feet, but the most striking thing about it were its eyes; these were nothing like the gemstone-like eyes of the amygdalines, but were solid yellow, reflecting the twilight like safety reflectors. It regarded her, and Paris backed away on shaking limbs. It seemed almost bemused as it took a step toward her, its red mouth opening like the mandibles of a giant insect.

Then it took her.

PART 3

OH THAT MAGIC FEELING
NOWHERE TO GO

November 2009

The two species that had resulted from the evolution of man were sliding down towards, or had already arrived at, an altogether new relationship. The Eloi, like the Carolingian kings, had decayed to a mere beautiful futility. They still possessed the earth on sufferance: since the Morlocks, subterranean for innumerable generations, had come at last to find the daylit surface intolerable.

—H. G. Wells, *The Time Machine*

November 16, 2009

Remarks by President Julian in Press Conference

EAST ROOM

8:59 P.M. EST

THE PRESIDENT: Good evening. I apologize for the late hour, but given the gravity of the situation, this could not wait. Before I take your questions, I'd like to first give a rundown of what we know about the plane crash in California that happened less than two hours ago.

A plane carrying the ETI entity known as Nikola Sassanian has crashed in the Sierra Nevada mountains at approximately 4:50 P.M., Pacific standard time. The crash was a whole loss and not survivable. While the fate of Nikola Sassanian is unknown, right now the ETI has been declared missing.

Our nation mourns for the families and friends of those who have been affected by this terrible event. At this time, investigators have recovered the remains of two private security personnel, John Fischer and Mark Villanueva, and a nurse practitioner, Stanley Cox. The other passengers on the plane have not yet been recovered.

The investigation is ongoing, but although the exact cause of the crash is not known, we do know that it was not caused by pilot error or by equipment malfunction. The crash is believed to have been caused by the second confirmed extraterrestrial species to have visited our world. This species is believed to be descended from the same common ancestor as amygdalines, and is code-named PH-ETI, also known as "physeterine."

If this is confirmed to have been the cause of the crash, this will have been by no means the first attack by ETIs on American soil that cost human lives, but it will be the first confirmed incidence of an attack from the species PH-ETI. Let us honor the memory of those who have lost their lives in this tragedy, and let us come together and agree that it is time to say "no more." We are under attack; now is the time to decide how we are going to defend ourselves.

I'm happy to now take questions.

Cora's helicopter couldn't land right next to the crash site; the mountain terrain was too rugged, and the nearest safe landing pad was a field several miles away, so it hovered a few feet off the ground while a couple of soldiers helped Cora hop down. She nearly fell out of the helicopter at the sight of the plane, burned and twisted metal the size of a house stomped into the side of the mountain as if by a giant boot. She didn't stop, didn't even thank them, just jumped out of the helicopter and ran toward the smoldering ruin of the plane.

She was among the first (humans) to arrive, the only ones who preceded her having come from a closer air force base, but even they couldn't have been here for more than ten minutes. Ampersand was standing in the middle of it, still wearing his dark gray raiment as he poked through the rubble. There were five soldiers nearby, clearly unsure how to handle the fact that the alien was doing something he very much was not supposed to be. They only got more agitated when Cora bolted right past them.

"Hey!" one of them shouted, starting toward her as if he meant to tackle her like a linebacker. She kept running, engaging neither with this soldier nor with the horror of the situation. This was only half the plane. She didn't see any bodies. Maybe there had been parachutes on board.

"Ampersand," she said, nearly smacking into him. "Are they here?"

"*There are no human remains here.*"

Ampersand, delicate and gravity-defying as ever, stepped up into the wreckage, balancing between what used to be the floor of the plane and one of the walls. He was looking down at something, but the innards of the plane were so fucked up she couldn't tell what it was.

"What is it?" Then her heart sank. No *human* remains, he had said. "Nikola?"

"*This is the gurney he was affixed to.*"

She moved herself around so she could get a look, unable to step up into the wreckage as he had. "He's not here?"

"*No. Three of the fasteners were unbuckled. The rest were ripped out.*"

"He escaped?"

"*That is most likely.*"

She swallowed the dry gunk in her mouth. Nikola was alive. *This isn't over. This isn't hopeless.* "What about Luciana and Paris? Is there any way—"

She stopped short when he looked at her, and she already knew what conclusion he had come to. "*The transients were here for Nikola. They would have no use for humans.*"

Cora was already shaking her head reflexively. "But they aren't here . . . and Nikola . . . Nikola's still alive. Maybe . . . this wasn't a commercial plane. It had security. There might have been parachutes on board."

Ampersand moved toward the front of the plane, which was even more of a mess than the open rear. The nose was visible, but the fuselage of the plane seemed to have folded up like a bent straw before disintegrating.

"The black box," said Cora, grasping for some hope to cling to. "737s have a device that records everything that happens in the cockpit to help with accident investigations. They're designed to survive plane crashes."

Ampersand was on it immediately, peeling away the parts of the front of the plane that were in his way.

"It won't be black," she said, remembering having seen one on the news and thinking it odd that it wasn't black, "but it'll be inside a sturdy case of some sort."

"Hey!" called out one of the soldiers. He may have tried to approach them, but seemed confused to have run into a force field. All of them started shouting when Ampersand stood back from the wreckage, put his hands down, steepled his fingers into a triangle, and opened what was left of the cockpit like a Venus flytrap from twenty feet away.

The soldiers behind her were apoplectic, but Ampersand was not about to humor them at this time by letting them take the reins. Cora looked at the troops and saw that they were even farther away than they had been when she arrived, gently pushed back by Ampersand's telekinesis.

She turned around to see that he had pulled something out of the wreckage, and indeed it was red, though not quite a box, more a metal cylinder attached to a box that read FLIGHT RECORDER—DO NOT OPEN. Ampersand opened it.

"Is it a tape recorder?" Since this plane hadn't exploded, it was untouched by fire. Ampersand crouched to put it on the ground.

"*It is a random access memory hard drive*," he said, pulling off the top of the cylinder and extracting what looked like a motherboard. Then the tips of his two middle forefingers morphed into something compatible with the device's port. She got down on her knees to get a better look, started to ask him if he could hear anything, but then she heard a staticky human voice in her earbud.

"Fresno Approach, Cherokee 8121K, 20 miles northwest of Las Vegas VOR at three-five-zero, en route to Sacramento."

Then another voice: "Cherokee 8121K." Fresno Approach.

"They must be talking to air traffic control," she said.

"When was this?"

"*Approximately six and a half minutes before the tape stopped recording.*"

"Cleared through Class Bravo direct Sacramento," said ATC on the tape. "Descend and maintain 5,500, maintain VFR, Cherokee 34K."

There was silence for about three minutes after that, each minute slowly boring another spike of anxiety into her chest. Then there was a click like the sound of a door opening.

"Excuse me."

Luciana's voice.

"Is there anything on radar?" said Luciana.

"You mean the weather radar?" said one of the men, either the pilot or the copilot. "No, clear skies ahead."

"Is there any way you could tell if we're under attack?"

"What's going on?" said the voice, suddenly very serious.

"Nikola's awake," said Luciana. "He said the sister species is attacking the plane. It is very likely that this is one of his many ploys to escape, but—"

"Attacking how?" said one of the pilots.

"I don't know! I don't know anything about planes."

There were a few seconds of silence, then one of the men said, "I don't know what to do with this."

"Me, neither," said the other, "Call a PAN-PAN?"

"PAN-PAN. Squawk—"

Just as he said that, Cora could hear Luciana in the very distant background yelling, "*What are you doing? Stop it!*"

"What the hell?" said one of the men.

There was a crack, an explosion, and then loud static.

"What is that?" asked Cora.

"*Explosive decompression. A hole must have been ripped in the fuselage.*"

The next two minutes were mostly white noise. Every so often, she could hear the voices of the pilot and the copilot shouting something, but nothing intelligible. Then their voices went silent. The recording ended a few seconds after that.

The muscles in her jaw hardened painfully; she shouldn't have let them go alone like this, she *knew* she shouldn't have let them board this plane without her and Ampersand to protect them. "Nikola's still alive," she muttered to herself.

"*Nikola was restrained to the aircraft,*" said Ampersand.

"What are you saying?"

"*The explosive decompression would have ripped them out of the aircraft instantly if they were not restrained. That is why there are no human remains.*"

"No." She grabbed his hands, pulled them toward her. "No, no no no."

"*I am sorry, my love.*"

She fell to her knees, shaking her head all the while. She wanted to ask him to sedate her, numb her, let her sleep forever. She felt his body over hers, his hands around her back, his garb shielding her like a tent.

Despite the overwhelming evidence, she was still in that same sense of disbelief she'd felt in those moments she'd held Kaveh's body in her arms, just before she felt the bullet wound in his head. This *had* to be a nightmare. If she tried hard enough, she would wake up from it.

She looked up into the woods, taking stock of where they were; giant red tree trunks intermingled with the gray-brown of the smaller ones, the unmistakable shadow of the great sequoia Kaveh had written about in his final essay. Fate could not possibly be this cruel. Luciana, who had finally gone the extra mile for her, who had been her rock during this last terrible year when no one else was. Paris, who still had so many stories to tell, whom she'd fallen for so fast she'd hardly admitted it to herself, whom she'd hurt so badly, and with whom she'd never made amends. This couldn't be happening, not again. She couldn't have Kaveh ripped away from her, only to lose Paris and Luciana *both* in one cruel swoop. She shouldn't have let them board this plane. She shouldn't have begged Kaveh to stay with her instead of leave the country like he'd planned. She shouldn't have walked out on Paris when she was angry, just like she walked out on everyone. All of this was because of her.

Ampersand stayed crouched on the ground next to her, his hands draped over her like a formfitting basket. The sound of another helicopter grew closer, the wind from its blades touching her skin. She wished he would send a telekinetic blast into those soldiers so they wouldn't see him touching her like this.

As the wind from the helicopter intensified, Ampersand stood up urgently. Cora looked to see what had caught his attention, and yelped, falling back onto Ampersand's digitigrade, therapod feet. A massive Similar stood before them, silhouetted by the setting sun, and the sight of him, in *this* forest, in *these* conditions, sent her already fried nerves into overdrive, and it was all she could do not to devolve into a sobbing panic. It took her a moment to recognize that it was Brako. Not Obelus. Just Brako.

Not that Brako was a huge improvement.

She knew that Similars did not *belong* to Oligarchs any more than a medieval knight *belonged* to a duke, but it felt to Cora like Brako did belong to Esperas, who was, if not Ampersand's nemesis, the person with whom he was on the most antagonist terms. On this planet at least, and this was a planet that was home to Todd Julian, Jano Miranda, and Bill Maher.

Ampersand had been convinced that, for lack of amygdaline personhood in the United States, Esperas would take advantage of that technicality and have both Ampersand and Nikola *eliminated* by Brako. Putting them out of their misery, as it were, and as Brako was more powerful than Ampersand, there would be little he could do to stop him. However, Esperas was nothing if not a follower of rules, and as long as he accepted American hospitality, he abided by their laws, meaning Brako would not murder Ampersand out here in the woods in full view of a bunch of soldiers.

Still, she'd hardly recognized Brako, and as far as she was aware, Ampersand had seen neither Esperas nor Brako since the "asylum" incident more than two years ago. The two just stared at each other, both still as stone. They were having a discussion, she figured. A silent exchange of information through their network language.

The nearby helicopter finally disgorged its inhabitants, all people in their civvies, but they hesitated before approaching the crash site. Brako was the first to move, surveying the carnage for about a minute. He only used his head, moving it like an owl as he kept his arms up in that half-mantid, half-velociraptor posture. Then he disappeared. She looked up at Ampersand, who crouched back down next to her, or rather, next to the black box.

"What does he want?" she asked, barely managing a whisper.

"*The situation concerns Esperas as well, but at the moment, our top priorities are not in alignment,*" he said, examining the black box intently. "*The pilots stopped speaking fifteen seconds before impact. They were fastened to their seats in the cockpit. But their bodies are not here.*"

"What does that mean?"

"*They exited the aircraft fifteen seconds before impact.*"

"How is that possible?"

"Sabino!"

She turned to see Sol jogging toward her. "It's Luciana," he said. "They found her."

Cora closed her eyes, face contorting as she braced for the inevitable.

"No," he said. "I didn't say they found her *body*. They found . . . they found *her*. She's alive."

"How?" said Cora, shooting to her feet. "Ampersand said he couldn't . . ."

Sol stopped short, looking at Ampersand and shaking his head dumbly. "It wasn't him."

23

From an intelligence perspective, Sabino's transportation method, which had never been disclosed to Sol, was one of the biggest pains he had to deal with. The trip from the mountains to the hospital where Luciana Ortega had been taken was an occasion he'd assumed would never happen—not only could he observe and report an occurrence of electromagnetic transport but actually participate! Participation meant being shrink-wrapped by 46 in a sort of liquid metal and going into the tiniest of comas, and then waking up seven-ish minutes later outside of the hospital in Fresno. Somewhere down the line, Sol knew this was going to mean an ungodly amount of paperwork.

Sabino was already there by the time he got de-shrink-wrapped, but 46 was not, and when Sabino asked the nurse at the check-in station to see her aunt, she gave no indication that 46 was even here. He technically had the *right* to be here, in the same way a homeless tweaker had the *right* to enter a Neiman Marcus, but that didn't mean that bringing the alien cyborg into the middle of a hospital during peak hours was a good idea.

They took the elevator to the third floor and found Ortega alone in her room talking to a doctor, who excused himself when he saw that family had arrived. Beyond her extra-wild hair and frazzled demeanor, Ortega looked perfectly fine. Sabino took a moment, as if scanning to make sure her aunt wasn't a doppelgänger, and then rushed to the bed, throwing her arms around her.

"Shut the door," said Sabino, and Sol obliged. Not one second after the door latched shut, a cloak of invisibility melted off a ceiling-height alien standing over Ortega's bed like candle wax in fast motion.

"How did he—" Sol looked at the window, which was slightly ajar. He knew these things didn't have the capability to teleport, but sometimes it sure looked like they did.

Sabino sat on the side of the bed, taking Ortega's hand, and her expression flipped to concern as she listened to something from 46. "He wants your consent for him to examine you."

"Oh," said Ortega, her voice fragile. "Sure—ah!"

46 pushed Sabino out of the way, grabbing Ortega's neck with one hand and her head with the other, turning it in all directions that looked just shy of painful. To her credit, Ortega did not shriek in terror.

Sol chuckled despite himself. He hadn't been Vincent Park's friend, not really, and Park had been far from the first person Sol had known killed in action, but Sol had slipped into a mentor role without realizing it, and that had been the first time he'd felt like he'd actually lost someone, and it was hard. And now, two years later, watching Nils Ortega's sister, a woman he'd taken a perverse pleasure in terrorizing just for pure guilt by association being poked and prodded by the very reason for their knowing each other in the first place, he was relieved. More than relieved, he was *glad*.

"Ortega the Younger," he said. "Glad you're okay."

Ortega tore her gaze away from 46 (presently peeking up her skirt) and looked at Sol like she was anticipating some mean-spirited punch line.

"Looks like you're not the only one of the Ortega lineage with a penchant for surviving un-survivable situations," he added.

"How did you—" Sabino stammered. "Nikola . . . Did Nikola—"

"It wasn't him," Ortega breathed. 46 seemed to have gleaned all there was to glean from a surface examination and backed away from her to a comfortable distance of a few feet. "He's gone."

"What do you mean, 'it wasn't him'?" asked Sabino, gesturing toward 46. "Ampersand said Nikola's still alive."

"Oh, thank God," said Ortega, completely clueless. "You have him."

"We don't know where he is," Sabino clarified. "Just that he's still alive. What about Paris?"

Ortega looked at her sadly and shook her head. "I don't know. But Nikola—"

"Ampersand can't use his bond with Nikola to track him down, but he does know that Nikola's still alive. And if Nikola's alive, Paris might be, too. But how are you here?"

Ortega hesitated, the memory already a painful thing to revisit. "Okay, so. The plane's been in the air for maybe thirty minutes. Paris and I are having a conversation, then Paris stops abruptly, and says that Nikola is telling her to remove his restraints, because the plane is being attacked. At first, I think it's just a trick, but then there's this loud creaking noise, and Paris starts to unbuckle him."

"Paris did?"

"Yeah. I don't know what instinct drove me to do this, but as soon as Paris started unstrapping him, I dove for the seat next to Nikola's gurney and buckled the seat belt, not a second too soon, because then the decompression happened and I blacked out, I'm not sure for how long. Anyway, I come to and I look at Nikola's gurney, and he's gone, and there's just . . . half the plane is gone! I grab at the space where he was, figuring he might be cloaked, but he wasn't there. And then . . ."

She moved her mouth for a moment like she was trying to speak but had forgotten how. "It was like the gates of hell had opened up and were crawling into what was left of the fuselage. About a dozen of them. They were these dark . . . lizard things. Their eyes were black; I couldn't tell what was suit and what might just be a natural protrusion of the body. They seemed to get around like . . ." She mimed a hump on her back like she was Quasimodo. "I think it was something like jet packs—no flame or smoke or anything, but they had some device on their backs that kept them in the air, helped them climb around in the fuselage.

"One of them checked out the restraining table while the other ones combed the cabin. It seemed like it was double-, triple-, quadruple-checking that Nikola wasn't there. And then it—*they*—the physeterine looked at me. We locked eyes, and . . . it was . . . a moment?"

Sol chortled. "A 'moment'?"

"Yeah, they seemed surprised, like perhaps they had never actually looked at a human in the flesh before?"

"Not one that lived to tell the tale, anyway," muttered Sol.

"I will tell you now that being near them is nothing like being near an amygdaline," Ortega continued, ignoring him. "Their *faces* . . ." She formed her hand into the shape of a claw, positioning it over her mouth. "I don't think we really appreciate just how much not having a mouth can make an alien seem less . . . *alien*. Anyway, that one joined the others toward the cockpit, and I unbuckled the seat belt and followed them. And . . ." Her voice was growing tense, shaky. "And I was about to die, and I knew amygdalines could be reasoned with and have been known to show mercy to humans, why not their sister species? So I grabbed at one of them, and I think they must have thought I was attacking them, because they threw me against the wall almost into one of the other ones, the same one I'd locked eyes with a few seconds earlier. So I reached out to that one and took that one by the arm, didn't lunge, I just took them by the arm, and I looked in their eyes and I said, 'Please, save us.'"

Her eyes grew glossy. "They just look at me for what was probably two seconds, but felt like an eternity. And then they throw me across the cabin into the arms of the one I'd lunged at, and then that one goes into the cockpit. And that one just kind of . . ." She reached out in front of her like she was grabbing two invisible cans of soda. "Held me by the arms. And the fuselage is disintegrating, the tail is going, the wings are going, structure's falling apart. And then I see the one I'd locked eyes with exit the cockpit, and they've got the pilot and the copilot, one in each arm like . . . fucking . . . prizes they won at the carnival.

"Then both of them just jump out of the plane, using their jet pack things to propel them, with me and the two pilots, and before I know it, I'm out of the plane, still being held by my arms. And I feel like my legs are being restrained, and I look down, and they are, by their tail. It was prehensile like . . . the trunk of an elephant, only pointed at the tip. Their tails are completely prehensile! And I see the fuselage keep going in a straight nosedive, but I couldn't see the crash from that angle. And they gently lower us to the ground in this grassy area in the middle of the mountains. I look over, and the pilot and copilot are a few feet away, just stunned. More stunned than I was. The physeterines looked at us for a few seconds. And then they kind of lifted off using their little jet packs, and then they were gone, and I mean *fast*. They were going so fast, I'm surprised they didn't break the sound barrier." Her nostrils flared and reddened, and she looked at Sol with puppylike, glassy eyes. "And . . . I just started to cry."

He knew she expected him to say something mean or dismissive. He didn't feel particularly inclined to, but the problem with a lifetime of being the biggest asshole in the room was right now he didn't know what to say. Then he got a buzz on his BlackBerry—a message from Macallan.

> Turn on CNN.

"Fffffff—"

He didn't get out the "uck" before Sabino snapped, "What is it?"

Sol did as he was instructed and turned on CNN. Macallan never contacted him, so this couldn't be good. Sure enough, there was Julian giving a press conference, the chyron reading PRESIDENT JULIAN ADDRESSES ETI-INVOLVED PLANE CRASH. Julian seemed to be divulging every piece of intelligence he'd been given, and possibly some ad-libbed bullshit for seasoning.

"What a child," said Ortega incredulously. "Who discloses this level of intel with the investigation still ongoing?"

"Someone who doesn't have the votes to pass their defense bill," said Sol. Stranger still, Julian named names. Usually in press conferences like this, the president just gave "thoughts and prayers" to the "loved ones" we lost, but here he listed the names of the bodies that had so far been recovered—three of a known eight humans on board. Wells, notably, not among them.

"I'm sure it's a total coincidence that he didn't mention the names of the survivors," said Ortega bitterly.

"But he didn't list Paris among the dead," Sabino said urgently.

"He didn't list Paris among the recovered," said Sol in as sympathetic a tone as he was able (so not very). "They still have a lot of square mileage to search."

"Nikola is still alive. It's possible he has Paris with him." She said it with such sureness, like she'd solved a puzzle.

"I . . ." Ortega swallowed. "I saw her get sucked out." She exchanged a glance with Sol, and he knew they were on the same page. The survivors were accounted for; all that remained was the recovery, and that had already begun.

"Yeah, but against all odds, you survived. They haven't found her body. Nikola talked to her when he wouldn't talk to anyone else. She might be different to him."

Sol just shook his head. A few days ago, 51 (who went by the stage name "Nikola Sassanian") had been a heartless monster with no path to redemption, but now that he represented the only hope for her hopeless cause, then he must be the golden-hearted antihero just waiting for the chance to redeem himself by rescuing her fair maiden. Poor kid.

"Why do you think they would do this?" asked Ortega, looking at 46.

Sabino took a moment to take in what she was hearing. "He doesn't know. Physeterines are like humans; they have dozens of cultures with competing habits and values. They could have done it for any number of reasons."

"But they saved us, it felt like on a whim," said Ortega. "And now we know that they probably didn't mean for the plane to crash. Maybe they had a crisis of conscience."

"He doesn't . . ." Sabino winced, shooting 46 a perturbed look like he'd used an ethnic slur. "He doesn't think they had a crisis of conscience. He doesn't think they *have* a conscience, at least as far as a human would define it. They must have done it for some other reason."

"I think you're wanting to give credit to your rescuers," said Sol. "Anthropomorphizing."

"You're anthropomorphizing, too," Ortega retorted, almost offended. "Thinking like a spy, giving them motives like a spy."

"Sentimentalizing, then."

"What about Nikola?" asked Ortega. "Is it possible the physeterines kidnapped him?"

"He thinks probably not," said Sabino. "If Nikola found a way out of the plane, it's more likely that this was a failed assassination attempt, and Nikola's just on the loose somewhere."

"Jesus Christ . . . ," said Ortega.

"Well, what with the inevitable reign of terror, shouldn't take too long to figure out where he is," said Sol.

"We need to go," said Sabino, standing up. "He says that Brako is still in the mountains. He found—" She swallowed. "He found another body. A 'Eurasian male.'"

Sol bit his tongue; to Sabino, this was just evidence that Wells had miraculously survived, and she was setting herself up for a bad fall.

"He's going to go back to the mountains, try to see what he can find," Sabino continued.

"Is there a polite way we can ask for intel?"

"Sol, he is *right here!*"

He sighed, looking at the alien who was not even looking at him (or anyone). Why did it feel like Sabino was asking him to address her ventriloquist dummy? "Mr. Atheatos," he managed, "all branches of the intelligence community want to help you. We want to find both Nikola and any physeterines, but we don't want to harm either of them. Will you please share any intelligence you find with us, even if you feel like it might not be relevant?"

Sabino threw on her jacket. "He's . . . hesitant."

"There's no benefit to him keeping things from us."

"On the contrary—failures in U.S. intelligence have caused quite a bit of pain! Instead of sitting back and waiting for him to do all the work, why don't you see what you can do to help *us* first?"

Sol crossed his arms, annoyed but also intrigued by the challenge. The last thing he wanted to do was rely on 46 for . . . anything, really, but it wasn't like there was nothing doing. If anything, this could be the excuse the agency had been waiting for to really let loose and do all sorts of Geneva Convention–violating stunts to find out what else the international intelligence community had been holding out on them.

"Fair enough," said Sol. "I've got some leads. I'll see what I can find."

24

Paris was conscious of the splitting headache before she got a grip on where she was, and where she was appeared to be a hole in the ground.

She sat up, her mouth sticky from dehydration and her head throbbing. She was in a hole about ten feet deep and about six feet in diameter. Above the hole, the branches of trees spread across the overcast sky like witches casting a spell over the pot she was in, their bright green leaves blocking most of the sunlight.

"Nikola?" she said weakly, blinking hard. She put her pinkie into her ear, hoping that maybe it had just gotten jammed, but no. Her earbud was not jammed, nor was it malfunctioning. It was just gone. It was that feeling of the absence in her inner ear that hit her like a bucket of ice water; she'd survived a plane crash. Nikola had been the one who'd saved her from it. But then he'd been taken.

They'd *both* been taken.

She pulled her knees to her chest and backed up against the mud wall. There was something smooth and white poking out of the dirt on the other side of the hole. *Just a rock*, she told herself, but could not screw up the courage to check. Was this the human pit? The pit in which they tossed any poor unfortunates who got too close? The walls were too smooth to attempt climbing, and she sometimes thought she heard movement on the forest floor above. A few times she heard the physeterine language, muffled as though it were coming from a neighbor's house. The white thing in the dirt taunted her, illuminated by the last vestiges of the setting sun.

Night fell. During the day, it had been hot and muggy, and with the dense, humid air came the mosquitoes, descending into her hole like an invasion of tiny evil helicopters. If it was this hot in November, that meant she was in a tropical rainforest, and here she was without any antimalarials. She covered her arms as best she could with her shirt, draped her braids around her face and neck like a curtain, and prayed that the sickle cell trait she'd inherited from the ancestors would protect her.

Then, like some goddamn dinosaur ninja, one of the physeterines hopped into the hole with her, causing her to yelp in surprise. In the darkness she couldn't see what was happening, but she felt something wrap around her wrist and then another rodlike device grab her by her other wrist. It seemed like a distant cousin of one of those grabber tools old guys use to pick up trash on the beach, only the grabbing end of this thing felt *alive*. The physeterine drew her wrists together with the two rods. Then they grabbed her by her bound wrists and lifted themselves straight out of the hole as if by a jet pack.

Once on level ground, they pulled her along by the wrists like she was a horse to be broken, hissing and clicking at her as if they were giving instruction. There were artificial lights out here, very dim by human standards and probably not visible by aircraft or satellites, but enough that she could see that she was in some sort of settlement. The physeterine dragged her through some brush, and suddenly she was inside some sort of antechamber that was almost as dim as it was outside. A second opening appeared, and the physeterine pulled her through.

Now she was indoors, as it were, though it felt and smelled like being inside a giant wet walnut, surrounded by dozens of them in heated conversation. Then the one who'd taken her threw her to the ground, and the rod detached from the thing binding her hands. She finally got a look at it and couldn't help but cry out in disgust. If not alive, it definitely looked the part, conforming to her wrists and even expanding and contracting with them, an organism that was part tentacle and part tree root.

The light in here was low and red like a darkroom, but she could see her captors clearly now that they weren't wearing the dark, wet suit–looking garb they'd been wearing before. Their skin was a sort of jaundiced albino off-white the texture of latex, smooth and translucent. Their skin color darkened at their extremities, fading into a dark purple on their muzzles, fingertips, tails, and head crests.

Their eyes were no longer the black, rodent-like ones she'd seen before, but yellow like transparent glass over a retinal satellite that gave it almost the effect of a pale topaz. They caught the light in much the same way as amygdalines' did and stood in contrast to the dark skin around them. It had the effect of looking at their retinas through a giant teardrop, and dozens of those lemon teardrop eyes were staring down at her.

Then one of them grabbed her by the wrist, guided her to an adjacent chamber, and threw her to the floor, which felt alive in the same way her hand binding did. It moved with footfall and then sprang back into place, less like a natural spring and more like a plant growing in fast motion. Then she saw another pair of eyes staring out of the wall, not yellow but the multihued colors of a cloud nebula, brighter than any of the physeterine eyes.

"Nikola!"

It was as though tree roots had grown around him and then congealed into a mass, but in a perfectly symmetrical way that reminded her of Celtic knots. His hands were bound behind him, as were his legs, and all of him was covered with the stuff, though his head was mostly free, poking out like a kid in an iron lung.

Throughout the diatribe in which several physeterines participated, Nikola's eyes betrayed no expression, the crest on his head standing alert like the petals of a sunflower. Then Nikola responded to them in the physeterines' language, and they conversed for several minutes, the physeterines growing more and more heated. Then one of them grabbed her by her braids, exposing her throat as though they were going to slice it open. "Nik!" she squealed again as if he could do a goddamn thing. Then after what felt like an hour but couldn't have been longer than a few seconds, they pushed her back to the strange, living floor.

She took a deep breath, and another, but felt no matter how deeply she breathed, she couldn't get enough air. She pulled herself to her knees and scrambled toward Nikola, but he shook his head in slight, barely perceptible gestures, and she froze.

"What should I do?" she whispered.

Nikola's eyes widened, and he bowed his head like he was praying. Paris mimicked him, bowing her head as their captors talked among themselves. Whatever Nikola was telling them, they weren't happy.

So this was the home of the Semipalatinsk pod, named after the most radioactive place on Earth. She thought of the one who spoke the most as Castle Bravo, since if not the biggest, he seemed to have the biggest personality. Tsar Bomba was another big one, who, while verbose, did not speak with quite so much gusto as Castle Bravo. Trinity she reserved for the one who had fished her out of the hole; that one was physically smaller than the others and spoke less, but commanded a certain authority when they did.

As this went on, she found she could easily tell them apart; they wore different clothes, had different ornamentation, even unique markings on their skin. Most notable were their veins, which were visible under their translucent skin, all making distinct patterns up their necks and on the edges of their faces. *Like a human fingerprint*, she figured.

The back-and-forth with Nikola continued. The sound of their language was making her dizzy with exhaustion, and she rested her eyes. Before too long, Trinity pulled her to her feet using that rod thing, keeping her at a distance from their body like her bite was poisonous. It almost felt absurd to her, given their size difference, like she was a radioactive rod being held at arm's length by Shaquille O'Neal (as he might be one of the few humans approaching these guys in size and stature). They dragged her back to the antechamber and back outside.

The second she was in the open air, she took a deep breath, and her head cleared immediately. Trinity marched her over the small grassy space and then threw her over the ledge and into the hole. The binding detached once she'd been tossed in, and she fell, landing next to the thing that was definitely not a bone. She landed on her upper right leg, her hip taking the brunt of the fall, and groaned in agony as her still-bruised ribs and lungs let their displeasure be known. She pulled to the other side of the pit and wept.

She knew there was little chance of getting out of this alive. Even in the best of circumstances, she wouldn't be allowed to go free simply for the crime of having seen too much, to say nothing of being a known ally of their mortal enemy. Eventually, she cried herself out. Keeping her knees to her chest and laying her head down on them, she dozed.

She woke when the sun rose, and listened. No movement in the daylight. Maybe they were nocturnal. That certainly jibed with the dim lights and the giant yellow eyes. Again she looked at the white object and decided enough was enough and moved to examine it.

It was a bone.

She was in the Sarlacc pit, naught but the latest that Jabba had tossed down for his own amusement. *It is entirely possible these are not human bones*, she thought. *Yes, entirely possible this isn't just the human pit but also the deer pit. Maybe a deer got unlucky and fell in.*

And then she wondered, *Why do people delude themselves like this?*

She dug out the bone—a femur, one that looked like it had been here for a while. There was also a tibia and what looked like a couple of arm (or forelimb) bones. No skull or rib cage, which natural erosion would have left, meaning these bones had to have been planted. She couldn't tell if the bones were human but then decided that it did not matter; whatever (or whoever) this was was long dead, and had given her some tools. If she could turn the bone into a foothold, she might be able to climb out.

The first twelve tries only resulted in the side of the hole becoming more unstable. Few options though she had, she decided that the knobs on the femur were doing her more harm than good. Really all she needed was two of the bones to give her a stable foothold and handhold.

Using a rock, she managed to split the two femur-ish bones in twain and use them as two footholds, employing one more bone like an ice pick to pull her over the top. She carefully dug a perfectly sized hole in the mud wall using one of the smaller bones and jammed half of the femur in as far as she was able, and then a smaller one in with it for stability. She did it again on the second foothold, and then she went for it. She slipped a couple of times, but using the forelimb bone as an anchor, she made it to the top and pulled herself out into the jungle. She didn't waste an instant, didn't even look back to test her theory that they were nocturnal, that they weren't all sitting there with a bucket of tentacle-tree popcorn watching the show. She just picked a direction opposite to where she had been dragged earlier, and ran.

· 25 ·

Nearly twenty-four hours had passed since the plane crash, and in not one of those hours had Cora slept, bringing her time awake somewhere into the thirty-six-hour range. Ampersand had left her to her own devices in their Fukushima house, so she did the only thing she could do: scour the internet for leads.

What had once been the domain of middle-aged crazies using Geo-Cities was now a profitable industry, one of the few that had grown in the last two years. One of the establishment alien-sighting websites, DeceptiNation.com, had exploded both in membership and in new hires so much since the physeterine news broke that the site had crashed three times in the last forty-eight hours. But the deluge of "reports" made her dizzy, even with the website vetting what they could into "reputable," "feasible, and "unreliable." Exhausted as she already was, she did not have the brainpower to suss out what was possibly useful and what was obvious bunk (which was, needless to say, the vast majority). Moreover, since Julian had not named Paris, anything that didn't at least include her description was probably a nonstarter.

The buzz of her phone nearly made her jump out of her skin, and the dulcet tones of Denis Leary singing, "I'm an asshoooooyyooo-yooooyooyole," piped out as the ringtone. She nearly fumbled it in her haste to answer. "Sol?"

"I was just asked to accept any charges I might incur for an international call."

She deflated. Not the tone of a man with urgent news to share. "What is it?"

"Well, I know the challenge here was for me to supply *you* with intelligence for once, but the truth is I have about a dozen very weak leads and am willing to admit that I may need help following up on what I do have."

"I'll do what I can."

"I was hoping you'd be in the States."

"I can be in the States."

"How soon?"

She looked down at her hands, shaky from both lack of sleep and blood sugar. "Do you have something?"

"I have one idea for where to start. But you aren't going to like it . . ."

"Just tell me."

"Well, Nils won't answer my phone calls, but he might answer yours."

Cora groaned. "Why him?"

"Because he indicated to you that he might have more goods from the Russians. If he does, that's where I'd like to start."

"But it's been two years since they were seen in Ukraine."

"That's two years more recent than the Philippines."

Cora looked at the thin light of the rising sun, her eyes dry and stinging. Twenty-four hours. Paris had been gone for twenty-four hours. She knew from personal experience that Nikola knew how to keep a human alive, and Paris was tough. If Nikola had Paris and she was still alive, then Cora wasn't doing either of them any favors barging into this with days upon days of missed sleep.

"How time-is-of-the-essence is this?" she asked.

"If we're digging up years-old Russian records, I'm going to guess not very. If we find anything, my guess is that it would be more helpful to your boy than for us."

Had she had her wits about her, Cora might have been shocked to see that Ampersand had silently appeared right next to her. He took her by the wrist, sharpening the tip of one of his digits into a needle so sharp she couldn't even feel it when it entered the tip of her forefinger.

"You could have asked," she slurred, putting the phone on mute and looking outside. Before the sun had risen, several times she had looked into the wooded darkness that surrounded the house and thought she'd seen two eyes glowing like cloud nebulae. "Is there any way Nikola could find this house?"

"*Unlikely. Have you eaten since yesterday?*"

"I had . . . some juice."

"*Eat, now. And you must sleep.*"

"I—"

"*Choose a form of sustenance, or I will choose it for you.*"

Cora nodded, unmuted the phone, and stumbled toward the kitchen. "Okay, I'll come as soon as I can, but I think I should probably try to get a little sleep. I haven't slept since yesterday."

"All right, so what am I looking at, time-wise?"

"Maybe . . . ten hours?"

"Ten hours . . . okay," said Sol. "That gives me enough time to get to New York. I'll meet you there."

"Where ar—"

The click of him ending the call came before she could finish. She dragged her carcass to the tiny Japanese fridge in the kitchen and withdrew a bottle of green Naked juice—a good compromise for when she needed quick calories. She returned to the living room to see Ampersand looking at her laptop to see if there was something on DeceptiNation.com that she'd missed.

"I'll go to sleep now, I promise. But first, will you tell me what your plan is?"

"*I must gather what I have that is operational.*"

"Your drones?"

"*Yes. I must also utilize man-made satellites, as my drones do not provide adequate coverage.*"

Cora took a seat on the floor by the short Japanese-style wood table and cracked open the bottle of juice. "Where do we start?"

"*I had a tracker on Nikola, but he found some way to scramble it not long after he reached the ground.*"

"He shouldn't be able to do that, right?"

"*No.*"

Cora forced down a few gulps of the Naked juice. So much thought and energy had gone into preventing Nikola from outsmarting everyone and escaping, no one was humoring the possibility that Nikola might have been kidnapped. Or worse, what if Nikola was *in league* with the physeterines? What if he had known the plane was going to be attacked? What if he'd been in on it? She wanted Ampersand's theory to be correct—it was much harder for her to imagine a reason the physeterines would keep Paris alive. Mean and spiteful as he could be, she didn't think Nikola would harm Paris just for kicks. It felt totally in character for Nikola to keep Paris as his "pet," especially if she had followed his instructions to unbuckle him. Though that scenario would be horrible for Paris, it was vastly preferable to the alternative.

An alternative that Ampersand was not presently entertaining.

"Would transients be able to scramble a homing signal like that?"

"*It is possible.*"

"Well, maybe—" Cora gasped as a large figure appeared in her peripheral vision, a Similar whom for an instant, silhouetted against the morning fog, she mistook for Nikola. She shot to her feet, grabbing Ampersand with one hand and her energy pulse emitter, which she had with her at all times in case of hostile Similars, with the other. But it was not Nikola, nor was it Obelus. Only Brako. (Well, "*only*" Brako.)

Brako was so huge that she initially missed that Esperas was standing right in front of him, ignoring her as he always did. At around six and a half feet tall in his neutral posture, Esperas was taller than most humans, but next to Brako, who was twice the height of an average human, he looked like a paper crane.

Ampersand for his part was stony (both physically and metaphysically). She didn't get a sense of upset or panic from the other side of the wall, so Cora had to assume they were communicating through network rather than spoken Pequod-phonemic. Amygdaline communication through network felt to outside observers more like a staring contest than talking.

"Ampersand, what's going on?" she asked after about a minute of staring.

Ampersand spoke out loud, in "common" Pequod-phonemic, while also translating into her earbud: "*I am requesting that Esperas speak in common. He is in my domicile, and he knows speaking in a language you cannot understand is considered rude.*"

Esperas hesitated, looked at Ampersand as if to say, "Fine, I'll humor you," then spoke in Pequod-phonemic. This didn't initially seem like much of an improvement, and in her delirious state, it took her a moment to remember that her earbud could translate Pequod-phonemic through her ocular overlays. She closed her eyes, trying to remember how to pull up the translation function, then, in the lower right of her vision:

[It is our intent to establish diplomatic contact with this physeterine pod or pods. We entreat you to do the same, or if you will not, we entreat that you will commit to doing them no harm.]

That was not where she had expected this to go.

Ampersand responded in Pequod-phonemic, and a heated (by their standards) conversation ensued:

[*I will commit to nothing at this time.*]

[If Brako had arrived at the scene of the accident sooner, he may have been able to track the physeterine pod as well as your symphyle, but these physeterines use a sophisticated form of scrambling to obscure their location. We will have to divine their location through other means.]

[*My first priority is to find my symphyle. These transients failed in their attempt to kill him, and now he has escaped.*]

[It's possible that this pod has your symphyle in captivity.]

[*They would kill a Similar on sight. They likely endeavored to kill him to remove the threat to their young, and failed, as they likewise failed to assassinate me.*]

[You should be open to the possibility. There are myriad reasons why he has more value to them alive than dead, perhaps to parties not on this planet. But this pod hasn't left the planet yet.]

[*How do you know that?*]

[We have a surveillance net around the entire planet capable of penetrating their cloaking. They haven't departed. We would have known.]

The empathic wall between herself and Ampersand, the one that ebbed and flowed with no rhyme or reason, was neither particularly thin nor thick at the moment, but Cora felt an unmistakable *whap* of what could only be described as indignation from the other side.

[*Was it your intent to ever reveal the existence of this surveillance system to me?*]

Esperas was calm, his eyes bright but not alert. He looked downright sassy.

[Noble peer, I implore as to why I would share such sensitive information with one who would keep from me the nature of their bond with Obelus, who killed our other Similar, and nearly killed this one? I would not share sensitive information to you unless it was relevant.]

[*This is highly relevant.*]

[Therefore, I have shared it with you.]

"This is good," said Cora, deciding it was time to step in. Funny, at first, she'd been brought on to make Ampersand more diplomatic to other humans; now, she was having to do it for his own kind, too. "I understand why you would hesitate to trust Ampersand with this information, but I am grateful you have chosen to share this with us now."

"*I do not trust his motives,*" said Ampersand to Cora alone. "*Esperas has wanted and continues to advocate for Nikola to be euthanized.*"

"But we are concerned for Nikola's safety," she added.

[Your symphyle is your business. If indeed you believe that these physeterines failed in their objective and that your symphyle has escaped, we will do him no harm, but we will not aid you in his recapture.]

[*I do not ask for your aid in his recapture.*]

"Esperas, would you explain to me why your first priority is to set up diplomatic relations with this pod? They've killed almost a dozen humans that we know of and tried to kill Nikola."

[It is my function.]

"*Esperas is a rare caste of diplocrat,*" Ampersand explained. "*There were very few Oligarchs bred to the purpose of expanding potential diplomatic relations with intelligent aliens.*"
Then why the hell has he been such a dick to humans? she wondered. "You have been . . . less than receptive to human attempts to establish diplomacy with the Fremda group."

[I was not bred for the purpose of diplomacy with humans.]

"*When he says 'bred,' he means that he was born with high-language abilities that others of our kind do not naturally possess.*"
"High language," she said, looking at Esperas. As far as she knew, physeterines did not *do* the high-language thing as amygdalines did— only spoken language and possibly network (which was really just a higher-tech version of spoken). "So physeterines *can* do high language?"

[They could, if they did so with me.]

"*Esperas and other Fremdan diplocrats were designed, in theory, to be capable of communicating through high language with physeterines, provided these hypothetical physeterines received the necessary implants.*"
"You mean like—" Cora tapped her temple.
"*If I were to try to communicate with a physeterine through high language, it would be a painful and arduous process not unlike the one I have done with you, one that would take months of work. But for Esperas, it could be done in a matter of hours.*"

Cora looked at Esperas, sensing a level of skepticism coming through the other side of the wall and sharing it. "In theory."

"*In theory.*"

[I haven't stayed alive for you, or for the humans, or for our inferiors. I have stayed alive that I might fulfill my function, that we might communicate with our cousins and show them that we are capable of peaceful intent. I have capabilities that you lack, while you have medical skills that I lack.]

"Skills?"

"*I believe he refers to the implantations required to make a non-amygdaline brain capable of high language. A moot point, as they would first need a physeterine to consent to such a procedure.*"

[In order to gain trust to obtain consent, we must first assure them that we mean no harm. Will you commit to doing them no harm?]

[*I will commit to no such thing. I will defend myself if they prove hostile, and they have so far proven hostile.*]

Cora looked at Brako, whose dim focus was right on her, and she inched closer to Ampersand. Esperas spoke again:

[Is this your statement of intent to do harm?]

[*It is a statement of intent to defend myself and any under my care, amygdaline or otherwise, from any outside force that proves hostile.*]

[Any outside force.]

Esperas was reading between the lines—*any* outside force, be it physeterine, human, or amygdaline, and at present, there was no force with more potential to do harm than Esperas and Brako. The pair stayed silent for a moment, then Brako lowered himself in a movement that almost looked like a bow and disappeared into a cloak of invisibility. Esperas said his last piece:

[Then we have nothing left to discuss.]

Then he, too, disappeared.

· 26 ·

Paris had imagined herself making a mad dash through the jungle, but the problem with jungles was while they did lend themselves to madness, they did not lend themselves to dashing. She'd been slogging through the brush for at least three hours, and the sun high in the sky told her it was probably around noon by now. She was also dangerously dehydrated, the heat squeezing what little moisture was left in her body out like a sponge and the humidity caking it on her skin. Could chewing on leaves provide hydration? Why hadn't she watched more than zero episodes of *Man vs. Wild*? What brain-space wasn't dedicated to trying to figure out how to remedy that problem was spent trying to suss out where the hell she was. About an hour ago, she thought she might have seen a few monkeys, but she wasn't exactly a monkey expert, and besides, knowing whether she was in Borneo or Brazil wouldn't do her much good if she didn't find help.

Then she stopped, ears pricking at what could be an aural mirage. It sounded like water. Big water. Rapids, perhaps, or a waterfall. She walked in the direction of the sound until she was convinced that this wasn't an illusion. Salvation in the short term, and a possible human contact, too. After all, where do towns and villages crop up but besides rivers? She followed the sound of the water, which was growing louder and louder with each step, until at long last the jungle opened up, and a river lay before her.

She slithered through the tree roots and rocks to the bank, falling to her knees so hard she probably bruised them, and shoveled water into her mouth. She looked upstream and saw the likely cause of the sound she'd heard—a large plume of water vapor coming up from behind the trees. She followed the river upstream until she came within sight of a massive waterfall, a river outlet spreading over several cliff faces falling down dozens of feet in thick, frothing lace.

For a moment, she was overtaken by the beauty of it, and it struck her that this must be an attraction of some sort, that a natural wonder this beautiful would have some sort of infrastructure, but from her vantage point, there was nothing, only some old, weathered garbage lining the river's edge that had come from somewhere upstream. That struck her as odd—there was garbage, meaning she couldn't be that far from civilization, but even in incredibly remote places, a potential attraction like this would be swarming with rich white people who helicoptered in to see it. Could this be protected land of some sort? As she pondered, she caught something out of the corner of her eye lounging on a rock about a hundred feet away, something she initially mistook for a sunning leopard, although given the choice between the two, she would have taken the leopard.

Going by the size of them, she recognized this one as Castle Bravo. They were seated in that manner she had seen Nikola do before, hind legs tucked up to their sides and forelimbs planted in front of them like the Great Sphinx, one wrist daintily draped over the other like they were sitting at afternoon tea. Their eyes were covered by bulbous, shining black domes, which she now realized she'd only seen them wear during the day—they must have functioned as something like sunglasses. The two stared at each other, the human calcified in fear and the alien observing her casually. Then Castle Bravo jumped to their feet, and Paris stumbled backward. She turned to run, but instead fell ingloriously into the river.

This river ran deceptively deep for how narrow it was, and the current dragged her down so violently and so quickly she didn't have time to catch her breath. She tried to get a sense of up and down, tried to find the bottom of the river so she could use it to springboard back up to the surface, but the water was moving too chaotically and too quickly, and all she did was bang her feet and head a couple of times on the rocks.

This lasted as long as thirty seconds before the river calmed enough that her head broke through the surface. Hardly able to remember what few swimming lessons she had at the Y some two decades earlier, she flailed and fumbled to get to the other side, which had widened to the point where it was shallow enough for her to stand. She barely managed to do so before the current knocked her off her feet again, and twice more she tried and failed until she made it to the shore, coughing and spluttering the whole way as she ran toward—

Toward what?

Paris looked behind her, and the sight of Castle Bravo not more than thirty feet away made her stumble to her knees again before scrambling back to her feet. She had no strategy; this was fight or flight, and fight was not an option. She ran toward a grassy area half the size of a football field, periodically looking behind her and seeing Castle Bravo there each time, not quite gaining ground but not quite losing it, either. Distantly, she knew she was being toyed with. Then there was a blast from behind her, and the shock wave knocked her flat on her stomach. She didn't look back, just scrambled to her feet and kept running. She had almost made it to the tree line before she looked behind again.

Castle Bravo wasn't there.

She stopped by a tree and fell to her knees, looking over her shoulder and preparing to switch to "beg for mercy" mode, but Castle Bravo was gone. There had been an explosion, one that could have been caused by any number of things. Perhaps it was a human air strike. Perhaps this was an act from a rival pod. Maybe even Nikola had done it. Then, over the sounds of her heavy breathing, she heard a noise that sounded like a dying animal. As she carefully backtracked, a part of her wondered if this was some sort of trick. But no, why would they bait her? They obviously could have caught her at any time during their little cat-and-mouse game. Something had happened.

There was a noise like dolphin whirs and clicks in extreme slow motion. The grass was tall, so it took her a few moments to figure out where Castle Bravo even was, complicated by the fact that they were no longer in one piece.

She saw the majority of them before she saw the leg that had been severed at the knee lying about ten feet away from their body. Centered between the limb and the rest of them was a small crater created by the source of the blast: a land mine. The blood in her veins curdled like bad milk.

She was in a minefield.

She looked down at the alien, who was grasping at the stump where their hind leg used to be, seemingly confused as to what had even happened. Like, this was clearly a mistake—*Could you please reattach the limb I have misplaced? I think it's right over there.* And there was so much blood, the same red as human blood, pooling and soaking into the dirt. Paris looked around, realizing how lucky she'd been, having traversed this field twice and avoided any land mines. Even knowing that, Castle Bravo's fellows would be looking for them soon, and they would find her as easily as Castle Bravo had. She would likely get blamed for this and be punished accordingly, and she couldn't pit that against the absolute madness of trying to escape a minefield, one that for all she knew could stretch on for miles. Castle Bravo was bleeding out, but wasn't gone yet, and if their circulatory system was anything like a human's, she might be able to slow the bleeding. Better for the pod to find her with their maimed fellow than their dead fellow.

As she knelt next to them, Castle Bravo tried to do a weak intimidation move, swatting at her with their claws and hissing with their mandibles. She couldn't say it was ineffective, but she shook it off and moved closer, and they calmed, less as a gesture of trust so much as the fact that they seemed to be losing consciousness. Paris took off her outer shirt and struggled to rip off a decent-size strip. Eventually, she managed a few strips about an inch wide and tied them together. Finding a stick to act as a windlass was tricky, as she did not want to move around and risk triggering another mine. She found one, but it was so brittle it broke. It took a few tries and not insubstantial risk to find a stick that worked.

Where Castle Bravo had been fading, the pain from the tourniquet jolted them back to consciousness, and they shoved her away with what strength they had left. Fortunately, this was something she'd trained for; humans tended to react in a similar fashion, as there were few things more painful than a tourniquet. They didn't understand that she was trying to help, and the fact they had been drifting in and out of consciousness for several minutes, while a very bad sign, was working to her advantage.

After she had tightened it as much as she was able, the bleeding had slowed but hadn't stopped. By this point, she was already in preprogrammed EMT mode. Second tourniquet necessary? All right, we'll figure it out. She still had most of her button-up shirt left and began the process of ripping off some more strips when she heard a storm of alien language behind her. She crab walked herself away from Castle Bravo before freezing in place, because she was *still in a fucking minefield.* Castle Bravo's backup moved around them cavalierly, like the only danger here was from Paris.

"Holy shit," she muttered. "You guys don't know."

There were four of them, but only two she recognized—Trinity and Tsar Bomba. Bomba grabbed her and threw her a few feet away as they tried to figure out what had happened and how to handle this. In short order, Bomba took the initiative and unfurled a spare transport device, which spread like blown glass, conforming to the body of the physeterine until they resembled something like a manta ray. When their transports were close to the ground, they seemed to hover, but once in the air, it looked more like controlled gliding.

Bomba loaded Castle Bravo onto their own manta, which swiftly enveloped their body and made its way back toward the settlement. From a distance, it might look like a machine, but up close, it felt almost alive. Within seconds, Bomba had taken off on their own manta, leaving Paris alone with Trinity. As Trinity regarded her, she took stock of just how covered in blood she was and how very incriminating that looked. Trinity spoke in their alien language, which could have meant any number of things—giving instruction to a computer, communicating with the settlement remotely, a spiritual incantation, wondering aloud to themselves—but Paris couldn't help but wonder if Trinity might be talking to her in the way one might talk to a wild animal they were trying to subdue. *Easy does it, fella.*

Then Trinity grabbed her by the neck and threw her down so quickly she didn't have time to react or cry out before her back was on the ground. She grabbed their wrist on instinct, felt the strange joints underneath the layer of garment and skin that felt almost like hinges made of bone rather than the dense puzzle of metacarpals that made up human hands. Trinity stared her down for a long moment and then shifted their head to look at a patch of ground a few feet to her right. She kept looking up at the alien, kicking and grunting, but then she saw the small, square plastic block poking up through the dry grass that had caught Trinity's eye.

"We have to get out of here," she said, looking at it like it was a rattle-snake. "This is a minefield."

She looked at Trinity, now regarding her instead of the mine. She couldn't see any shifting in their expression or focus underneath those black sunshields that lay over their eyes like obsidian shells. Then, not loosening their iron grip on Paris's neck by even a hair, they reached to grab a large stick about the size of a long, wizened baseball bat. *No, you are not about to . . .*

Oh, but they were.

Still watching Paris, they moved the stick toward the square poking out of the grass, what could only be another detonator. "No!" Paris cried out. "No, it will kill us both—stop, *stop!*" She pointed at the mine, and getting no reaction, she mimed an explosion with her hands.

Trinity did stop, still eyeing Paris, and it occurred to her that they never intended to poke the mine but to test her reaction. They held the stick over the mine a few more seconds, then placed it harmlessly a cou-ple of feet to her right, carefully so there was no possibility of it coming into contact with the mine. Then they just looked at her. It felt like an hour, but it probably wasn't longer than a minute of staring, no sound from either of them, just the song of the bugs in the jungle, the birds having been chased away by the blast.

Then Trinity unfolded their own manta device and loaded her up.

"You said you might have more for me," said Sabino, holding her iPhone between herself and Sol. "But I don't have anything for you in return. Not right now, anyway."

"This isn't a transaction," said Nils Ortega's voice from the iPhone, which was muffled by the sound of a nearby honking match between two sedans. Sol didn't want her to know where he lived and wasn't wild about the idea of meeting in a dorm, so the compromise was a field in Central Park, far from prying ears. "This isn't about who breaks a story first. This is serious. But I do want you to tell me one thing."

"What?"

"How did Luciana survive that plane crash?"

Sabino looked at Sol. That Luciana and the two pilots had survived was public knowledge by now, but had been totally drowned out by Julian's war against the alien menace. "Well, I don't know specifics . . ."

"You can tell me you're not at liberty to say, but please don't lie to me."

Sabino winced. "It's an active investigation, so I'm not supposed to tell you anything, but off the record, it didn't *not* have to do with aliens. Happy?"

"No," said Ortega. "But I'll accept it, if you tell me what it is you need."

"I have to tell him, or he won't cooperate!" she mouthed.

Sol rolled his eyes. "Tell a half-truth," he mouthed in return.

"We need to know more about Semipalatinsk."

"Does this mean that Semipalatinsk was responsible for the crash?"

"Paris is missing," Sabino blurted. "You know that, right?"

"I heard—but this has to do with Semipalatinsk?"

"We don't know, but here's the truth. Paris was on that plane. She is missing, presumed dead. But I don't think she's dead."

"You're saying that you think Paris Wells may have survived the plane crash because she was kidnapped by aliens?" He sounded a little disappointed, like yes, he might have some intel for them, but he had hoped it would be for something a *little* less cartoonish than this.

"I don't know, Ni—" She bit her lip, and Sol couldn't help but smile. He wondered if Ortega knew he hadn't been "Dad" for many, many years (not that he'd care). "I don't know. We don't know anything; we're just trying to learn as much as we can."

"Okay, come right over. I can't tell you anything over the phone, and I certainly can't send you anything. You aren't being a CIA mole right now, are you?"

Sabino paled, looking at Sol. "Yes," she squeaked. "Sort of."

"I said *half-truth*!" he mouthed.

"Glad you said so," said Ortega. "I would hate for us to get off on the wrong foot with you lying to me. So if there are already CIA agents listening in on this call and they're in town—the Flatiron office, I assume—I think it might be in our best interest that you come pay us a visit as well."

Sol planted his face in his hands. How. *How* had that location leaked already?

"Why?" asked Sabino.

"We need to be pooling our resources," said Ortega. "Much as I would like to continue this dick-wagging contest, I'm a little more concerned about the extraterrestrial threat than corrupt government agencies. We have had our differences, but I think now might be the time to put our differences aside."

"Okay," said Sabino. "We'll be there in about half an hour." She hung up, looking at Sol worriedly. "This feels like a trap."

"That it does."

"Do you really think you'll be able to be civil with him after what he did to you?"

"I think I might be able to pull off solemnly contemptuous."

"What would he want you there for? What . . . entrapment could he possibly have worked out?"

"I don't know, but he is right about one thing—it's still an existential threat, so we should nut up, head over there, and see what he's got."

· · · · ·

"Sol Kaplan, I had a feeling it was you," said Ortega, pronouncing his name like it rhymed with *hole*. "Welcome in."

Ortega waved them into his apartment and shut the door behind them. It wasn't a huge two-bedroom, but it was a good size for the Upper East Side, meaning he was still pulling in a fair amount of cash through donations to *The Broken Seal*.

"*Sol*," said Sabino like a kindergarten teacher correcting a five-year-old. "*Sol* is short for *Solomon*."

"The Hispanophone in me," said Ortega. Yeah, that mispronunciation had been deliberate. "I'd say we've met, but . . ." Ortega trailed off.

"It's cool," said Sol dryly. "I didn't need my identity protected. Not like I worked in counterterrorism for ten years."

"'Counterterrorism'?" Nils chuckled. "Is that what you want to call it?"

"Where is Felix?" interjected Sabino.

"I imagine he's just getting out of school." He looked at Sol. "I have a feeling you are well acquainted enough with my apartment that I don't need to give you a tour." He said this in a friendly tone, as if Sol had simply been a former roommate.

"Look," said Sabino. "I know you two have a weird history, but I'd like for you to table that for now. This isn't CIA mole stuff; I'm just working with Agent Kaplan because he has a better chance of finding intel than I do on my own."

"What about your . . ." Ortega made a gesture like he was trying to draw an outline of a T. rex in the air. "Friend?"

"He's got his own business right now. Please, if you have anything that Agent Kaplan might be able to look into . . ."

"Stay put," said Ortega, heading into his bedroom.

Sol peeked in and saw that Ortega was digging around in a modest little office setup that looked distinctly impermanent. Everything he'd required to cut and run if the need arose. Doubtless his major hardware was at the office, though Sol figured his most sensitive stuff he'd keep with him at all times—that cell phone in his pocket, for instance.

"Now, the original source that leaked Semipalatinsk, I don't know who that is," Ortega said, pulling out one of his several laptops and returning to the living room. "They seem to have been disappeared by the Russians, but I got more yesterday from my anonymous source. I haven't had the chance to translate it yet, because I don't have anyone to translate it that I can trust—"

"Let me see it," said Sol.

"You speak Russian?" asked Sabino.

"Couldn't say," he said, taking the laptop without giving Nils the chance to object.

It was mostly pretty rote stuff, discussing Semipalatinsk in a way that could be mistaken to the untrained eye for the actual Semipalatinsk region in Kazakhstan, a place the Soviets had used as their nuclear testing ground with such rapturous frequency that it was now the most irradiated place on Earth. But whatever they had, it was not being stashed in Kazakhstan.

"Hooboy," sighed Sol. "Of course, it would be the one country that's a bigger pain in the ass than Russia."

"What do you mean?"

"Belarus," he said. "Those photos weren't from Ukraine, they were from Belarus, and this says that the files detailing what they actually found at this location are in Minsk."

"What's wrong with Belarus?" asked Sabino.

"You mean besides the military dictatorship? It's just hard to get in and out of, and the locals—the city folk, anyway—are generally a suspicious bunch, harder to get intel or sources."

"You've been there before?" asked Ortega.

"Couldn't say."

"Could your source maybe find those files?" Sabino asked Ortega.

"Doubtful," said Sol. "These are of a classification that says these documents are within someplace called the Chiksulub Institute and nowhere else. And the fun thing about Belarusian intelligence is they almost pride themselves on their dogged, Luddite love of hard copies. I can have some of our guys look into it, but my suspicion is that if you want to see these files, you're going to have to go to Minsk."

"Then . . . you should go," said Sabino, her meaning unmistakable: *I should go.*

"It could be a big nothingburger."

"It's the only nothingburger we have," she said. "And I know enough about missing persons that the longer they're missing, the less likely they are to be found alive."

"I know she and Kaveh were really close," said Ortega.

"Yeah, I . . ." Sabino's voice caught in her throat. "I only met her a couple of months ago. I didn't know her when he . . ."

Sol could hear the gears in Ortega's head turning as he saw the way Sabino talked about Paris Wells, the desperate tremor in her voice, her fervent denial of the reality of the situation. Ortega moved closer to her on the couch, and oh, the way he moved in, slipping so effortlessly into the role of absent father who was finally stepping up, made cold worms crawl up Sol's neck.

"She was away on assignment last year, if I recall," said Ortega. "But they weren't just friends; he was her mentor. It must have been really devastating for her to lose him. For both of you."

Sabino looked at Ortega, half like she wanted to claw his face off and half like she wanted to be held by her father.

"I know I didn't know him as well as either of you did," he continued. "He and I were all work and no play."

Again Sol chafed, as if the work they did was just being paper pushers for accounts receivable and not leaking sensitive national security, as if he wasn't even in the room, as if the very work he did with Mazandarani *didn't expose his own fucking identity*. Ortega slithered his arm over her shoulders like an eel. "You couldn't have saved him. No one could have seen that coming. But maybe we can still save Paris."

"I know, I know it was my fault," she said, tears spilling down her cheeks.

Gaaaahhhhhddamn it, thought Sol, trying to get her to look at him. *Abort, abort!*

"No, it wasn't your fault," said Ortega. "His blood is on the hands of the men that killed him."

"No, you don't understand. He said, 'I have to leave the country. I have to go.' And he begged me to go with him. Kaveh was going to go to Iceland. I told him to go without me, but he wouldn't go. He wouldn't leave me, so he said, 'You don't have to go alone. I'll go with you.' And that was all I wanted; he told me that and it was like the weight of the world—the weight of the Senate hearing—lifted, he was going to stay with me, but then—"

Her face curdled, and she broke down. "He begged me to go with him," she said, now sobbing. "He begged me to go with him. He's dead because I didn't go with him!"

"No," said Nils sternly. "He's dead because a bunch of rednecks were shooting at something they did not understand. He wouldn't want you to feel this way."

"I know he wouldn't want that," she sobbed. "But it doesn't matter. He's gone. He asked me to go with him, and he's gone. He's gone!"

Nils pulled her close, and she cried into his shoulder, her body uncomfortable and flaccid, as if she still wasn't quite ready to accept comfort from him.

"Can I use your bathroom?" she said after a few minutes.

"Of course," he said, guiding her to her feet and leading her toward the bathroom. Her vulnerability had presented Ortega with an opportunity, and he certainly took it. Then Sol noticed that Ortega had left his cell phone on the end table next to his sofa.

"Do you have a printer, by chance?" asked Sol.

"I do," said Ortega.

"I know it would be the pinnacle of irony to ask for this, but would you mind printing me a copy of the Belarusian documents?"

"Sure," he said after a pause that was just long enough to be rude. Then he went into his bedroom, his cell phone still alone and vulnerable in the living room.

Sol waited until he heard the click of the printer before grabbing the phone, slipping out the SIM card, and putting it into the "external phone battery" into which was installed a SIM card–cloning tool for just such an occasion. Ideally, he'd be able to get it done before Nils realized he had done it, rather than having to steal it outright. Fortunately, Nils stayed in the bedroom long enough that he was able to pop the SIM card out of the cloning tool, back into Nils's phone, and back onto the end table in one fluid movement. He was proud of that movement. It was too bad no one was watching to be fooled by it.

Nils returned seconds later, documents in hand, and within about ten minutes, Sabino had calmed down enough that she could come back out of the bathroom.

"I'm sorry for all that," she said. "I guess I'm still processing it."

"It's okay," said Ortega, handing the documents to Sol but keeping his eyes on her. "It's a lot to process. I can't even imagine."

"I, uh . . . need to step outside for a minute. Get some air." She looked at Ortega. "I'll be in touch."

She exited the apartment, but Sol stayed put. Ortega looked downright chuffed that he now had the chance to speak with him alone. "I don't know what I expected you to be like, but this wasn't it."

"I'm surprised you expected anything of me at all."

Ortega sauntered toward the still-ajar door to his apartment, hands in his pockets. "When we were working on the piece that exposed your black site, we had to wonder what type of person . . . does what you do. Like do you really believe the ends justify the means when you do the sort of things you did, or are you just an agency of bullies and being a cop wouldn't be a hard-core enough outlet for those tendencies?"

"I do have trouble getting erect nowadays without at least imagining a waterboard first," said Sol flatly.

Ortega chuckled. "I don't begin to understand the culture at the agency—"

"It's all Mormons. They're the only people in the country with the correct combo of patriotism and never having smoked pot. Huge flaw in the recruitment process, to be honest."

"—but I want to believe that we agree that the world needs to change for the better, and maybe even how it needs to change. Where we disagree is the means."

"Sure."

Sol continued to look at the man coolly, not for one millisecond entertaining the idea that Nils Ortega's first and only priority wasn't the elevation of Nils Ortega; tricking dupes into believing he was doing it for the greater good was simply his method.

· · · · ·

Plenty of the data on the SIM card was incriminating, less for Nils than for his sources. There were only a few, but boy if they weren't some of the exact names the agency had been looking for. Some little diphthong

NSA contractor had leaked a bunch of code names for hacking programs, another CIA contractor had been ferreting out classified documents on burned CDs labeled "Lady Gaga." He hoped for their sake that they had skipped the country already, because if they hadn't, they were going to be in for a world of hurt. After about an hour, he got back as far as spring of 2008 and almost did a double take when he saw his own name.

> (3/4/2008 10:36 PM PST) Nonce: Sol
> Kaplan is here. He works with ROSA.
>
> (3/4/2008 10:36 PM PST) Nils: Wow, I
> thought the conspiracy nuts just made
> that up.

The contact was listed only as "nonce," probably a burner, and the number's area code, 575 (Roswell, New Mexico, har har), didn't exactly help. *Sol Kaplan is here*—on March 4, 2008, "here" would have been Los Alamitos, during that two-week span they had Nikola Sassanian on the air force base.

> (3/4/2008 10:49 PM PST) Nonce: CIA-
> Bedford, VA. I couldn't find anything
> on NORAD, but there was an incident
> in Bedford, VA, that happened the day
> after NORAD involving two vehicles.
>
> (3/4/2008 10:50 PM PST) Nils:
> Casualties?
>
> (3/4/2008 10:50 PM PST) Nonce: I don't
> know.
>
> (3/4/2008 10:50 PM PST) Nils: Death?
> Sightings? What?
>
> (3/4/2008 10:51 PM PST) Nonce: I think
> people died.
>
> (3/4/2008 10:51 PM PST) Nils: What kind
> of people? Bystanders?

(3/4/2008 10:55 PM PST) Nonce: No.
CIA people. I overheard Kaplan talking
about losing agents in Bedford, VA, the
day after NORAD. Two vehicles were
recovered. That's all I know.

(3/4/2008 10:56 PM PST) Nils: And do
you have any clue as to the identities
of these individuals?

(3/4/2008 10:59 PM PST) Nonce: No. I
don't have any documents, I'm just
telling you what to look for.

Sol hadn't even gotten to the end of the conversation before he figured out who "nonce" was. He'd been surrounded by Americans for so long, he'd forgotten that *nonce* meant something different in Europe—*cradle robber, pedophile, pederast.* And whom would Nils Ortega be calling a *nonce* but the thirtysomething fucking his twenty-one-year-old daughter?

So everything that had gone down at the Senate trial, Nils had known about, and Mazandarani had been his source. The guy who finally got his precious fucking Pulitzer, if only posthumously, for delaying a vote on a bill *just* long enough for it to become politically inexpedient when a nonperson status meant they could not extradite the alien cyborgs for a murder trial.

And the whole time, Mazandarani had been feeding intel to Nils.

In a way, Mazandarani was even more loathsome than Ortega, who at least made no pretense about the fact that he was his own first and most precious priority. Genius, scholar, and martyr, Kaveh Mazandarani, who was now enshrined in marble in the pillar of everyone's mind. Paris Wells was a nonstarter and a waste of time, and most probably dead anyhow—*this*, this was something he could work with, and Sol could not wait to knock this perfect, infallible dead angel off his pedestal.

All he needed was the right opportunity.

Trinity shoved Paris onto the floor in front of Nikola *right* on her hip, *right* on the bruise they'd given her the night before. Nikola's head was cocked at a weird angle, his eyes focused on nothing, like he'd been put in a trance. It was so dark in here, and coming from direct sunlight, it was taking some time for Paris's eyes to adjust. This time, a bigger crowd had shown up to bicker about . . . whatever it was they were bickering about.

Then a shove from behind her from Tsar Bomba, the loudest of the bunch, knocked her onto her face. She curled into a fetal position as Bomba stood over her, addressing their peers in that spitting alien language. It was so strange watching them speak with their mouths closed, all the noise coming from the air holes in their necks. She chanced a look at the crowd that was gathering. Some of them were smaller than the group that was standing over her and bickering loudly, smaller even than she was. *These must be juveniles*, she thought.

The adults were clad in black skin suits, but the skin suits the juveniles wore were all over the place, the garbs covering them so diverse in color, style, and amount of clothes it made her think of the Lost Boys from *Hook*. The veins under their alabaster skin were much darker than what she'd seen on the skin of the adults, snaking up their necks and faces like vines crawling up old houses.

One of the other adults grabbed Paris by the shoulder and pulled her back onto her knees, and she tried to flinch away when they jammed something into her ear.

"DEAR GENTLE CREATURE."

"Nik!" she gasped, and the shoulder-grabber let her go. "Tell them I didn't . . . I didn't know about the land mines!"

"I KNOW, DEAR GENTLE CREATURE. YOU DON'T EVEN KNOW WHERE WE ARE."

"Do you know where we are?"

"WE ARE IN THE NORTHERN HEMISPHERE. THAT IS ALL I CAN TELL."

Northern Hemisphere, she thought, her mind racing; *Northern Hemisphere. Tropical rainforest. Land mines.* That narrowed it down considerably; they must be somewhere in Southeast Asia. "What's happening? What are they going to do?"

"THEY HAVE REQUESTED THAT I ACT AS TRANSLATOR. THEY WANT YOU TO EXPLAIN YOURSELF."

"Yes, anything they want! I'll tell them whatever they want."

Nikola paused, looking at the group behind her, still bickering. She wondered if she should frame it more as an act of altruism than the fact that she had been more terrified of being discovered with a dead Castle Bravo than a maimed Castle Bravo. The others quieted until only Bomba was speaking to Nikola. Nikola was still in that trancelike state, his focus on no one and nothing.

"THIS ONE BELIEVES YOU DELIBERATELY LURED THEIR FELLOW INTO THE MINEFIELD. THEY WANT TO KNOW HOW YOU STAGED IT."

Paris looked at the creatures behind her incredulously. "They think I planned this?"

"THEY HYPOTHESIZE I DID."

"That's absurd!"

Nikola's head straightened, and he finally said something. He hardly got a word (or whatever their word equivalent was) out before Bomba cut him off. Then another cut *them* off, and then the bickering started all over again.

"Do they not know they're in a literal minefield?" Paris whispered.

"NO, THEY DON'T."

"Tell them . . . there are . . . thousands, maybe millions of these things called land mines all over the world." She swallowed nervously as Nikola translated for her. *Please, God, let him be wording this well.* "They're explosives that are buried underground. They're designed to go off when somebody steps on them—"

A physeterine voice cut her off.

"THEY WANT TO KNOW WHAT PURPOSE THESE BURIED CHARGES SERVE."

"They're used in wars," Paris explained. "They're a cruel, terrible device used in wars. I don't know what country we're in, so I don't know exactly why these land mines are here. I think in this region they were probably to make this land unusable for guerrilla fighters. That's why the Americans buried them in Vietnam, to make the land unusable for the Viet Cong. Or if we're in Cambodia, it was the Khmer Rouge. Those wars are over, but the land mines are still there. And they kill thousands of people, thousands of *human* people, every year. Innocent people. Mostly children."

She looked toward the entrance, to a sliver that indicated the presence of sunlight. "This land is unusable. That's probably why it's uninhabited."

Paris braced herself as the group talked among themselves. "They don't believe me?"

"THEY ARE SKEPTICAL."

She looked to the juveniles near the entrance, who were having their own quiet conversations. She wondered what their relationship was to their parents. Given the totalitarian nature of the Pequod Superorganism, were these kids likewise indoctrinated, kept under lock and key to protect them? Or were they free to romp and cavort as they pleased?

"How long have they been in this region?"

"NOT MORE THAN A FEW MONTHS."

"If this is a minefield, it's a miracle they haven't had any accidents before now." She looked at the juveniles, all of whom had their wide eyes on her. "I don't know if they have the technology to do it, but they need to do a thorough demining of this area if they're going to stay here, or they should move." She shook her head, a wave of dizziness hitting her. "I feel like I can't breathe."

"THEIR AIR IS DEADLY TO YOU WITHOUT A FILTER. THE HIGH PROPORTION OF CARBON DIOXIDE IN THEIR AIR WILL ASPHYXIATE YOU."

"Do they know that?"

"YES."

"What can I do to get them to let me back outside?"

"I CANNOT COMPEL THEM, DEAR GENTLE CREATURE."

"Please, just ask." The asphyxiation was putting her head in a vise.

Nikola did ask, but there was no movement from the group of adults besides continued conversation.

"YOU SAVED THEIR FELLOW'S LIFE. THEY WANT TO KNOW WHY."

"I only realized this was a minefield when I saw the injury, and knew that any misstep meant that I would be next. I know I could have run, but I was in a minefield, so I stayed with . . . with their fellow."

"WHY THE TOURNIQUET?"

"I'm an EMT." It was getting harder to breathe. Harder to *think.* "They were bleeding out."

"YES, BUT WHY?"

"Are they going to kill me?"

This, Nikola didn't answer, and her face grew hot, her eyes stinging with tears.

"Nikola, what is it they want to hear? Tell me what it is they want to hear and I'll say it."

"DEAR GENTLE CREATURE, I DON'T KNOW WHAT ANSWER WOULD PLACATE THEM. I AM UNSURE WHY THEY ARE KEEPING YOU ALIVE OR WHAT THEIR PLAN FOR YOU IS. TELL ME YOUR TRUTH, AND I WILL RELAY IT TO THEM AS ACCURATELY AS I AM ABLE."

Her head lolled forward, and she forced it back up, tried to stay conscious. "Because it's what I would do to a human in the same situation."

"EVEN AN ENEMY?"

"Yes . . ."

Nikola relayed this, but before he was even done talking, she was grabbed by the shoulders, hoisted to her feet, and led back to the entrance. The exit from this chamber was almost like an air lock, stepping through one door, the door closing behind them of its own power, like the petals of a flower at sunset, and another door opening into the sunlight. As Trinity led her to her hole, she tried to get a lay of the land, but it didn't *look* like a settlement—she couldn't see the entrance to anything, not even the chamber from which they'd just emerged. Only . . .

The Hole of Death.

She stopped where she was, wondering if there was some way to indicate that she was willing to comply, only to *please* not shove her into the pit. Trinity did shove her down, but kept a grip on the strange root-thing that was binding her wrist. This time, they did not remove it, leaving her trapped in a hole *and* bound.

The bones were gone.

She backed up to the shaded side of the hole and slid down it until she was sitting. She took in deep breaths, feeling like her lungs were coated in the toxic CO_2. Then something that looked like a whoopee cushion fell with a *splat* right in front of her. She looked up and saw nothing but an empty sky and a few tree branches. She picked it up in her bound hands; it was a water pouch. It took her a moment to figure out how it worked, that it wouldn't come out with the help of gravity but needed to be sucked out. She looked up again and saw one of the juveniles peeking over the edge of the hole. They locked eyes with her and then disappeared.

· 29 ·

Sol stepped out of the janky Flatiron elevator, charmed by it now that he'd had some time away. "After you," he said to his reluctant companion and nascent CIA contractor.

Cora followed him into Macallan's office, which was about ten degrees cooler than the rest of the fifteenth floor. The leaves outside in the park were beginning to turn to bright yellows and reds, the autumn air leaking in through the cracks in the air conditioner, but she still had not taken her AC out of the window for the season.

"Ms. Sabino," said Macallan, gesturing to one of the chairs on the other side of the desk. "Agent Kaplan. Got something for me?"

Kaplan handed her the documents Ortega had printed, as well as the translation he'd banged out last night.

"Nils Ortega as a cooperative asset," she said. "Wonders never cease. Do you know what he wants?"

Oh, Sol knew what he wanted, all right. No intelligence agency in the world could take him down, but Cora Sabino sure could. She would only need to call him out for the deadbeat piece of trash he was in order to ruin him, or at least drive him out of the mainstream. But if he scratched her back, made her indebted to *him*, well, that was a great way of inoculating himself against the threat she represented. If he played his cards right, he might even get her on his side. Hell, he'd already managed that with his son. One down, two to go.

"Not exactly, but . . . that doesn't really concern me right now," said Sabino.

"I wasn't asking you," said Macallan, and Sabino shrank into her chair.

"I suspect this is a play at social capital, if you will," said Sol. "He wants her on his side."

"He's been trying that for years," added Sabino.

"Yeah, I'm not buying that he had a sudden crisis of conscience about what constitutes sensitive information," said Macallan. "So whatever they have at this institute in Minsk . . ."

"At the least, it should show us specific locations of 'incidents,'" said Sol. "They might even have some 'specimens' there, but based on the language they use, I'm doubting it's anything near as juicy as a physeterine corpse."

"So," said Macallan, twirling her ballpoint pen between her fingers, "is the plan to tell the KGB we know what they have and demand that they share?"

"The KGB?" asked Sabino, like Macallan had made a mistake.

"Yes, the Belarusians actually kept the name KGB," said Macallan. "If that tells you anything about the intelligence culture in Belarus. Sometimes we wonder if they realize the Cold War is over." She arched an eyebrow at Sol. "So what's your play? Seduce some KGB greenhorn at the institute and talk her into doing your dirty work for you?"

"No, that would take too long."

"I can get us into the institute," said Sabino, now surer of her footing. "But I don't speak Russian, or Belarusian, or whatever it is they speak in Minsk."

Macallan leaned forward, intrigued but skeptical. "What do you mean you can 'get in'?"

"You know I have means of travel that you don't. So does Jude. You know we use them all the time. I'm not going to tell you what it is or how it works, but I can get Agent Kaplan wherever he needs to go."

"You're saying you want to go with Kaplan to Minsk."

She nodded fervently. "Right now."

Macallan crossed her arms and leaned back into her chair. "We don't have time to create an identity for you. Faking IDs take time, passports take time, you *learning* your identity takes time."

"You won't need to," Sabino said. "I can get us into Minsk."

Macallan's eyebrows popped.

"That same method of travel, it can take me anywhere on Earth," Sabino continued. "Wherever he needs to go, I can get him there."

Macallan's eyebrows remained popped. "Kaplan?"

"I am in the process of filing a report detailing my experience with this mode of transport, and I can confirm that it does exist."

"So your plan is for her to sneak you into Belarus, and her with no cover?"

He shrugged. "Time is of the essence."

"Kaplan, she's the subject of one of the most famous photographs in the world."

Right. He always forgot about that. "Since this is going to be so quick and dirty, and I'm not going to be in the business of building connections or trying to find assets, her lack of a cover won't be a factor here."

"And if you get caught by the KGB?"

"I . . . ah . . ." Sabino stammered. "Well. . . ."

"Spit it out," said Macallan.

"Jude wouldn't let us get captured," she said. "Or at least, he wouldn't let us *stay* captured. Wherever he is in the world, whatever he's doing, if I'm in danger, he'll extract me quickly."

Macallan looked at her with pity. "You really believe that?"

"Trust me," she said. "I can call him from anywhere in the world. If we need extraction, he can do it far more quickly, stealthily, and efficiently than the CIA can."

"Kaplan?"

"I am inclined to believe her," he said.

Macallan scanned him, surprised. She had clearly been ready to maybe, *maybe* craft a long game that saw them maybe, *maybe* trying to infiltrate the Chiksulub Institute in six months or so, but she trusted his judgment, and if he believed Sabino had an alien guardian angel, great, a contractor they didn't have to even pay.

"You were the one who wanted me to get back in the field."

"All right," said Macallan. "When do you want to leave?"

"Now," said Sabino before he could respond. "Right now."

Macallan chuckled, almost amused. "Right now, then." She stood up, and Sabino shot to her feet. "You'll both go downtown for a briefing, and then you're off the grid. We don't know you, we disavow your activity, and we never had this conversation."

"I understand," Sabino said faintly. "Thank you." With that, she exited the office and headed down the hall toward the elevator, and Sol moved to follow her.

"Kaplan," said Macallan. "A moment."

Sol twirled on the balls of his feet and turned back to her.

"She seriously thinks Wells is alive?" asked Macallan.

"It's not that I don't have the heart to break it to her, she just refuses to believe the inevitable."

Macallan gave her right temple an exhausted rub as she shuffled through some papers on her desk. "You sure she doesn't know something you don't?"

"On this topic? Yes."

Macallan gathered a few of the papers on her desk—photocopies, from the looks of them—slid them into a manila folder, and held them out to Sol. "Wells had some journals on her when the plane went down. NTSB recovered some that contained notes she took the day of the crash. Might turn up something useful."

Sol took the manila folder with a curt nod, promptly shuffled this to the bottom of his to-do list, and turned again to leave.

"Kaplan."

He stopped in the doorway, turned to listen to her.

"She's just a kid."

Sol didn't bother to mask a look of disbelief; all this time, from the second he'd laid eyes on her, he'd been the only person in this agency or any other to keep an eye out for her, and every motherfucker in the agency interpreted that as some clumsy maneuver to get her into bed. As if he needed to go through all this trouble to do it. Fuck's sake, an insecure, lonely kid like that? If seducing Russian spies was vector calculus, Cora Sabino was first-grade math. Insulting to think he'd have to go to any real effort to do it.

"What do you care?" he said. "You've helped organize drone strikes against 'enemy combatants' that we now know were just poor schmucks who happened to be in the wrong place at the wrong time, *including* children, and now you want to grow a conscience?"

Macallan glared at him coolly. "She's just a kid."

Sol regarded her for a long moment, then smiled. "If you're so concerned, maybe you shouldn't put me in charge of her."

Macallan kept her cool glare in place, but said nothing. He followed

Sabino to the elevator, which arrived just as he got to the door. He gave her a wry smile as he smacked the down button for the lobby, looking her up and down. She was much slimmer now than she had been two years ago when he'd met her, and her hair was no longer that goofy blue but a natural color cut by actual hair shears. Now that she dressed herself in clothes designed by something other than Goodwill, she almost passed for an adult.

"Everything okay?" she asked, trying to hide the nervousness in her voice as he stepped into the elevator alongside her. Funny thing was that in any other context, the very thing Macallan had instructed him *not* to do might even be expected of him; half the job at the CIA was a form of seduction, and that sometimes meant literally. Sometimes getting in good with assets meant *getting it in*. It had been a long time since he'd done that sort of thing, and the truth was, it was fun. He liked doing it.

But he didn't *need* to here, even though she was eminently vulnerable and exploitable as ever. Macallan saw it; Mazandarani had seen it and taken advantage of it. All these people knew how to do was exploit, and he was no better than they were, he knew that. He'd stooped far lower in the past, but he hadn't done it with her. Not that he would. He was the only person in this whole operation who'd looked out for her, and nobody got that, even Sabino herself. If he'd wanted her, he'd have had her already.

But, said a little voice that was always in the back of his mind when Sabino was around, *it would be very, very easy. If you wanted to.*

"Everything's just fine."

Paris took a sip from her water pouch, rationing it for the hot day ahead. She wondered what Cora was doing right now, if she and her alien soul mate had already left Earth. Why had she gotten so mad? Why had she been so damn *mean*? If she'd kept Cora on her good side, that would have been her best bet for being saved, but now? Why would anyone waste effort on someone who'd just hurt them so deeply? Tears started to form, and she thought, *Don't you dare. I cannot spare the hydration right now.*

On day one, she had clung to the hope that someone out there might be looking for her before she accepted that, if anything, they were looking for a body in the Sierra Nevada where the plane had crashed, by this point a recovery and not a rescue. Her family was probably keeping hope alive as families so often do in these situations, but the people with the power to search for her wouldn't. The possibility that Jude might be out there searching for Nikola was her only hope, because no one was searching for her.

The stars were bright here despite the humidity. Paris had lived in New York her whole life, and it occurred to her that she'd never seen such bright stars. In the city, one had to make special effort to see this sort of thing, perhaps go camping, an activity her family had never had any interest in. She was so transfixed by the stars that she didn't immediately notice the head that had appeared over the edge of the hole.

She gasped, backing against the opposite wall as another head popped up. Then another. Then there were six of them, six alien heads silhouetting the stars, their bright yellow eyes reflecting the moonlight

like cats, peeking over one another like they were looking into a zoo enclosure. Hell, she supposed, for all intents and purposes they were. She
pulled her knees up to her chest and rested her head on them. Then she
felt something smack her on the shoulder, and she nearly jumped out
of her skin. A few of them scattered, but three were still there, looking
down into the hole as she realized what they'd done.

They'd thrown a pebble at her. Those little fuckers had dropped a
fucking rock on her.

She had hoped to sleep, but now that wasn't going to happen. It was
one thing to deal with the adults, but these were kids who had no clue
what might be harmful (or even lethal) to a human. If a big enough rock
beaned her in the head, that would be that. She curled back up, now
holding her arms over her head, and every so often, *plonk*. A pebble
would land somewhere on her, or right next to her.

Variations on this theme went on all night.

By daybreak, they were gone, and she was able to capitulate to her
exhaustion, which in that moment was greater than her hunger. It was
the middle of the day when she woke up again—this time, more fucking
rocks. She put her arms over her head. Another one fell. Then another.
Finally, she snapped, "*What?*"

There were two juveniles standing at the edge of the hole, but this
time, they weren't holding rocks but something like a rope or a vine,
at the end of which was a stiff device that looked like a large fishhook,
which they lowered into the hole. They deliberated quietly—alien whispering, perhaps, less like dolphin clicks so much as hissing. Then they
seemed to agree on their method of communication with her: panto-
mime. One of them curved up their hand into the shape of the fishhook,
and the other, mimicking her own bound hands, placed them onto the
hook.

Understandable enough.

Paris stood up and approached the hook and looked up at them.
These guys were nocturnal. These kids were supposed to be in bed.
What she was witnessing was, in all likelihood, not something they were
supposed to be doing.

This could be a very bad idea.

On the one hand, kids were evil. From deer fawns to kittens to baby
humans, every stripe of youngling were little bastards. But on the other

hand, her survival odds at the mercy of the adults were not great, either. If she was doomed either way, what was this but a lateral move?

Paris moved carefully, imagining that if she were in their place, she would be very, very on edge. She hung her bound hands on the hook, and they reeled her up the side of the hole like a fish on a line. It wasn't a graceful reeling, and it ended with her having to scramble over the side using her elbows as one would normally use their hands. The two juveniles stood a few feet away, both ready to beat her into submission if need be with sticks, of all things. Big sticks. Paris rose to her knees and stayed there.

Both juveniles were a bit smaller than her, about the size of human adolescents. Now that she had a good look at them, there were elements of their body language that weren't hard to read. The most familiar was the tail—from reptile to mammal, anything with a tail tended to behave in similar ways when excited, and these were no exception. The tail belonging to the one on the right was sticking straight out behind them, twitching every few seconds like a muscle tic, and the one on the left had theirs wrapped tightly around their foot.

More conspicuous were the crests on their heads, something they had in common with their amygdaline cousins. The crests, according to Cora, were sensory organs that detected both sound and electromagnetic waves. They were also a means of communication in the same way humans communicated with facial expressions or dogs communicated mood with their ears. The crests on the heads of these two were splayed out about as far as they could stretch.

The pair backed away from her, sticks still at the ready but now less braced for an attack. Then Righty reached into a pouch they had on the ground next to them and pulled out a large, spiky object the size of a football. They held it up as if they expected her to know what it was—some kind of alien egg, perhaps? Or an extraterrestrial seedpod? When Paris didn't react, the two conferred, and then the one holding it pulled out a shiv of some sort, planted it in the green spiky football, and pried it open, revealing bright white and yellow innards that looked like inflamed kidneys. Then the smell hit her, like athlete's foot that had been crème brûléed, and she realized what it was—not a giant alien seed but a durian fruit. They must be trying to tempt her with it. When she didn't immediately react, the second one disappeared into a copse, reappearing seconds later with another green nut that she did recognize—a coconut.

The one with the durian continued backing away from her, waving the spiky fruit like she might forget it was there if they were too subtle with it. The smell of the durian was like a punch to the face, but she was so ravenous that she'd gladly hold her nose and go for it if they let her. Coconut, meanwhile, kept their fruit close to the chest. She got the impression that Durian was the brains of this outfit, the Tommy Pickles to Coconut's Chuckie Finster. The two backed into a copse of trees and then seemed to disappear altogether.

Paris wondered if the exhaustion had gotten to her. Had they camouflaged? She hastily followed them into the copse and stopped dead when she realized she was in that "air lock" space that led into the chamber where they were keeping Nikola. "Fuck," she muttered as the outer doors closed behind her like two leaves sealing shut with a magnetic zipper, the promise of hypoxia already dotting her vision. Hopefully, they'd make this quick.

The inner door opened, and there stood Durian with the durian. Paris blinked as her eyes adjusted to the dark, and Durian and Coconut took off their black sunglass coverings. Out of the corners of her eyes, she saw other juveniles doing the same, then suddenly, one of them grabbed her from behind, and another grabbed her legs. It was hard to tell, as her eyes still hadn't quite adjusted to the dark, but there were at least ten of them. On instinct, she fought, but held still as she noticed that one of them was holding her earbud at the end of a pair of large tweezers. Realizing what was happening, she turned her head, presenting her ear to the one with the tweezers. They'd clearly been expecting a struggle, but then they went ahead with the plan, holding her fast all the same. Then, as if they had counted to three and acted in unison, they all let her go, all save Durian, who was holding her bound hands with that hook.

"Nik?" she whispered.

"DEAR GENTLE CREATURE."

Durian unhooked her and then went back to luring her with the durian until she was right in front of Nikola. Then Durian dropped the fruit at her feet and hopped away like she might bite if he stayed in her sphere for too long.

"Do they want you to translate again?"

"Yes."

She glanced around, feeling much less menaced by this crowd than the previous one. No bickering here—they were all quiet, curious. She tried to pick up the durian with her bound hands, but it was even spikier than it looked, like holding a medieval mace made out of wood. So she held her breath, bent over, and just ate from it like a goddamn dog from a goddamn bowl. It smelled like feet and ass, and tasted like warm feet and ass custard. After days of no food and barely any water, it was the most delicious thing she'd ever tasted.

"I'm going to go out on a limb and assume they aren't supposed to be doing this," she said after a few bites.

"The adults do not know they are here."

She sat up, having scooped some of the slippery stuff out of its spiky encasement. "I'll tell them whatever they want, but could they please give me some more water?"

Nikola relayed the request, and without hesitation, one of them left the chamber, returning a few seconds later with a water pouch much bigger than the one they'd given her yesterday, about a quart's worth. They seemed to be weighing the wisdom of giving it to her directly, but then gave it to Durian, who dropped it in front of Paris like they had the durian.

Paris held up the bottle, sucking the water into her mouth, feeling it expand inside her capillaries like she was a dried-out sponge. As she did, the group chattered among themselves, and she hastily finished the durian before she lost her chance.

"They had been keeping you alive because they assumed you of some potential value to me, but now there is serious debate among the adults about why you applied the tourniquet to their fellow. The adults feel they cannot trust my translations, but the juveniles say they will decide for themselves if my translations are trustworthy. They want to know why you applied the tourniquet to their mentor."

She'd had some time to think before she was asked again, but now that she was being put on the spot, what progress had she made? She couldn't possibly anticipate what would and wouldn't play well to an alien audience. Even humans were wildly inconsistent with what was and was not the appropriate thing to say.

"I'm afraid your people are going to kill me," she said, eyes growing hot. "I hoped you would show me some mercy if I showed you mercy."

As Nikola translated her she looked back toward the juveniles, who were standing in a group some fifteen feet away. A few of them whispered to one another, but most just watched, with Durian ostensibly speaking for the group to Nikola.

"This land is dangerous," she added. "They need to demine it, or they need to leave."

Durian spoke, and Nikola translated. "'HUMANS DID THIS.'"

Paris nodded. "Humans did this."

"'AND THE LAND IS UNUSABLE, EVEN TO HUMANS,'" said Nikola, continuing to translate. "'JUST AS THIS LAND IS BOOBY-TRAPPED AND UNUSABLE. AND OUR LAST HABITAT, IRRADIATED. UNUSABLE, EVEN TO HUMANS.'"

"Irradiated," she repeated. *Last habitat*, she thought, wondering if that referred to the photos Nils had shown them from 2007. "Ukraine. Chernobyl?"

"'THEIR PREVIOUS SITE WAS CHOSEN BECAUSE IT HAD BEEN ABANDONED BY HUMANS. IT WAS SIMPLE ENOUGH FOR THEM TO AVOID AREAS OF RADIOACTIVE FALLOUT, BUT THEIR CROPS ABSORBED TOO MUCH OF THE RADIOACTIVE ISOTOPES. THEY HAD TO REJECT TOO MUCH OF THE HARVEST FROM THAT AREA, AND SO THEY CAME HERE ONLY TO FIND THIS LAND HAS BEEN RENDERED UNUSABLE BY HUMANS AS WELL.'"

Then Coconut joined in on the diatribe, lecturing not just Nikola but Paris as well. Nikola responded to them in their language, but with nowhere near the length or vigor.

"'THEY ADDRESS ME, 'YOU THINK WE ARE THE SCOURGE, THAT WE DESERVE TO BE DRIVEN TO EXTINCTION, AND YOU WANT TO LET THESE BEASTS RUN ROUGHSHOD ALL OVER THE GALAXY?'"

"'Beasts,'" she said, holding the pouch to her chest like they might take it away. "They mean us."

"'THEY THEN ASK, 'WHY IS THE SUPERORGANISM GROOMING THE HUMANS TO ADVANCE SO QUICKLY?'"

"Grooming—*what*?"

"THIS POD WAS CONFOUNDED BY HUMANITY'S RAPID TECHNO-
LOGICAL ADVANCEMENT BETWEEN THE EIGHTEENTH AND TWENTY-
FIRST CENTURIES. THEY BELIEVE THE MOST LOGICAL EXPLANATION
IS THAT IT IS OUR DOING. I TELL THEM, 'THE SUPERORGANISM IS NOT
HERE. I AM DETACHED FROM IT. MY BELOVED IS DETACHED FROM
IT. THE SUPERORGANISM DID NOT KNOW HOW THE HUMANS HAD
ADVANCED, EITHER, BUT WHEN THEY DO ARRIVE, THEY WILL SHOW
THEM NO MORE MERCY THAN THEY SHOW YOUR KIND.'

"THEY TELL ME, 'THE HUMAN SUPERORGANISM IS RENDERING
THE PLANET UNUSABLE. IT SHOULD BE OURS. IF THE HUMANS ARE
GOING TO KILL IT, ANYWAY, WHY NOT LET US HAVE IT?'"

At this point, almost all of them were butting in, talking over one
another.

"'THIS IS THE ONLY HOME WE'VE EVER KNOWN. WE WOULD BE
BETTER STEWARDS TO IT.'

"'IF WHAT YOU SAY IS TRUE, AND THE SUPERORGANISM WILL HALT
THEIR ADVANCEMENT AND END THEIR CIVILIZATION, WHY NOT LET
US HAVE THIS PLANET NOW? WHY WAIT?'

"'IF THIS CIVILIZATION IS DOOMED, AS YOU SAY IT IS, THEN THIS
PLANET SHOULD BELONG TO US, BEFORE THEY RUIN IT BEYOND
RECOVERY. WHY WAIT?'"

The fear holding her body rigid dissolved into despair. Paris had assumed that the worst of what they had seen had happened in the Philippines, an incident that had left two of theirs dead as well as six humans,
but human bodies didn't even need to be present for them to bear witness
to human barbarity. One wilderness was too close to human settlements
and led to death on both sides, and they had to move. Another wilderness was only uninhabited because it had been blanketed with radioactive fallout caused by human arrogance, and so they had to move. Now
their new wilderness was uninhabited because of land mines that had
been buried decades ago.

There is no saving this, Cora had said.

It wasn't even her faith that right would ultimately win out that had
made her dismiss the idea that there was no hope for humanity but
the fact that there were so many people who were fighting for a better

world. No just universe could see those people who had dedicated their lives to the betterment of the world slaughtered for the sins of those at the top.

But this was no just universe.

December 7, 2009
Los Angeles Times

Julian Unveils Broad Defense Spending Plan

By Joanna Kobierska

President Todd Julian called for a radical increase in defense spending to invest in military technologies in a bid to invigorate his agenda as he nears the end of his first year in office.

With Wednesday's proposals—which includes a 10% year-over-year increase in defense spending, and a nearly 40% increase in the budget of the Department of Energy, which manages the nation's nuclear stockpile, and a bailout of banks that are not yet insolvent—Mr. Julian hopes to speed up economic growth, make his mark as a historic tax cutter, and develop technologies to defend the nation from unknown threats.

"We must not take any option off the table," Mr. Julian said. "Our most cutting-edge technologies were made with human enemies in mind, but the technology that delivered us the greatest power man has ever harnessed has been stagnant for decades. We may not have the luxury to allow that stagnation to continue."

Julian's critics have interpreted this as a commitment to develop new forms of nuclear weapons. When asked if he was willing to end the U.S.'s commitment to nuclear nonproliferation, Mr. Julian reiterated, "We must not take any option off the table."

· 31 ·

When choosing a location to travel to, Cora used her ocular overlays to draw up a schematic that was based on the planet's electromagnetic field; Earth, after all, was spinning, so simply plotting the coordinates of a point on the other side of the world wouldn't work, as by the time you got there, the spot would have moved around five hundred miles to the west, depending on how close one was to the equator. The 3D manifestation of that electromagnetic field in her viewfinder looked like gray, formless blocks, which was what she expected Minsk to look like: blocky Soviet buildings, all the same color, with a grayish-blue filter haze casting a pall upon the joyless Belorusian masses as they moved robotically from work to home and back again.

What she saw when she opened her eyes was a modern European city, the weather cool and brisk, the sky bright and blue, the reds and yellows of the trees reflecting the afternoon sun. The streets were clean, a little *too* clean, and the one they had landed on was lined with cafés at which people read newspapers in their autumn jackets. This portion of the city looked like Berlin, if Berlin had hammers and sickles everywhere.

Right after they'd left Macallan's office and gotten their briefing, Cora ran to CVS, got the cheapest black hair dye she could find, and hastily dyed her hair in her dorm's bathroom before collecting Sol to depart. Despite this, she still felt like she was sticking out, as she assumed Minsk didn't get a lot of Western tourists. The city was still adorned with the remnants of the Soviet Union, but alongside those were also the trappings of Western capitalism. Here was a large stone edifice of Soviet workers marching forth at least two stories high, under which stood a KFC.

"Let's figure out our cover," said Sol, surprising her by looping his arm through hers.

She shook off her surprise, and they continued to walk down this lovely street dotted with cafés like an elderly couple out for a stroll. "Our cover?"

"You speak Spanish, right?"

"Badly."

"Good enough. You're my wife."

She started and looked at him. "I'm your what?"

"We're a newlywed couple from Spain, and you're my uncomfortably young bride."

"Why do I have to be your bride?"

"What other believable reason would the two of us have to be alone together in Minsk?"

She shuddered. "Maybe we're brother and sister."

"I am twenty years older than you, and we look *nothing* alike."

"Maybe I'm your daughter, then?"

"See above likeness problem."

"Business . . . associates?"

Sol laughed. "Please, that only means one thing in Eastern Europe. 'Business associates.' Wink wink, nudge nudge, say no more." He pulled out a little tin flask and took a sip from it. "When in Minsk, *nazdarovye!*"

They rounded a corner, and she stopped at the sight of a group of teenagers dancing a dance that looked an awful lot like the Vengadance, in front of a bus that looked an awful lot like the Vengabus, in front of a large marble bust that looked an awful lot like Lenin. She caught Sol smiling at her condescendingly. "What were you expecting?"

Cora shrugged. Any former Soviet country elicited a certain mental image, but informational tidbits like "military dictatorship" and "still uses the moniker KGB" even more so. "I guess something a little more, I don't know, totalitarian."

"What do you think totalitarian states look like? People don't stop living their lives."

"Kaveh worried that's going to be us someday," she mused. He had told her more or less the same thing about Iran. The regime was brutal, there was no freedom of speech or movement, assassinations were routine, and people went about their lives. They still laughed and partied and tried to make the best of living to see another day. "The way Julian is pumping all this money into the military, and if the Third Party wins all those Congress seats that are up for grabs next year . . . A military dictatorship, but one with the most powerful military in human history."

"Funny you're so concerned with *our* power, but I never see you interrogate yours."

"*Mine?*"

Sol nodded his head toward the Vengabus, and Cora saw the abstract mural painted in bold, bright reds, blues, and blacks on the side of the building behind the Vengabus.

Of her.

More specifically, the Pulitzer-winning photo of her throwing her body between the inert forms of Ampersand and Nikola and the gunman pointing at all three of them called *Human Shield*. It wasn't the first artistic rendering she'd seen of the photograph—really, they were all over the place—but she'd never seen one in real life before, let alone so big.

"You've got a bigger presence on this block than Lenin."

"What's that supposed to mean?"

Sol shrugged. "What is that if not power? You have but to reach out and take it."

She looked again at the kids in front of the mural, finishing up their dance and gesturing to the hats in front of them they had set out for change; the presence of the mural did not seem to play into their act, but at the same time, if it was there, someone felt strongly enough that it should be. "Are you saying I should?"

"Only that you could, *amorcita*," said Sol, wrapping a firm arm around her shoulder. "Only that you could."

· · · · ·

The Chiksulub Institute, according to Sol, was a KGB front purporting to be a privately run research institution funded by pharmaceutical companies and academics. It was in a central area in Minsk with a fairly active nightlife, where institute employees were likely to drown their woes. He wanted to see if he could gain any intel from these woe-drowners before marching into the institute blind, so he picked a bar nearby to hole up in.

As they sat down, the only word she understood from Sol as he spoke to the bartender was *"wood-keh."* As her software could not figure out human language algorithmically like Ampersand's could, and she had not thought to ask Ampersand to program her ocular overlay with Russian and/or Belorusian, that remained just about the only word she understood. He chatted up the bartender in halting Russian tinged with a Spanish accent, his demeanor changed to the point where she felt like she was looking at a completely different person. Equally surprising was the bartender, who was very friendly, and immediately introduced Sol and Cora (well, Javi and Isabel) to several of the other bar patrons, who were equally friendly and interested to meet him. They especially seemed charmed that he spoke Russian. Sol gestured to Cora and said something that she assumed was, "She doesn't speak Russian, but isn't she cute?"

"*¿No te diviertes, amorcita?*" he said to her, wrapping his arm around her waist. Then leaning in so close to her ear he was practically kissing it, he whispered, "My young bride should at least *pretend* to enjoy my company."

"Your young bride is considering that maybe she made a huge mistake marrying someone so *old.*"

Sol got a look on his face that made her stomach sour, that said, *If you don't play along, I'll make you.* Then without warning or preamble, he kissed her, *hard,* and she had to stop herself from pushing him away. He broke the kiss and looked at her smugly, the bartender and patrons laughing riotously at the display of spicy Spanish marital drama. "*Las cosas que hacemos por amor,*" he said with a chuckle.

The things we do for love? She refrained from smacking him long enough to ask, "*Por amor?*"

He leaned in again to whisper in her ear, uncomfortably close, painfully close, and said, "Your girlfriend?"

Right. She had to keep sight on *why* she was even here. She *had* to endure his bullshit. Sol's behavior seemed to charm the bartender and his three patrons, who laughed like they were all sharing an in-joke. Sol smiled at her in a way that made her stomach sink further, a look of affection. Not genuine, she knew, as he was deep in the Method, but she'd never seen it on him before, never even imagined him capable of it. He brushed his thumb across her cheek and then handed her a shot of vodka. "*Nazdarovye!*"

"*Nazdarovye!*" echoed the barflies, and they all took a shot.

Cora braced herself and took the shot, only to find it tasted like water. It *was* water. She looked at Sol, who smiled at her knowingly. He must have replaced it at some point, though how, she did not know. However he did it, it was some impressive sleight of hand.

This went on for about three hours, the bar filling up and everyone else (including the bartender) continuing to down shots of vodka, while Isabel and Javi continued to down shots of water. As everyone got drunker, Sol pretended to get drunker, and Cora followed suit, worrying with every touch, each more intimate than the last, that he was going to do something really inappropriate under the guise of "being drunk." Maybe it would give her the opportunity to slap him. It would be appropriately *picante* for whatever "cover" he was going for.

There was a part of her that was disappointed. Of course if she was here with him, in public, the idea that they were a couple was the most convincing and least suspicious to any KGB agents, but he was also taking advantage of the situation under the guise of "*What? We have to act the part!*" Now he was just one more person she had to defend herself from, both emotionally and physically.

And here they were, alone together in what was effectively still the Soviet Union.

"*Nazdarovye!*"

Smooch!

This was going to be a long night.

"I'm not sure how well my skills will serve us here," Cora whispered. Getting into the building had been easy enough, as there had been some open windows on an upper floor, but as they got closer to where the pay dirt was purported to be, it got trickier.

"Well, maybe mine, then," said Sol, pulling something out of his pocket that at first she mistook for a nail clipper container—lockpicks. "Use your 'skills' to make sure there isn't any surveillance."

Large-scale electromagnetic surveillance was easy for her, but the kind that required feeling out small objects like cameras was tough. Even so, in the two-odd minutes it took Sol to unlock the door, she had sussed out no fewer than five security cameras.

"Are there any security guards between here and the lab?" asked Sol.

"No, but there are several cameras."

"Damn, and me without my infrared gun."

"What would that do?"

"Take out the cameras, but that carries its own set of risks because that's the first thing they look for when someone's breaking in."

"Get down!"

Cora whispered the order as soon as she saw the security guard on the other side of the glass, though she wasn't sure if they had moved quickly enough to avoid being spotted. Sol must have figured the same, as he nodded for her to follow him, and they speed-crawled while staying underneath the windows looking into the hallway, turning the corner *just* in time for the security guard to open the door and shine a light in their direction, barely missing them. He shined it around and then spoke into his walkie-talkie. He got a response on his walkie and retreated from whence he came, shutting the door behind him.

"Shit," whispered Sol.

"What'd he say?"

"That was Belorusian, so I didn't catch all of it, but I'm pretty sure he just asked whoever was on the other side of the line to check the security cameras."

"Shit." Cora felt around in her jacket pocket. "I always keep this on me," she said, pulling out her pulse emitter, "in case of Similars."

"In case of . . ." He looked at the pulse emitter like she'd pulled out a black market kidney, and shook his head. "What does it do?"

"It creates an electromagnetic pulse keyed to the energy signature of Similar power cores, but it also shorts out most man-made electronics."

"Most?"

"The really simple ones it doesn't, like old cars. But those security cameras, I'm guessing, are not from the Soviet era, and it will short them. Even on the lowest setting, it should take out everything in the building."

"But it won't take us out?"

"No, it doesn't have much effect on humans, except it might make you black out for a sec."

"Why didn't you tell me you had that before?"

"I'm only going to help you commit espionage under a very specific set of circumstances!"

"*Ooh, muy caliente!*" he said, and she swallowed. "It's a risk. We'll have to move quickly, but it'll draw less attention to this site specifically if it takes out power to the whole building before they can check the security camera footage."

"It'll probably take out the whole block."

"Even better. Hope we aren't next to a hospital."

Cora hesitated, wondering if there *was* a hospital nearby. The correct thing to do would be to, you know, check, but that would take time. *Ticktock, motherfucker.* She pressed the button on the pulse emitter, and as far as times she'd seen EMPs deployed, it was certainly the least dramatic. The hum of the heater fell into silence, some lights on the street went out, and the security cameras, innocently moving back and forth, stopped.

"Well, that worked," said Sol.

They kept their heads low as they ran down the hallway, and once again, Sol had to break out the lockpicks, only this time (having now gotten acquainted with this type of lock), it took him less than a minute. They entered the lab, and he whipped out a flashlight, but not of the conventional variety; it didn't seem to be emitting any light.

"What kind of flashlight is that?" she asked. "Infrared?"

"No, UV—whoa."

Cora looked at what he was whoa-ing about and saw that there was something under a glass that glowed brightly within the UV light. These were plants with black leaves, frozen in what looked like clear resin, that positively luminesced.

"What is this?" asked Sol. "It looks like they've been charred."

They looked like cheese burned to blackness when left on a pan for too long, but they were too intact to be something that had actually burned. "I think they're plants."

"Burned plants?"

"No. I think they might be . . ."

"Alien plants?"

"Yeah, I think they might be alien plants."

"Why are they black?" asked Sol, taking out the flask he'd been sipping from earlier, or apparently pretending to sip from, as he removed a center panel, revealing a lens—not a flask but a camera.

"It has to do with the color of the sun these plants evolved on. Part of the reason why amygdaline eyes are so big relative to their bodies is because they evolved on a planet that didn't get anywhere near as much light as we do here on Earth. Their atmosphere also had *way* more CO_2 than Earth has. So they just had a much dimmer, redder planet."

"Red sun equals black plants," muttered Sol, eyes through the tiny viewfinder as he took pictures of the plant from every angle. "Have you seen plants like this?"

"Not these exactly, but I've seen images of the kind of plants that grew on their ancestral world. This is probably some genetically engineered descendant of a crop they evolved tens of thousands of years ago."

Sol located the file attached to the plant, then opened the file cabinet attached to the file, pulling out papers and taking pictures of them, one by one. "They'd better let me retire after this," he muttered.

"Does it say where they found it?" she asked.

"It's in the exclusion zone, rural eastern Belarus," said Sol, scanning the papers one at a time before putting them back.

"The exclusion zone?" she repeated. "Is that some Soviet thing?"

"Oh, it's some Soviet thing, all right," said Sol. "The *Chernobyl* exclusion zone."

"You mean, the radioactive part?"

"That's the one."

"Okay, let's go."

"We're not frolicking in the radioactive forest in the middle of the night."

"*Ticktock, Sol!*"

"Much as we at the agency like to have first dibs on discovery, I think you and I aren't going to be the best interpreters of whatever's out there, *comprende*?"

Her shoulders fell. "I guess so."

"Tell *nuestro amigo* the coordinates, but ask him to *please* give us any intelligence that we don't already have."

"Right." Of course Ampersand should know before anyone else. "But you and I can go tomorrow."

"Yes, I definitely plan on going for reconnaissance, but that's it."

She nodded nervously. "Okay."

"But we go in the morning, hard enough doing reconnaissance in the dead of night. I need to file a report, anyway."

"Okay."

"Let's go find a hotel room."

Her stomach sank further. *A* hotel room. Singular. "Right."

· · · · ·

The city center was a fairly nice part of town, yet somehow the "hotel" Sol picked was little more than a glorified hostel. "Agency budget isn't what it used to be," he said. He had Belorusian rubles on him, which the old man at the desk accepted before leading them to their room. It was about the size of her college dorm and likewise only had one bed.

"Why'd you get the one with one bed?"

"It's all they have at this place."

Sol took off his jacket like she wasn't there as she looked at the bed, which wasn't even a queen. He took off his outer clothes and went into the bathroom, and she continued standing there uncomfortably looking into the bag she'd brought while he brushed his teeth. She'd been instructed to travel extremely light, only things that would fit in her government-issued "purse," meaning the pajamas she'd brought were quite sheer. Maybe she could sleep on the floor. Maybe she could sleep in the tub. Maybe she could grow a spine and draw some boundaries, and then he would laugh at her that she would even consider such a thing. Maybe he could stop being such an asshole and reassure her that nothing was going to happen. He took his sweet time, so she hastily changed into her pajamas and got into bed, just in time for Sol to emerge from the bathroom wearing nothing but a tank top and boxer briefs.

"What?"

She just stared at him. *What do you mean, what?*

"You're not the first contractor I've shared a hotel room with," he said. "I've got to file my report."

He took a seat at the little desk that faced the window not three feet away from the bed. *I should sleep in the tub*, she thought, pulling back the bedsheet and lying down. She told herself that she stuck with the bed because there didn't seem to be any other blanket options in the room and the tub would be freezing, but really, it was the thought of him ridiculing her that stopped her. *What is wrong with you?* he would laugh. *You are the last person on Earth I'd have that kind of interest in, even though I sure did enjoy performatively putting my hands all over you tonight!*

Eventually, he turned off the light and slid into the opposite side of the bed. She could feel the heat of his body, his skin on hers, and she shifted uncomfortably. He lay on his back, so he wasn't spooning her, but the bed was too small for them to both be on it and not be touching. So this was how it was going to be.

"*Buenos noches*," he whispered coyly. "*Amorcita.*"

· 33 ·

The thunder started around sunset, and the rain had been going at a horrifying clip ever since. For a little while, Paris tried to dig a divot for the water to divert into so her hole wouldn't turn into a swimming pool, but it didn't take long for that plan to fail. She was doomed to the squalor of the sewage of her own making. At least it made the mosquitoes take the night off.

"Send all the things from ashore / Let all the breezes blow / I'm so sorry that I can no longer stay . . ."

She had known the song as "The John B. Sails," and her father had sometimes played it on the guitar. One meager silver lining—he wasn't alive to see her go missing-presumed-dead, especially after he was the one who'd supported her going into journalism at one of the most expensive schools in the country instead of medicine, like all the other good children of immigrants. Only Renée, and soon she'd be the only one of her immediate family left alive.

"Let me go home / Let me go home / I feel so break-up / I want to go home."

She looked up toward a sky she couldn't see. "Nikola, can you hear me?"

"YES, DEAR GENTLE CREATURE."

"Can I ask you a question?" she asked, sliding down onto her haunches. The mud was by now up to her ankles.

"YOU MAY ASK ME ANYTHING. I DO NOT THINK YOU HAVE LONG TO LIVE, REGARDLESS."

Paris swallowed a hard lump in her throat. "Why did you save me?"

"I HAD HOPED TO RELAY TO OTHERS WHAT HAD HAPPENED ON THE AIRPLANE AND WHERE I HAD GONE, AS I KNEW THERE WAS LITTLE LIKELIHOOD OF MY OWN ESCAPE. I DID NOT ANTICIPATE THAT THESE TRANSIENTS WOULD CONSIDER YOU WORTHY OF CAPTURE."

Paris rose to sit on her knees, leaving her shins submerged and giving her another few inches before she'd be up to her lap in water. This was the first time in her life that she was actually glad to be experiencing travel constipation; at least she wasn't about to be submerged in fecal matter. "Can you tell me what they want with you?"

"I SUSPECT IT'S BECAUSE I POSSESS A METHOD OF TRANSPORT BOTH UNIQUE AND VALUABLE, AND THEY CANNOT EXTRACT IT FROM ME IF I AM DEAD."

"And you're letting them take you alive."

"I INTEND TO DIE ON MY TERMS, NOT THEIRS."

She looked up just in time to see a pair of yellow eyes disappear over the lip of the hole, and she shot to her feet. "Hey!" she whispered in a high-pitched voice. "Please help me!"

The owner of the eyes reappeared shyly. It was a juvenile, although it was too dark to tell which one. Paris reached her arms out pitifully to the juvenile, a hopefully transparent plea for help.

"Weird, this one doesn't have any veins on their face."

"THE TRACING OF THE VEINS UNDER THEIR SKIN IS COSMETIC. THE RAIN WILL HAVE WASHED IT AWAY."

Paris couldn't help but smile. "Even alien teenagers experiment with eyeliner." The juvenile said something and disappeared. Paris dropped her hands to her hips and slid back down to her knees into the ever-deepening water. "What did they say?"

"PHYSETERINES HAVE A COMMON LANGUAGE, PHYSETERINE-COMMON, BUT INFORMALLY, THIS POD SPEAKS IN ITS OWN DIALECT. THE JUVENILE USED THEIR COLLOQUIAL SEMIPALATINSK-CREOLE TERM FOR *HUMAN*. PERHAPS *SIREN* IS AN APPROXIMATE TRANSLATION OF THEIR VERNACULAR TERM FOR *HUMAN*."

"Siren, as in, Greek Sirens?"

"CORRECT, AS IN A MONSTER WITH A BEAUTIFUL VOICE THAT USES THAT VOICE TO LURE PEOPLE TO THEIR DEATHS. THEY CONSIDER HUMANS PHYSICALLY REPULSIVE BUT YOUR VOICES BEAUTIFUL. THEIR NARRATIVE FOLLOWS THAT ANY TIME ONE OF THEM HAS

HEARD THE BEAUTY OF THE HUMAN VOICE AND FOLLOWED IT, THE MONSTER POSSESSING THAT VOICE TRIED TO KILL THEM AND OFTEN SUCCEEDED."

"That's so sad," Paris whispered, fat raindrops falling on her face as she watched for movement up on the ground. "Why are the kids doing all this behind the adults' backs?"

"I CAN ONLY SPECULATE, BUT I BELIEVE YOUR BEHAVIOR IS CONTRADICTING THE NARRATIVE THE ADULTS HAVE BEEN GIVING THEM."

"How so?"

"IMAGINE YOU ARE BORN ON AN ALIEN WORLD YOU WILL EVENTUALLY HAVE TO LEAVE. YOU CANNOT HELP BUT SEE THIS WORLD AS YOUR HOME, YET YOU ARE TOLD YOUR WHOLE LIFE THAT IT IS NOT, BECAUSE THE NATIVES ARE EVERYWHERE, AND THE NATIVES ARE MONSTERS. SOON, THIS WORLD WILL BE UNUSABLE BECAUSE OF THE NATIVES' HUNGER. YOU WOULD HAVE TO WONDER THEN—WHY LET THESE MONSTERS KEEP THIS WORLD?

"BUT THEN YOU LEARN THAT THE SIRENS ARE NOT THE ONLY MONSTERS OUT THERE, THAT EVEN IF YOU DID EXTERMINATE THE NATIVES OF EARTH, THE WORSE MONSTERS WILL FIND YOU EVENTUALLY, AND WHEN THEY DO, THEY WILL RENDER THE EARTH UNUSABLE MORE COMPLETELY THAN THE SIRENS EVER COULD. THEY HAVE DONE IT BEFORE. THEY COULD DO IT AGAIN. NO, DEAR LITTLE ONES, WE CANNOT WREST THIS PLANET FROM THE NATIVES. IF WE TAKE EARTH NOW, THE SUPERORGANISM WILL STERILIZE IT LATER.

"BUT NOW YOU HAVE LEARNED THAT YOUR AMYGDALINE COUSINS ARE ALREADY HERE, AND WORSE, THEY APPEAR TO BE IN LEAGUE WITH THE NATIVES. IT WAS ONE THING TO CONCEIVE OF THESE TWO NEBULOUS EVILS AS DISTINCT AND SEPARATE, BUT TOGETHER? THIS CHANGES EVERYTHING.

"AND NOW YOUR POD HAS ONE OF THE NATIVE SIRENS CAPTIVE. YOU ANTICIPATED A WILD, SLAVERING BEAST, BUT SHE IS CURIOUS AND COOPERATIVE, POSSIBLY EVEN COMPASSIONATE. STRANGER STILL, SHE HAS SAVED THE LIFE OF YOUR MENTOR, WHO WOULD HAVE DIED IF NOT FOR HER QUICK THINKING. AND YOU ARE OF AN AGE WHERE YOU CANNOT HELP BUT BEGIN TO QUESTION THE NARRATIVES THAT HAVE DOMINATED YOUR LIFE.

"AND SO WE COME TO OUR LITTLE REBELLION—THEY SEE YOU AS

AN OPPORTUNITY TO LEARN THE TRUTH THAT HAS BEEN DENIED TO THEM."

"Their ancestors have been to Earth before."

"YES, MANY TIMES."

"And they'd have had run-ins with earlier humans."

"YES."

"Then those historic humans must have thought they were demons. It must have been nothing but conflict every time there was even a passive interaction."

"THAT IS A REASONABLE ASSUMPTION."

"So now they won't even consider trying to communicate with us."

"CORRECT."

Paris looked up, and a raindrop beaned her right in the eye. "Is there no way to un-fuck this?"

"THEY BELIEVE THAT THE SUPERORGANISM IS GROOMING YOUR CIVILIZATION TO ACT AS THEIR WEAPON WITH THE KNOWLEDGE AND UNDERSTANDING OF YOUR POTENTIAL FOR GREAT HARM. THIS POD ALREADY HAS SEVERAL CONTINGENCIES IN PLACE TO INCAPACITATE HUMAN CIVILIZATION, OR ERADICATE IT ALTOGETHER, SHOULD THE NEED ARISE."

"Like what?"

"MOST OF THEM ARE BIOLOGICAL IN NATURE. MASS CROP FAILURE IS ONE. FLESH-EATING BACTERIA ANOTHER. THEY'VE DEVELOPED SEVERAL DISEASES. THIS METHOD THEY VIEW TO BE MOST EFFICIENT."

"Do they have any plans to deploy one of these?"

"I DO NOT KNOW."

An adult landed with a soft *thunk* in the mud directly in front of her, and she shrieked in surprise, covering her head like she expected an avalanche to come down on her. She then felt the strange sensation of the tentacle-plant thing sliding around her wrist like a hand before locking in place, and then the adult nonchalantly picked her up, and before she knew it, she was out of the hole, being carried.

"What's happening?"

"IT WOULD APPEAR THE JUVENILE HAS PETITIONED FOR YOU TO BE MOVED."

Once on the other side of the "entrance," she realized it wasn't a copse at all, or at least not in the traditional sense. It was shaded, but hidden by some sort of hologram like the entrance to the other settlements. This area, however, was not airtight, air from the outside flowing into it freely. There was some sort of filter over the roof propped up by poles like it was a big invisibility cloak tent. It was covered with a material that looked like the black fabric of an old screen door, and under that material were crops. Rows and rows of crops, but not like any plants she had ever seen. The soil beneath her feet was more like sand than the rich sod of a rainforest, and the crops themselves weren't green but black.

This must be some sort of greenhouse.

Once inside the greenhouse, the adult put her on her feet, and the juvenile led her by her bound hands. Given that it was the middle of the night (what she assumed was the middle of their workday), there were dozens of them scattered throughout. The two took her to a corner of the greenhouse that appeared far more active. Over here was a new feature, what looked like daisy petals the size of Hula-Hoops pulled taut and emanating a soft glow. On closer inspection, Paris saw that they were displaying images, like televisions.

"THE ADULT IS USING THIS AS A LEARNING OPPORTUNITY FOR THE JUVENILE TO PRACTICE FORMS OF CONTROLLED PLANT GROWTH."

The adult stood back and watched as the juvenile placed their hands over a spot a couple of feet away from the corner, the tips of their fingers glowing almost like cheap fiber optics. Then something flowered out of the dirt, and Paris figured this was how those alive-feeling floors were formed, not built but grown. It looked something like the cap of a flat mushroom, but forced out like it was a pool of oil being pumped from below. As the floor spread out millimeter by millimeter, the juvenile planted some strange bulbs that looked like little nuclear bombs around its edges. They then pushed Paris on to the freshly grown flooring, which in its fresh state felt like something between cork and silicone. She turned to face the juvenile, but gasped when she saw little black tendrils curling up in front of her like grapevines crawling along an invisible pole. The few bulbs the juvenile had planted in the dirt sprouted, forming thicker tendrils that rose in front of her until they met with the ones growing from out of the wall, grasping them like hands and then growing along one another, until they had formed a sort of cord. Once they had created what was obviously a cage, Paris carefully touched the "bars." It was taut, like thick, massive violin strings tuned just a bit too tightly. Even now in its early growth phase, it felt more like metal than the bark of a tree.

"THE ADULT CONGRATULATES THEM ON A JOB WELL DONE AND INSTRUCTS THE JUVENILE TO LEAVE THEM TO THEIR WORK."

The adult turned from the newly grown cage and went to join two others near those giant glowing screens. Paris squinted to look at them and could make out that the screens displayed images or perhaps video of some sort. The juvenile cast a quick glance at the adult, reached into their suit, and slid a water pouch through the "bars" of her cage before slinking away.

Paris hid the pouch in what was left of her own overshirt and crawled up to the sides of her birdcage, fingers poking through as she tried to see what was on those screens that had the adults fascinated. The images looked like surveillance of other greenhouses, or at least former greenhouses that appeared to be abandoned. The angle of the sun was different in each one, as was the climate; perhaps these were live feeds.

There was some growing hubbub over one of the screens; she tried to peek through her vine-bars, and blocked though her view was, she could get enough of a glimpse to see what had interested them—there were humans in one of their abandoned greenhouses.

This must have been no big deal, or no rare occurrence, as the adults seemed interested but not terribly upset. They examined the feed, discussed it for a bit, then after a few minutes went about their business. The botanists stayed inside the greenhouse, and the rest departed. Paris strained to look at the two human figures in the feed, and suppressed a gasp. The man she didn't recognize, but she did recognize Cora.

34

Sol had kept his satellite phone conversation short and low on details, lest any Russo-ears might be eavesdropping. He gave Macallan the co-ordinates and put his phone away to survey this find, and it was an *incredible* find.

Probably.

"Well, whatever was here," said Sol, "the Belorusians have pretty well cleaned it out."

46 had come and gone during the night and, according to Sabino, told them all there was to know—this had been a greenhouse the Semi-palatinsk pod had used to grow resources that had been abandoned about two years ago, not long after those security photos were taken. The Belorusians had turned it inside out before abandoning it with a several-kilometer-radius electrified barbed wire fence (easy enough to get around if you could fly).

"Weird that they didn't leave anything," said Sol. "There's no evidence of those black plants."

"These plants would need special conditions to grow here," said Cora. "Filters to keep out some of the light—it's easy to subtract light where there's too much; it's hard to add light when there isn't enough."

"So they cover their greenhouses with . . . plant sunglasses." Sol looked at her. "I take it *nuestro hombre* didn't find anything useful?"

"Nothing that gives us any clues about where Nikola and Paris might be."

He took a seat on a log, one that must have bordered the greenhouse before they packed up. "This isn't a waste. This is incredible intelligence."

She sat down next to him. "I know."

Some shriveled, weak voice in the back of his brain that some might call a conscience said that he should show some sympathy, but his over-riding emotion was irritation that she was wasting both of their time when she *could* be using her alien panopticon for all sorts of cool (and more importantly, useful) shit.

"I know what you're thinking," she said curtly. "She's dead."

"That . . . is the likeliest scenario, yeah."

"But I've seen enough things that are improbable to the point of im-possible that I don't see why I should accept it just yet."

"What do you mean, you don't see the point?"

"I mean, I have nothing to lose by trying to find her."

Time, he thought. *You are wasting your time when you could be al-locating your hopes and prayers to a cause that isn't completely hopeless.* "It's only going to make it harder to accept in the long run."

"That doesn't make any fucking sense, Sol. Do you think it's going to be any less traumatic to me if we find her dead at the end of all of this, rather than if I just accept it now? Yes, I understand, by any meaningful statistic, she is dead. But we've never seen a plane crash caused by aliens before, either."

"That we know of," added Sol in a playful tone that she clearly didn't appreciate.

"*I've* been kidnapped by aliens. *I've* been kept alive because I was useful."

"I'm guessing you're referring to Ampersand: Mark 1." He'd suspected as much, but that's not exactly something you can interrogate without just cause (at least within U.S. borders). "You never told us that."

"Because my agreement with Ampersand was to try to make him appear as unthreatening to you as possible. You were always going to assume the worst, and what he did to me was my business."

"Then why are you still . . . you know . . . ?" He limply gestured in the direction of Japan.

"What?"

"Why are you still *working* for him? Why did you ever agree to work for him after your initial . . . whatever gentlemen's agreement you had?"

"Because I forgive him."

Sol arched a confused eyebrow. "Did he deserve forgiveness?"

She looked at him, weirdly furious. "That's not how forgiveness works! 'Deserve.' Do you even know how to human? Forgiveness isn't meted out by who deserves it or not."

"Ah, right. I forget you people do things differently."

"He understands what he did to me was wrong. I *choose* to forgive him. That's all there is to it."

"Hey, calm down. I didn't mean anything by it."

"Just because you waste your life holding eternal grudges doesn't mean everyone else does."

He blew a stream of air between his lips. Easy as it was to push her buttons, it was time to de-escalate. "Are you two in some . . . disagreement as to how to proceed?"

"It's just . . . he's making a lot of assumptions based on physeterine behavior. He's convinced that the physeterines couldn't have colluded with Nikola—or kidnapped him, for that matter—because he thinks they would only ever kill a Similar given the chance. And obviously he knows more about their behavior than we do, but he's been wrong before. He doesn't know what they're about, he doesn't know anything about their culture, and he doesn't know if there is something they might want with Nikola. And I've seen Nikola make deals with the devil before, too. He might have helped them plan this."

She slumped over, burying her head in her hands. "I should *hope* that Nikola escaped and has her as his prisoner. If my theory is correct and the physeterines kidnapped Nikola, or colluded with him, she's probably dead. Nikola might keep her alive for his own Svengali reasons . . . but why would physeterines?"

Sol bumped her shoulder with his. "Well, maybe now you're being narrow-minded."

She smiled a joyless smile.

He shook his head and nearly placed his hand on hers before thinking better of it. He may as well keep playing along, he figured. Maybe her motives were a big waste of time, but motives didn't matter if they turned up something useful.

"These two species are . . . related," said Sol. "Distantly. They're 'sisters,' but really they hardly know each other at all. So you're right. We don't know. And this might be a road to nowhere, but any intelligence is better than zero. Unless Nikola or the physeterines or whatever . . . skydiving Colombian drug cartel plucked her out of the sky just decide to let her go."

She laughed quietly, then her expression grew sad again. "Have you ever . . . seen someone who'd gone missing come back alive?"

"Yeah," he answered honestly. "Yeah, I have." He strapped on his satchel, whipping out a Geiger counter and turning it on.

"Are those standard issue?" she asked.

"No, I bought it this morning while you were asleep," he said. "Half the country is radioactive; they're pretty easy to get."

"What for?"

He rose to his feet. "I heard some interesting rumors at the bar last night. Disappearances out here in the exclusion zone. Of course, that's just any given Tuesday in Belarus, but it might also be worth checking out."

Sol had marked some spots on the map he wanted to investigate based not just on rumors from the barflies but also info he'd gotten back from the office once they'd had a chance to look at the photos he'd sent them.

"Can you carry this in your bag?" he asked, handing her a bottle of vodka. His satchel was already pretty heavy, and he wasn't about to go porting three bottles of vodka around all day.

"Is this water?" she asked.

"No," he snorted. "It's vodka."

"What's it for?"

"Bribery."

. . . . .

They walked along a dirt road for hours, deeper and deeper into the exclusion zone, and every so often passed a biohazard sign warning of radioactivity. The houses out here were all long abandoned and for the most part spaced fairly far apart, each one on an acre or two of subsistence farmland. These were a different kind of time capsule— farmhouses that had been built with little or no help from the state.

The first few they explored were long gutted, the furniture either sto- len, decomposed, or even scrawled with graffiti, and the wood floors so rotten they weren't safe to stand on. But a few hours later, they found a house that wasn't quite so decrepit as the others, one that still had that postapocalyptic vibe but hadn't yet rotted to the point of near collapse. This one hadn't been looted like the earlier houses, either, and even still contained some ephemera that must have belonged to the family who had lived here.

"Interesting," said Sol, holding up a little egg-shaped, long-dead plastic toy he found on a table.

"A Tamagotchi," said Cora bemusedly. "You think it's possible someone came back after the fact and left it here?"

"Extremely unlikely."

"So that means that this house was abandoned . . . sometime after Tamagotchi became a thing. Sometime after the late nineties."

"Maybe even later," said Sol. "I imagine it probably took time for Tamagotchi to make it all the way out here."

"And it hasn't been looted. So this house was abandoned less than ten years ago." She took the Tamagotchi from him and examined it.

"It's certainly possible it's an alien-related government-mandated evacuation," said Sol. "Anyone who'd been booted because of the radiation would have been long evacuated by the time Mr. Tamagotchi got here."

As the sun approached its zenith, they came upon more signs of civilization, only this time not abandoned. There was one empty farm on one side of a dirt road, across from which was a shack with a couple of goats baaing placidly in the cold autumn breeze. An elderly woman with a red kerchief over her hair came outside to tend to the goats, spotted them, and bellowed out what Cora assumed to be a hearty, "Good morning!" Sol responded in kind, and the two had a brief back-and-forth, the old woman treating him like he was some nephew who didn't visit as often as he should.

"What's she saying?"

"Well, her Russian is about as good as my Spanish."

"What language does she speak?"

"Belorusian," he said, gesturing to the trees like they were eavesdropping the two of them. "We are in Belarus."

The old woman spoke slowly, biting each word in large chunks and speaking with her hands. Sol regarded her with incredible fondness, calling her *babushka* and talking with his hands in turn. He pointed at the bottle of vodka and said something to her in clearly enunciated Russian. "*Oh!*" she said, and gestured for them to follow her.

The inside of the shack couldn't have been more than five hundred square feet, the kitchen barely the size of a large walk-in closet. The babushka bade them take a seat at her tiny kitchen table, all the while gleefully professing gratitude at the gift of vodka.

"Am I still your nouveau riche barely legal bride from Madrid?"

"Oh yeah, you are, but we're Canadian now, so we can speak English."

"So, Ottawa barely legal bride."

"Calgary, and yep."

The babushka took out three glasses and put one in front of each of them, keeping one for herself. Sol moved to pour the vodka, but the babushka stopped him, went to the small refrigerator, and started digging things out. Bread, yogurt, cheese. *Ah, grandmas*, she thought. *The world over, they are all the same.*

"*Yest,*" said the babushka, putting her fingers to her lips, gesturing the international grandma instruction—*Mangia! Befarmain! Yest! Eat!*

"Would be rude not to do as she says," said Sol.

Hoping the . . . flora of this yogurt wouldn't upset her stomach, she accepted it as well as the bread and cheese. Then she sipped the vodka, surprised to find that it was actually vodka this time.

"What's she saying?" asked Cora.

"She's explaining the living situation, why they're allowed to stay but the people across the street had to leave," he said. "'On this side of the street, they are forced to leave. On our side, they leave us alone. You want to tell me that that side of the street is radioactive, and this street is fine? It doesn't make any sense, but they didn't force us to leave.'"

Sol and the babushka continued speaking in simple, widely gestured Russian, while every couple of minutes or so the babushka told Cora to *yest*. Then a man stepped in through the kitchen door. Sol stood to meet him, bowed, and the two shook hands. "Boris," said the man, putting his hand on his chest. Cora rose to her feet, and he did not shake her hand but instead pulled her in and kissed her on both cheeks.

Sol laughed, wrapped his arm around her shoulder, and kept it there. She figured now that there was another *man* around, it was Belorusian de rigueur to get all grabby again, just so it was clear who belonged to whom. Then he took a seat. Boris actually seemed to speak fluent-ish Russian.

"That second bottle of vodka," said Sol. "Time to whip that out."

Cora did as he said, apparently gaining Boris's favor, because he cracked it open, and after a couple of drinks, he also got grabby. Sol said something about Cora, wrapping his arm around her waist, and then Boris laughed, petting her on the shoulder and even once on the cheek. And then Babushka did the same thing.

I'm undercover, she reminded herself. *This is a CIA thing. Deal. Deal. Deal. Apparently, Belarus is a nation of touchers.* But at the same time, even if he was rationalizing it as some "cover" thing, it didn't need to be like this. Why couldn't his cover be a jealous husband who allowed no other man to lay hands on her? The wall with Ampersand felt thick at the moment, so he wouldn't know about her discomfort unless he thought to check, which, why would he? He was busy. No, she was on her own with Solomon in the nation of touchers.

This went on for what felt like hours, and after a while, they went outside, and Boris showed him their property. He told them all about how they watched their little community slowly die. The original evacuation in the late '80s had taken a huge chunk of it, and many more happened organically as they left to find better opportunities elsewhere. They were mostly subsistence farmers out here, but they did need to engage in some commerce to survive. Boris raised pigs and goats, selling the pigs for slaughter every year and the goats for milk, cheese, and yogurt. It was a tiny operation, and they couldn't even say it kept the lights on, as blackouts happened out here all the time.

"I asked when the people up the street had to move," Sol told her, "since the house looks newly abandoned. He says they left two years ago. I asked if it was because of radiation, he said the government said it was, but he knows that's not true."

"What do they think it was?"

Boris said something in a suddenly serious tone.

"He says they saw things, too, more recently than that," said Sol, asking him a question in Russian. "I asked, why didn't you inform the government?"

Boris responded, using big caricature-esque gestures with his hands as he spoke, and Sol translated: "After what happened to their neighbors, they were careful not to tell. No one in the community has said anything. When the government relocates, they don't give anything, they just tell you to leave and give you a few hundred rubles."

Sol responded in Russian, then said, "I asked if they know what's happened with the ETIs."

Boris caught the word *ETIs* and got excited. He translated to Babushka in Belarusian, and she got even more excited.

"They said they always knew it was aliens. The government didn't evict their neighbors because of newly discovered radioactivity but because their neighbors saw things. They saw monsters. They're very religious, and they thought they were demons. But they—Boris's family—knew better."

Boris and Babushka gestured to each other assuredly, that yes, indeed, they knew better. Sol asked a question, then said, "I asked if they could show us what they saw."

Boris shook his head emphatically as he responded to Sol.

"He says no, they don't go out there. It's too dangerous. Especially now that they heard what happened in the Philippines. I asked if they could tell us where it is."

Boris looked at Cora and shook his head, his red cheeks burning brightly as he smiled at her and patted her on the cheek.

"He says he's worried for you," said Sol. He and Boris negotiated for a moment, and then Sol translated, "He says he's happy to let me know where it is, if you stay here, where it's safe."

She didn't want to make a noise of incredulous horror, nor did she want to wear an expression of one, so she turned to Sol and said, "You wouldn't do that to me."

Sol smiled, shaking Boris's very drunk hand, intimating that yes, he absolutely would do that to her. Then they went outside, and Boris gave Sol directions. He nodded once the directions were complete, then stuck his index finger in the air, and Cora heard the word *wood-keh*. Boris clapped in delight. Oh, so he was going to get Boris even *drunker* before he left her alone with them. Great. She was going to have to call Ampersand for an extraction.

Sol poured Boris and Babushka another shot of vodka. Cora reached for hers mechanically, by this point *wanting* the vodka. "*Nazdarovye!*" said Sol, and they all took a shot.

"Okay, I'm going to get my coat," he said. When he came back a few seconds later, he looked at her. "Where's yours?"

"Where's my what?"

"Your coat? We're wasting daylight. Chop, chop."

Cora turned around and saw Boris now slumped over on the table, snoring into a piece of bread. Babushka, a little drunk herself, shook her head and laughed as she pointed at Boris.

"Poor Boris," said Sol, biting his lip mischievously. "Guess he just can't handle his liquor!"

Babushka did not press as Boris had, and so Sol took her by the hands and gave her many kisses on the cheek (and the last bottle of vodka) before he took his young "wife," and the two went on their merry way. Babushka didn't let Cora go as easily as that, giving her a cloth full of bread and cheese before she left (and no fewer than ten kisses per cheek). Then she waved them goodbye and shut the door behind her.

Without a word, Sol marched on in the direction Boris had pointed. Cora just stood there, staring. Eventually, he turned around, gesturing for her to follow.

"Oh, come on," he said, looking at her like she was the idiot. "I wouldn't do that to you."

35

Paris had been upgraded from hole in the ground to cage in a green-house, and it felt slightly, well, more civilized? But it was way, way hotter and had way more traffic, and given the fact that her nerves currently had the sensitivity of a hair trigger, every movement in the greenhouse, even the slightest rustle of leaves, caused her to jump, so sleeping at night was impossible.

Their movements weren't the abrasive thing; it was their language. Even spoken softly, it was just so hissy and clicky, and when they were being particularly loud it almost sounded like a human choking. It was one of these conversations that woke her up for at least the fifth time that night. The space itself was too small to stretch out properly, tall enough only for her to stand on her knees, about the size of a small love seat, so she had to stretch her body out in sections.

"You awake, Nik?" she said, rolling onto her back and giving her spine a twist.

"I HAVE NOT SLEPT, DEAR GENTLE CREATURE."

She rolled her legs to the other side. "They haven't taken my earpiece."

"I DON'T BELIEVE ANY OF THE ADULTS ARE AWARE THE JUVENILES HAVE RETURNED IT TO YOU, SO USE IT JUDICIOUSLY."

She tilted her head toward the screens that surveilled the other greenhouses. The one where she saw Cora and the other guy had been flooded with what she assumed to be CIA agents, but Cora was long gone. She sat back up and leaned against the wall of the greenhouse. Two of the botanists were looking at her, talking in their version of "hushed" tones. She could only imagine the speculation as they tried to figure out what it was they were looking at—*Is it sick? Is it dying? What, are we supposed to feed it every day?*

The two returned to their business, which looked like a miniaturized pile of autumn leaves stacked into almost a cylindrical shape. The stack took up almost the entirety of the botanists' work table, which looked to Paris like a mushroom-tree hybrid. The botanists observed the pile in front of them and then put on a set of gloves like the one the juvenile had used to create her cage of vines. They ran their fingers around the edge of the table, and then slowly, almost imperceptibly, more table grew.

Paris put her face up against the "bars" of her cage, straining to get a better look. Satisfied at their handiwork, the botanists began working through the pile of roughage before them, using the new table space to organize the pile, even as the table was still growing. It was like watching a high-speed camera capturing the growth of a mushroom.

"Nikola," she whispered, "correct me if I'm wrong, but it seems like almost everything I've seen of their living spaces is made from plants."

"Most of their tools come from organic life taxonomically similar to plants or fungi."

"Wow," she whispered as the table continued to expand. It had a white edge that glowed slightly, like the rim of a coral under black light. "Is that how they're able to move around so easily?"

"It is in part how they are able to remain transient. They likely have a large vessel capable of space travel somewhere on Earth, but they need it for the transport of their bodies, food, and little else."

Even as Nikola was explaining, gears turned in her head. They'd figured out how to grow pretty much everything they needed out of the ground like goddamn reptilian elves. These guys could probably cure world hunger in a weekend if they wanted to.

About an hour later, Durian came back, eager to toy with the human they had tamed, which was almost charming until one of the botanists popped up behind them, causing Paris to back away from the vines and into the wall. The adult practically loomed over her tiny prison, and she wondered if they really, honestly saw *her* as the monster in this scenario. The juveniles were on average a few inches shorter than she, owing to their forward-leaning birdlike stature, but the adults were the size of grizzlies.

The botanist, still wearing the gloves with the slightly blue glow at the fingertips, touched the vines of her cage, and they slowly parted to form a hole big enough for Paris to climb through.

"They've opened my cage. I think they want me to go with them."

"THAT IS WHAT THEY WANT, DEAR GENTLE CREATURE."

"Should I be worried?"

"YOU SHOULD ALWAYS BE WORRIED."

"Should I do what they *want*?" Goddamn, this fucking guy.

"FROM WHAT I CAN HEAR OF THEIR CONVERSATION, IT IS SIMPLY TO INDULGE CURIOSITY ABOUT YOU AND HOW YOU WILL REACT TO CERTAIN STIMULI."

"Stimuli?"

"CROPS THAT THEY HAVE DESIGNED. IF YOU INDULGE THEM, YOU MUST BE CAREFUL; IF THEY PERCEIVE THAT YOU ARE BEHAVING AGGRESSIVELY, THEY WILL NEUTRALIZE YOU."

Paris didn't even ask what he might mean by that. She squeezed out of the hole, and another lively discussion ensued between Durian and the botanist. Paris stayed absolutely rigid, but the botanist wrapped their massive claw around her forearms, and within seconds, the other, squishier form of vine had wrapped around her wrists. The juveniles, led by Durian, excitedly gestured for her to follow them.

"THE ADULT DOES NOT APPROVE OF YOU BEING UNLEASHED IN THEIR GREENHOUSE AND HAS ABDICATED RESPONSIBILITY FOR ANY DAMAGE YOU MIGHT CAUSE."

Unleashed. He may be algorithmically translating an unfathomable alien language, but he still had a way with words that was just shy of insulting. "Do they not have parents?"

"THEIR SYSTEM OF CHILD-REARING IS MUCH MORE COMMUNAL THAN IN MODERN HUMAN SOCIETIES. THE JUVENILES ADDRESS ALL ADULTS IN THE POD AS *PARENT*, EVEN THOSE WHO ELECTED NOT TO BREED DURING THIS GENERATION."

She followed Durian, who was flanked by their little squad while the adult brought up the rear. On the way, they passed several other botanists, each one stopping and inquiring an obvious, "What the hell?" before doing the alien equivalent of shaking their heads in resignation and going about their business. Durian led her into another large chamber, and Paris stopped dead. Just inside was a ledge that dropped into darkness, as though she were standing at the top of a maze. Its walls were almost like bookstacks, dozens of them, *hundreds of them*, only instead of shelves, there were cubbies like honeycombs, perfectly hexagonal and interlocking. She could scarcely see the majority of whatever was down there.

"What is all this?" Paris wondered aloud.

"FOOD STORAGE. THEY WILL NOT ONLY LIVE ON THIS STORE BUT WILL BARTER THIS WITH OTHER PHYSETERINE PODS WHO DON'T SPECIALIZE IN HORTICULTURE."

There were a few dozen adults in here and even a few juveniles processing harvests. She heard a chirp from behind her like a little toucan and then a tug at her arm. Durian beckoned her to another one of those mushroom tables piled with what looked to be alien produce.

"THE JUVENILE WANTS TO SEE HOW YOU REACT TO SOME OF THE FOODSTUFFS THEY HAVE DESIGNED."

"Designed?"

"ENGINEERED FROM TERRAN FRUITS THAT ARE THEMSELVES DOMESTICATED BY HUMANS."

Okay, so alien-ified Earth fruit. If she wasn't convinced she would never live to see another human being, this would actually be pretty cool.

Five juveniles surrounded the table, four of which kept a comfortable distance of a few feet as Durian picked up one of the fruits and placed it into her still-bound hands. It looked like a bright yellow plum the size of a grapefruit. Then one of the other juveniles picked up another of the same varietal, opened its mandibles, and took a big bite.

Paris couldn't help but stare, fascinated by the mechanics of their jaw. The closest comparison was probably a praying mantis, although these guys seemed to have the ability to unhinge their jaw equivalent if they wanted to. She figured that they probably saw something equally gross when they watched her eat, especially given how they were staring at her like she was a lion and they were paying customers on a safari.

Bon appétit, she thought, and plunged her teeth into the fruit. Texturally, it reminded her of a red bean paste she'd once tried in a Japanese market, and the fruit was almost as sweet. If this was a modified plum, it wasn't *just* a modified plum; it seemed to have some potato grafted into its DNA, and possibly also some legume. She didn't know or care if it was safe to eat, devouring the thing in less than a minute, while the kids presumably remarked on how disgusting she was.

"Why did they engineer this . . . fruit?" she whispered.

"THIS POD HARVESTS POTENTIAL CROPS FROM PLANETS THEY IN-HABIT, AND EARTH IS A PARTICULARLY RICH RESOURCE BECAUSE OF CROPS THAT HUMANS HAVE ALREADY DOMESTICATED."

"We've already done the work for them." Paris swallowed the last of the plumtato as another adult approached them. "We have company."

"THAT IS AN ANTHROPOLOGIST. IT IS THEIR JOB TO STUDY HUMAN BEHAVIOR."

A lively discussion erupted, the juveniles surrounding the anthropologist like they were Ms. Frizzle and Paris was the topic of this week's adventure on *The Magic School Bus*. "Can you give me a rundown of what they're saying?"

"THE JUVENILES EXPRESS SURPRISE AT HOW SMALL YOU ARE. THEY THOUGHT SIRENS WOULD BE BIGGER. THE ADULT EXPLAINS THAT YOU ARE FEMALE AND THAT FEMALES ARE SMALLER. THE JUVENILES WANT TO KNOW WHY HUMAN FEMALES HAVE BREASTS AND MALES DON'T."

The juveniles erupted into an excited noise like a flock of parrots.

"THE ADULT HAS EXPLAINED TO THEM HOW MAMMARY GLANDS WORK. THEY FIND IT BOTH DISGUSTING AND COMICAL."

Figures, thought Paris, unable to suppress a smile. In another life, they might fit right in with human tweens.

"THE ADULT IS NOW EXPLAINING HUMAN REPRODUCTION AND HOW IT MORE RESEMBLES THE REPRODUCTIVE SYSTEM OF THEIR NATURAL PLANET-BOUND ANCESTORS THAN IT DOES MODERN PHY-SETERINES. THE JUVENILE WANTS TO OBSERVE YOUR SECONDARY SEX CHARACTERISTICS MORE CLOSELY; THE ANTHROPOLOGIST SUG-GESTS THAT THAT WOULD BE AN EFFECTIVE WAY TO GET BITTEN."

"So they're—*you're*—hermaphroditic, but didn't used to be?" she whispered.

"AMYGDALINES ARE NOT HERMAPHRODITIC. THE ANTHROPOLO-GIST EXPLAINS THAT PHYSETERINES NOW FAVOR HERMAPHRODITIC REPRODUCTION BECAUSE IT IS MORE EFFICIENT. AMYGDALINES RE-TAINED BIMODAL SEX, BECAUSE THEY NEVER HAD A NEED TO DE-VELOP SUCH EFFICIENCY, BECAUSE THEY ARE COLONIZERS."

It was all Paris could do not to laugh.

"THEY ARE EXPLAINING AMYGDALINE REPRODUCTION TO THE JU-
VENILES. THEY ARE MAKING WILDLY INACCURATE STATEMENTS."

Again, Paris bit her tongue and suppressed a smile. If a computerized voice were capable of expressing indignation . . .

"THEY ARE TELLING THE JUVENILES THAT WE HAVE RETAINED
THE RIGID GENDER ROLES OF OUR ANCESTORS AND KEEP OUR MALES
CONFINED WITHIN PHYLES TO PROTECT THEM FROM OVERDOMI-
NANT FEMALES. I CANNOT TELL IF THEY ARE PROPAGANDIZING OR
SIMPLY IGNORANT."

"Maybe they're trying to piss you off, Nik."

"SEX IS NO LONGER RELEVANT TO AMYGDALINE CASTE OR FUNC-
TION. WE ARE BORN STERILE. WE USE GENOMES TO REPRODUCE. I
AM MALE, AND I AM IN THE OLIGARCH CASTE. WE NO LONGER AD-
HERE TO ANCESTRAL GENDER ROLES. THERE ARE MANY MALES BRED
TO BE OLIGARCHS. EVERYTHING THIS ANTHROPOLOGIST IS TELLING
THEM IS EITHER FALSE OR WILDLY MISREPRESENTATIVE."

This went on for a little while, with Nikola so indignant that she was
beginning to suspect that this anthropologist was well aware that Nikola
could hear them and was doing this on purpose. The juveniles fed her
several more of their GMOs before the adults told them it was time to
put their toy away. When Durian returned her to her little cage, she du-
tifully got inside. Durian removed the vines around her wrists but didn't
close the cage immediately, instead approaching the wall adjacent to it,
stroking the wall like they were giving it a massage. The wall contracted
like skin that was tensing, and then it turned black. No, not black, she
realized—transparent. It was showing the darkness from the outside.

"My God," Paris whispered.

"WHATEVER THEY DID, THEY WANT YOU TO REPEAT THEM."

She carefully mimicked the motion they had used on the wall she
had backed against, rubbing it like a pencil eraser. Durian turned to
their buddies and chattered at them, downright chuffed. One of the juveniles looked through the "window" Durian had just made, and the
tone of the group changed wildly. Then all of them but Durian disappeared, with Durian only staying long enough to close the hole in Paris's
cage. Then they, too, were gone.

As the transparent segment of wall faded back into opaqueness, Paris
leaned back against the vines that comprised the bars of her cage and

released a long, frustrated breath. Once again, she wondered *why* this was happening at all. Why was not just the story of human civilization but apparently *all* civilizations simply the long, sad tale of artificial scarcity? Whatever the debate was about their extremely finite resources, they were having it on a planet that was home to a civilization that could solve all their problems, at least in the short term.

"We could help them," said Paris. "At least, we could shelter them. They don't have to live in the wilderness."

"WHO IS 'WE' IN THIS SCENARIO, DEAR GENTLE CREATURE?"

"Humanity."

There was a slight hesitation before Nikola responded. "ANY KIND-NESS YOU OR ANY OF YOUR KIND SHOW THEM WILL ONLY BE EX-PLOITED."

She watched the last of the moonlight seeping through the window disappear. "Nikola, I have a favor to ask."

"I WILL DO WHAT IS IN MY CAPABILITY TO DO, DEAR GENTLE CREATURE, WHICH IS VERY LITTLE."

"I want to communicate with them. I want you to speak for me. Be my voice for them."

Uncharacteristic silence from the other end of the earbud. A silence that lasted seven, maybe even eight seconds. Then: "WHAT WOULD YOU HAVE ME COMMUNICATE TO THEM, DEAR GENTLE CREATURE?"

"That right now, the proportion of Earth we have rendered unusable by war or negligence or radioactivity or greed is still fairly small. Most of the earth isn't irradiated or pocked with land mines. There could be safe land for them somewhere. We have the resources to help them, even protect them, and that's something they haven't considered."

"THEY HAVEN'T CONSIDERED IT BECAUSE THEY WOULD NEVER HUMOR IT."

"I just want you to communicate it to them, and you said you'd do anything you could if it was in your capability to do it."

"IT'S A FUTILE ENDEAVOR."

"I don't care! It's something I want to communicate to them, even if they never choose to act on it. I don't know about the adults, but the kids are clearly curious and might be open to the idea."

"THE JUVENILES BEING OPEN TO THE IDEA IS MOOT IF THE ADULTS FORBID IT."

"Nikola, I'm not asking for your input. I'm just asking you to do for me what Kaveh did for you. Now will you do it?"

It was a little while before Nikola gave her some indication that he'd executed his version of, "Hey, kid, c'mere . . . Wanna talk to a human?" How long it might take for said kids to sneak away from wherever their bunks were she could not say, only that Nikola had told her the package had been delivered in the middle of the night. It was getting late in the day, and she was beginning to fear that they wouldn't show at all, but eventually, two of them arrived; it was the usual suspects, Durian and Coconut, the cosmetic vein-tracings on their skin freshly applied.

"Nik," said Paris. "They're here."

Durian put on a pair of those fiber-optic gloves before approaching her cage of vines, and ran their fingers along their roots. Within a minute, the entire cage expanded like a balloon. There was nothing big enough for her to escape from, but now they could see each other. And now, the money question, the WIIFM—what was in it for *them?*

The answer was obvious and manifold—they wanted the threat of humanity mitigated, they wanted land where they could safely mind their own business, they wanted to feel safe. But to suggest any of these things as possibilities to them would be akin to suggesting to a human that the U.S. was eager to go all in on anarcho-syndicalist communism, or that Bill Maher might start being funny. What they wanted was simple and obvious, but to convince them that getting it might be a possibility? Less so.

Paris put her hand up to her ear. "Now what, Nikola?"

She shivered when she felt the earbud rubbing against the skin of her inner ear before sliding into the center of her palm. She held it up in front of her, cradling it like it was a baby bird that had fallen out of its nest. "Will it be loud enough?"

"I WILL BE UNDERSTOOD, DEAR GENTLE CREATURE," said the earbud. At that volume, if that had been in her ear, it might have blown out her eardrum. Durian and Coconut turned from her, whispering to each other, which sounded like tiny handclaps. Then they faced her, and Durian spoke.

"THEY WANT TO KNOW WHAT YOUR PEOPLE INTENDED TO DO WITH THE CAPTIVE SIMILAR BEFORE HE WAS CAPTURED BY THEIR PARENTS."

"I take it they mean you."

"THAT IS CORRECT."

She pushed past the awkwardness of having to translate this sensitive information *about* Nikola *through* Nikola. "He is mentally unwell. The people at the facility were trying to rehabilitate him."

Nikola conveyed her words, and the two practically cut him off with their response.

"What's going on?"

"THEY ARE ASKING ME TO VERIFY THE TRUTHFULNESS OF YOUR ASSERTION. I AM TELLING THEM THAT IT IS TRUE." Then a bit more back-and-forth, something that seemed to make the two juveniles either giddy or livid. "THEY SAY, 'THE HIVE PEOPLE WOULD KILL ONE SUCH AS THE CAPTIVE SIMILAR.'"

"'Hive people'?"

"THAT IS WHAT THEY CALL US. THEY CONSIDER US ALL MINDLESS DRONES, LIKE ANTS."

"Is that true?"

"NO, WE ARE NOT MINDLESS DRONES."

This. Fucking. Guy. "I mean, is it true that your people would kill you?"

"YES, THAT IS TRUE. THEY ASK YOU, 'HOW MANY OTHER SIMILARS ARE THERE ON THIS PLANET?'"

Somehow this felt like a trick question. She knew enough to know that it was not accurate to call Nikola a Similar, despite the fact that he was running around in the body of one, though he didn't seem keen to correct them. Jude was, likewise, an Oligarch in the body of a Similar. Which meant, technically, there was just the one she'd only heard about in the realm of myth and maybe: Brako, the Similar they had in custody at ROSA.

"One, I think," she said.

Durian and Coconut conferred, and then Coconut moved to one of the surveillance consoles, replacing the surveillance feed of one of their former greenhouses with another, more familiar image—*Human Shield*. The photograph of Cora defending Jude and Nikola from a gunman in Pershing Square.

Durian approached the screen, pointed to Jude, and spoke.

"THEY ASK, 'WHY IS THIS IMAGE SO UBIQUITOUS ON HUMAN NETWORKS?'"

Paris's mouth ran dry. *Ubiquitous* was indeed the word, like the *Mona Lisa* or the face of the one-dollar bill, she had seen that picture so many times she had completely divorced it from the fact that it featured someone she *knew*, someone she cared about deeply despite everything. "That's a picture of the first time the public ever saw an ETI. It's a very . . . important moment."

"THEY ASK, 'IS THIS THE OTHER HIVE PERSON?'"

It almost felt like she'd been caught in a lie, and she did not want to lie to them. But then again, Nikola said *hive person*, not *Similar*. "Yes, that's another . . . hive person."

Durian's two clawlike forefingers moved to the barely visible image of the inert Nikola. "'AND THIS IS THE CAPTIVE SIMILAR?'"

"That's Nikola, the one you have in captivity." Not confirmed as a Similar, but not a lie.

Durian then moved his forefingers over the image of the man holding the gun to Cora's face. "THEY ASK, 'WHO IS THIS SIREN?'"

"They know what guns are, right?"

"THEY KNOW WHAT GUNS ARE."

"That's a gunman. He was threatening to shoot the . . . girl—" She just couldn't call Cora a 'siren'; somehow she figured that their term was way more derogatory than it came off in English. "—and the two . . . hive people. The gunman was killed a few seconds after this photo was taken."

"THEY ASK, 'DID THE SIMILARS KILL THE GUNMAN?'"

"No, the police killed him. The LAPD. Human police."

"They ask, 'The human police defend the Similars against a human gunman? They murder one of their own?'"

"Yes."

Coconut and Durian scrutinized the image shining in soft light up on the screen as if trying to find holes in Paris's story, then spoke.

"They want to know who the female is."

She bit her lip, feeling like despite a chasm both in language and millions of years of evolution they could tell how concerned she was for this "siren." That even though they had parted on terms that in normal circumstances likely would have led to them never speaking again, she was still afraid for Cora, just wanted to know that despite everything she'd be *okay*.

"She works as Jude's . . . interpreter. She communicates to other humans for him."

"They say that she is his pet."

"No." Paris laughed humorlessly. "No, they're friends. He cares about her very much."

The juveniles met Nikola's translation with a noise that sounded almost like an indignant Donald Duck.

"They don't believe hive people are capable of love and presume that my little cousin must be extremely gullible if he convinced her that they are."

The Donald Duck noise stopped abruptly, and then Durian moved toward her, standing directly over her cage, sliding their fingers through the vines as they looked down at her kneeling on the floor. Coconut pulled up another image on a screen adjacent to the one showing *Human Shield*—the footage from yesterday of Cora and the tall, dark-haired guy in the greenhouse. Coconut pointed to Cora in *Human Shield* and then to her image in the greenhouse footage.

Fuck, she thought. They knew the figures in the two images were the same person. Way too much interest in Cora for comfort.

"They want to know what this human was doing at the site of one of their abandoned settlements."

"I have no idea."

"They think you are lying."

"Nikola, I genuinely have no idea."

"I HAVE AN IDEA, DEAR GENTLE CREATURE. THEY ARE SEARCHING FOR YOU."

She sat up straight. "For me? Why not you?"

"MY DEAR LITTLE COUSIN WOULD SOONER SEE ME DEAD THAN EXPEND ANY EFFORT TO SEARCH FOR ME, BUT I DO NOT BELIEVE THE SAME HOLDS TRUE FOR YOU. SHE IS SEARCHING FOR YOU, AND THE CIA AGENT IS AIDING HER."

She looked again at the image of Cora, this time through the lens of someone who hadn't convinced themselves that there was no one out there looking for her. The tall, dark-haired guy, the "CIA agent," looked bored, but Cora's expression was a potent combination of worried and determined. Paris could not know if that determined expression was for her, but it was hard to imagine that Cora was wearing it for Nikola.

"Nikola, I *don't know*. You can tell them your theory if you want, but I don't know who that man is or what they are doing at their old greenhouse."

The two stepped away to confer quietly, then Durian turned back to her and spoke.

"THEY'RE CURIOUS ABOUT YOUR HAIR AND THE MARKINGS ON YOUR SKIN."

"Oh . . . well . . ." She ran her box braids through her fingers; they were still completely tight, locked in, a perfect style for alien abduction. "My hair, I just do it because it's pretty."

"AND THE MARKINGS?"

"The tattoos are permanent skin art. Do they have a concept of art?"

"THEY DO. THEY WANT TO KNOW HOW IT IS ACCOMPLISHED."

She eyed the black markings on their pale skin that accentuated their veins and noticed there was something almost like latticework on Coconut's.

"We use needles to inject ink into the skin. That makes it permanent."

Coconut kept his distance, but Durian leaned in close, stopping just short of threading their fingers through the bars. They seemed particularly fixated by the butterfly on her collarbone.

"THEY ASK, 'DOESN'T IT HURT?'"

"Yop."

"'AND YOU DO IT VOLUNTARILY?'"

"It doesn't hurt *that* much."

Durian continued to stare, and again, she spied the carefully applied lines that ran up their necks and framed their faces like vines on the side of an old building. It was possible that they were looking down on her primitive ways as the Europeans had upon discovering the tradition of Polynesian tattoos, exotic and savage, but she suspected the overriding emotion here was envy.

Durian backed away and asked another question.

"THEY WANT TO KNOW THE SIGNIFICANCE OF THE INSECT ON YOUR CHEST."

She swallowed, again cornered by a sensitive piece of information that she earlier had not wanted Nikola to be privy to. "It's a species of butterfly from Jamaica, where my father is from."

"WHAT MAKES IT WORTH PERMANENTLY ADORNING YOURSELF?"

"It's a painting my father did. Toward the end of his life, he became interested in painting wildlife. He painted this not long before he died, the biggest species of butterfly in the Western Hemisphere. It's also incredibly rare."

"WHAT MAKES IT INCREDIBLY RARE?"

"Their habitat has been severely reduced since . . ." Paris blinked, a stampede of words representing an even more complex history than she could easily articulate to a human let alone to an alien parading before her—*slavery, colonialism, imperialism, genocide of the Indigenous, mass slaughter of the enslaved, deforestation, poverty, exploitation, globalism, climate change.* How to crack that nut when, as things stood now, these guys saw humanity as a single, unified monolith, which could not be further from the truth?

"Their habitat has been severely reduced in the last few centuries."

"THEY WANT TO KNOW WHAT REDUCED IT."

At first, she hesitated at yet another topic that would only make humanity look bad, but then realized that this could be the entry she was looking for. "The last few centuries have seen a lot of human development on the island of Jamaica. That's led to mass deforestation on the island. For lumber, for development, most of it is for farmland."

"'THERE ARE TOO MANY OF YOU.'"

She'd hoped that they'd know better than to ascribe humanity's ills to a nebulous, eugenicist concept of "overpopulation," but then again, they were literally children. "That's far too simplistic an explanation, don't you think?"

"'YOU CONSUME TOO MUCH; THERE ARE TOO MANY OF YOU.'"

"I agree with things as they are now that our civilization is not sustainable, but that's not a reflection of the population, which is already leveling off, but of inefficiency."

"'YOUR POPULATION SHOULD BE CULLED IF YOU WANT TO SAVE YOUR BUTTERFLY. THERE ARE TOO MANY OF YOU.'"

Children, she reminded herself. *Literal fucking children.* "Don't your amygdaline cousins say the same thing about you?"

"'BUT THAT'S NOT TRUE OF US. WE ARE ON THE VERGE OF EXTINCTION.'"

"So are we. At least your species is scattered—if this planet gets sterilized like the hive people did to one of your planets, we are done. We are extinct."

This put both of them on alert, and again Durian grabbed the vines of her cage excitedly. "THEY ASK, 'YOU KNOW ABOUT THE ERYTHRAN STERILIZATION?'"

Paris backed against the wall. "Yes, I do."

"'AND YOU STILL ALLY YOURSELF WITH THE HIVE PEOPLE?'"

"We don't 'ally' ourselves with their civilization. We have no diplomatic relationship with their civilization. My understanding was that their Superorganism committed genocide against some of your people. Not every single amygdaline agreed with the genocide, just like not every human is pushing for deforestation, just like you don't agree with everything your parents believe."

"'HOW DO YOU KNOW WHAT OUR PARENTS BELIEVE?'"

"I know that you don't want them to know you're talking to me."

Durian let go of the vines and retreated to confer with Coconut out of earbud-shot. Then they turned back to her, stood up straight, and spoke.

"THEY SAY, 'YOU ARE INEFFICIENT. YOUR AGRICULTURE IS INEFFICIENT. IT CANNOT BOTH FEED YOUR POPULACE AND SUSTAIN YOUR BUTTERFLY. ONE MUST DIE FOR THE OTHER TO SURVIVE.'"

"You're right," she said, rising to her knees and threading her fingers through the holes of her cage. The two juveniles paused and looked at each other, then back at Paris before speaking again.

"They express confusion that you agree with them."

"It's not just that we're consuming at a rate that's unsustainable," said Paris, hanging her fingers on the vines. "We just don't know how to be efficient about it. I wish there was a way for us to be more efficient about our agriculture—then we could feed our populace and restore the butterfly's habitat."

"'To remedy those inefficiencies would be simple.'"

"What is the solution?"

"'Simple for us. Complex for you.'"

"Do you have ideas on how you could make our systems more efficient? More resistant to drought and climate change, use less land, produce less greenhouse gas?"

"'Many ideas.'"

"Do you ever imagine what it would be like if you could come in and reform our agricultural systems to be more efficient, like yours?"

This almost seemed to prompt some indignation, as Durian puffed up, and the two retreated to confer for a solid two minutes before returning.

"They say, 'Of course we do. But it could never happen.'"

"Why not?"

"'You would not accept it. Every time we have tried to interact with you, you've attacked us.'"

"I don't deny that humans have seen your kind and reacted with violence; they were afraid because they didn't know what you were. But we know what you are now—you aren't monsters, you aren't demons, you're just kids. You were born and raised on Earth, same as I was. You're the children of immigrants, same as I am. If you have ideas on how to improve our agricultural technologies, many of us would be glad to listen to them. Our species has a terrible problem with hunger, and we're facing a catastrophic climate crisis that our civilization created. But maybe you could help us."

At this, the two conferred in that tiny-handclap version of whispering. At last, they approached her cage.

"They ask, 'Why should we help you?'"

"Because we could help you in return."

"'How could you help us?'"

"Imagine not having to move anymore, not having to live in fear of us, but working with us." She leaned her forehead against the bars, looking them right in the eye. "Imagine if you didn't have to hide from us."

Durian and Coconut looked at her, the silence of the enclosure almost suffocating. If there was a play, this was it. "Even something as simple as warm food and shelter, there are so few of you, there isn't a country in the world that doesn't have the resources to make you more comfortable than you are now. Think about how much we have to learn from each other."

"'WHAT COULD SIRENS POSSIBLY TEACH US?'"

"Would you like to learn how tattooing works?"

This appeared to hit both of them right where they lived, with Coconut even tracing some of the patterns they'd drawn along their neck.

"I'd be happy to show you—"

She was shocked into silence by the sight of the dark-haired girl and her surly companion appearing on another one of the greenhouse feeds, one in which up to now she'd seen no human activity. Durian and Coconut immediately clocked her preoccupation and turned to look at the screen.

"They're looking at a feed of Cora and that CIA guy again. This looks like a different location."

"THE IMAGE IS A LIVE FEED. MY LITTLE COUSIN AND THE CIA AGENT HAVE FOUND AN ABANDONED GREENHOUSE HITHERTO UNDISCOVERED BY HUMANS IN THE IRRADIATED ZONE."

Fuck, this was a live feed of the Chernobyl exclusion zone, and Cora was there *right now*. The two were chittering to each other, those tails twitching in that universally excited animal way. Paris didn't like it.

"THEY SAY THEIR PARENTS WILL NOT SUFFER THEM TO DISCOVER ANY FURTHER; THEY ARE GETTING TOO CLOSE."

"Too close to what?"

"ONE IS TRYING TO CONVINCE THE OTHER THAT THEIR PARENTS WILL BE INTERESTED IN MY LITTLE COUSIN, GIVEN HER SIGNIFICANCE BOTH TO MY BELOVED AND TO MYSELF."

Nikola then used the earbud to say something in Semipalatinsk-creole, a sharp, loud noise designed to get their attention. A warning, she assumed. She hoped.

"Please, leave her alone!" Paris threw herself against the vines of her cage, and Durian and Coconut started in response, then Durian stepped up to read her the riot act.

"They say, 'You cannot tell us why she is in our old green-houses. Therefore, we will find out for ourselves.'"

"No, please, no!"

Nikola tried to tell them something, whether it was translating her or his own harsh words she did not know, but it didn't matter; the two juveniles were gone.

Cora stood in the middle of the former greenhouse, staring absently while Sol made another satellite phone call to Langley. This place didn't look terribly dissimilar from the other former greenhouse—it was carefully deforested, with room for dozens of rows of crops but with the trees covering most of it in such a way that it would not be notable from above. Only difference between this greenhouse and the last one was this one hadn't yet been scoured by former Soviet spies.

"We . . . should probably tell your boy," said Sol, flipping his satellite phone shut.

She nodded as she flipped out her phone and sent a message:

> Could you come back? We found another greenhouse.

> En route.

Cora couldn't help but smile. French, but in the way that English speakers use French. "Aww."

"Aww, what?"

"I still don't understand a lot about how his language algorithm works, but he's getting better at using idioms and foreign words and whatnot."

"Yeah, the cyborg death machine is adorable."

Cora glared at him, but he did not see, as he was investigating something between a pair of trees. "Whoa!"

"What is it?"

He moved between the two trees, and like a magic trick, he just disappeared. It happened so quickly and strangely that she wondered if he was pulling some kind of prank. Then he reappeared as if from behind an invisibility cloak. "Okay, this? Is a find," he said. Then he disappeared again.

"Sol!" she yelled, following him and stumbling through that shield of invisibility. Not invisibility—it was a holographic screen concealing the entrance to a structure not meant to be seen by human eyes. This, however, was not a greenhouse. This was an entire chamber.

"Whoa," said Cora, unintentionally channeling an excellent Neo impression.

It wasn't huge; size-wise, it felt like entering the foyer of a Red Lobster. The walls looked like they were made of giant leaves that had weathered into a substance like dried leather. "It kind of reminds me of the inside of a giant sequoia," she said.

Sol snorted, running his fingers alongside the wall as he ventured farther in. "You would think of that."

"What do you mean?"

"I recognize that you are still in mourning, but you do take any opportunity, however tenuous, to bring him up."

She had a soft spot for great sequoias since they had been such a centerpiece in Kaveh's essay, but that hadn't been why she'd brought it up. It genuinely felt like the closest physical point of reference. "Does that bother you?"

Sol laughed a laugh that she knew was bait. "Your boyfriend wasn't as perfect as you think he was."

Cora looked outside, and thought, she should just get out of this chamber. Go outside and take a seat. And if he tried to egg her on, she should just ignore him. Ampersand was on his way. Her long Belarusian nightmare was ten minutes from being over, fifteen max.

Instead, she engaged.

"I know what you think about him, Sol."

"That's not what I mean," he said with a chuckle. "There's plenty you don't know."

Again, her Shoulder Angel begged her, pleaded with her not to take the bait. "What do you mean?"

His camera made the tiniest *click* as he took a photo of something on the floor. "Well, did you know he knew about Agent Park's death before *el presidente* did?"

Bait. Bait. Bait. This is bait. "No. How could he have known?"

"I'm not sure how he knew, but he did know. Because he told Nils all about it."

"Are you sure?"

"Yes," he laughed, almost cruelly, taking another picture. "I do have hard evidence on this, believe it or not."

Her body was moving toward him of its own volition as he stood up to his full height, taking another picture of something on the wall. "You know, I should thank you, by the way, for that crying spell at Nils's apartment," he said, still not looking at her. "Got him out of the way just long enough for me to copy his SIM card. And I found a very interesting conversation between your boyfriend and your dad, in which one told the other all about an incident where I lost my junior agent, as well as three other agents, at the hands of an alien death machine. An incident that was classified top secret and was never meant to be made public."

She just stood there, waiting for him to look at her, to do something other than smugly take pictures of a wall. "Does this sound at all familiar to you, or . . . ?"

"When?" she asked. "When is your 'hard evidence'?"

"The conversation is dated March 4, 2008."

She stilled, again wondering if Sol was just making things up. She knew the date—that was the day Kaveh wrote about going into Sequoia National Park with Nikola.

"Why would he do that?" she asked.

"One would presume that he wanted something from Nils."

"What could Nils *possibly* give Kaveh?"

"Plenty."

He continued taking pictures, bopping along as if dancing to a tune only he could hear, and it struck her—he was getting off on this. Same as he watched her squirm at the bar, same as he watched her squirm when they were in bed together, same as he watched her squirm at NORAD, same as he watched her squirm at Langley, same as he watched her squirm as fucking Boris put his hands wherever he wanted. He fucking *got off* on it.

"Wasn't it your boyfriend's last great mountain to climb, getting a Pulitzer? Closest he ever came to getting one was with Nils. Well—"

"Why do you treat me like this?" she cut him off.

He turned to her, eyebrow arched. "What do you mean?"

"Why do you treat me like this?" she repeated, voice trembling from exhaustion. "What have I done to you?"

"I don't know what y—"

"You've always treated me like this. You knew you were making me uncomfortable yesterday, first with your little 'wife' charade and then with the hotel thing."

"We are undercover," he said like she was a child.

"I've never done this before. I'm alone with you in a foreign country. You didn't even begin to give a shit about how I felt."

"We don't have the luxury to care about your *feelings* when we're undercover."

"*Bullshit!*" she snapped, stepping up to him and coming a hairs-breadth away from punching him in the head.

"Keep it down, this area might be—"

"*Fuck you!*" she yelled. "This isn't fucking Afghanistan; we weren't hanging on to life by a thread, we were in a major fucking European city and *nobody* knew we were there! You could have gone over what you were planning to do with me ahead of time! You could have gotten my permission to touch me before you did it! You could have asked me if I was comfortable sharing a bed with you! You could have taken thirty seconds to do any of those things, and none of it would have blown your precious 'cover.'"

"Listen—"

"You don't gloss over basic human decency because it's fucking 'pro-tocol'; you do it because you get off on it! You've always gotten off on it, because all you've ever wanted was to get revenge against them, and you can't get it against them, but you can get it against m—"

"*Cora!*"

He grabbed her by the shoulders, and before she could protest, he turned her around, and she saw what he was looking at.

A physeterine. A live one.

The part of her that was always connected to Ampersand turned to jelly at the sight of his longtime tormentors, and she had to remind her human self that she was still in charge. The adults she knew to be the size of lions, but this creature didn't look much bigger than she was—probably one of the juveniles. They were standing on a ledge near the entrance, crest on their head splayed out like shortened peacock feathers, eyes covered in shiny black shells.

"How far are we from extraction?" whispered Sol, keeping his hands on her shoulders.

Cora swallowed. "Maybe another ten minutes."

The juvenile moved like a large cat, keeping their back low and balancing themselves on their forelimbs. This had very quickly become a staring contest, Cora and Sol stone-still while the juvenile prowled on the ledge.

"Okay, then you'll have to extract us," he said.

"Right." She nodded, and tried to pull up her viewfinder. She was nervous, so the first few tries to do it with eye movements didn't work. Then she tried to do it manually. A few blips, then nothing, just regular old human vision.

"It's not working."

"What?" said Sol. "It can just break?"

"I don't know. Something must be scrambling it."

She felt his arm move behind her to his belt. "I have a gun," he whispered so quietly she could barely hear it.

"No, don't. We can either wait here until Ampersand arrives, or we can get out of here. This . . . chamber must be what's scrambling my viewfinder. Maybe if we get outside—"

"Yeah, I don't want to chance that we have ten minutes."

The juvenile slithered down off the ledge, right into the open doorway, and was now blocking the exit. Their hands were still partially raised, crest up and alert.

"All right," said Sol, "I'm going to fire a warning shot at the ground, okay?"

"I . . . I think maybe we should wait. We don't know if they're armed."

"It doesn't look armed."

"We don't know what *armed* physeterines look like," she whispered. "Amygdaline armament is completely invisible to the human eye. Same might be true here."

"Is it possible they use energy weapons that are affected by your pulse emitter?"

"Possible, I guess. In that 'with Jesus, all things are possible' kind of way."

"It might also unscramble whatever is scrambling your systems."

"Worth a shot," she sighed.

"Okay, one-two punch," he said. "I'll fire the emitter, then fire the warning shot. If he doesn't move, I'm going to fire another warning shot."

"Sol—"

He had something in his hand, and she realized that somehow he'd gotten the pulse emitter out of her bag while she wasn't looking. "Count of three."

"How did you—"

"One, two . . ."

A flash of white crossed her vision. The pulse made her light-headed, and the sound of the gun going off made her stumble. She looked up and saw that the juvenile had not moved from the entrance, but did look very surprised, as if *something* in their systems wasn't working correctly. Sol picked up on this, and aimed his gun directly at the juvenile. They seemed to realize what they were dealing with, because they dove out of the way of the entrance and down into the shadows of the chamber before the shot went off.

"Go!" said Sol, and Cora dashed for the entrance, Sol right behind her, gun trained in the way she'd so often seen in cop shows, casing every angle for potential threats before training his gun back on the entrance to the chamber.

She stayed close as he continued backing away from the entrance, gun still trained. She tried to split her attention, half scanning for threats, half trying to get her viewfinder to work, but it was still scrambled.

"Any luck?" he said.

"Nothing," she said. "I think it's probably going to need some repairs before it works again."

"Fuck. Okay. Watch my back."

"Okay."

Watch my back. She hadn't given much thought to what that phrase actually meant, and she was in such a heightened state of panic that a part of her took that literally. Turn around and look at his back? No, but that wasn't what that meant, was it? It meant that he was watching from his front, and she was watching *from* his back. But then she felt that he was no longer at her back, and turned to see that he had moved a few feet away. She hadn't had her back turned for a second when a pair of limbs reached around her from behind.

"*Sol!*"

He whipped around, gun trained right on her as the limbs dragged her away. She started to yell at him not to shoot, but then something that felt like silicone film came down over her entire head, over her nose and mouth, and in moments, she was in both complete darkness and silence.

· 38 ·

"How long has it been?"

"ONE HUNDRED AND EIGHTEEN MINUTES. WOULD YOU LIKE FOR ME TO GIVE YOU UPDATES ON TIME ELAPSED EVERY TWO HUNDRED SECONDS, DEAR GENTLE CREATURE?"

Paris could not help but read this as shade. "No. Thanks," she said, hugging her knees to her chest. Her instinct was to come up with contingencies, a list of if-thens. The sun was only just setting, so if the juveniles returned with Cora in tow, maybe she could communicate with them through Nikola before the adults woke up. If the juveniles returned without her, maybe she could give them a fuller picture, explain that going after Cora was a Very Bad Idea. But could she really influence anything? In so many ways, this was just like the feeling of falling from thirty-six thousand feet; she was truly helpless, and any mental gymnastics she did was just bargaining.

"WHAT DO YOU THINK YOU MIGHT SURMISE BASED ON THE AMOUNT OF TIME THAT HAS PASSED, DEAR GENTLE CREATURE?"

"Maybe I'm lonely and I just want to talk to you, Nik." She had meant it sarcastically, but there was some truth to it. She had traveled over metaphorical hill and dale, crossed the rope bridge, and answered the troll these riddles three just for the opportunity to talk to him. Why would that have changed just because they were prisoners?

"AND YOUR DESIRE TO TALK TO ME IS WHY YOU ARE HERE AT ALL, DEAR GENTLE CREATURE."

"What, is that supposed to make me feel bad?" she snapped. "Is this some sort of 'I told you so' moment? That everyone warned me that talking to you would get me killed?"

"I WARNED YOUR MENTOR, AND HE DID NOT LISTEN TO ME, AND NOW HE IS DEAD. WHY WOULD YOU BE DIFFERENT?"

"I'm not different," she said, throwing her head against the wall as she rubbed on the space that gave her the best view to the clearing. She'd done this for the first forty-five minutes nonstop since Durian and Coconut had left, and by now, her fingers, fists, and palms were raw.

"WHY WERE YOU CREATURES SO INVESTED IN MY REHABILITATION? IT WOULD MEAN NOTHING TO YOUR SURVIVAL ODDS."

Paris released another long, beleaguered sigh. "Because by deciding you are a person, we have effectively adopted you. Quirk of the species, I guess."

"JUST LIKE YOUR MENTOR, I KNEW THAT YOU WERE STILL DOING HIS WORK. YOU HAD NO INTENTION OF EVER HELPING ME GET WHAT I WANTED."

"What?" Paris breathed, a little hurt despite her fried nerves. "That's not true. I don't think that we have the right to impose our cultural norms onto you. I absolutely feel like you should have the right to choose when you die. But I also believe that you are not of sound mind, and you don't have the capacity to make that sort of decision right now. But I didn't say anything to you that I didn't believe."

"WHY WOULD YOU ADVOCATE FOR MY WISHES IF YOUR CULTURE FINDS THEM SO REPULSIVE?"

"I don't find them repulsive," she said, punching the wall in frustration. "I don't understand them, but our long, sad history of colonialism has been one group after the other saying, 'I don't like this thing you people do; change it and do what we do.' It never works out. I don't care if in the greater sense amygdalines are space colonizers; it would be the height of hypocrisy if we did the same to you. So if in some extremely unlikely scenario we do find some way to coexist, then we will need to figure out ways to incorporate your customs and biology and beliefs into our laws. We can't impose our shit on you any more than you can onto us."

Paris stopped rubbing the wall, her arm exhausted, and she leaned her head into her knees as the translucent wall started to fade back into opaqueness. *If they do something to her, am I going to spend the rest of my short life trying to reassure myself that it wasn't my fault?* She thought what she had said to Cora the first time they met—"*It wasn't your fault.*"

"Nikola, what did you do to them?" she asked.

"WHOM DO YOU MEAN, DEAR GENTLE CREATURE?"

"Cora and Jude. You said you did something unspeakably terrible to them. What did you do?"

Nikola was always ready with a response to even the most damning questions, so his silence at first raised a red flag. She sat up straight. "Nikola?"

"IT CONFERS NO BENEFIT ONTO ME TO TELL YOU."

"You are constantly giving me information it confers no benefit on you to give me."

Again, an uncharacteristic nonresponse.

"You tried to kill them, didn't you?"

Nothing.

"You tried to kill them, but they were somehow able to overpower you. Whatever you did hurt them so badly they couldn't deal with you, so they abandoned you to Bella Terra."

Again, no sound from her earbud, only the sound of cicadas gearing up for their nightly cacophony in the jungle outside.

"Am I wrong?"

Then she heard a voice outside, a *human* voice making a sort of half choke, half cry. Paris vaulted into the wall, rubbing it violently until it was translucent; Durian and Coconut were back, and they had human cargo.

Paris couldn't see her at first, as the two juveniles were in the way, and then didn't immediately recognize her, hands bound and lying prone on the forest floor with her black hair that looked like a bad wig from Halloween Express. Cora raised her head, shocked and trying to get a grasp on the situation, but she looked okay for the moment.

"Cora!" Paris cried without thinking. "I'm here! I'm here!"

Cora's eyes popped, but she didn't make a sound. Suddenly, a dozen adults descended on the two juveniles and Cora, Trinity among them.

"Nikola, what's going on?"

"THE TWO JUVENILES HAVE TAKEN MY LITTLE COUSIN CAPTIVE."

"Yes, I can see that. What is happening?"

"THEIR PARENTS ARE NOT PLEASED."

"Cora!" she cried again, clawing frantically at what she could possibly do or say. "They have Nikola here! I'm in the greenhouse! I'm . . ." But she couldn't even direct Cora as to where she was—the entrance to the greenhouse was invisible by design.

At that moment, Trinity grabbed Durian harshly by the shoulder in an action that Paris could only interpret as disciplinary, leaving Cora lying on her stomach bound only by the vines tying her hands together. Then it seemed as if a sheet of liquid metal spread out from underneath her, covering her limbs, her body, her clothes, but as fast as the liquid metal was, Trinity was faster, grabbing Cora by the neck before the liquid metal shroud sealed her up. The sheet of metal didn't close over her head but slid up Trinity's arm, confusing and enraging them. In a swift motion, they pulled out a tool, with their other hand, a blade, and brought it down on Cora's neck.

"*No!*" Paris screamed. None of them paid her any mind, all eyes on Cora as the group that surrounded her talked over one another. Trinity pushed her over onto her stomach, their hand still covered in the liquid metal, which now seemed to be receding into the back of Cora's neck. This was where Trinity brought their blade a second time, and the noise Cora made was the sort of haunted thing they tell about in legends. Paris could feel that scream ringing in the marrow of her bones, vibrating painfully like nails on a chalkboard, and she closed her eyes. Whatever they were doing to her, Paris couldn't look.

"THEY HAVE DISCOVERED MY LITTLE COUSIN'S IMPLANTS."

"Implants?"

"MY BELOVED HAS BEEN IMPLANTING HER WITH CYBERNETICS FOR SOME TIME, WHICH I PRESUME WOULD INCLUDE A TRACKING SYSTEM. THE JUVENILES CAPTURING HER AND BRINGING HER HERE MEANS THE LOCATION IS COMPROMISED."

Paris opened her eyes and rubbed the wall furiously. There was blood everywhere. Cora wasn't screaming anymore, but her ribs were heaving up and down painfully. Suddenly, there were dozens of adults flooding into the greenhouse, grabbing things left and right. Some grabbed cuttings, others tried to harvest what was there, jamming what they could into pouches.

"Nikola, what's happening?"

"THEY ARE EVACUATING."

There were physeterines everywhere now, in the small clearing, in the greenhouse, running in and out of the main dwelling where they were keeping Nikola. It was too crowded now for her to see anything, and she saw no sign of Cora or even the two juveniles.

"Cora!" Paris yelled, too terrified, too nauseated for tears. She tried to listen over the commotion for something, *anything* that might indicate that Cora was still here.

"WHAT A TERRIBLY FOOLISH THING THESE JUVENILES HAVE DONE. MY BELOVED WILL HAVE NO INCENTIVE TO SPARE THEM NOW."

"What do you mean?" Paris demanded. "Did they kill her?"

No response, only the fading sound of physeterine chatter.

"Nikola, is she still alive?" she whispered.

"I DON'T KNOW."

"What'll it be?"

"Vodka, neat," said Sol.

The bartender looked at him like he'd made a bad joke. "Are you sure?" he asked. For a bartender of the New Depression, he looked like a bartender of the old one with his goofy suspenders, bow tie, and page boy hat. Only thing un-period about him was his big red beard. "Would you like to look at the menu?"

"I can see vodka right behind you."

"Perhaps a vodka drink? Do you prefer more fruity or more savory?"

"Just vodka," said Sol, exhausted. It had taken him a while to finish his paperwork, which he had filed in great detail, even though the details did not serve him. Macallan was pissed, obviously, but not, shall we say, *disappointed*. She, of course, assumed Sabino dead because that's how these things go, but that outcome was preferable to the one where he fucked her. Probably because the CIA was full of rapists who took advantage of assets all the time, and she was constantly putting out fires. A dead asset was preferable to a raped one, because dead people can't make public accusations.

"Okay, then. Got a preference?"

"Whatever's most expensive."

The bartender looked at the shelves behind him. "I got this Crystal Head."

"Not that one."

"Grey Goose okay?"

"I'd prefer Russian."

"Stoli?"

Based on the goofy label, Stolichnaya didn't *look* expensive, but whatever. The swill of his ancestors was no more than he deserved. "Fine."

He knew Luciana Ortega had been flown out to DC for roughly the hundredth endless interrogation she'd gotten in her career and was therefore still on the East Coast, so he'd told her to meet him in New York on a whim, half expecting she wouldn't show up. But given the subject was her missing-presumed-dead niece, she was on the next train. Meeting at the local diner Veselka he'd vetoed—it was Ukrainian, and he was not ready to face that culture again. Bar None she'd vetoed because apparently there were fights there all the time, so this was the compromise, a trendy East Village speakeasy with some ironic name about death or dying, where ordering something as simple as straight vodka was an affront to the mixologists. *Twelve* dollars for a cocktail? Who could afford this?

The bartender (sorry—*mixologist*) slid him the vodka, and Sol looked at it curiously. There were agents who occasionally drank a little bit of alcohol in the field to maintain a cover. That was never a problem in Muslim countries, where *everyone* always had their wits about them, but he had been in and out of the Russosphere so many times and had grown so skillful at swapping vodka out with water that he had never actually taken a shot. Forty-one years old and had never had a shot of vodka. Hell, to this day, the drunkest he'd ever gotten was on Manischewitz at his cousin's bar mitzvah when he was sixteen.

Down the hatch it went. *Woof*, he thought. *Not missing out.*

"One more."

It surprised him how quickly the bartender went along with it. No questions, just gave him the poison. He figured that was how drunkards like Mazandarani ended up the way they did. At least junkies had to do a little bit of work to get their fix; for drunks, they practically throw it at you.

"Hey," said the voice of a harried redhead taking a seat on the barstool next to him, shedding her coat and scarf, just dripping with concern. If he didn't know any better, he'd have thought she wanted to hug him as if *he* were the person who'd lost someone and not the other way around.

"Why aren't you more freaked out?" asked Sol.

"I am extremely freaked out," said Luciana. "But I've been through this before a few times. She has a way of turning up."

Sol shook his head, agog. Luciana was just as delusional about Sabino as Sabino had been about Paris Wells. "She has a way of turning up with 46. I think for their mortal enemies, different rules may apply."

"Did you see them kill her?"

"I shouldn't be telling you anything."

"Are you *kidding* me?"

He hung his head, shoulder blades jutting out behind him. "You're in the private sector now, you *know* I can't tell you anything."

"Jesus, how many have you had?" she asked, looking at the empty glass in front of him.

"Two."

She blinked. "Really?"

"Two."

She released a frustrated sigh and signaled for the bartender. "Can I get a . . ." She looked at the menu, seeming to pick one at random. "Dr. Strangelove? And he'll have another . . . whatever."

"Stoli," said the bartender as if Stoli were an *insult* to his artistry.

She looked at him quizzically as the bartender departed to fill the order. "Stoli?"

"I'm never going to Russia or any of its former colonies again," he said. He couldn't look drunk, could he? He didn't feel drunk. "May as well try it."

"Is she dead, Sol?"

"And you know what that alien . . . fucking . . . you know what that *thing* did when I told him they'd taken her? He just left me there. Just left me in the middle of enemy territory."

"Sol—"

"I had to hitch a ride to the Ukrainian border in a Soviet farm truck from the 1960s, sneak over the border, hitch yet *another* ride from the exclusion zone to Kiev—"

"*Sol*—"

"—and then forge a Ukrainian entry stamp onto my cover's passport before I could get—"

"Sol, did you see them kill her?"

"No," he choked as the bartender slid him another glass of vodka.

This time, the guy had actually filled it *more*, so he sipped it instead of shot it. It was still gross. Yes, junkies clearly had the right idea (he assumed).

"What did you see?"

"They grabbed her while I wasn't looking, two of them. They put like . . . this film over her face. And it all happened so fast, I had a gun, but even if I'd had a clear shot . . ." He shook his head helplessly. "And then before I could do anything, they were gone. I saw some grass move, I could hear them running away, but . . . that was it."

"Where was it?"

"Eastern Belarus." He took another swig of vodka, and she took a long drink. "You really should be more freaked out."

"Sol, physeterines saved my life. They are capable of some measure of compassion for humans. And you said it yourself—they took her, they didn't kill her. And she has . . . those implants, whatever they do. I'm sure some of them track her. He probably has her with him already."

"And you think she wouldn't tell you if she was okay?"

"When they disappear together, and have some reason they want to stay hidden, they go off-grid. She does it all the time."

"*All* the time?"

Luciana nodded, a little unsure but surer than she should have been considering her niece, probably the person closest to her in the world, just . . . *disappeared* sometimes when her alien overlord needed to lie low for a while.

"You should be more furious with me," he said.

"Why?"

"Because I lost her."

"It wasn't your fault."

"It *was* my fault. I was treating her like a trained field agent who was armed, and she was neither of those things. I had her at my back like she could defend herself, but she couldn't, and they took her when I had my back turned. It is my fault."

"You can't predict these things."

"No, it . . ." He laughed angrily. "I goaded her. I pushed her buttons like she was a reluctant informant, and that got her guard down, and that's when they took her." He looked at Luciana. "It *was* my fault. I was using tactics on her that are used to destabilize informants."

Luciana was looking at him like a tiny third arm had just sprouted from the side of his face. "Why?"

He chuckled, a strange pressure building behind his sinuses. "Because I like doing it."

He looked at her and was greeted with this expression like every worst thing she'd ever suspected about him was being proven in real time.

"Macallan thought . . . my *superior* thought I was trying to fuck her."

"What the hell are you talking about?"

"She thought I was going to take her to the former Soviet bloc and get her alone so I could have my way with her. And that's . . . why I endorsed the whole mission. I wouldn't have done that, even though that was exactly what Mazandarani did."

Luciana continued staring dumbly.

"What, you didn't know? He did it the night she hurt herself, back at Los Alamitos. *You* should have taken her home, or I should have taken her. I wouldn't have done that to her, not to someone who'd just sliced themselves open and almost gotten committed. But he took her right back to his little Persian palace in the Orange County hills, and he got her alone, and he fucked her little brains out. And he did it practically every night, until he got his head blown off."

Luciana recoiled. "May he rest in peace."

"May he rest in . . ." He chuckled, shaking his head incredulously. "I thought you dropped out of Catholic school."

"Sol . . ."

"So you know that Mazandarani was spilling state secrets to your brother, the most unscrupulous bag of wet shit on this planet, human or otherwise, all while he was fucking your very young, extremely volatile, very vulnerable niece, and you are not upset by this?"

"You are right that I should have taken her home that day. I know that. But he really loved her."

"You *really* buy that?"

She furrowed her brow. "Sol, you are so fucking full of venom, but it doesn't seem to occur to you that there might have been a reason *why* Kaveh did what he did?"

"Does he need a reason?"

"Yes! A very good one. He loved her, Sol."

"*He loved her, Sol*," he repeated in an obnoxious nasal tone like he was five. He finished his vodka. "Well, tell me, oh Speaker for the Dead, do you know what that reason is? Did you know that Nils knew about those *things* killing *my* agents before Julian did, because Mazandarani told him?"

"How do you know?"

"I have evidence."

"What evidence?"

"From your brother's apartment. When I went there with . . . with Cora, too . . . I cloned his cell phone while he wasn't looking—"

Luciana looked at him with the pity one might reserve for some dummy who didn't know their fly had been down for the whole conversation. "You mean this all comes from a cell phone that you found in my brother's apartment?"

He sat up straight. "What? What is the issue?"

"I just . . . If it were me, I'd be skeptical of anything I found in Nils's apartment."

"What, are you saying he fabricated it?"

"No, but if he knew you were coming . . . maybe he wanted you to find it?"

Now that he was three drinks in, he actually found himself tempted to order another. *This is how it starts*, he thought, thinking again of Mazandarani, the drunk with a redemption arc. "What fucking difference does that make?"

She shook her head, giving him that expression that women often use when the person they're with is drunk, but they're too polite to say so. "I'll tell you if I hear anything," she said, sliding off the barstool and putting on her jacket. "Thanks for the drink."

It was only after she was out the door that he remembered, he had *not* offered to buy her a drink.

· · · · ·

Sol had never been this drunk in his life, although in the grand scheme of drunk, he wasn't that drunk. This was the kind of drunk normal college kids get at typical college parties—more than was wise, but less than was dangerous. Still, he actually stumbled a time or two on his walk home, so that was new.

He picked up his mail on the way in, which he'd forgotten to do when he'd gotten back earlier but wasn't a huge pressing thing, anyway; he rarely had mail that wasn't bills, and he never got anything at his Alphabet City address that was work related. He was surprised, therefore, to find that he had a package.

Goddamn it.

Smart protocol would mean calling in a bomb squad, but he was just drunk enough that he figured he could do it himself. He had the equipment, after all, and he probably deserved to get blown up, anyway. So he put on his silicone gloves and did the bomb test (the same one the TSA does), and then opened the box to find a computer hard drive. On the hard drive, a note:

> HOPE YOU HAVE BETTER LUCK WITH THIS THAN I DID.
> —A FRIEND

He didn't recognize the handwriting, but it looked like it had come from a human. As far as he could tell, there were no shenanigans—this wasn't a bomb or a bug (or if it was, it wasn't a human one; it could have alien shit in it for all he knew). He got out his hardware, plugged in the drive, and opened it—regular old Mac OS.

He opened the mail app first. Most of the emails in the inbox had the subject "Inquiry." He scrolled down to the "Sent" tag, and when he saw the name from whom all the emails were sent, he thought this must be drunk hallucinations. It could very well be a sick joke or, more likely, a misdirect from the person who appeared to be the owner of this hard drive.

Nils Ortega.

· 4 0 ·

Cora woke with a sense memory; the feeling of her skin being ripped off felt so real and present, her back arched on instinct, as if doing so would keep the seams of her skin together. She opened her eyes in a familiar dim light, back still arched, the ghost of the injury still there.

"Ampersand?"

"*You are home.*"

She was in bed, the *downstairs* bed that he preferred, and Ampersand was standing over her. She felt some sense of urgency, perhaps a sense of carefulness, like if he moved too quickly, she'd break apart again.

"*Did you see Nikola?*"

She covered her face with her hands. So, that was that. She'd come so close to finding Paris only to once again become the victim of unspeakable alien violence. "No, but I heard Paris's voice. She's alive. She said they had Nikola there, too." She let her eyes de-blur and find their focus. The lights in his lair were barely brighter than night-lights. "What happened?"

"*I arrived in the physeterine settlement in Belarus two minutes and forty-five seconds after you were taken. Your intelligence colleague told me that you were taken by two juveniles, and I was able to use what data I had to track them to the Himalayas, but no farther, as they were able to use the mountains to their advantage, and their scramblers disoriented my ability to track you. This scrambling came in and out until you came back on line in a mountainous region on the Malaysian peninsula. I followed your signature there, fearing it may have been removed from you altogether, a move that would likely prove fatal if not treated. To my immense relief, you were intact, albeit wired with an IED.*"

"A what?"

"*The juveniles—two of them, I believe—told me they would release you alive and intact if I would answer their questions.*"

"A fucking IED?"

He looked at her as if he was confused as to why that little tidbit might be upsetting. "*Not of the human-made variety you are familiar with.*"

She took a deep breath and closed her eyes. "The last thing I remember before I passed out was one of the adults finding the implant. And when they did, they . . ."

"*I know what they did.*"

She felt long fingers lightly brushing against the skin of her face. "I think the juveniles didn't know about the implants. It seemed like the adults were really angry about it, like they knew you could track me down with the implants, because right after they . . ." She shuddered. "After they figured out I had them, there was this huge commotion. Then it seemed like they almost forgot about me." She looked at him. "Didn't you catch them?"

"*The juveniles conducted their interrogation remotely. It was clear that these juveniles were acting alone, as adults would never have been so careless. The operation was clumsy, their questions both lacked strategy and were incredibly revealing; therefore, I was able to quickly retrieve you, but I was not able to capture them, nor was I able to find their settlement.*"

"What did they ask you?"

"*They asked why we were here on Earth—I told them a simple, abridged version of the truth. They were particularly fixated on humanity's rapid technological advancement in the last two centuries. They seemed convinced that it was the Superorganism's doing; I told them it was not. They asked of what significance you were to me; I told them you were my liaison and my interpreter. Then they asked several questions about our legal personhood under human law; I told them that what countries have granted us legal status equal to humans have done so of their own volition and without coercion. It was at this point I was able to circumvent the explosive they had implanted you with—*"

"Jesus."

"*—and was able to extract you before any more harm came to you.*"

Cora reminded her muscles to relax, the distant ache in her upper back much fainter now than the memory she was finding difficult to shake.

"*I need to know what you saw and heard at the physeterine settlement.*"

"Well, I can tell you as best I can, but I was—"

"*You misunderstand me. I need to know what you saw and heard. I need to know it through your senses.*"

Then it sank in what he was asking. "What?"

"*Your lover and my symphyle are still their captives. The transients do not know I'm capable of accessing your memories through high language—*"

"Ampersand, no, please—"

"*Your memory is fresh; you may not have been able to understand what was going on, what was said, but if I am able to experience it as you did, I may be able to understand what they said to one another.*"

"It isn't ready. We're not ready. *I'm* not ready. Please. It will kill me."

"*Moreover, if I am able to see the setting, I may be able to deduce where they are.*"

"You said you wouldn't do it again until I was ready!"

"*That was an extension based on personal comfort, before the lives of our loved ones were on the line.*"

He said it with such intensity she wondered if he would force her to do it if she continued to say no.

"*I have no other leads, my love. We know they are both alive, but we do not know for how long. We must act quickly, and my best intelligence lies inside your memory. You must let me see it.*"

· · · · ·

It was even darker in the sensory-deprivation chamber than it had been in Ampersand's bedroom, like it was lit by fireflies, and she stared into that dimness like it was the last time her eyes might see light at all.

"*Remove your clothing.*"

She did as he said, one of the many tiny concessions she made for him that made her feel even more vulnerable. She could feel him behind her, the slight pressure as he hooked up the implants in her brain to whatever machinery was going on in his.

"*I can sense your discontent.*"

"I've already had to come to terms with my mortality once in the last few hours," she whispered, hugging herself tightly. "I feel like it's more economical to just stay there."

"If you've agreed to this and you're committed to going through with it, there is no benefit to expecting you're going to die. You won't."

How to explain? It wasn't literal death that she was afraid of, but rather a death of the mind, death of the *self,* that her consciousness was far more fragile than he anticipated and that his barging into hers would burst her apart like a water balloon filled too full. She wouldn't die, but she would no longer *be.*

"We should not begin with a memory of physical trauma; I want you to concentrate on a memory in which you felt safe."

She closed her eyes, tried to sense what was going on in him, tried to see if there was *any* sense of hesitation on his end, but as always, no. Right now, the wall was thick, and the only thing she could sense even distantly was a strong sense of urgency.

"I'm still really scared."

"Your fear will only make this more difficult. Concentrate on a memory of safety."

As he said that, the room fell into complete darkness. She felt the water slide into her ears like puzzle pieces falling into place, and breathed deeper, not because she needed the oxygen so much as she needed the sound, sound being the only sense she had tethering her to her physical body. She knew he didn't *want* her to die, but she wasn't his top priority right now.

"You'll wipe me out to find Nikola."

"No. I am your caretaker. You are both mine. I would not sacrifice one for the other."

He would, though. He's done it before. He's done it with Obelus, and he hates Obelus. He'd do it with Nikola, whom he doesn't hate, only fears, only pities. She wanted to believe him. She wanted to be able to put her life in his hands and feel secure in it, tell him, *It's okay, do what you need to do. We are in this together. I trust you.* But every fiber in her being was telling her that she wouldn't *be* after he was done. He'd be left with an empty shell like a hermit crab's, a lovely, unliving thing he could crawl inside whenever he wanted.

"Will you save her?" she choked. "If I don't make it, will you save her?"

"*You will make it.*"

"What if I don't?"

"*You won't be harmed.*"

"Promise me. Just promise me you'll save her."

"*I will, dear one.*"

He said it so quickly. Like he didn't take it seriously, either the possibility of her being irreparably damaged or even killed, or the impetus to save Paris.

Formless, senseless darkness. That was the intent of this exercise, to disembody her, to make it seem like she was floating in nothing.

And then the darkness beginning to take shape. She tries to wave her arms around where she knows there to be water. Tries to take in air, tries to speak, but can't. She is already in it.

No, no, it will kill me!

It won't.

You've been wrong before. You were wrong about this before!

She tries to cry out, but her body, wherever that is, isn't responding. Then she sees it, like a hurricane against a deep black sky and just as huge. It hasn't seen her yet, but it is searching for her.

She remembers that she has some instruction, but she must get away from this presence. It is too big, it will consume her, crush her. She opens her mouth to scream but only draws its attention.

By now, she feels like she is on solid ground, but the ground is like molasses. The spirals of the hurricane are taking shape, lighter from the dark sky behind it, and begin to resemble fingers, each one a mile long as it coalesces and reaches toward her. She tries to move through the black molasses, knowing that if they touch her they would crush her like an ant.

Then it is as if two mountaintops are trying to come together to pick her up. She knows that she cannot outrun them, cannot fight them. They have her now, pinching her body between them, her impossibly fragile body.

Again she recalls there was an instruction to go somewhere, somewhere safe—where could be safe? She can't see the ground. It is miles beneath her, and she begs the force holding her to let her go. She had instructions; she was supposed to go somewhere.

She sees a pair of eyes in the hurricane, each eye the size of an island miles wide and the color of lava burning in the darkness. She feels the wind on her as the hands that belonged to those eyes move toward her. And there is a voice belonging to the eyes, the eyes that are now the size of oceans, and it says:

You had your instructions.

*What was the word? **Safe**, safe was the word. Go someplace **safe**. But safe is a concept she could not imagine any more than she could imagine a dimension outside of space-time.*

Go someplace safe.

I don't remember where I was supposed to go!

Let me inside you.

No, I can't! You'll kill me!

She tries to pull away as another mountaintop comes toward her, the two holding her together offering her up to the third, and she realizes that this one isn't going to hold her in place like the other two; this one is going to crush her. She is a gnat, and it is going to smear her on the side of the mountain like she is nothing.

Let me inside you.

I can't, I can't, I can't!

You had your instruction.

She stops holding the mountaintop back and allows it to crush her, smear her against the rocks, dash her into nothingness.

41

The first sensation they are aware of is the feeling of the cold, hard floor beneath their feet. Their feet are flat, which gives them more surface area to experience coldness. Stranger still are their upright legs, their upright posture. The bright light isn't harsh, but pleasant to their eyes, which aren't sensitive to bright light at all. It is indirect sunlight reflecting into this kitchen through a window. They are in a kitchen they have never been in before.

Some of their senses are muted; their vision is dulled, their color spectrum narrowed. They are unable to sense electromagnetic fields at all. But enhanced are other senses—they can sense volatile chemical compounds in the air with every breath they take in. Those chemical compounds don't register as data but as smell because they possess the ability to place those chemical compounds with specific objects projecting the smell.

"Just like college," says a voice. "That's all right. I'm not above it. I liked college."

They look up at the source of the voice. Their color vision is limited, but it is heavily attuned to the color of human skin, human hair, human eyes. To their eyes, her skin is dark brown, her irises a lighter shade of the same, her hair a halo of black curls framing her heart-shaped face. Then an intense swell of emotion, so *sudden*. A deep fondness, combined with excitement at the possibility of being with their partner. No, not their partner, not yet—they have not yet formalized any sort of partnership, have not yet consummated any sex acts. But they want to, their entire body is buzzing with anticipation, *excitement*. It is overwhelming.

"I've never actually done one of these before," they tell her.

"Snap," she says. "Milestones left and right. Give me your hand?"

Their prospective partner is holding a small container full of sodium chloride crystals, and she pours some of the crystals onto the back of their outstretched hand, which only seconds prior they have swiped with their tongue, leaving a small patch of saliva. Some of the sodium chloride crystals cling to the drying patch of saliva; most fall to the floor.

"First salt, then the shot, then lime," says their prospective partner, pouring some of the crystals onto a saliva patch on her own hand.

They look down; their left hand has the salt crystals held in place by their rapidly drying saliva, in their right, a phial of poison—ethanol. This is not the first dose they have ingested so far on this day. "This is to make it bearable?"

"It's more the ritual," says their future partner. "This is Patrón—not the best, but not the worst."

"I'm honored that I was worthy of the Patrón."

"Oh, I wouldn't subject you to Señor José," she says. This is a joke. José is not a person. She is referring to an inferior brand of the same poison.

Their future partner licks the salt crystals from her hand, ingests the phial of poison, and then sucks a wedge of a green citrus fruit to extract the juices. At the same time, they use their own tongue to lick the crystals off their skin, and the taste of the sodium chloride explodes across their mouth. The taste is distinct to this mineral and this mineral alone—the only mineral that they are able to distinctly taste. They have barely had time to grasp the effects of the sodium chloride when they swallow the poison in one painful gulp.

It is the most revolting thing they have ever experienced.

Immediately, they can feel their body rejecting the poison, their salivary glands pumping saliva in their mouth as they push the fluids down their esophagus. The effects of the sodium chloride are dwarfed by the effects of the ethanol, which cause an innate gag reflex that might precede the regurgitation of both the poison and the rest of their stomach contents. The taste is intense and bitter, the smell distinct to this poison alone—*tequila*. Then they bite down on the citrus fruit—a lime—and suck hard. Again, an explosion of sensation, this time the sting of acid and the taste of sour. It immediately overwhelms most of the taste and smell of the tequila, which is still quite strong in their mouth.

"Actually pretty smooth," they say, a lie. It is not smooth. It is not smooth at all.

But they are mostly unfazed by the unpleasant effects of the ethanol, much more driven by desire for the person whose home they are in. Their feelings of desire are intense, *too* intense, manifesting in a wave of emotion so strong that it is surprising they possess the restraint not to act on it immediately. But of course they have the restraint not to act on intense emotion. They must use this restraint every day. All humans do.

Their partner brings her body close to theirs, and a thrill of excitement goes through their chest. They can actually *feel* their heartbeat, which is a rare occurrence. Their partner runs a digit softly over the skin of her clavicle, sending an even greater thrill of excitement through them.

"You sure you want to do this?" she asks.

Yes, yes, they desperately want to touch her, to be touched by her. They feel an intense urge to slip their hands underneath her shirt and put their hands on her midsection, imagining her skin to be warm and soft. They have been so deprived of contact since they lost their previous partner. Their previous *human* partner. They have a current partner, but he is not human, and he does not make them feel safe. He frightens them.

He *frightens* them.

They are backing themselves up against a wall, an invitation that their partner accepts as she runs her soft fingers over their hairline and moves her body close to theirs. This makes them even more excited, and blood rushes into their genitals. The sensation is warm, tingling. The unpleasant effects of the poison have receded, and now its intended effects are taking place; their inhibition is lowering, their self-doubt receding. They lean forward and place their lips on their partner's.

A part of them is enjoying this torrent of emotion, of desire, and the other part of them is overwhelmed. The arousal has heightened their senses from their human baseline, which are already extremely sensitive and impossible to control. Their sense of smell has become acuter, their sense of touch keener, and the nerves in their lips are particularly sensitive. They desire to *sense* their partner in every way—taste, smell, touch. They enjoy the sounds she makes, the sweet taste of her lips on their tongue, but especially her smell, a comforting blend of vanilla and her natural pheromones. A part of them has never experienced such intense desire.

Now they have moved into another room. Now they are lying supine on a couch, struggling to remove their clothing and undergarments at the same time. Now their partner is mounting them and taking off her own clothes. Her tongue is long and red, her teeth sharp and white, it is the mouth of a carnivore, but they aren't frightened at all when she brings that mouth to their breast. This elicits an even stronger sensation. They are overwhelmed with the sensations. Their genitals are now slick with naturally occurring lubricant, and they are possessed by the desire to run their digits over their partner's genitals to find if they are in a similar lubricated condition.

They are.

Their partner makes an emphatic noise, one that could be easily mistaken for one of pain but they recognize as a noise of encouragement, that she wants them to keep making these movements with their digits, to increase their intensity. They insert two digits into their partner's vulva while simultaneously rubbing their thumb over her clitoris. She moans—not of pain or anger but of approval—and grinds her genitalia into their hand. Seeing the pleasure they give their partner gives them an even more intense sense of arousal, and they plunge their digits even deeper. Their partner gasps in delight.

"You've done this before," she says.

They have.

She kisses them again, moving her hips in encouragement as they continue the rhythmic movements. Their partner places her own hand on their genitals, causing an explosion of new sensation, an intense desire that she will do *more*. They intensify the rhythmic movements of their hand.

"Fuck, you're going to make me come," she says. This is a euphemism. She is referring to orgasm.

They are delighted that they have induced such feelings of arousal in their partner, and so quickly, and move their digits with even more fervor. Their partner cries out, and they can feel the muscles expanding and contracting over their digits as she experiences an orgasm. They look into their new partner's eyes and feel safe here. They feel *correct* here. Their partner looks down at them with satisfaction.

"Baby girl," she says, "you just need someone to take care of you."

The words touch them with an intensity that physical contact never could, and for a moment, they are incapable of a coherent response, only nodding eagerly as their partner leans in to kiss them again. It isn't that their new partner desires to be a caretaker, it's that she makes them feel safe, feel desired, feel *seen*.

Their other partner has never done that.

Their partner kisses them on their lips, their cheek, their neck, and then begins moving her mouth down their body—their breasts, their torso, their—

A part of them realizes that this carnivore is putting her mouth on their genitalia, stroking her tongue around the outer vulva in small, teasing strokes, and is appropriately horrified. But the other part, the part whose body this belongs to, is delirious with joy and arousal, moving her hips forward in encouragement, feeling their partner's tongue run over their vulva, *inside* their vagina. This carnivore is thrusting a tool primarily evolved to taste and manipulate food *inside* their reproductive organs.

"Mmm, you're so sweet." She is referring to the aforementioned naturally occurring lubricant.

They run their hands through their partner's hair, over her soft skin. Their fingers are *incredibly* sensitive—so much information simply from their fingertips! Simply taking in the sensory information is a source of pleasure.

"Don't stop, please," they say, and their partner intensifies her tongue movements, inserting her digits inside them, and they begin to experience their own orgasm. They have felt sensations this intense before, but they weren't pleasant ones. If pain was the most extreme negative one could feel, this was its inverse. They make a series of involuntary noises, *loud* noises, their back arching, the muscles in their vagina contracting. The feeling from the orgasm subsides, and their mind begins to clear. A part of them feels a deep sense of urgency, reminds the other that this isn't real. They reach for their partner, but she is gone.

"Paris?"

They sit up, now completely alone. This feels like a dream. *Dreams,* manifestations of the subconscious while asleep. Humans have dreams. They are in a memory of safety, but this memory is not why they are here.

"Please," they say, from one part of themselves to the other. "Please, don't make me go through it again."

They open their eyes, and their partner has returned, not as she was in the memory but as she is right now. She is covered in sweat and dirt and mud. She's hardly eaten in days. She is dehydrated, and starving, and alone, and frightened. She *needs* them. They have to leave this pleasant memory and go into a terrible one in order to save her.

Then another deep, intense emotion. Motivation. They so desperately want to save her. They want to save both of them. Paris and Nikola, they're both alive, they're both in pain, they both must be rescued. They regret the way that they parted with them, the way they treated them. Nikola was their charge, their youngest. Nikola had been in pain, suffering, and they left him in that place alone. Nikola ripped open spacetime itself to be with them, and they abandoned him. They have to save them. Both of them. They have to bring them both home, nurse them back to health, care for them as they should have before. Both parts of them feel this desire, but only one part of them knows the pain that awaits in that other memory.

They close their eyes in a warm house in Brooklyn.

They open their eyes in a jungle.

The sun has only just set, and there is enough light that they can still see their surroundings, but won't be for long. They are diurnal; their eyes are attuned to sunlight. They try to take in air; the air they've been breathing before this isn't made for them, the CO_2 levels are too high, it has been asphyxiating them. Now they are back in the open air, can breathe, but can hardly see. Where are they? Settlements, those are physeterine settlements. Their captors are speaking to one another as they gasp for air.

This is the one, the siren from the ubiquitous image.

The one protecting the Similars.

Shall we deliver her?

Our sires may kill her.

Though they didn't kill the ornamented siren?

The ornamented siren seemed to know this one.

The juveniles take them by the forelimbs and drag them toward one of the structures of the settlement, one of the greenhouses. They drag them into the open as their sires arrive, then they hear a human voice. At first they think they imagine it, but no. Paris's voice, trying to give them instruction—she is being held captive here, and so is Nikola. Another overwhelming experience, the relief at hearing their mate's voice. They *knew* she was alive. No one else believed she was still alive for statistical reasons, but they kept hope alive, and they are now vindicated. But they cannot see where she is.

Then they are grabbed. They can't see by whom. An adult transient, no, two adults.

This is one of the Similars's pets!

The juveniles reply in affirmation; they know that. That is why they took them.

Did you know this one has been implanted by one of the Similars? the adult asks.

Then they rip into their skin.

It is a pain unlike they've ever experienced—no, a pain unlike *part* of them has ever experienced, the other part of them, the one whose body this is, has experienced far worse.

The implants will have trackers. The Similars will find us, they will kill us all!

We can kill this one.

It is too late! Dead or alive, she must be removed!

Then we will remove her.

In the chaos, the two juveniles manage to drag her away, out of sight, into a cover of trees. They don't realize what they've done, don't realize that perhaps their scramblers weren't enough. In their haste and irresponsibility, they may have led the powered Similar right to the settlement, and the powered Similar will kill all 835 of the pod in an instant.

They want her destroyed.

Our sires may kill us.

They won't kill us.

Abandoning the harvest will mean starvation. It was our transgression that caused it. We will be the first to die.

They bleed like we do. It's the same color as ours.

They are in a copse now with five of them, all juveniles. The agony is terrible, so terrible it's all that the part of them capable of understanding the physeterine language can do to concentrate on what the juveniles are saying to one another.

We cannot save ourselves from punishment, but perhaps this might be redeemed.

If the implanted siren is so valuable, the Similar will want her alive.

If we use the implanted siren as bait, we can see what the white Similar tells us. Then we could know if they are truly detached from their Super-organism.

Why does that matter?

The ornamented siren offers us sanctuary.

The sirens gave sanctuary to the hive people, then why not to us?

They fear us.

They can learn not to fear us.

Perhaps the sirens gave the Similars sanctuary out of fear.

Then we can make the sirens fear us.

Our parents have the means to kill all the sirens if the need arises.

Fear will breed resentment. Fear is unsustainable.

It doesn't matter—we only need the time and resources.

Perhaps instead of bartering the dark Similar to another pod, our sires can use him as ransom.

The transients' motivation for taking Nikola instead of killing him becomes clear to them now. These transients are desperate. And so they took an incredible risk by taking Nikola alive so they could barter him to a rival pod.

Our parents will leave this planet before begging for sanctuary from the natives.

We will die in space more quickly than we would here, even with hostile natives!

Our sires will kill the natives with their plague before they are forced to beg them for sanctuary.

Killing the natives with their plague will only guarantee that the Similars on Earth will kill us all in turn. We can't kill the sirens. Truce is our only option.

You forget our history. Every attempt at truce with the hive people has led to our kind slaughtered. They want us exterminated.

We are transient because of the Superorganism.

But this is a new scenario in all our history.

We can't allow you to do this. You'll expose us all. The powered Similar will find us here before we can evacuate and kill us all.

They don't see or hear anything else.

42

Paris had expected the act of chewing through synthetic hair to be easier than it was; the top half of her braids were her natural hair, but the bottom half was a synthetic burgundy so bright it bordered on fuchsia, and it resisted being cut by teeth in the way that most plastics do. She doubted they would leave her where she was in this evacuation; she'd be either taken along or, more likely, killed, but she wanted to leave something to show that she had been here, and she was fresh out of business cards. After about ten minutes of trying, she managed to get one braid free, pushing it through the vines of her cage.

The evacuation had been going at a frantic pace for several hours, and now the sun was finally coming up, forcing the adults to don gunmetal-colored daysuits. They used the mantas she'd seen earlier to move resources out of the honeycomb-bookstack storage area, ferrying them to bigger manta rays the size of sedans. She'd been rubbing her wall transparent during the entire operation; either it operated like a two-way mirror, or the adults outside didn't care, as none of them reacted to the fact that she could see what was going on outside.

"I don't see any kids anymore," she said.

"THEY EVACUATED THE JUVENILES FIRST, AND NOW THEY ARE EVACUATING THE STOCKPILE, BUT THEY WILL LOSE THE MAJORITY. THEY MAY NOT EVEN HAVE ENOUGH TO FEED THEMSELVES ONCE THEY DEPART THE PLANET, LET ALONE BARTER WITH IT. AND NOW THEIR PRESENCE ON EARTH IS WELL KNOWN TO THE TERRAN SUPERORGANISM. BUT THEY HAVE STRATEGIZED POORLY. TAKING MY LITTLE COUSIN WAS A FATAL MISTAKE ON THEIR PART."

"It was the kids that took her, and I really don't think they were being strategic. I think they were trying to impress the adults."

"IF SHE IS DEAD, THERE IS NO REASON FOR US TO SPARE ANY OF THEM."

Paris stopped rubbing the wall, her arm slowly falling down into her lap, and her back fell against her prison of roots and vines. She almost felt guilty for suggesting to the juveniles that there might be some hope for coexistence. "You really do mean to kill them."

"WE HAVE LITTLE CHOICE."

Through the wall, which was fading to its normal opaque state, she saw a few of the adults suddenly drop their load and turn their attention to something. She got back up to see what had caught their attention—Durian and Coconut had returned.

"The two juveniles who took Cora are back."

"CAN YOU SEE THEM?"

"Sort of. They're surrounded by adults."

The two had their heads down, arms tucked in a mantid way that felt more amygdaline than physeterine, tails between their legs like dogs, with Durian's wrapped around their right leg like a corkscrew. The crests on the two juveniles' heads splayed like spirit fingers as they timidly spoke to Tsar Bomba and Trinity.

"THE TWO JUVENILES RANSOMED MY LITTLE COUSIN IN EX-CHANGE FOR ANSWERS FROM MY BELOVED."

"Holy shit." Paris nearly gagged on her relief. "She's alive?"

"SHE WAS WHEN THEY DELIVERED HER."

The adults listened to them for a minute, two at most, before Bomba grabbed Durian and Coconut violently by their necks, throwing both of them flat on their stomachs and holding them there.

"One of the adults is practically standing on top of them," said Paris. Durian tried to cut in on Bomba's diatribe, while Coconut curled up like a roly-poly. Bomba again cut them off. "What are they saying?"

"THE JUVENILE IS TRYING TO MAKE A CASE THAT THEY ACQUIRED USEFUL INTELLIGENCE FROM MY BELOVED. THE ADULT IS ENRAGED THAT THEY MAY HAVE GIVEN MY BELOVED A SECOND CHANCE TO TRACK THEM TO THIS LOCATION. THE JUVENILES HAVE NEVER SEEN HOW SIMILARS KILL; THE ADULT HAS. A SIMILAR WILL KILL YOU

BEFORE YOU EVEN REALIZE YOU'RE DYING, AND THAT'S HOW THE WHOLE POD WILL DIE IF MY BELOVED FOLLOWED THEM."

"Is that true?" asked Paris, cowed again by the thought of a re-powered Nikola, of a Jude who had never lost his power.

"YES, DEAR GENTLE CREATURE, A FULLY POWERED SIMILAR IS CAPABLE OF FAR MORE THAN THAT."

Coconut offered a timid rebuttal, which Nikola translated: "THE JU-VENILES INSIST THAT THEY ESCAPED FROM HIM SUCCESSFULLY."

Bomba lifted the two by the neck, holding them in the air, covering their breathing holes completely. They couldn't get any noise out, let alone any air in.

"THE ADULT SAYS THESE JUVENILES WON'T BE GIVEN THE CHANCE TO TEMPT FATE AGAIN."

Durian managed to flip their tail up around Bomba's neck, taking them by surprise, and then kicked the adult hard enough in the chest that Bomba dropped both of them. Without hesitating, Durian fled. Bomba stood stunned for a moment and then followed them into the jungle, their outraged chittering fading into the distance.

"The kid ran away."

"THE JUVENILE WAS AFRAID FOR THEIR LIFE."

"Of the adult? Their 'parent'?"

"YES."

Paris stayed glued to her window, needing to rub it back into translu-cency about once every thirty seconds. Before long, Bomba returned to the clearing and was intercepted by Trinity. Durian was nowhere in sight.

"THEY SAY THE EVACUATION CANNOT WAIT. THEY MUST ABAN-DON EVERYTHING AND LEAVE NOW."

Paris backed as far into the corner as her body would go, closing her eyes, thinking invisible thoughts. They only took her *just in case* she might be important to either Nikola or Jude. They only kept her alive *just in case*. She didn't matter anymore. Surely, she would be of the lowest priority. Surely—

A pair of powerful claws pierced her cage of vines, ripping the whole apparatus out by the roots, and Paris screamed. Bomba flung the vine bars into one of the rows of crops and, before she could react, grabbed her by the neck, announcing something to the others.

"THEY SAY THE SITUATION IS DIRE, AND THEY MUST ENACT THEIR CONTINGENCY. FOR THAT, THEY NEED A VECTOR; YOU ARE THE ONLY OPTION AVAILABLE."

"A vector for what?" she cried as Bomba bound her hands behind her back using that vine restraint. Then they picked her up in one arm, carrying her like a sack full of grain to one of the larger mantas.

"Nikola, a vector for *what*?"

T O P S E C R E T _____ **TOP SECRET**

MEMORANDUM FOR : SA Solomon Kaplan

VIA : Deputy Director for Operations Susan Macallan

SUBJECT : New Physeterine Settlement Discovered in Cambodia

An anonymous source has provided us with the location of a recently abandoned physeterine settlement in the mountains of Cambodia approximately fifty-three miles northeast of Phnom Penh. The director has requested your immediate presence at the site to deliver your expertise on the subject.

You are instructed to board flight KAL 86 00:50 out of JFK, transfer in Seoul flight KAL 678 08:20 to Phnom Penh.

U.S. armed forces have already arrived in the region and are currently conducting surveys under the command of Major General Wesley Porter.

Att: CIA Intelligence Report, 11/24/09, Subj: PHY-ETI Hostiles

· 4 3 ·

Sol stepped over a log and looked down into the hole where the foren-sics team was gathering evidence. It was deep and wide like an old-fashioned well, less a "this is where the dogs got a little too rowdy" hole so much as a "this is where Buffalo Bill lotions up his victims before he skins them" hole.

"Human remains?" asked Sol, trying to sound impartial.

"Not out of the realm of possibility," said Agent Makkonen. He was young and fresh-faced, one of the extremely rare Black guys in the agency. "There's definitely urine. Might be human, might not be."

"How old?"

"Less than a week, more than a few days," said Makkonen. "It's been raining off and on pretty heavily."

Sol pulled his aviators over his eyes and quickly surveyed the sur-rounding jungle again and saw a scrap of red sign poking out from behind some trees. A scrap of a red sign with a skull and crossbones. "Have they swept this place for mines?"

"Not yet."

"Get a minesweeper before you step one toe outside of this imme-diate vicinity. I'm guessing that's a big reason why they haven't had any run-ins—no human in their right mind is going to come out here."

Sol looked to the sky when he caught the sound of another helicop-ter arriving. He'd never been to Cambodia, but there was something about seeing American helicopters flying and landing in this part of the world that put him on edge, like the land, still scarred from Amer-ican bombing, might produce some immune response and repel the invaders. The helicopter touched grass in a clearing some fifty feet away, and out hopped his department head, Susan Macallan, while the blades still whirred. The helicopter took off just as Macallan and a few other CIA personnel hit the ground, making room for the next helicopter to disgorge.

"Kaplan!" yelled Macallan against the noise of the blades, holding her cap in place as the helicopter took off behind her. "AG-2 and AG-3 have gone rogue."

"Surprised they didn't do it sooner." After all, AG-2 and AG-3 (by night known as Esperas and Brako) had been gallivanting as they pleased ever since the Sierra plane crash; it was only a matter of time before they stopped coming home to their government security complex altogether. "What about the rest of them?"

"Same as always," said Macallan, donning her own pair of sunglasses and jamming her fists into her jacket. "Just parked in their semi-inert state, awaiting instruction, one assumes."

"Instruction from whom?"

"From whomever they're taking instruction from this week." She looked at Sol, and he thought he saw an air of suspicion. "46 didn't relay anything to you?"

"46 does not *speak*—that's his thing. Sabino speaks for him."

"There are other ways to communicate."

"Well, he declines to utilize them. I told 46 that they took her; he barely looked at me before he disappeared again. I didn't see him again after that." He looked at Macallan. "I assumed 46 must be how you even found this place."

"It might well have been," she said with a dry laugh. "I don't know how we got the intel, and I doubt it was from the transients. What all do we have?"

"We have what look like the remains of . . . let's call them dormitories. But they're all incinerated, destroyed, hardly recognizable as something alien if you don't know what to look for."

"Is that it?"

"So far," said Sol. "But it is strange; all the other settlements had some evidence of horticulture."

"This one doesn't?"

"I suspect we haven't found it yet."

"Have they done infrared scan?"

"Yes, but I'm pretty sure these guys have ways of evading those," said Sol, wandering toward the tree line near the Buffalo Bill pit.

"What is it?" asked Macallan.

"The remains of the settlement we found in Belarus had hidden entrances." Then he spotted a pair of trees that were positioned similarly to the ones he'd seen in Belarus. He put his arm between them and froze when, optically at least, his hand ceased to exist.

Macallan noticed it, too. "Kaplan . . ."

Without waiting for her to say yea or nay, he stepped through the two trees and found what he had been looking for. "I need a containment team!"

Here was the greenhouse, their "garden." They'd departed in such a hurry, they'd left a stunning amount of evidence: living spaces, tools, laboratories, even what looked like some half-eaten food they hadn't had the chance to finish. They had left part of the filter that hung over the black plants, and it was only here that he saw what Cora meant about subtracting sunlight rather than adding it.

Within minutes, the greenhouse was flooded with operatives in hazmats, with more on the way now that they realized the scope of all they had discovered. All Americans, he noted. No Cambodians. With America heavily leaning into its image as a nation of bullies that didn't care about the sovereignty of other nation-states, *that* would play well on the international stage.

While the forensics team gathered more biological specimens, Sol and several other agents continued through the greenhouse itself. It was stunning how seamlessly it wove into the natural fabric of the jungle, as though they wanted to sacrifice as few trees as possible to build it. The crops were in rows, but the rows weren't in straight lines at all, instead conforming to the natural flow of the jungle, making it all that much more difficult to spot from the sky. What was strange was that it didn't seem more inefficient than traditional human irrigation, just laid out in a far more complex pattern.

"Kaplan," called Makkonen, following Sol as he walked back to the greenhouse entrance. "How's this compare to what you saw in Belarus?"

"It looks to me like the Belarusian location was abandoned deliberately, over a period of time—they didn't leave anything behind that they couldn't afford to lose. This looks like—"

"An evacuation?"

"That's my read."

"Agent Kaplan?"

Sol and Makkonen turned to the source of the voice—an agent on his knees, scraping some dirt into a test tube.

"What do we got?" asked Makkonen.

"Blood," said the agent, looking at the test tube clinically.

"Human?"

"Can't say."

"Send it out."

Sol returned to the greenhouse and explored for a bit. Before long, out of the corner of his eye, he caught something pink—a hair braid. A pink-and-black hair braid the diameter of a drinking straw and about twelve inches long. A few feet away, he found another. There was, he supposed, a possibility that another, different creature had found Paris Wells's corpse and chewed off one of her braids before both Wells's corpse and this unidentified third party had been removed. But that was exceedingly unlikely.

Sol put the braid into a plastic bag and handed it off to forensics. "Send this off to DNA testing, too." The second braid he pocketed.

"Human hair?" asked Makkonen.

"The red is synthetic, though the black is probably real. There may be saliva here, too. This looks to me like it was chewed off, not cut."

"So Wells was here."

"At least her body was," said Sol. "Find out what cut it. When it was cut."

"On it."

As Makkonen left with the braid, another helicopter was touching down to disgorge a new batch of personnel, which Sol decided was his chance for an exit.

"Kaplan?" said Macallan, walking with him toward the helicopter.

"I'm heading back to Phnom Penh," he said. "There are some things I want to research."

As Sol walked toward the helicopter, he recognized the head officer of the army contingent. Joy, oh, joy. The former brigadier general Wesley Porter, who had been upgraded to major general and wanted everyone to know it. Sol swallowed his pride and saluted the man.

"Kaplan!" yelled Porter over the noise of the blades. "At ease. Any stragglers?"

"Physeterine stragglers, sir?"

"No, Khmer Rouge stragglers."

"They were all gone by the time we arrived," said Macallan before Sol could offer some smart retort that would get them both in trouble.

"Sir," said one of Porter's junior officers, "what if we find any stragglers?"

"We engage the way we engage with any hostile."

Sol tilted his head, wondering if he'd heard the man correctly. Once a force was declared "hostile," units could engage that force without observing a hostile act or demonstration of hostile intent. The basis for perceived hostility was no longer conduct but status, and unless they were to surrender (and only then due to injury), a "hostile" force could be killed for the sheer crime of existing.

"Are you declaring these ETIs hostiles, sir?"

"How many people have these things killed, Kaplan?"

"Sir, human hostiles might at least speak Pashto or Urdu—we presently have no means of even attempting communication with physeterines."

"They don't need to speak Pashto to kill children in the middle of the night."

Porter moved toward the tent that was being pitched, and Sol retreated to the helicopter before turning back one last time and asking, "Major General, do the Cambodians know we're here?"

"They know no more than they need to know, Agent." Porter didn't even look back at him.

Sol shook his head, boarded the helicopter, and buckled up, watching Porter as the helicopter lifted off.

· 44 ·

As Cora dipped back into consciousness, every cell in her body told her no, she should stay asleep for at least another eighteen months or so. She had a vague sense not just of having relived some intense memories but having been in an altered state while doing it. Having not been alone in her own head when doing it.

And then she remembered why.

Her eyes shot open, the second time she'd woken up in this dim bedroom on this giant bed. This time, Ampersand was not standing over her but was lying right next to her.

"How are you feeling, dear one?"

"Did it work? Did you find—"

She stopped mid-sentence, already knowing the answer. After all that, after reliving the experience of having her very flesh ripped open like wet tissue paper, it didn't work. He hadn't found her.

She flopped back down onto her pillow, clapping her hands over her eyes. She felt like her body had just been used as a glove in a boxing match. Why, she wondered, did her muscles ache so when they hadn't after Ampersand repaired her injuries before? Had every muscle in her body been in a persistent stage of tension since he'd . . .

Let me inside you.

Well, that had happened. The eldritch horror demanded to be let in, and she let him. She opened her eyes to look at him, to see if those residual feelings of revulsion and horror were still there. They weren't, but she couldn't place a finger on why. She strained to sit up. She did not have the luxury right now to process these feelings. "Is Nikola still alive?"

"*He is.*"

She released a breath. He hadn't found them, but it wasn't over yet.

"*I did find the settlement, but it had been abandoned. There was one straggler in the woods nearby, though. I have a captive. The same who kidnapped you.*"

She threw her legs over the side of the bed and stood up. "Take me to them."

· · · · ·

Ampersand threw back the curtain as Cora pushed the sliding glass door open, flooding the living room with sunlight and causing their new captive to cry out in hissing, clicking terror like a frightened cobra. Cora scrunched up her nose. "The smell—did they piss themselves?"

"*They have glands that secrete ammonia as a stress response.*"

Ampersand had bound their arms behind their back in the way she'd seen him do to Nikola before, not by the wrist but more the whole arm tied behind them like chicken wings. They turned their face from the sun, eyes closed tight.

"Where are their clothes?"

"*I removed them.*"

Just like Johnny the Alien Corpse in the Philippines, the juvenile's skin was a faded canary yellow that transitioned into dark black-purple patches on their extremities—the tips of their crest, muzzle, fingers, toes, tail, and even the lining of their eyes appeared so dark it was almost black.

"Have you tried interrogating them yet?"

"*Not directly. I am not an expert in interrogation techniques.*"

The ammonia smell hit her again, purer than urine normally was. It smelled like old jewelry cleaner. "Seems like the Superorganism isn't huge on interrogation."

"*Certainly not with transients.*"

She almost wondered what Sol might say—he'd intimated to her before how annoyed he was at how cavalierly the CIA employed all sorts of torture before they got found out, but she didn't know what his level of participation in said torture had been, let alone if any of it actually *worked*. "I can't help but think that there's not much to be learned from human 'enhanced interrogation' techniques."

"Hypnosis and drugging is also an option, though that will take some time and may yield unreliable information."

The juvenile writhed like a worm on a hot driveway, shaking so violently as to almost jerk every few seconds or so. All the while they seemed to be *trying* to stay silent, despite the occasional coughing-choking noise.

"What's wrong with them?"

"Their eyes and skin can't tolerate the UV light; at the same time, the ambient air temperature is too cold to maintain thermoregulation."

"They're burning and going hypothermic at the same time," she said, surprised at how cold and detached she felt. In a way, this almost felt like retribution. *You kidnapped me. You let them torture me. Now how do you like it?*

Ampersand stayed where he was, speaking in physeterine-common, and the translation appeared on Cora's optical overlay:

[*Where has your pod gone, young one?*]

The juvenile didn't respond, only writhed and jerked in miserable silence. The smell of ammonia hit Cora so hard she shielded her face.

"The one alarming thing I did learn from your memories was that their pod has engineered a 'plague' as a contingency against human civilization and are considering deploying it. In order to deploy their plague, they need a living human vector. And we know they have at least one living human."

This hit her like a punch to the chest. A living human vector.

Paris.

Ampersand spoke again:

[*Your pod has an escape vessel hidden somewhere. Tell me where it is, and I will shield you from the starlight.*]

The juvenile gave them nothing but pained silence. This was getting nowhere fast. She closed her eyes, thinking back to what she had overheard during the high-language memory of her captivity. *What do they want?*

The ornamented siren offers us sanctuary.

The part of her that had been attached to Ampersand during the memory was able to parse the nuance of that translation, that *ornamented siren* was in reference to a human nearby, which could only be Paris. *Ornamented* in this context meaning in a superficial way—they must have been referring to her tattoos or her braids. Paris must have told them that humans had given sanctuary to the Fremda group and suggested that Semipalatinsk might be able to get the same deal. Ampersand didn't really have anything to offer them in exchange for information, but humanity might.

"Hold tight," she said, going back into the master bedroom and pulling out a spare blanket from the closet. She then came back into the living room and unfurled the blanket, shielding the juvenile from the sun. "It's called good cop / bad cop. A very basic human interrogation technique. They're scared shitless of you, but they might talk to me if it feels to them like I'm on their side."

She wrapped them up in the blanket, and tried several times to get the juvenile to their feet, but they remained twisted in the fetal position, eyes clamped tight. Eventually Ampersand got impatient and grabbed the juvenile, wrapping them up in the blanket like a burrito and carrying them inside the house.

"Can you give me a way to communicate with them?" she asked, ushering the juvenile toward the living room table. "Maybe through the tablets?"

Ampersand retrieved one of their old tablets, a device they hadn't had use for in over a year, and spent a few minutes updating it with physeterine-common. Cora took a bottle of distilled room-temperature water out of the pantry, as well as a couple of ceramic bowls, and set them down on the table in the living area. By now, the juvenile had gotten up on their haunches, shivering and trying to wrap themselves up in the blanket, but unable with their hands bound behind them as they were. Their eyes were still closed—not out of fear, she realized, but because they couldn't stand the sunlight.

"It's still too bright for them—could you draw the curtains?"

Ampersand did as she asked, though she could sense that he was skeptical. He handed her the tablet, and she placed the tablet right in the juvenile's line of sight. "It's okay. I'm not going to let him hurt you."

The juvenile looked down at the tablet, their eyes no longer yellow but a dark orange verging on red.

"Why are their eyes red?"

"*A stress response.*"

"Can I get you some water?" she asked. "Maybe some food?"

The translation appeared on the tablet, and although the juvenile looked at it, she got no response. This went on for about half an hour—Cora tried to ply the juvenile with basic needs—water, food, protection from the sun, blankets, *more* blankets, but the juvenile didn't budge.

"*No amount of incentive or pain inflicted will make them volunteer information on the whereabouts of their pod,*" Ampersand decided. "*I will have to drug them.*"

She nodded. It was unethical, but the stakes were too high, and besides, Ampersand had done the same to her the literal first time they'd met for more or less the same reason, and unlike this little twerp, she had been completely innocent.

Ampersand stood up. "*I must first devise a drug specialized for physeterine juvenile brains. That will take some time. You recall how much trial and error it took for me to formulate a similar drug for humans.*"

"Yeah, I try *not* to think about that." She often forgot that two years ago she had only been the latest in Ampersand's long, sad string of human abductions/druggings, and the ones who had come before her fared far worse than her. "How long will that take?"

"*Days, at minimum.*"

"Fuck," Cora whispered, glaring at the juvenile. They didn't have hours, let alone days.

Then came another voice from just a few feet away, speaking in Pequod-phonemic, which translated on her viewfinder:

[That won't be necessary, noble peer.]

Ampersand turned, hands curled up in an antagonistic stance. There was Esperas, and a few feet behind him in the shadows, Brako. *This* caused a reaction in the juvenile, who chittered miserably in their own language and cowered under the blanket.

[Noble peer, they are terrified. What have you done to them?]

Ampersand didn't move but responded in Pequod-phonemic:

[*The presence of your Similar is the source of the juvenile's agitation. They have been brought up to fear Similars above anything else. You know this.*]

Esperas regarded the juvenile, eyes brightening, as though this were a treasure he'd found after long weeks of searching. He spoke:

[Noble peer, I commend you for taking this captive alive, but I request that you remand them to me.]

[*No.*]

[I overheard your dilemma; you need information from this juvenile but have no means of gaining it from them in a timely fashion. I do.]

[*I will not remand my captive to you.*]

[You take this poor child's clothes and expose them to the sun. You do not treat this child humanely. These are our only living cousins.]

Something about this phrase—*our only living cousins*—set something off in Ampersand, something that felt to Cora somewhere between disgust and embarrassment. "What does he mean?" she asked.

[You haven't told your liaison, have you? What makes us unique, what makes us a liability within the Superorganism.]

Esperas looked at her, and she quavered. It was one of the only times he'd ever looked at her directly, and his gaze was intense.

[What do you know, simple creature? Only that we are a genetic subset, that we were bred with the intent of an expanded genetic pool, but he never told you what made us unique? Or did you never guess? For you to invest so much in this human, I had assumed she would be cleverer than that.]

Ampersand finally put his hands down into his more neutral, mantid posture, and Esperas relaxed as well. "*Esperas retains some genomic memory, same as I do,*" Ampersand said to her privately. "*Only he contains memories from non-amygdaline ancestors as well.*"

"You mean your distant ancestors?"

"*No—Fremda were bred to respond to the crisis in genetic diversity. The only beings that could provide genetic diversity are our only living cousins.*"

"Your only living cousins . . ." Cora looked down at the juvenile as they continued to shiver. They tried to sneak a frightened look at her, only to jerk their gaze away when they saw she was staring. "Oh," she breathed. "Oh, wow."

"*This is what made Fremda unique within the Superorganism; we are hybrids.*"

Cora looked at Ampersand, who was staring at her as if daring her to say something. All this time—the "genetic defect" that had been the excuse for the Fremdan genetic purge had been physeterine DNA. It hadn't been just a political purge but a genocide in the purest sense. "That's why Fremdan Oligarchs opposed the Erythran sterilization."

"*No, dear one, most Fremdans did not know they were designed with some physeterine DNA. Most never learned before they were killed.*"

[There is much that the Superorganism does not know about us, if indeed they remember anything at all, but few physeterines know about us, either. And of course, communicating this truth would be difficult, but through high language, I could communicate it effectively and without mistrust.]

That didn't sound right to her at all; she'd just been down that road and knew firsthand how horrifying it was to go through high language with someone you *did* trust, let alone someone you were terrified of. Esperas watched the juvenile, his eyes brighter than she had ever seen them.

[They will not volunteer the information you seek. You have the materials and the technical skill to place rudimentary implants into their brain, and then I will communicate with them. It is unfortunate that I must do this to them without their consent, but in the process, they will see that I do not mean them or their pod any harm.]

Ampersand took a moment before moving toward the juvenile, never taking his eyes off Esperas and Brako. And through the wall, she felt nothing but contempt—contempt for Esperas, for his militarist Similar, and for every single one of the transients for whom Esperas showed so much compassion where he had none for him, or for Nikola, or for any human. Likewise, she didn't love the way Esperas was looking at the two of them, as though he hadn't quite abandoned the hope that he might be able to get rid of Ampersand if the opportunity presented itself.

Ampersand tore off the blanket, causing the juvenile to cringe and make some noise of protest as they balled back up into the fetal position, their tail wrapped tightly around their right ankle. Ampersand picked them up by the midsection and carried them toward his fallout shelter. Esperas spoke again:

[Do them no harm, caste-peer. It will only make my endeavor more time-consuming.]

Ampersand didn't look at Esperas again before taking his captive down into his lair. Even the juvenile didn't protest, their body hanging limply as they disappeared with him into the darkness.

Brako moved outside onto the patio that overlooked the mountains, while Esperas stayed inside. Brako even relaxed into a roosting position, which she'd never seen him do before. On its face it looked like he was sitting sentry, but it almost felt like he was giving them privacy.

Cora jumped at the sound of an animal screaming from the fallout shelter—no, not an animal, it only sounded like one. She couldn't help but feel like she *should* feel bad about this. It wasn't even that she felt a desire for vengeance for what the kid had done. They were just a dumb kid, and it hadn't been the kids that had ripped her open.

[I will accept distilled water.]

"Oh," she said, realizing that Esperas was talking to her. Was this some gesture of good faith? Like humans, the form of sustenance they needed in greatest quantities was water, even if it was far less water by volume than a human needed (somewhere in the neighborhood of about a liter per week). But for them, it was like changing one's oil filter, not the ceremonial thing that was eating and drinking in human culture.

"Um, sure."

She got some of the nicer ceramic cups gifted to her by one of Kentaro's associates from the kitchen, then poured a cup for each of them like this was sake service. The height of the table really was strangely perfect for this sort of thing. The few humans who had been in this house besides Luciana had all been Japanese, and they were positively chuffed at the fact that traditional Japanese furniture (particularly the seating arrangements and tables) were much more egalitarian than Western-style dining tables, serving needs both human and alien. She pushed the bowl in front of Esperas, who lowered the tip of his muzzle into it and imperceptibly took in the water like a deer at a forest pool.

"*Kanpai*," said Cora, lifting her own cup of water to her lips. Another swinelike wail emanated from below, but whatever it was, it was either too muffled or too incoherent for her translators to pick up on. She looked to Esperas for some cues, but he didn't seem particularly upset by Ampersand's methods, either.

"I've never seen Ampersand so . . . contemptuous before."

[This pod is the same that attacked and killed the phalanx of Similars that was guarding him, and his symphyle, and also killed and consumed his symphyle.]

"The same ones?"

[Not the same individuals. Those individuals are long dead. But they are of the same pod.]

"Do the ones here know that?"

[They likely know that said sub-pod did kill and consume those Similars. They do know that this sub-pod spared one Oligarch for the purpose of barter and did barter that Oligarch away before they were killed by a larger phalanx of amygdaline Similars. They would not know that said Oligarch and your symphyle are the same person.]

Cora was at that moment too drained, too tired to really be surprised that Esperas used that word—*symphyle*. That he knew. Hell, the secret she was supposed to take to her grave had been either divulged to or deduced by several people by now. Why not also by the one person who above all who was not supposed to find out?

"How did you know?"

[I surmised it.]

At this, she drained her water, walked into the kitchen, and filled her sake goblet with a cold, unfiltered ¥40,000 Nigiri she'd been saving for a special occasion. Then she returned with two fresh matching sake cups. "Can you drink this?"

Esperas regarded it.

[Such a high ethanol concentration is poisonous to us.]

"Well, it is for us, too. *Kanpai.*" She finished the cup in one gulp upon hearing another miserable screech from below. To her surprise she *hated* it in a way that she had never hated the taste of alcohol before.

[Your relationship is perverse, but it is a perversity that has led to some innovation of great potential consequence.]

"What do you mean?" She poured herself another cup of sake.

[Have you had any success with your high-language experiment?]

No one, least of all Esperas, was supposed to know about this. But at this point, what did it matter? "Yes."

[This is a tremendous discovery.]

"How so?"

[Physeterines are our cousins. There is no debate as to their personhood. Of course, with the right engineering, they could be made capable of high language. But you have no relation to us. Your neurology is completely foreign to ours. That one of our kind is able to communicate with one of your kind through high language at all is a discovery of great consequence.]

Esperas lifted his gaze toward her, and she froze as if it were his telekinesis holding her in place, a power that she knew for a fact he did not possess. His gaze was just so intense, like she was an amoeba looking up into the eye of a microscope.

[Would you consider allowing me to know you?]

She nearly choked on a sip of sake, still overwhelmed by the intensity of that gaze, and it took her a moment to get, really *get* what he was asking. "Wouldn't it be considered perverse?"

[Not perverse. Dynamic fusion bonding with you is perverse, but communication in itself is not perverse. I wonder, I wonder.]

"What?"

[I wonder if your capability were known within the Superorganism, that humans are capable of high language with the right engineering, would that change anything? If this situation with our physeterine cousins resolves peacefully, and we are all consigned to stay on Earth for the time being, would you allow me to know you, little one?]

There was a bigness to the request, not just that Esperas was curious for himself but that this somehow might change things. Like if humans weren't just cold, monstrous intelligences to be dealt with but were capable of their most intimate form of communication with the right engineering, it might change the way the Superorganism saw humans. And the cost to her, the only thing he was asking, was to allow him to know her in the most intimate way imaginable.

"I . . ."

"*The juvenile is prepared.*"

Cora took in a sharp gasp as she saw that Ampersand had reappeared, his eyes sharp and fixed on Esperas.

"*Do with them what you wish,*" Ampersand continued. "*Only do it quickly.*"

· 4 5 ·

Sol had never felt as out of place and uncomfortable in any country, even much more hostile ones that his own country had violently destabilized, as he did in Cambodia. It wasn't just the fact that there were American forces in the east without the government's knowledge and that sort of thing had ended very, very badly here in the past; really, it was how goddamn *nice* everyone here was. Always smiling and bowing with the hands together and the "Safe travel, sir? Are you on holiday, sir?" Bow, bow, bow. Didn't these people just have a genocide that his very agency had an indirect hand in facilitating? Would they be so *nice* if they knew he was CIA?

The Lucky Star Hotel in Phnom Penh did not charge hourly rates despite seeming like the sort of place that should, though for the price of five dollars a night, why would one need to cut corners? It was far from the worst room he'd ever rented—sure, the last person here hadn't flushed the toilet and there were stains on the comforter, but it was a lateral move from the one in Belarus. The room was a bit claustrophobic, as the only thin window looked into the hallway rather than outside, although given his line of work, he preferred it.

There was a very tiny writing desk onto which he unfurled his laptop and satellite internet station. There was even a "minibar," which was just a few snack items on a dresser, like candy and potato chips, and two cans of room-temperature Angkor-brand beer, one of which Sol cracked open. Funny he had judged Mazandarani so harshly, as he was rapidly starting down the same road.

Almost the instant Sol opened his laptop, he got a ring, not on one of his burners but on his main. In a way, he wasn't sure which he was dreading more. He put the phone to his ear. "Speak."

"We got a match on the blood." It was Makkonen.

"Human?"

"Yeah."

He leaned forward onto the writing desk. Nice of them to have a writing desk here. Maybe the Lucky Star Hotel got more CIA agents than Sum, the smiling, bowing receptionist, had let on. "Sabino?"

"Yeah." A pause on the other end of the line. "A 99.8 percent match."

He threw his head back against the chair and smiled bitterly. *Fuck you, Luciana Ortega, purveyor of false hope*, he thought. To think, she had been so irrationally convinced that Cora would escape this one, same as she always did, he'd almost believed her.

"What about the braid?"

"In the process of getting a DNA sample from Wells. We should get a result within a few hours."

"Thank you, Agent," he said calmly. "Please keep me updated."

He put the phone down on the little desk. Luciana Ortega had been in New York two days ago. What time was it there? Eleven, twelve, thirteen hours behind? Middle of the day, probably, and this news would be a good way to ruin it. He decided to let Luciana enjoy her last few hours of delusion before her world got shattered.

All the same, this whole time, Sabino had been right. Wells had been alive. Might *still* be alive.

He reached for his satchel, remembering the photocopies from Wells's journal that Macallan had given him before they'd departed for Belarus. He'd quickly ruled them irrelevant (at least pertaining to the current mission). The only interest he'd had in Wells's notes was for dirt on Mazandarani, one passage in particular.

Jannaham — Blackmail??

Sol did not speak Farsi, but knew enough vocabulary words from the Islamosphere to know the meaning of that word—"hell." It had also been the last word she'd written before her plane exploded. Something that the alien had said to Wells had indicated that Mazandarani had some correlation with hell and blackmail.

Then another buzz, this time to his burner. He flipped it open and put it to his ear. "Speak."

"Kaplan." It was a guy he knew at the NSA named Henry whose real name was not actually Henry but was unknown to Sol.

"You find something?"

"You in town?" said NSAHenry.

"No, I'm abroad."

"Oh, dang. I've got some stuff for you, but . . . I'd rather give it to you in person."

"Is it a lot?"

"It's a lot."

"Is it going to take a lot of time to *send*?"

"Data-wise, we're looking at a few kilobytes."

"Just send it to me."

"All right, dude. But I'm telling you right now, this is above my pay grade. It's all from private servers, so we're not violating any clearance for this, but it's a lot. We may as well be violating clearance."

"Is any of this classified?"

"No."

"Then we're not violating clearance."

Sol tapped his fingernails on the desk like he was sending Morse code as those few kilobytes crawled their way over the open ocean. It took almost three minutes. No body in the email, but several attachments, the first of which was a police report for a domestic disturbance in Yorba Linda, California. The perpetrator: Kaveh Mazandarani. The victim: Cora Sabino.

On 02-29-2008, at approx. 0415 hrs, I, Officer Lanning, along with Officer Turner responded to a domestic advised that victim Cora Sabino (DOB 8/21/86) had arrived at hospital with a superficial gash on her forehead and bruising all over her body, and a nurse suspected domestic violence.

I arrived at the hospital to interview the victim at 0546 at Anaheim Regional Medical Center.

Sabino stated that she had been living with Kaveh
Mazandarani (DOB 06/05/72) for the past two weeks.
When I asked about the nature of the bruising, that
some of the bruising on her fist, arms, and face were
more than a few hours old, she stated that she had
fallen before.

I then with Officer Turner interviewed Mazandarani,
who said that her injury came from her falling down
the stairs and that the multiple number of bruises on
her body came from repeated falls. He corroborated
her claim that the injury to her head had come from a
fall. Sabino did not consent for hospital to release
any medical records to PD. Sabino declined to press
charges. Arrest was not made for lack of probable
cause.

"That police report is wild, dude," said NSAHenry. "I don't think even your people knew about it. Looks like the FBI scrubbed it."

"How did Ortega get ahold of it?"

"Fucking Jano Miranda bribed some corrupt cops into giving him a copy of the police report before it got scrubbed and then sent it to Ortega!" NSAHenry said Miranda's name like he was talking about an NBA star scoring an awesome dunk. "Do you think he did it?"

"Do I think who did what?"

"Do you think Mazandarani beat her up?"

The police report was dated to the early morning of February 29—less than two weeks after she'd nearly cut her own arm off to get a reaction out of 46. Clearly, the self-harm had not stopped that day. "No, I don't think he did."

"Really? Wasn't he Iraqi or something?"

"Iranian."

"You know how they treat their women."

"Mazandarani wasn't like that."

"Don't they stone women to death for 'fornicating' in Iran? Like even rape victims? She might have stepped out on him."

"He wasn't a hitter. Trust me, I'd know."

"Okay, well, apparently, Ortega used that police report to blackmail something out of Mazandarani, some sort of intel."

Sol read the next two emails in the chain:

Mon, Mar 3, 2008 at 6:21 PM
From: Kaveh Mazandarani <KavehMaz@gmail.com>
To: Nils Ortega <nils@thebrokenseal.org>
Subject: Re: Interesting . . .

Nils

I may have something for you, but if I give it to you, will you
give me your word that you'll leave her alone?

...

Mon, Mar 3, 2008 at 6:24 PM
From: Nils Ortega <nils@thebrokenseal.org>
To: Kaveh Mazandarani <KavehMaz@gmail.com>
Subject: Re: Interesting . . .

Shoot it to my burner and we'll see.

The burner.

That had been the SIM card he'd copied from Nils's cell phone. The cell
phone that Nils had left conspicuously, even conveniently, in the living
room alone with him when Cora had fallen into hysterics at his apartment.
The cell phone that Nils, in all likelihood, had *intended* for him to find.

"Did you get to the April emails?" asked NSA Henry.

"No, not yet."

"Well, I include them because whatever intel Mazandarani gave him,
it must have happened over the phone because I don't have those records, but I *do* have these, and boy, they are a doozy."

Sol read through them—they were short, but damning, not one day
after the "nonce" conversation between Ortega and Mazandarani teasing the big government cover-up of four dead CIA agents at the cyborg
hands of a few superpowered space aliens in Bedford, Virginia. Who
had Ortega run to with that information?

The future president, Todd *fucking* Julian.

That wasn't the worst of it, though. The worst was Julian's response:

Your work has been nothing if not the work of a true patriot.
When I am president, if you choose to return to the United
States, you will be met with a hero's welcome.

"This is above my pay grade," said NSAHenry. "But I'm pretty sure that Mazandarani told Ortega about the Bedford agents killed in action, and then Ortega traded that intel to Julian for amnesty."

Sol's gaze glided back to the photocopies of Paris Wells's notes, the phrase he had circled at the end of the page.

Jannaham — Blackmail??

"Mazandarani was Julian's source." Sol chuckled, honestly surprised he'd found proof that his suspicions had been correct. All this time, Mazandarani had been Julian's source, and he'd felt so guilty about it he confessed his sins to an alien, because he knew the alien was the one being on the whole planet who could not give one rat fuck about his sins. Sins so damning, they made an atheist fear hell.

"It's a good thing you got that hard drive," said NSAHenry. "Ortega'd erased these from the cloud, but I was able to extract them."

"Yeah," said Sol airily. "Good thing."

"What are you going to do with it?" asked NSAHenry.

"I don't know."

"In a normal administration this . . . *could* end a presidency, but Julian is . . . you know."

"Yeah."

"Does Sabino know about any of this?"

"I am fairly certain that Cora Sabino is dead." No use keeping a lid on it; it will be news soon enough.

"Whoa," said NSAHenry. "Well, that sucks. Anyway, I'm wiping my machines. We never had this conversation. And if they ask about it, we never met." He said it like it was a joke, but he absolutely meant it.

"Got it. Thanks, Henry."

He snapped the phone shut. He had, in the past, been known to crush burners in fits of frustration, and this burner was just lucky he was too tired right now. He glanced at the end of the text conversation, the last Mazandarani and Ortega would ever share.

(3/4/2008 11:00 PM PST) Nils: Okay. If this leads to something, then let us consider our business concluded.

(3/4/2008 11:05 PM PST) Nonce: You're
going to burn in hell for this.

(3/4/2008 11:05 PM PST) Nonce: This
will be the last time we ever speak.

(3/4/2008 11:09 PM PST) Nils: I don't
doubt it.

Nils had played him.

Someone was bound to home in on Nils as Julian's source one of these days, but if he could deflect it to Mazandarani—Mazandarani, who was dead; Mazandarani, who couldn't defend himself; Mazandarani, who was even more loathed within the agency than Ortega was—well, that would mean there was no mystery left to be solved, then, didn't it? They'd have all the scapegoat they'd need with Mazandarani, meaning they'd leave Nils Ortega the hell alone.

He loved her, Sol.

And there it was—Mazandarani had indeed leaked classified information to the corruptest personification of the human taint that ever lived. Yes, he had done something extremely illegal and extremely stupid, but hadn't he done it for the most noble of reasons? For ~ * ~ *luuuuuuuuurve* ~ * ~?

What was this feeling again? How did the hu-man describe this churning unrest in his gut? Ah yes, nausea, a feeling so foreign to him he couldn't immediately place it. *Okay, fuck it*, he thought, now regaining the energy to slam the burner he'd been using to communicate with NSAHenry into the floor into a dozen pieces. NSAHenry had already cleaned out his systems of any of this stuff, anyway, and also, fuck that guy. Now only Sol had these documents, and what could he do with them?

He could fucking destroy Nils Ortega, that's what. He could fucking destroy Jano Miranda, too, the opportunistic little fuck. Hell, he might be able to knock that Ken Doll Juan Perón of a president down a peg. He couldn't do that through the agency, though. He'd have to find a journalist to help him, irony of ironies. If only . . .

He looked again at the scrap of pink-and-black braid on the corner of his little desk lying atop the photocopies of Wells's journal he'd been mindlessly toting around with his other documents. They'd found Cora's blood, but they hadn't found Wells's—only her braid, the only evidence that she had recently been at the scene, and alive at that, trying to leave a trail of bread crumbs. Wells didn't even know Special Agent Sol Kaplan existed, but she'd left this for someone, and he was the only person on the ground who'd noticed. Therefore, she'd left it for him.

He slammed shut his laptop. Cora would have wanted him to destroy Ortega, but that was such a secondary priority. Ortega could wait. Wells might still be out there, alive. And for that matter . . .

Goddamn it, Luciana Ortega.

They'd found Cora's blood. They hadn't found a body. If Cora was dead, then she was dead, but if she was alive, then any moment spent doing nothing was a moment spent not saving her. And as of a day ago, Paris Wells had been alive. If Cora was dead and Sol could have saved Paris Wells but didn't, her spirit would cling to this earth to torment him with that crunchy acoustic lesbian music she loved so much. She'd haunt him with a ghost guitar playing Melissa Etheridge or Indigo Girls or whoever the fuck for the rest of his days, and that would not do.

He called Agent Makkonen, told him based on what they knew about the way Semipalatinsk hopped from site to site, from greenhouse to greenhouse, that they probably had other active sites, and evidence from those. To look for evidence of *human* activity, that they had a missing person who might still be alive and should be top priority.

"Log anything that might be from another part of *this* planet," he said. "They might be going *back* somewhere. See if there's any nonnative soil, some sort of unusual plant, or mold, or seed that is distinct to somewhere else."

"Got it. I'll do my best. But, Kaplan . . ."

"Yeah?"

"Porter's calling in the big artillery," said Makkonen. "You need to get back out here."

Cora sat outside on the patio next to a silent Ampersand, letting the sunlight wash over her. They'd left the juvenile looking utterly defeated with dozens of little fiber-optic lines coming out of their head like they were in the electric chair, alone in the fallout shelter with Esperas and Brako. She turned her face to the sun, letting it warm her skin. The thought of never seeing the sun again hurt. She didn't need a filter to survive under that star, not like she would for other stars, not like *they* did for this star. Were there other suns out there on life-bearing planets where she would be able to just go outside, or were all living beings specially tuned to the planets they evolved on, always requiring special equipment to set foot on another world, no matter how advanced their genetic engineering?

Fall was almost over, and a light snow dusted the limbs of the trees, frosting the few leaves that remained. Olive had asked her when she would get to come to Japan; money wasn't the issue so much as school, and Demi, who wouldn't let Olive come by herself. Now, she may never get the chance. If a plague really did get deployed, she had to get them out of LA, get them ... *somewhere* isolated. Somewhere where they could hide while the world burned.

"Has Esperas ever done this before?" she asked.

"*I don't believe he's ever attempted this with a live transient, let alone a juvenile. Their brain may not yet be developed enough.*"

"I'm surprised mine was."

"*You are an adult; your brain is fully developed.*"

"That's very charitable of you."

"Your brain is fully developed."

"I was joking."

She ran her fingers over her head, over the base of her skull and the nape of her neck. What few "entry points" were there were hardly perceptible to her fingers, like the holes of an ear piercing. She imagined a future where the world *didn't* burn, where she could talk things out with Paris, where she could watch Olive graduate high school and go to college, where she might become a mother *here* and not as Ampersand's repopulation broodmare, where Ampersand would continue to refine the high-language process, where they would do it again and again and—

"Do you still fear me?"

She snapped her gaze to him, taken aback. "Still?"

"In your memory of safety, when you thought of me in contrast to your new partner, there were thoughts of fear. There is a gap between your feelings of me, where they are and where they should be."

She couldn't help but take offense, like it was *her* fault she was afraid of her mind being invaded by the hyperintelligent alien cyborg brain. Then she realized it wasn't her initial feelings of fear he was referring to but her memory of being glad she was away from him when she was with Paris. He knew how she'd felt about him at a time when she verged on never wanting to see him again.

"Listen," she said. "That memory . . . that was from several weeks ago, and that was *right* after the whole . . . I mean . . . I'm not afraid of you. I was afraid of going through high language again. You don't . . . It's not . . ."

"Calm yourself, my love."

"I'm just trying to explain—"

"I am your caretaker."

She sighed. No interest in listening, only lecturing. "You keep saying that."

"But you do not see me as such."

"Yes, I appreciate that you give me a place to live and a place to sleep, and make sure I'm eating and sleeping, but, like . . . a robot could do that. You didn't show me any empathy or concern when Nils waltzed back into my life. You didn't care how scared I was after the first high-language . . . . 'success,' if you want to call it that."

"I knew that fear would recede when we integrated fully."

Cora's fingers stiffened into a frustrated cage in front of her. "But that's the thing. '*I knew you'd get over it*' is not the excuse or explanation you think it is. And it's not just that," she continued before he got the chance to respond. "You don't let me in on, like, 99 percent of your life. I don't know where you are or what you do most of the time, and *yes*, I always am expecting you to abandon me again, and it is—"

"*You should trust me.*"

"You should be *trustworthy*. It is *wild* that you think I should trust you completely just because we are 'bound.' I know how you are."

"*Clarify your meaning.*"

"I mean I've seen the way things played out between you and Obelus, and then you and Nikola—I know dynamic fusion bonding doesn't guarantee that you won't do to me what you did to them."

It was in that moment she felt something from the other side of the wall that she'd never felt before—*hurt*. That she had not foreseen, let alone intended. "Not that you didn't have your reasons to do what you did with them—"

"*We are bound until death regardless.*"

"Yeah, and that was an accident!" she snapped. "One, which by your own admission several times, you regret."

He watched her, uncharacteristically still and silent for a long, tense moment. "*Indeed, I did not think it possible to successfully bind myself to you, and I did not expect it to succeed, but I would not characterize my initial feelings as 'regret.' Even so, I now consider it a gift. None of my kind would ever have thought such an act with a human was possible. We have much to learn from each other, but through our bond, we are able to learn so much more than we would be able to otherwise, high language or no.*"

"Yeah, well, you never communicated that little epiphany to me."

"*An oversight on my part, my love.*"

"My love," she repeated in a tone walking the line between mocking and affectionate, but tipping to the latter. She didn't want to stay upset at him.

"*But understand that my kind utilizes high language to communicate internal states, not words as humans do. Thus, my oversight. Material needs are relatively simple; interpersonal needs are not, especially between two so disparate as us. This is why I felt successful high language integral* for us. I knew the experience would be illuminating, but I did not know in what ways. For instance, that a stranger could declare themselves your caretaker and elicit such feelings of submission."

"*Submission?*" She scoffed, a little incredulous. "There you go, always framing everything as a function of your caste system."

"*You know our caste systems do not operate like human caste systems— superiors serve their inferiors. We are beholden to one another, but I more to you than you to me. I am your caretaker.*"

"If superiors do all the work, what do you get out of it?"

"*Your devotion and your obedience.*"

She couldn't help but snort at such a brusque and, well, authoritarian answer. "You can't just dynamic fusion bond your way into that with us, bucko," she said with a wry smile. "Devotion and obedience are earned."

"*I agree, my love,*" he said, and a long, slender finger ran its tip over the skin behind her ear at *just* the right pressure to send a thrill down her spine like a xylophone. It was only here that it really hit her that it wasn't just that he knew what she did and didn't like with being touched, now he knew what it felt like to have human skin, to have someone touch it. He knew *exactly* what touch would elicit what response. "*There is no satisfaction in obedience if it is coerced.*"

"Satisfaction," she repeated, more to herself.

That finger ran down the skin of her neck at exactly the right pressure to cause a full-body shiver. He wasn't just going to use this new-found knowledge to his advantage, he was going to have fun with it. "*Your devotion, and your obedience, and your trust. Of course, there are times when obedience must be coerced. But not between us, my love. Never between us.*"

"Times like what?"

Ampersand didn't get a chance to respond before he became alert, like a deer that sensed a tiger nearby. She looked back into the house, and there stood Esperas, Brako standing behind him like he was a high-ranking capo. The juvenile was nowhere to be seen.

[I have their location.]

"Where's the kid?" asked Cora.

[Unconscious. The process was taxing to them.]

[*Were you able to confirm whether they enacted their contingency to remove the threat of human civilization with a pandemic virus?*]

Esperas watched Ampersand, his eyes brightening like he anticipated a fight and was eager for it.

[As they see it, they have no choice but to stay on Earth, and their biological weapon contingency may be the only means they have to keep their pod safe until they are able to leave.]

[*We must neutralize them before they have the chance.*]

Cora didn't know how accurate the translation was, but if it was anywhere near as loaded in Pequod-phonemic as it was in English, Esperas would not take it well.
Ampersand spoke again, and her overlay translated:

[*Give me their location.*]

Esperas gave a curt response, and one word, simple, clear, and crisp, popped up on Cora's overlay:

[No.]

Ampersand retorted in a language that didn't translate on Cora's overlay, something to the tune of *What do you mean, "no"?* Esperas responded in Pequod-phonemic:

[You mean to exterminate them.]

[*They are prepared to implement a mass slaughter of humans.*]

[My mission does not prioritize human lives over theirs.]

[*Transients are not restricted to one planet; humans are. Their plague could become an extinction-level event.*]

[Then humanity's extinction-level event may come only marginally sooner than it might have from the Superorganism.]

[*The transients must be neutralized.*]

She felt the air become thick, and saw that Ampersand was immobile, all except for his eyes, and she felt a frothing mix of anger and panic bubbling from the other side of the wall. Esperas moved toward Brako, and not for the first time, Cora thought that it was they, not the physeterines, who were the real danger.

Ampersand responded:

[*They will kill you.*]

Esperas only seemed to be hardening, and he spoke:

[You will say anything to dissuade us from warning them of your intent. You do prioritize human lives over those of our cousins'. For that reason, our goals are mutually exclusive.]

"Esperas!" Cora dashed between the two warring parties, stopping short at the sight of Brako snapping his gaze to her. "If they haven't seeded their disease yet, then there's still time—nobody has to die! Please, don't kill him!"

Esperas looked at her with that overwhelming glare and spoke:

[Even if his abilities had outlived their usefulness, I would not kill him. We are not like him. But we can't have you following us.]

The light went out of Ampersand's eyes, and he collapsed. Brako and Esperas left with a nonchalance usually reserved for leaving a store after one decides not to buy anything. Cora ran into the bedroom, scrambling to find her backpack. Sol had her pulse emitter, but she still had the pill bug device that could resuscitate Ampersand. She ran back into the main room but found she didn't need to apply it—Ampersand was already struggling to stand.

"Do you have any idea where they might be going?"

"*I have no locations beyond the ones we have already discovered.*"

She put the pill bug down. "I guess we can only hope they know what they're doing."

"*They don't. They have no experience with this species. They have no experience with this pod. They should know better than to try to engage in truce talks; no physeterine would see such an attempt as anything other than a ploy to entrap them. Their good faith will get them killed.*"

· 47 ·

Paris tried to scramble to her feet after she was thrown to the ground, and when that was thwarted by Bomba, she kicked at them until, for the briefest moment, they let her go. That she fought back at all seemed to surprise them, as if they had just taken for granted that their captive would behave like a doormat indefinitely. But she was done cooperating; fat lot of good being "compliant" had done for her, and it wasn't going to do her any favors now. They had transported her and Nikola to another location using that big manta, which she only knew because Nikola was still within range of her earbud. They were still in some subtropical region, though this was not a physeterine settlement. There were a few dozen here, including a few juveniles, though none that she recognized.

When Bomba regained their bearings, they grabbed her again by the arms, forcing her down onto her stomach, and out of the corner of her eye, she caught Trinity approaching with the stick that grew the binding vine, which was promptly applied to her feet. Apparently satisfied that this would keep her down, Bomba let her go, only for Paris to sit up and attempt a headbutt (key word: attempt). She didn't make it anywhere near Bomba's head, and they grabbed her braids in turn, holding her fast and rendering her nearly immobile.

"Nik?"

"THEY ARE STRATEGIZING HOW TO DEAL WITH AN UNPRECE-DENTED CRISIS. A HUMAN MILITARY CONTINGENT HAS DISCOVERED THEIR PREVIOUS SETTLEMENT. THEY ARE DEBATING WHETHER THEY SHOULD ATTEMPT TO CULL THE HUMAN POPULATION TO IMPROVE

THEIR OWN CHANCES OF SURVIVAL. RIGHT NOW, THE MOST POPULAR SUGGESTION IS THROUGH A PANDEMIC."

"That's what you meant by *vector*," she said, and swallowed. "I'm the vector."

Once again, Bomba threw her onto her stomach as the others conversed, only this time, they put their foot on top of her.

"What would this disease do?" she whispered, although if any of them noticed that she was talking to Nikola, they didn't care. What could Nikola possibly tell her that would help her situation, anyway?

"IT CAUSES HEMORRHAGIC FEVER. IT IS DERIVED FROM A NATURAL VIRUS."

She looked at the ones who were participating in the conversation, straining to see if she recognized any. Most were unfamiliar, but Bomba and Trinity she recognized, as well as the anthropologist from the greenhouse. Even Castle Bravo, maimed but ambulatory, hobbling around like a three-legged dog. "So they took a native virus and . . . supercharged it."

"I IMAGINE THEY MADE IT ESPECIALLY DIFFICULT TO DETECT, SO THAT BY THE TIME IT WAS A PANDEMIC, IT WOULD BE FAR TOO LATE TO PREVENT COMMUNITY SPREAD, EVEN WITH A STRICT QUARANTINE IN PLACE NEVER BEFORE SEEN IN HUMAN HISTORY. ONLY REMOTE POPULATIONS WOULD REMAIN UNTOUCHED, AND SUCH POPULATIONS WOULD POSE NO THREAT TO THE POD."

"What's the fatality rate?"

"ACCORDING TO THE ONE WHO DESIGNED IT, IT WOULD BE BETWEEN 97 AND 99 PERCENT."

"I'm guessing they've tested this on humans."

"THEY SURELY HAVE."

She looked again at Castle Bravo, who handed something to Bomba that looked like a grenade with a pointy tip. This, she surmised, contained the virus. "I'm guessing also there is no cure."

"THEY WOULD HAVE DESIGNED IT TO BE INCURABLE. IT WOULDN'T DRIVE HUMANITY TO TOTAL EXTINCTION, BUT IT WOULD PUT AN END TO HUMANITY AS A SUPERORGANISM."

She tried to get a beat on which of them was talking. It was animated, which indicated to her that there was some disagreement, though on what she had no idea. "So what's stopping them?"

"THE HUMAN PROBLEM CANNOT BE DEALT WITH UNTIL THEY DEAL WITH THE PROBLEM OF THE OTHER SIMILAR."

"Other?"

"THEY DO NOT KNOW THERE ARE TWO, IGNORING THE FACT THAT MY BELOVED IS NOT, ON TECHNICALITY, A SIMILAR."

As Nikola said this, Bomba looked down at her, and she bucked when she saw them readying a phial, like a doctor about to inject a syringe. She struggled and squirmed, trying to communicate that she wasn't an animal, that she knew *exactly* what was going on. Suddenly, the anthropologist piped up, like they were standing up to Bomba.

"They seem to be in disagreement," observed Paris, breathing heavily from the struggle.

"THEY DISAGREE AS TO WHETHER THIS PANDEMIC IS NECESSARY. THE ANTHROPOLOGIST SAYS, 'WE SHOULD TAKE INTO CONSIDERATION THAT WHAT THE JUVENILE REPORTED WAS TRUE. THAT THE PEQUOD SUPERORGANISM HASN'T BEEN GROOMING A NASCENT CIVILIZATION TO DO THEIR BIDDING BUT THAT HUMANITY HAS ADVANCED ON ITS OWN MERIT, AND THAT ANY AID, COMFORT, OR LEGAL RIGHTS THEY HAVE GIVEN TO THE AMYGDALINES HERE THEY HAVE DONE OF THEIR OWN ACCORD.'

"ANOTHER RESPONDS, 'WHY WOULD THEY DO SUCH A THING VOLUNTARILY?'

"THE ANTHROPOLOGIST RESPONDS, 'WE DON'T KNOW; THEREFORE, WE SHOULD NOT ENACT A PLAN THAT CANNOT BE UNDONE.'

"ANOTHER RESPONDS, 'THIS IS IRRELEVANT—FOR OUR OWN PROTECTION, THE POPULATION MUST BE CULLED AND THEIR SYSTEMS CRIPPLED FOR AT LEAST ANOTHER FIFTEEN YEARS. THE HUMANS ARE SO NUMEROUS THAT EVEN OUR MOST ADVANCED PLAGUE WOULDN'T DRIVE THEM INTO EXTINCTION.'

"ANOTHER ADDS, 'THE AMYGDALINES HAVE DONE THE SAME TO OUR KIND.'"

The anthropologist took over the conversation, now seemingly surer of themselves.

"THE ANTHROPOLOGIST SAYS, 'DO YOU NOT SEE HOW WHAT YOU ARE PROPOSING IS FAR WORSE? IF THEY ARE BEING GROOMED, THEN THEY ARE IGNORANT OF THE FULL SCOPE OF OUR HISTORY. IF THEY ARE NOT BEING GROOMED AND HAVE ADVANCED ON THEIR OWN,

THEN THEY HAVE NO STAKE IN OUR CONFLICT AT ALL AND ARE INNO-
CENT. EITHER WAY, THIS PLAGUE IS A MORAL EVIL.'

"ANOTHER RESPONDS, 'THE AMYGDALINES STERILIZED AN EN-
TIRE PLANET WITHOUT WARNING. THEY DIDN'T JUST KILL ALL ON
THE GROUND, THEY RENDERED IT UNINHABITABLE.'

"THE ANTHROPOLOGIST RESPONDS, 'WHEN ERYTHRA WAS
STERILIZED, THERE HAD BEEN A LONG HISTORY OF INTERSPECIES
CONFLICT—HERE THERE IS NONE. HERE OUR ENEMIES BARELY EVEN
KNOW WE EXIST, AND LIKE THE AMYGDALINES, WE ARE DEBATING
WIPING THEM OUT BASED ON THE HYPOTHETICAL THREAT THEY
MIGHT POSE, NOT HARM THEY HAVE ALREADY DONE. IF THEY ARE NOT
BEING GROOMED, THEN THIS IS ONLY THE SECOND TIME ANYWHERE
IN THE KNOWN UNIVERSE THAT A CIVILIZATION HAS ADVANCED TO
THE POINT OF SPACE TRAVEL. THIS IS A PROPOSAL THAT WILL END
IN THE DECIMATION OF SOMETHING SO RARE AND PRECIOUS IT HAS
ONLY HAPPENED TWICE, AND IT IS BEING MADE IN IGNORANCE.'

"THEIR LEADER SPEAKS: 'THE PRESENCE OF THE REMAINING SIM-
ILAR RENDERS THIS UNFORTUNATE PLAGUE NECESSARY.'

"ANOTHER DISAGREES WITH THE ANTHROPOLOGIST, STATING,
'WE HAVE HIDDEN OURSELVES FROM THE SIMILARS FOR FOURTEEN
YEARS; WE CAN HIDE FROM THEM FOR FOURTEEN MORE. WHAT WE
NEED NOW ARE LAND AND PROTECTION FROM THE HUMANS. WE
CANNOT SURVIVE TO REPLENISH OUR RESOURCES IF AN ENTIRE CIVI-
LIZATION IS HUNTING US.'

"ANOTHER SAYS, 'WHAT DO YOU THINK THE REMAINING SIMILAR
WILL DO IF THE HUMANS ARE WIPED OUT? THEY WILL ONLY BECOME
MORE OF A THREAT, NOT LESS.'

Then all fell silent except for one, but Paris couldn't tell where the
voice was coming from, and apparently neither could anyone else. The
voice seemed to be coming from all directions like surround-sound ste-
reo.

"Who is that?"

"THAT IS NOT PHYSETERINE."

At first, a burst of hope exploded in Paris's chest—the likeliest candidate in the Venn diagram of "not physeterine" and "can speak their
language" was Jude, meaning that they might be saved! He'd found them
before they could infect her, before they got Nikola off-world, before

any harm could come to any other human at their hands. The amygdaline speaker prompted body language she hadn't seen in the adults before, squatting with their backs parallel to the ground. Bomba didn't move, their foot still holding Paris down, and she entertained the idea of trying to escape again, but every time she tried to wriggle her wrists out of their restraints, they seemed to tighten as if they were designed to prevent that very thing. Trinity stood next to Bomba, scanning the trees and taking the initiative to reply to the amygdaline.

"THE PHYSETERINE ASKS IF THE SPEAKER IS A SIMILAR. THEY REPLY THAT THEY ARE NOT; THEY ARE INTRODUCING THEMSELVES AS A DIPLOCRAT FORMERLY OF THE OLIGARCH CASTE OF THE SUPERORGANISM—THAT WOULD BE ESPERAS."

Paris's heart nearly fell out of her chest. Not Jude. Not salvation. If anything, the opposite may be true. Cora had never said anything positive about Esperas.

"ESPERAS IS PLAYING A DANGEROUS GAME—HE IS NEVER WITHOUT HIS SIMILAR. HE SPEAKS TRUTH THAT HE HIMSELF IS NOT ONE, BUT HE IS DECEIVING THEM BY IMPLYING THAT THERE ARE NO SIMILARS NEARBY."

Paris was close to tears at this emotional roller coaster, to say nothing of Bomba, who was incrementally tightening their grip, micrometer by micrometer.

"THE POD REQUESTS THAT THEY SHOW THEMSELVES. ESPERAS RESPONDS THAT HE WILL WHEN HE HAS ASSURANCES THAT NO HARM WILL COME TO HIM."

Trinity and Bomba conferred quietly for a moment, and then Trinity responded.

"THE POD REQUESTS THAT HE DELIVER HIS MESSAGE. HE BEGINS WITH A WARNING—THAT HE COMES IN PEACE BUT THAT THERE IS AN AMYGDALINE SIMILAR ON THIS PLANET THAT MEANS TO EXTERMINATE THEM. HE MUST BE REFERRING TO MY BELOVED."

"Does that sound right to you?" Paris whispered.

"IT IS CERTAINLY POSSIBLE."

Nikola continued to translate Esperas, and what precious little she had learned of physeterine body language told her that not a single one of them trusted this. Trinity and Bomba whispered to each other while Esperas spoke as if they weren't even listening.

"Whatever these two are talking about, I don't like it."

"THEY ARE AWAITING A SIGNAL FROM ONE OF THEIR TECHNICIANS— THEY ARE TRYING TO FIND ESPERAS'S LOCATION."

She watched Bomba and Trinity as Nikola continued to summarize what Esperas was saying, but within a minute, Trinity perked up like someone had just called their name, blurted something, and left.

"Something is happening."

"THEY BELIEVE THEY HAVE FOUND THE SIMILAR'S LOCA—"

Nikola went silent, and Paris felt like her heart had skipped a beat. Her wits returned in a flash when Bomba removed his foot and several others disappeared into the trees. Paris didn't wait, knowing she had absolutely zero to lose by trying to worm her way out of this situation, especially now that the pod was distracted. Then she realized what had happened—one of the physeterines had detonated an EMP.

"Nik? Nik!"

No response. The EMP had affected Nikola as well. And now, she was truly on her own.

A few seconds of worming were largely fruitless, and so she switched to rolling. All of them were too preoccupied with finding "the Similar" to do anything about her (likely because they knew she could roll to her heart's content; they'd catch her whenever they could spare the attention). Then Bomba and the half a dozen that had disappeared into the jungle returned, dragging a very large amygdaline body behind them. The body of a Similar.

Bomba and the others pulled Brako's body into the center of the group like a lion pulling a buffalo carcass. She looked around wildly for Esperas, whom she assumed would be smaller than Brako, but only Brako emerged from the woods. She remembered something else Cora had told her—those EMPs only affect those in the bodies of Similars. Esperas must have escaped, leaving Brako to the wolves.

The pod was in an absolute furor, loudly and aggressively talking over one another in what looked like intense disagreement, until Bomba, ready and willing to use their size advantage, had enough. They put their fingers underneath the top of Brako's carapace and ripped it off. Brako's innards looked nothing like the red of physeterine or human innards, but instead were gray, mechanical, and gelatinous, somehow still alive and grotesque in its own way. She could see the post-natural outline of the equivalent of a spine, a rib cage, skin, veins, capillaries. Then Bomba ripped the spine out, plunged their hand into Brako's inert body, and pulled out something round and glowing like it was radioactive, about the size of a bowling ball.

His power core.

Bomba didn't seem interested in Brako anymore, but many of the others did, and in seconds, Brako's corpse was surrounded. Paris was so transfixed by the crowd surrounding Brako, she didn't notice Castle Bravo behind her until they grabbed her by the neck, forcing her onto her back. Before she could protest, they injected a phial straight into her heart.

PART 4

ISN'T IT A PITY

November 25, 2009

Ages ago, thousands of generations ago, man had thrust his brother man out of the ease and the sunshine. And now that brother was coming back changed! Already the Eloi had begun to learn one old lesson anew. They were becoming reacquainted with Fear. And suddenly there came into my head the memory of the meat I had seen in the Under-world.

—H. G. Wells, *The Time Machine*

48

"It's back here," said Agent Katalinic. She was young, the (extremely) rare fellow Jew, and he suspected she was probably on one of her first assignments and was already in way deeper than she had anticipated. "They found the entrance at the back of the greenhouse."

As a few agents in hazmats came into view, Sol noticed a sweet rancid smell, like fermenting fruit. "You'll need to put on a hazmat," said Katalinic. "Ignoring what toxins might be in there, the air itself isn't breathable. CO_2 levels are insanely high."

Sol shuffled into his hazmat and respirator while Katalinic quick-changed into hers like she was in a stage performance. Once strapped in, Sol followed a jittery, eager Katalinic through the hidden entrance, which led into a subterranean chamber like the mouth of a cave the size of a small bedroom. At the end of the entrance, Sol shined his flashlight in the direction that Katalinic was pointing, and nearly dropped it.

It was as if he were standing on the wall that rimmed a giant underground maze, only the walls of the maze plunged so deep into the earth he couldn't see the bottom through the haze. This chamber was so big that with the haze in the air, he couldn't even see to the end of it.

"Agent Kaplan."

Sol turned to see his superior officer Susan Macallan walking toward him, Major General Porter right behind her. "Guess this shocked even you, huh?"

"What do you make of this?" asked Macallan.

Sol tried to shake out of it. "It looks like storage."

"We figured," said Macallan humorlessly. "Storage of *what*?"

Sol looked back into the maze at the intricate swirls of honeycombed bookstacks like a vast alien library. Some of the combs close to the entrance had been torn open, their contents ransacked, but not much of it relative to the sheer scope of what all was down here.

"Some form of industry," said Porter.

"They're, ah . . . horticulturalists," said Sol. "Whatever they're growing in the greenhouses, they're storing down here."

"But what was it?" said Porter. "Weaponry? Was this their breeding containment cells?"

"No," said Sol, focusing on the conversation at hand. "No, the way they breed isn't too dissimilar from the way we do, as I understand it. They don't lay eggs or use birthing pods."

"What could possibly create such an intense smell?" asked Macallan.

Occam's razor, he thought. Maybe the thing that smelled like rotting fruit *was* rotting fruit.

"If I had to guess, this is probably food," said Sol. "This is probably more than a decade's worth of work." This gave him an even deeper sense of foreboding—if there's one thing more dangerous than desperate people, it's *hungry* desperate people.

Porter nodded, glaring at the expanse of storage towers beneath him like it was an infestation he was contemplating how best to exterminate. "Kaplan, with me," he said, heading to the cave entrance, and Sol followed.

Once back into the greenhouse, Porter tore off the hood of his hazmat. "What are the odds they'll come back here within the next few days?"

"Sir, I have absolutely no way of knowing that," said Sol, removing his own hood and continuing to disrobe.

"Then give us a guess based on what you know," said Porter, hastily shuffling out of the rest of his suit.

"I don't even know where AG-3 or 46 are, let alone what's going on within the Semipalatinsk pod. If I had to hazard a guess, I think this is an incredibly volatile situation. I have no idea what their assessment is of humans as a potential threat, but they've got to be feeling backed into a corner."

Porter nodded, heading back toward the open daylight without a word, and Sol followed. "Amygdalines use energy weapons," said Porter, putting on his sunglasses as he stepped into the muggy sunlight. "What do physeterines use?"

"I think they're like us; they've got a mélange they'll choose from depending on the situation."

"I'll rephrase, then; amygdalines *prefer* energy weapons. What do physeterines *prefer*?"

"Biological weapons." As the words came out of his mouth, a part of him wished he could put them back in.

"Biological weapons," Porter muttered with a seriousness that bordered on theatrical, like he was doing a George C. Scott impression.

"Have you made any inquiries to Cambodian intelligence?" asked Sol.

"Isn't that an oxymoron?" asked Porter with a dry chortle.

Sol wasn't immediately sure how to respond or what Porter even meant. Was he implying that Cambodia had no intelligence service? The country's intelligence agency was new, but it did exist. But he suspected that Porter wasn't referring to government-run intelligence agencies.

"Have you been here before, sir?" asked Sol. "This part of the world."

"Yes, I have," said Porter. "Four tours in 'this part of the world.' Getting the locals involved never does us any favors."

"I see," said Sol. "If it's all right, I'd like to do a quick survey of the area—see if there's anything else I might find that your boys missed."

Porter gave a curt nod without looking at him, and Sol returned to where he had left his satchel, withdrawing his sidearm as well as a few clips. As he left the clearing where Porter's unit had set up shop, he glanced at the soldiers patrolling about with their assault rifles; he was trained in their use but had never used them in the field. Assault rifles were tools of indiscriminate killing, and if he had reason to shoot at anyone or anything, it was probably because anyone or anything was trying to kill *him*, and for that, one needed a more precise, short-range weapon.

As the sun poked through the trees and mottled the ground, Sol stepped lightly, treading on tree roots wherever he could. The land was lousy with antipersonnel land mines that were, by design, nearly impossible to see. He froze when he saw an unnaturally colored protrusion jutting out of the dirt like the tin wheel of a toy truck. Pins and needles spread over his entire body like he'd seen a poisonous snake, even though he knew the response was irrational. It was a decades-old explosive, and a man-made one at that—harmless as long as he didn't touch it.

Slowly, as if it *were* a poisonous snake, he approached the device. It was the color of old bathrooms, a faded sea green buried in the mud by years of rain and erosion. As he got closer, he was better able to make out the shape—it was like a round metal fan at the end of a bowling pin. He was even able to make out a serial number. This wasn't a mine at all; this was unexploded ordnance. This was not a remnant of Pol Pot. This had been dropped by the Americans.

Distant popping made him jump, an almost innocent sound like firecrackers. Then came the yelling from soldiers barking orders, the sound of assault rifles firing. If this was a physeterine attack, then they were either taking a massive risk in returning to their settlement or they thought they were safe from amygdaline interference. He took out his sidearm and headed back toward the clearing. The gunfire had stopped. This could mean many things, none of which afforded him the luxury of caring about land mines.

By the time the clearing was in view again, he didn't see anything or anyone; no humans, but no human bodies, either. The soldiers he'd seen earlier must have fallen back into a defensive position somewhere. Hell, maybe they'd been vaporized, and the physeterines wanted to surprise everyone by demonstrating, *Hey, today actually we* do *prefer energy weapons.*

Then there was a deep rumble coming from the greenhouse, a hiss of air out of the earth like a giant was releasing a deep sigh, and then there was the sound of human voices—yelling, shouting orders, but mostly coughing and sputtering. A cloud of haze and dust came out from all sides of the greenhouse like a plume of spores had just been forced out. Everyone in the vicinity, CIA agent and soldier alike, grasped at their skin and coughed as they struggled to get away from the cloud, some so overcome they had to fall to their stomachs and combat crawl. Knowing that he couldn't be any help near the greenhouse and was only likely to get himself killed, Sol climbed a tree, unholstering his gun again once he had a clear vantage point. No sooner had he found one when the alien cavalry arrived.

Like amygdalines, these guys had the ability to cloak themselves, and also like the amygdalines, their preferred method of short-range transport seemed to be single unit and involved gliding, but the similarities ended there. Rather than the bullet shape he'd seen 46 employ, these things looked more like black stingrays while in flight, and rather than gliding back into the users' bodies, the riders left them on the ground like one would leave a motorcycle. The formfitting stingrays melted away from their riders as they hit the ground, and about thirty physeterines stood up from them.

The group was in some sort of militaristic formation, wearing matte all-black bodysuits that covered everything but the crests of their heads, which themselves were so dark they were almost black. The coverings on their eyes were the only things that stood out, black but bright and shining in the sunlight. They seemed much more careful than hurried, as if waiting to see what their little smoke bomb had accomplished.

Then the shooting started, not from the greenhouse but from the forest. A few of the physeterines formed a barrier between the gunfire and the rest of the group, and some bullets deflected as if they'd been smacked right out of the air. The group split up, some into the greenhouse, some into the forest, and the rest forming a defensive line. Several of them raised their arms toward the trees where the soldiers were firing from, palms forward like they were giving the air a high five (six?), and projectiles came out from their wrists, exploding like shrapnel when they hit their targets.

Sol couldn't see clearly from where he was, but he did see a couple of those projectiles hit soldiers in their arms, knocking their weapons out of their hands. It was a rapid one-two punch: first came the hit, and less than a second later, the hit exploded, ripping a hole in the soldier's body. He witnessed this happen to three of them, although God knows how many more there were, and Sol was so transfixed by this he hardly noticed the physeterine combatant until it was right under him.

Sol moved his head to look at it but didn't dare move his gun; having seen that invisible defensive line, he was pretty sure his itty-bitty Glock wouldn't be much use, anyway. The physeterine watched him but hadn't pointed its hand shrapnel gun at him just yet. Without moving any other muscles, he released his grip and dropped the gun to the forest floor. The physeterine's gaze followed the gun, and for at least an entire second, they seemed to be searching for it. Sol took advantage of the distraction and jumped out of the tree, landing right on the physeterine's

LINDSAY ELLIS

back. A horrific, shocked screeching sound came out of the holes on the creature's neck as Sol's fingers found the border between its head and the cowl that covered its eyes, and he ripped it off.

This time, an even ungodlier scream as the creature used one hand to cover its eyes and the other to try to get Sol off its back, but Sol was already diving for the gun at the roots of the tree. He grabbed it and, still on his back, aimed at the creature.

It had stopped wailing by now, desperately clawing at the ground with its free hand to find its cowl while covering its eyes with the other. Sol took a few seconds to gain his composure before approaching the creature. Belly to the ground, the physeterine kept feeling around frantically, and as soon as its back was to him, Sol pressed the barrel of the Glock into its head, just beneath the crest.

"You know what this is," he whispered.

The creature stilled. It did indeed.

Sol stayed frozen for a few seconds, just to make sure that, if even in this brutal fashion, what was being communicated was clear. He then backed into a tree, keeping his gun trained on the creature, and pulled out his walkie. "Macallan, this is Kaplan, over."

"Kaplan," she replied.

"I've got one neutralized, over."

"What?" Macallan's voice was almost unintelligible through the static.

"I've got one of the physeterines neutralized. Alive and neutralized. Requesting backup, over."

More radio static from Macallan's end. Then something that sounded a lot like, "Air support is on its way, over."

"What?"

Then the air rang out with the sound of gunfire, causing Sol to nearly jump out of his skin despite years of training for situations like this. His instincts assumed that this was hostile gunfire, *Taliban* gunfire, and he scrambled away from the body of the physeterine, which was now being riddled with bullets. "Stop!" he yelled once he realized what was happening. "*Stop!*"

The air was thick with the sound of it, and not just the one that had shot his prisoner. He bolted to his feet, waving his arms to catch the attention of the marine firing the assault rifle. The physeterine's skin suit, clearly designed to withstand this sort of thing, had one major weakness at the head, which was now spewing red, red blood.

"What are you doing?" demanded Sol.

"It's still moving!" The marine didn't even look at him, raining down a second volley of rounds into the alien.

"Stop it!" bellowed Sol, and after about a dozen more rounds, the marine stopped.

"It was still moving!" he yelled.

"This isn't a *fucking* video game! Where is Porter?"

"Bird's nest," said the marine, not deigning to look at Sol again as he eagerly headed back into the heat of battle.

Sol fell to his knees next to the creature, muttering, "Fuck fuck fuck." Even now, having spilled at least a liter of blood onto the forest floor, it was covering its eyes with its hands, gurgling something in that clicky, cetacean language. Sol tried to apply pressure to the wound, succeeding only in making blood spurt all over him, and pressed harder. "C'mon, they told me you were hard to kill," he said. In a way, he supposed it was true. He counted three shots to the neck and head, and it was still moving.

And then it wasn't.

Sol kept applying pressure for almost half a minute after he knew it was no use. Then the smell hit him, that coppery smell that results from the oils of human skin making contact with the iron in blood. Blood he was now covered in.

Bird's nest.

They'd set up a command post on a small ridge about a kilometer away. That must be what the marine had been referring to. Sparing no thought to land mines or unexploded ordnance, Sol ran up to the bird's nest, making it in a little less than five minutes. Porter was there, as was Macallan, as were several injured soldiers only just arriving, bleeding and ported by their comrades. He found the major general at a table, looking over a map, yelling orders into a satellite phone.

"Porter, what the fuck is going on?" he demanded, blowing right through the man's entourage. "What are their orders?"

"You are way out of line, Agent," said Macallan.

"What did you mean, 'air support is on the way'?"

"She meant what she said," said Porter, putting the phone down.

Before Sol could respond, he heard the engines of fighter jets. He looked into the sky helplessly as the pilots of those jets did the exact same thing their fathers had done to the exact same land. The forest erupted into a fireball. Then like a tiny nuclear bomb had gone off, the ground pulsed up slightly and then fell inward like a sinkhole. Sol looked at Porter, who was stoically watching the whole thing through a pair of binoculars. Macallan shot him a glare before raising her own pair of binoculars.

"Do you realize what you've done?" said Sol, gazing dumbfounded at the now smoking crater where the resource cache had been. A few black dots rose out of the forest, and from this distance, it almost looked like giant black crows who'd learned to fly without flapping their wings. Sol thought back to the marine who had fired so indiscriminately. *It's still moving.*

"We are meat to them," said Porter, putting his binoculars down. "We are prey. They've killed seven of my men, three of your agents, and God knows how many civilians."

"These things aren't some tribe in Pakistan that have no choice but to retreat; these are post-natural aliens whom we know to be experts in biology, and you just destroyed all the resources they've spent the last thirteen years accruing."

"These things are a threat, to the nation and to the world."

"They weren't storing weapons! Did you even consider what they were hiding here? To check?"

"We don't have intel—"

"We have *plenty* of intel!" yelled Sol. "I am that intel! There is *zero* tactical benefit to destroying their cache! And I had one, *alive*, and one of your guys gunned it down."

"One more word, Kaplan, and you're sidelined," warned Macallan.

"We could have had a live asset. I *had* a live asset. And they—"

"*Kaplan,*" Macallan snapped. "I want you out of here."

Sol stopped and looked at Macallan, jaw square.

"Fall back to Puerto Princesa," she said. "We'll debrief there."

49

"*Cannibals.*"

It was the only word Ampersand had said in the last few minutes. At first, he'd gone into shock at the sight of Brako's body, left there on gruesome display, and it was only here that Cora truly understood that yes, amygdalines could very much be cannibalized. Brako lay prone, back split open from the head all the way down the middle, not in a neat line as if cut by a knife but frayed, like he had been torn apart by lions. His nervous system, brain and all, had been scooped out, a black hole in the center of him from where they had dug out his power core.

They'd set off the EMP to incapacitate Brako, and a side effect was that any scramblers the physeterines had been using to obscure their location also became inoperable, making Ampersand instantly aware of their location. But it took him all of fifteen minutes to get to the scene of the crime from Japan and another half an hour to ascertain that there was no danger of Ampersand suffering the same fate.

And by then, it was far too late.

Not ten feet away were Brako's two physeterine porters, dead. They had barely gotten a look at Ampersand before they keeled over, their bodies twitching like they were receiving mild electric shocks, and then they lay still.

"What did you do to them?"

Ampersand finally moved to examine one of the porters, lolling their jaw open to get a look inside the mouth, jerking his fingers back like he was touching toxic refuse. "*I did nothing. They carry with them a suicide poison.*"

She knew she needed to focus, needed to stay strong, but she couldn't help but hold tightly on to Ampersand's forearm, weak in the knees at the thought that this could have been him. This could *still* be him. She held on to him more tightly with her right arm, clasping the pill bug defibrillator in her left, her one assurance that in the worst case, this wouldn't happen to him, because she was there. Esperas and Brako did not have human allies who could protect them from energy pulses, but Ampersand did. And as long as there were transients here on Earth trying to remove threats from their pod, this was always a possibility.

And with that thought came another: *Exterminate them all.* What other choice was there? And suddenly, she was struggling to see any reason at all to allow these things to live.

"How do we keep this from happening to you?"

"*I have one advantage; now that they have deployed their energy weapon, I am aware of the type and frequency they are using.*"

Ampersand moved away from her, surveying the scene beyond Brako and the two transients, and she held on to him for a few steps before letting him go.

"Where do you think they were taking him?"

"*I don't know, but given how uncharacteristically sloppy they were with their scramblers, they clearly didn't think they had anything to fear from me. It is likely they believe Brako and I are the same person, and having disposed of Brako, they now have all Similars on this planet killed or captive.*"

"Did they do this?" she asked. "Were these two the cannibals?"

The ground in front of Ampersand grew hot as he spread his hands over it, drawing out dirt and separating it, until he had some sand suspended in front of him. The sand melted into glass, which he formed into two long tubes, each about two feet long and the diameter of a pencil. He plucked them out of the air and jammed the two glass rods right into the porters' torsos.

"What are you doing?"

"*A biopsy.*"

With a quiet *schlorp*, he removed the two glass rods to examine them, now full of viscera and stomach contents and slick with blood so red it looked like food coloring. As he did so, Cora noticed that one of the porters had died with two fingers slipped in a pouch on the flank of their skin suit.

"*It wasn't either of these two*," said Ampersand, heating the glass until its contents were incinerated.

"What do you think that is?" asked Cora, pointing to the pouch.

Ampersand took a moment before examining it, slitting it open with the sharp ends of his fingers and withdrawing a phial from one of the pouches. "*This is a sample of the virus*," said Ampersand, eyes wide as he examined the contents of the phial for at least a minute. "*This strain appears to be engineered from a* Marburg *virus*." A protective casing slid out of his fingers like wax and sealed up the phial. "*I need you to return home.*"

"What if she's already infected?"

"*Then there is little we can do for her*," said Ampersand, sliding the phial under the carapace on his back. "*You must return home.*"

"Wait, what?"

"*Return home to Fukushima. I will come to you when it is—*"

"What do you mean there is little we can do for her? You're a xenobiologist. I've seen you do so many impossible things with—"

"*I am a biologist, not a virologist.*"

"What are you saying?"

"*I cannot cure it.*"

She shook her head in disbelief. A part of her felt that there must be some argument she could make to make this not true. That she could whip out, *You promised you would save her*, as if that were some sort of binding contract with the rest of the universe.

"*Biology is the study of life; viruses are not alive. I could cure a natural disease, perhaps, with enough time and study, but this is not natural.*"

There were times when he would indulge her, do the human thing of offering some form of condolences or comfort, but now was not one of those times.

"*Go home.*"

"What if you need me to resuscitate you?"

"*I won't risk you being captured or killed again.*"

"You might need me."

"*If I think I may have need of you, I will let you know.*"

In less than a second, Ampersand's metal plating slid over him, and he disappeared, leaving Cora alone with three corpses. At a loss, she did as she was told.

· · · · ·

Cora had googled "Marburg virus" when she'd gotten back to the house; that had been a mistake. Now there was naught to do but sit on the patio, staring blankly into the mist rising from the mountains, stewing in her own helplessness. Heat tugged at the corners of her eyes, the pressure in her chest building like a thunderstorm. Was this really how it was going to play out? That Paris would survive a plane crash, survive being a physeterine captive, come so close to Cora finding her, only for her to be turned into a biological weapon? That the best possible outcome they could hope for now was that Paris's body was a threat that might be nullified?

Cora stood up and went back inside the house. Esperas had implied that he had gotten all potentially useful information out of the juvenile, but she had no way of knowing that for sure.

After all, Esperas was probably dead.

Ampersand left the juvenile in an enclosure down in his lair that looked like a much smaller version of the one that Nikola had been held in at Bella Terra—a cube made of a material like acrylic in the middle of the room, about as big as a full-size bed and five feet in height. Cora approached the shivering, mewling horror inside the enclosure. Now she had a pet, a movie monster that would only grow larger and more dangerous with each passing day. What in God's name would they do with this pitiful, hateful little liability?

"Are you cold?"

The juvenile finally spoke, a translation appearing on Cora's ocular overlay:

[Not the light of the star.]

"I don't understand."

[Mercy. Mercy. Don't expose me in the light of the star.]

She noticed that the entire right half of the juvenile's body was redder than the other, the type of red one might see in superficial skin burns, and the smell of ammonia hit her, the chemical physeterines apparently emitted as a stress response. They chanced a look at her, and again their eyes were red, the result of broken capillaries, another stress response. It struck her that human eyes did something similar when crying, and it was only here that she realized that that was what they were doing.

Then her revulsion broke, and she was left standing in the cold reality of the situation. Physeterines didn't go about their day naked, but this juvenile had been without clothing since Ampersand had revealed to her that he had a captive. This wasn't an animal or a monster; this was a child, naked and freezing and hurting from the torture she had watched Ampersand inflict. She bolted upstairs, grabbed a bottle of distilled water from the kitchen and several large spare blankets from the bedroom closet. Then she went back downstairs, and the juvenile seemed to shrink even farther at the sight of her. Again, they spoke:

[**Not again, please, not again.**]

"I'm not going to hurt you," she said, opening the enclosure. She unfurled one of the comforters, and the juvenile cringed and buried their face in their hands as Cora wrapped them up in it. "I'm sorry; I don't know how to increase the temperature in here, or I would. Drink this."

She held the water in front of them, but they didn't budge.

"It's okay, it's distilled water. It's sterile. This is the water Ampersand drinks."

[**Are you going to kill me?**]

"No, no one's going to kill you."

[**Why?**]

"We don't have any reason to kill you."

[**He means to kill my people.**]

"He wouldn't kill your people unless he had no choice."

[Why spare me? I led him right to them. Please, kill me, not them. Kill me.]

"I don't think any of them have to die if they surrender."

[I should die with them. Please, let me go.]

"I can't let you go right now, but you won't be our prisoner forever, I promise."

[Where is diplocrat-Oligarch?]

"I don't know. I think he's dead."

Slowly, the juvenile uncurled. They didn't even look at the bottle of water, but they did pull the comforter around them more tightly.

[How dead? Why?]

"He tried to entreat with your pod, but your pod killed his Similar. We found his Similar's remains. We don't know where Esperas—diplocrat-Oligarch—is."

The juvenile just stared at her blankly, their bloodred eyes as wide as they would go.

"We found his Similar with two dead porters. They had a sample of a virus with them—a virus designed to infect humans."

The juvenile's head crest flared wide, then grew limp as they dropped their head back into their hands.

[Despair. Despair. They will unleash a pandemic to protect themselves. Similar-Oligarch will kill all of us to protect humans, or he will kill all of us in revenge. There is no saving us. Did not want this.]

"You need to tell me where your people are."

[**No, never. He'll kill them.**]

"He won't kill them if he doesn't have to, but they're planning to do something terrible with that virus. You need to tell me how to stop them."

[**Similar-Oligarch will leave me alive to know that I killed them. I killed my people. I killed them.**]

"If that disease gets released to the public and humans start dying, you are right that Ampersand is absolutely going to kill all of them. The only way Ampersand is going to spare them is if they surrender before they infect anybody. So if you want to save your pod, you have to prevent the plague from getting into the population. Do you understand?"

The juvenile stared at her, their shivering bordering on violent. Cora took the edges of the comforter firmly, as if she were taking them by the collar of their coat, and pulled them closer to her. "You need to tell me where they are and how they are planning on spreading that virus. *Now.*"

- **5 0** -

"Nikola?" she said for approximately the five hundredth time, fearing the worst. It had been hours since she'd heard his voice. If the wall of Paris's cell was of the variety that became transparent by applying pressure, then it was also a wall that faced complete darkness on all sides. She'd been in pitch-blackness for hours.

"DEAR GENTLE CREATURE."

She allowed herself a moment to verify that she hadn't imagined it, and released a sigh of relief into the stuffy air. "Oh, thank God you're alive."

"FOR NOW."

"Where are you?"

"I AM CLOSE."

"I can't see anything."

"THEY HAVE MADE A TERRIBLE MISTAKE. ESPERAS AND HIS SIMILAR CAME TO ENTREAT WITH THEM, AND THEY RESPOND WITH MURDER. TIME AND AGAIN, THIS HAPPENS. THIS IS WHY THE CYCLE WILL NEVER END."

"They injected me with something. I think I'm infected."

"ARE YOU EXPERIENCING ANY SYMPTOMS?"

"I don't know. It could be symptoms. It could be me freaking out."

"WHAT ARE YOUR SYMPTOMS?"

"I'm feeling a sort of pain in my gut. My skin is cold. I'm starting to have chills."

"THEN YOU ARE INFECTED."

Paris's breath shook as she took that in. *Viral hemorrhagic fever.* She knew what it did to the body. There were few worse ways to die. "Is there any way you could cure it?"

"EVEN IF I WERE TO REGAIN MY POWER CORE, THERE IS NOTHING I CAN DO, DEAR GENTLE CREATURE. I SPECIALIZE IN ENGINEERING AND THEORETICAL PHYSICS, NOT DISEASE."

Paris let her head fall back against the wall of her cell. There had to be *something* someone could do about it. She just needed to get out of this situation, and then maybe, *maybe* . . .

Psychologically, she was in the bargaining phase, and she knew it.

"How are they going to use me?" she asked. "As a vector."

"YOUR BODY WILL INCUBATE A VIRAL LOAD, WHICH THEY WILL THEN EXTRACT TO CREATE AEROSOLS, LIKELY OVER A MAJOR POPU-LATION HUB."

"Which population hub?" She thought of New York, of people packed on subway trains, of a crowded Times Square, of kids on her own block playing on the stoops of their brownstones.

"DOES IT MATTER?"

"Good point." She leaned forward, burying her face in her hands. "They killed Brako."

"I AM AWARE. DO YOU KNOW WHAT BECAME OF HIS POWER CORE?"

"They brought the power core into the vessel. I'm not exactly sure where."

"I WILL FIND WHERE. YOU NEED TO RETRIEVE IT FOR ME."

Paris blinked, wondering if his translator had gone wonky. "How?"

"YOUR CELL IS NEAR TO MINE—I LACK THE MOBILITY TO DESTROY ANY STRUCTURES IMPRISONING US, BUT I CAN WEAKEN THEM. IF I CAN WEAKEN A WALL OF YOUR CELL ENOUGH FOR YOU TO DESTROY IT AND ESCAPE, YOU MUST RETRIEVE BRAKO'S POWER CORE AND RETURN IT TO ME."

She found herself slipping right back into the bargaining phase at the thought that Nikola might be able to break her out, that they *both* might be able to get out. If she moved quickly, maybe it wasn't too late for her. But given all that Nikola had said to her on the nature of power and how he would wield it given the chance, wasn't deliberately giving him back his godlike abilities among the worst things she could do? But then again, what was this but a choice between the worst of two evils; one, despite possibly endeavoring to become world dictator and/or go on a murder-suicide spree, had no *desire* to see human civilization wiped out, but the other already had a plan in motion to do just that using a biological weapon.

One she was already infected with.

"I CAN ONLY ESTIMATE THE INCUBATION PERIOD OF THIS VIRUS, BUT IT MAY NOT BE LONG BEFORE IT INCAPACITATES YOU. EITHER WAY, I DO NOT THINK YOU HAVE VERY LONG TO LIVE."

Tears pricked at her eyes as it sank in; bargaining phase over, no time for depression or anger, only acceptance. And if she died in the process of getting the power core, hey, she was about to be used as a vector, anyway. Dying was probably the most noble thing she could do for mankind right now. Whether or not mankind deserved it, well, she didn't exactly get a say in that.

"Nikola, I have an odd request to make. Do you have any way of killing me quickly?"

"I AM QUITE RESTRAINED."

"Please, I . . . Hemorrhagic fever is one of the worst ways for a human to die. I don't want to die, but if there really is no cure for it . . . I don't know if you could imagine what it might feel like to have that body grow sick and weak. To have it break apart and rot with you still inside it, until after unimaginable suffering, your brain finally has nothing left to support it."

"I MAY BE ABLE TO IMAGINE SOMETHING SO TERRIBLE."

"I am begging you, Nikola, don't let me die like that. You're so advanced. There has to be a way to do it quickly."

"YOU MUST RETRIEVE MY POWER CORE, DEAR GENTLE CREATURE. WHEN YOU DO, I WILL ENSURE YOU ARE SPARED A GRUESOME DEATH."

She nodded to herself. If she succeeded in this likely very futile endeavor, she was putting her life in Nikola's hands and then asking him to take it. "Okay."

"RUN YOUR HAND ALONG THE WALL TO YOUR RIGHT—I WILL TELL YOU WHERE THE WEAK POINT IS WHEN YOU FIND IT."

Paris did as she was told, and given the small size of her cell it wasn't long until Nikola said, "THERE."

She held her hand still and felt subtle vibrations that she hadn't picked up before. "Now what?"

"A MOMENT."

She'd seen him do this twice now, but both times he'd been doing it to rigid structures, not this strange pliant material that felt more like stiff leather than solid rock or acrylic.

"YOU MUST STRIKE EXACTLY THIS SPOT EXACTLY WHEN I SAY."

"Okay, on the count of three. Should I count or you count?"

"YOU SHOULD COUNT."

"Okay, one, two, three." She struck the wall as hard as she was able.

"AGAIN."

"One, two, three." She struck the wall even harder.

"AGAIN."

This went on for at least twenty cycles, by which point Paris was sweating, her muscles aching. The sweat made her shiver, and this, she knew, was not psychosomatic. A sharp pain tore through her stomach at the next strike.

"AGAIN."

"Nikola."

"AGAIN."

So, she did it again. And again. And again.

And then the wall shattered. It was a modest shatter, as if the wall were made of leather so brittle that she was able to punch right through it. She pulled at one of the pieces and in short order had created a hole almost big enough for her to fit through.

"YOU MUST HURRY."

Her strength was already failing her. It was all she could do to squeeze out of this hole.

"WHEN YOU ENTER THE CORRIDOR, GO RIGHT TWENTY FEET."

"Right."

She kept low to the ground, but her legs shook, and even the act of moving silently was becoming more difficult by the second. Visually, the corridor wasn't a huge improvement over her cell. Being in total darkness meant that her eyes were as adjusted as they were going to get, so while there was minimal light here, it was still dim, and relative to the eyes that the ship was designed for, hers were at a tremendous disadvantage.

The vessel vibrated all around her, and she stopped herself from letting out a surprised yip. "Nikola, what's going on?" she asked as quietly as she could.

"THIS VESSEL IS PREPARING TO LIFT OFF."

"Yeah, I figured. Why?"

"ONE WOULD ASSUME THAT THEY ARE MOVING IT."

"Yes, I get that. *Where?*"

"I DON'T KNOW. YOU MUST FIND THE POWER CORE; TIME IS SHORT."

Whether it was the thought of population centers or the reminder of her mortality, she felt faint and nearly crumpled where she was. *Mankind*, she thought. Renée and her high school students who still had not yet learned to breathe life into Tucker the Mannequin. Her *abuela* in Puerto Rico, whom she always promised to visit but never did because she was always too busy. And Cora, who had continued the search for her despite the way that they'd parted, despite the hopelessness of the situation, who may yet still be alive. She pulled herself together and moved.

Nikola guided her through another few corners, each corridor shorter than the last. She was beginning to feel light-headed, and it took her a moment to connect—the air in the cell she had been held in was native Earth air. This air was not.

Fucking fantastic, she thought. Bad enough she was dying of viral hemorrhagic fever, now she had to worry about asphyxia? How long did it usually take before she started to seriously feel the symptoms of asphyxia? Five minutes? Seven minutes? Then again, if she failed Operation Power Core, at least she would asphyxiate before her organs ruptured and she bled to death from the inside. Silver linings all around.

"Nik, how much farther is it?" she whispered. "The air . . . I don't know how much longer I can take this air."

"IT'S IN THE NEXT CHAMBER."

It was only as he said this that she entered the chamber and found the lump with the light blue glow she had been looking for sitting atop one of those portobello-like tables. And then there was the physeterine guarding it, who saw her before she saw them. Even in this incredibly dim light, she recognized their stature, their size, the coloration and lines on their head and crest—Tsar Bomba.

Cognition already impaired from lack of oxygen, Paris froze. What to do? Run? Try to grab the power core, which was much closer to Bomba than she was? Attack? Bomba, for their part, seemed somewhat bemused. Whatever their reaction, it was short-lived, as they decided she needed to be dealt with and moved toward her.

Then everything went dark. At first, Paris thought that her vision had gone or that she had blacked out. Then came the same sensation of her stomach rising up into her throat that usually accompanies descent on a roller coaster, and she realized that she was experiencing the effects of gravity.

The ship was falling out of the sky.

Sol took a seat on the curb in the hot sun, glad he had been sent back to this Filipino-run air force base rather than the one operated by the Americans up in the north near Manila. The CIA used this base in occasional conjunction with the Filipino military, so in some regards, this was friendlier ground than if he were to be shunted back to the American base where Porter actually had the jurisdiction to chew him up and spit him out. At least down here, he officially did not exist, just like God intended.

He'd been here a couple of hours, and since he was the only person in any department who'd been in Cambodia ordered to fall back to this base, no one here was any the wiser about what had happened, going about their day performing aircraft maintenance and filing reports and whatever else it was people did on air force bases. Nobody knew that the American military had, in effect, declared war on a group of ETIs about whom they knew effectively nothing.

It was then that Estraton Catipay, director of science and technology for NICA, caught his eye. He wavered a moment as if confused as to why Sol was here at all. Then he donned a mask of faux civility and approached him. "To what do we owe the pleasure, Agent Kaplan?"

"Same as always," said Sol curtly. "Aliens."

Catipay took a seat next to him and pulled out a pack of cigarettes, taking one for himself and offering one to Sol, which he robotically accepted. Strange, how even a small gesture like this could feel laced with hostility.

"Odd times," said Catipay.

"Yep."

The cigarettes were good old Marlboros, and the entire bottom half of the box was dedicated to a graphic photo of a dying, emaciated man on oxygen, under which was a warning: SMOKING CAUSES EMPHYSEMA. He almost asked why it was in English, but then again, everything was in English around here.

Catipay lit his cigarette, drawing in a few puffs to keep it alight. "Can you tell me what's going on?"

"Nope," said Sol, taking the lighter to light his own.

"Can you tell me what *isn't* going on?"

Sol blew out a long stream of thick, freshly lit cigarette smoke. "I can't tell you that there are American troops on the ground in Cambodia. I can't tell you that the Cambodian government does not know. I can't tell you that there have been violent run-ins between the American military and hostiles in Cambodia."

"Human hostiles?" Catipay asked, concerned but not alarmed, like they were discussing bomb-obsessed high school kids who'd bought suspicious amounts of fertilizer.

Sol took a drag. "I can't tell you."

"You seem upset by this." Catipay's tone bordered on condescending. "Were you censured, Agent Kaplan?"

"I can't tell you."

"I'm curious, why does it bother you now where it didn't before?"

Sol looked at him coldly. "Why does what bother me?"

Catipay shrugged. "The way your country's CIA and military do whatever they want with such flagrant disregard for the sovereignty of other countries?"

"Of course it's always bothered me. It's thorny fucking business. You can understand how the ends justify the means and still be upset by the means."

"The ends justify the means . . ." Catipay shook his head, his chest moving like he was laughing without making a sound. "Did your president know about the . . . incident you can't say happened in Cambodia?"

"I can't say."

"Did he order it?"

Sol opened his mouth to repeat himself, but then for some inexplicable reason, he told the truth. "I don't know."

"Your president seems to believe that the only way forward is for America to be the shield that will protect the world from hostile ETIs. Do you believe that, Agent Kaplan?"

Sol didn't respond, didn't look at him, didn't even take a drag on his cigarette, just watched as it burned on its own, micrometer by micrometer.

Catipay took one final half-laughing big drag on his. "If the last ten years have taught your country anything, it is that they can do more or less whatever they want to the citizens of other countries, and only the outermost fringe will oppose them." He dropped the cigarette to the ground, putting it out with his boot. "What do you think they will do now that there are hostiles that aren't even human?"

When Sol didn't answer, the man stood up and walked back toward the administration building from whence he had come. He took another short drag on his Marlboro. This base wasn't more than twenty miles away from Bahura, the village where the first confirmed physeterine run-in had happened. Sol thought of that kid Lorenzo, who had been saved from certain death by 46, and wondered, why was his first instinct to try to dissuade that? Why had it been his instinct to default to noninvolvement? To expect a bleeding heart like Sabino to do the same?

His satellite phone rang, and he had the impulse to let this phone suffer the same fate as the burner he'd used to talk to NSAHenry rather than hear Macallan chew him out while defending Porter and Julian's cavalcade of stupidities.

"Kaplan," he answered.

"Sol?"

There was a long pause, both from him and the other side of the line as he processed whether this voice belonged to whom he thought it belonged to.

Fucking . . .

"Sabino?" He made a noise that was half-laugh half–enraged grunt. "You're alive?"

"I'm sorry. I've been indisposed." She sounded like she was in a hurry. "Sol—"

"We found your fucking *blood* all over the settlement! I thought you'd been—"

"I wa—I mean, I'll explain later. I'm fine now."

He resisted the urge to take his frustrations out on his phone. "Okay, cool. Glad you're alive. Next time I see you, I'm going to kill you. Why the hell haven't you gotten in contact with me?"

"Where are you?"

"Philippines. Where the hell are you?"

"Why are you in the Philippines?"

"Because I was ordered to fall back to the air force base in the Philippines after getting into an altercation with a commanding officer. *Where the hell are you?*"

"I'm in Fukushima. Do you have any idea where the Semipalatinsk pod is?"

"No. Do you?"

"No, we don't know where they've gone, but . . ." He heard her take a breath. "Brako is dead. The physeterines killed him."

"Are you sure?" asked Sol.

"I saw the body."

"What about Esperas?"

"We don't know what happened to Esperas, but Brako is dead."

"Are you *sure*?" After all, Brako had been incorrectly assumed dead once before.

"We're sure. And Brako . . . Do you remember what we said about Similars having power cores . . . power cores that are easy to remove if the subject is, well, dead enough?"

Sol's entire body stilled just at the mention of power cores. "I see. How did that happen? Did they use—"

"Energy pulse."

Sol took off his sunglasses, throwing his head back and rubbing his face with his hands. "So you're telling me these things have the body of a Similar."

"They don't have his body; we found the body. But they do have his power core."

"Fuck me." He closed his eyes. "We found the Semipalatinsk settlement in Cambodia."

"Yeah, we figured—"

"Porter destroyed it."

"*What?*"

"They destroyed it," said Sol, smearing his hand down his face and over his chin. "The whole settlement. Zero hesitation, they just did it."

"Fuck," she whispered. "*Fuck.*"

"A group of physeterines showed up, fighting broke out. They called in an air strike. They destroyed everything."

"*Why?*"

He shook his head, smiling incredulously. "The current policy is that they are to be handled like we would handle any hostile."

"This is very bad, Sol."

"I had a feeling you would say that."

"That power core isn't the thing we need to worry about. They have had a pandemic waiting in the wings in case things got too desperate. And things have gotten too desperate."

"What does that mean?"

"It means they're going to try to deploy a global pandemic to protect themselves from *us.*"

Sol didn't react immediately, mostly because he wasn't surprised. Why would these things stay on a dangerous planet like Earth without some contingencies for if the natives got too restless? What else but the wanton, careless destruction of their resources would be the last straw?

What in the ever-loving realm of fuck had that idiot Porter been *thinking*?

"Semipalatinsk doesn't know that Ampersand is still alive and is operating on the assumption that humans are now the only major threat," Sabino continued. "And now that humans have taken everything from them, they intend to mitigate the threat. Do you follow?"

"I follow. What's the move?"

"I know their main vessel is somewhere near Bahura. The juvenile says it's capable of spreading a biological weapon using the vessel's venting system."

"I'm at an air force base near Bahura."

"How soon can you get there?"

Sol's eyes darted to a small reconnaissance helicopter parked a few hundred feet away that was about to be refueled. "I could probably be there in a few minutes if I hoofed it."

"Okay, go. Now."

Sol sprang to his feet, almost jogging toward the helicopter. "What do I do if I see anything?"

"I don't know. But anything capable of spreading a biological weapon has to be grounded. It has to go down at *any* cost."

"Any cost, huh?" he said, pulling his aviators down over his eyes.

"Any cost."

"I'll do what I can." Then he remembered what he had learned from NSAHenry about her goddamn father blackmailing Mazandarani. "Unrelated, but I have . . . come into possession of some information that you might be interested in. It's about . . ." He pinched the bridge of his nose hard and winced. "It's about Kaveh."

Pregnant pause from the other end of the line. "Can it wait?"

"Yeah, it can wait."

"Then tell me later."

"I'm en route," he said. "I'll be over the village in a couple of minutes."

"Okay, I'll be there as soon as I can." Without another word, she hung up.

He was licensed to fly helicopters, though not this one in particular, and while he'd definitely yoinked helicopters from air bases that he wasn't cleared for, he'd never actually *stolen* one. Sol's trot turned into a sprint when he saw the refueling truck putting its way to the helicopter—helicopters were much easier to steal when they didn't have a fuel nozzle in them.

Once he was in the air, fuel truck guy looking on in confusion, he considered calling Macallan to brief her on the situation, then stopped. If he did that, she would go straight to the Pentagon, and the American naval base in the north would immediately send troops and equipment down to Bahura, and then what would happen? Wouldn't that be the perfect irony—little Lorenzo gets saved from certain death by the alien, only to become collateral of American cruise missiles.

He got clearance from ATC, figuring it would be another few minutes yet before ATC figured out just how stolen this helicopter was, and then called Cora on the satellite phone. No response. Well, that figured, didn't it? If she was on her way from Japan, that meant she was probably shrink-wrapped and incommunicado. He was on his own, then. Just like old times. He requested one thousand feet from ATC and sped toward Bahura. As he approached the village, he spotted some of the rock formations that made a sort of perimeter to the coast. He'd noticed them the last couple of times he'd been here, but then he saw that one of them was new, and a millisecond after that realized it wasn't a rock formation at all.

"Holy shit."

A craft, what he assumed to be a spaceship, was lifting out of the jungle. It looked like a flying saucer about the size of a 747 and was, for the most part, invisible, and the only reason he could see it was all of the dirt and debris sliding off it.

It has to go down, Cora had said. *At any cost.*

This was not an attack helicopter, wasn't even the sort one could open a door and shoot AK-47s out of like a badass. And even if it were, he somehow doubted the aliens would be flaunting their vessel if they thought there was a chance his piddlin' human weaponry might pose a threat to it. He had no way to get that thing out of the sky, except . . .

He reached for the pulse emitter in his pocket he'd been carrying with him ever since Belarus, examining it with his fingers, feeling the point in the center that acted as a detonator. He might, *maybe*, be able to take this ship down before it got anywhere, let alone to somewhere populated, but he'd be taking himself down, too. He initiated a descent to five hundred feet, pushing the throttle forward, but then a shot popped out from behind the alien craft, one he was able to almost dodge. Almost.

It hit somewhere in the tail, maybe one of the tail blades, sending the helicopter into a spin. A bad spin, yes, but not so bad that the tail had been blown off altogether so he might, *might*, be able to get it to the ground without it turning into a fireball. He was losing momentum fast, but that ship was still moving, gaining distance from him with every second. He knew using the pulse emitter would change his own outcome in this imminent helicopter crash from a probability to a certainty.

Even still, he had an instruction, so he did what he had to do and pressed the button.

Paris dated a pilot once, back when she was humoring the idea of dat-
ing men. He was still in training, taking night courses at an aviation
school on Long Island while working the day shift at a diner in Rock-
away Beach. One time, the very last time she saw the guy, he took her
up in a Cessna owned by the school. As he was preparing to land, he
nonchalantly stated at roughly 6,500 feet, "I'm going to turn the engine
off," and then he did.

The engine shut off, as did the electrical equipment, and the loud
sound of the plane's engine powering the propeller was replaced only by
the sound of the wind against the fuselage. He'd done it to impress her,
maybe, or perhaps because he wanted her to dump him to save him the
hassle of doing it himself and decided to do something shitty to hurry
things along. It scared the hell out of her and contributed to a lifelong
fear of flying she never overcame. That sensation was what this reminded
her of now.

She could hear and feel engines cutting out, could hear the naked
air against the hull of the ship, and was in near-total darkness, the glow
from Brako's power core snuffed out. Bomba could probably see more
than she could (which was to say, nothing), but she took the chance regardless; lunging for where the power core *had* been, she slammed into
the table and grabbed something the size of a bowling ball. All of this in
less than two seconds.

Then came the crash.

The crashing and gnashing of parts ripping to pieces created rips and
tears all over the ship, allowing in sunlight. Something slammed into

her rib cage, another blunt object into her thigh, and she howled. Paris fell into a ball, and gravity pushed her under a table.

Then it all stopped.

She didn't move for a few seconds, hands still firmly clamped over her head, convinced that the pain of whatever fatal blow she'd just been dealt hadn't really hit her yet. She took a couple of breaths—no puncture wounds, no lungs filling with blood. She opened her eyes and saw that she *had* grabbed the correct sphere, its radioactive blue dimmed considerably but still visible. Then she smelled smoke and remembered what usually kills people in plane crashes—*fire*. At this, she forgot all caution. "Nik?" she called, straining to move. She tried to go in the direction from which she'd come, but everything was bent and twisted. It was unrecognizable. "Nik, give me a sign you're still there!"

Nothing.

She heard one of the physeterines moaning, crying for help, perhaps. Now surer of her footing in the unstable structure, she began moving back the way she came just as Bomba grabbed her by the foot. She screamed and turned to see that while they had her by the ankle, they were unable to move owing to the large metallic rod that was now jutting through their right leg, their tail crushed by two walls. She tore her leg away, looking back only quickly enough to see that they had freed their tail and were struggling to free their impaled leg.

Paris scrambled through a small opening that she was pretty sure she'd been through before, holding the power core to her chest like an infant, unable to stop herself from screaming when she saw that one of the things she was stepping over was a dead physeterine body.

"*Nikola!*"

Nothing.

Bomba realized what she was trying to do and suddenly regained their vigor, trying to move the two pieces of the ship holding their tail down so they could get leverage to rip the pole out of their leg. They were no longer trying to rip it out the way it came in—they were trying to rip it out horizontally, through what in a human leg would be inches of fibrous muscle. Paris kept moving. Nikola had said his cell was adjacent to hers and it must have been, considering that he had been able to weaken the walls of her cell.

"Nik?"

She chanced a look into the jagged hole she'd punched into her cell once she reached it and saw that although it had been crushed, it didn't reveal to her any openings into Nikola's. She pawed around, looking into newly formed holes in the bent and broken walls. In one of them, she thought she saw something familiar, something beetle black rather than the slate grays and dark browns of the rest of the craft. Then she heard a growling noise, followed by scrambling in her direction. Completely out of her depth, she shoved the power core through the small hole, then dashed for the sunlight, once again just barely missing their claws.

It was only by virtue of her smaller size that she got out of the ship before Bomba did, as she was able to slide out of the holes Bomba had to struggle to squeeze through. She made it outside not into clean, fresh oxygen-rich Earth air but into thick black smoke, causing her to cough and gag. Two more adults had made it out of the wreckage before she had, loading onto their mantas, but they didn't even throw her a passing glance as she fled from them into the trees. Within seconds, they were gone, either unwilling or uninterested in pursuing her.

But Bomba still was.

Bomba's injury was the only thing allowing her to outrun them when they had been in the ship, but now in the open, it was a different story. Now they could get down and run with their forearms on three legs, holding their injured leg up. Even with three legs, out here in the forest and with her vigor already diminished from disease, they would easily overtake her, and within less than a minute, they did.

They swiped one of her legs right out from under her, sending her shoulder slamming into a tree and throwing her to the ground. She turned to see them reaching for her, and she threw up her arms and closed her eyes, bracing for the blow, but it didn't come. She heard a noise like bacon being fried. When she opened her eyes, Bomba was frozen in place, their lips tearing back against their mouthparts like an alien Cryptkeeper, eyes sinking back into their skull. They seemed to be trying to speak, but not for more than a few seconds, as that was about how long it took for them to turn to black carbon, and then to gray and white ash floating away on the ocean breeze.

Nikola stood about twenty feet behind where Bomba once was, beautiful and horrifying, black cloudy wisps surrounding him almost like tentacles. His focus at first was on the spot where Bomba had been and then brightened as it focused on her. Her horror compounded when she remembered their agreement; here he was, her angel of death, ready to fulfill his bargain, and she was too terrified to beg him not to, to plead, *Please, not like that. Please, some other way, please leave a body for my family to bury. Anything but that!*

Nikola's focus spread out like a dying firework, his eyes becoming almost as dark as the rest of him. Then his attention caught something to his left. He didn't spare her a parting glance before that strange darkness that surrounded him engulfed him completely and then disappeared. Paris's limbs stayed locked for almost an entire minute before they collapsed, burned out on adrenaline.

What have I done?

She sat up, repulsed by the spot of carbon right next to her, this organic matter that up until a few minutes ago had been a living being. She saw now that, even though it felt like she had fought through acres of woods to get away from the crash, she hadn't gone far at all and was still within eyesight of the smoldering vessel. The smoke in the air made her cough, reminding her that this wasn't a California-in-summer-level disaster yet, but it could still turn into a wildfire.

She followed what sounded like the surf of the ocean and soon saw that the vessel had gone down at the top of a limestone mountain that dropped a few hundred meters to the sea in a steep, sheer cliff. The trees hugged the edges of the cliffs, which dropped into the bluest water she had ever seen. She just needed to find clear access to the cliff and thought, *I guess this is just as good a place as any.*

"Sol!"

She paused, half thinking she imagined Cora's voice. Hell, maybe she had, the voice was so faint and distant. And who the hell was Sol? Had there been a Sol on that ship, too?

"*Sol, are you here? Where are you?*"

Paris hesitated to call for her. She had no idea how contagious she was, and any proximity could be dangerous. Furthermore, what was there to say between them but a more final form of goodbye? *Whatever was going to become of us, we don't get a say in that now.* She turned back toward the ocean.

"*Paris, are you here? Can you hear me?*"

But that was the thing, wasn't it? To keep on marching to the ocean would deny the chance to see each other one last time. Most people in situations like this don't get the opportunity for closure.

"Cora?" Paris called, surprised at the weakness in her own voice. Now it was catching up with her.

"*Paris!*"

"I'm here!" she replied.

She saw movement in the trees, then Cora's hair. It was still that jet-black she'd seen back at the settlement. "Stay back!" said Paris when Cora came into view.

Cora stopped about thirty feet away from Paris, looking at her like she'd just discovered her corpse. "Oh no."

"You knew?"

She nodded, her face knotting up like she was about to cry. "I knew they had a virus they were planning on deploying. I knew they might use you as a vector. I hoped . . . I hoped . . ."

Hands shaking from the effects of the fever, Paris took off what was left of her filthy, blood-spattered overshirt, wrapping it around her face like a mask. "Nikola said it's extremely contagious."

Cora nodded sadly. "I think they're gone. The ones that survived the crash, anyway."

"Where have they gone?"

"I don't know. To regroup with the rest of them, I think, maybe somewhere on the mainland."

Paris looked back toward the ocean. "You still came for me."

"Of course I did," said Cora, voice shivering. "I knew . . . I knew you weren't—"

"I thought you might have gone already."

"Gone?" Cora repeated, taking a moment to see what Paris was getting at. "No, no, we wouldn't have . . . I knew, the second I saw you weren't in the plane when it crashed, I knew you were still alive. That's why—"

"So you *were* searching for me," said Paris, smiling despite everything. Nikola had been right yet again.

Cora nodded, her face contorting painfully as the reality of the situation set in. Paris had no idea what all she'd done to find her, but in the end, she'd been too late.

"I'm sorry," said Paris. "I'm sorry for the things I said."

Cora shook her head. "No, you were right to be upset. It's true I . . . The plan is to abandon everyone and everything. And I feel rotten about it; it is cowardly—"

"It's not cowardly," said Paris, smiling at her own words as hot, silent tears slid down her cheek. "Maybe you were right. Maybe there's no hope for us. When you look at it from their point of view, how can you see this civilization as anything but an infestation that just destroys everything it touches?"

"Please, don't talk like that," said Cora. "This isn't you."

Paris shook her head, falling to her knees, her muscles trembling like strings on a violin. "I don't blame you now . . . for wanting to go with . . . him." She swallowed painfully. "When I'm gone . . ."

"No, don't even think it."

"Cora, I've seen hemorrhagic fevers," she said, looking at Cora sharply. "I know how this story ends. I can . . . I can already feel it. That's not how I want to go."

"Just wait," Cora whispered so softly she almost couldn't hear her. "Jude will be here any minute. You aren't gone yet. Just wait."

"Is there any hope?"

"I don't know."

Paris closed her eyes, more tears streaming out.

"But that's the thing—I *don't* know," Cora continued. "*I don't know* isn't the same as *no*." Cora looked behind her as if she expected to get jumped. "Where is Nikola?"

"He's gone."

"Where is he?"

"I don't know, he . . . I . . ." Paris swallowed. "He has Brako's power core."

Cora's eyes widened like Paris had just told her every nuclear reactor in the world was about to melt down. "Stay here. I'll be back!"

"No!" cried Paris. "Wait!"

But Paris couldn't even get the word out before the strange metallic film spread over Cora's body and she disappeared.

· 5 3 ·

"Ampersand? Ampersand!"

Cora shook off her daze from the transport—even traveling a relatively short distance required shutting her body down, and booting it up took more effort than simply waking up from a nap. "Ampersand!"

She was in a deeply wooded area, cooler and more deciduous than the Philippines had been but still very humid. She closed her eyes to pull up her viewfinder to see where it had taken her, as she had moved too quickly after commanding her plating system to go to his location to even check. *Location, location,* she thought, the nerves in her eyes fumbling with barely contained panic. The system didn't coordinate with international borders, so she had to deduce where it was based on what the land looked like. She zoomed out far enough to see that it was definitely mainland Asia, possibly Korea? No, too far south. Definitely China.

She opened her eyes, still looking for any sign of him. "Ampersand!"

"*Be silent!*"

Cora whirled around, scanning the greenery for that familiar silvery iridescent white. "Where are you?"

Cloaked, apparently, as when she turned again there he was, not five feet away. "*The majority of the pod was not on board the ship. I believe they are close by, but I have not yet homed in on an exact—*"

"Nikola has Brako's power core!"

Ampersand didn't move, but she could feel the shift in him. "*How do you know this?*"

"Paris told me. She's infected. They've infected her."

It took another few moments for him to move, his eyes brightening as he widened his scope, scanning his surroundings. She looked around as if there was something her primitive human eyes might catch that his wouldn't. "What do we do? She's isolated for now, she didn't look too bad, so maybe, maybe there's still time, but Sol has my pulse emitter, I don't have any way to . . ." She fell silent when she saw that Ampersand was not focused on her but on something behind her, and she turned to face it.

Nikola was undeniably back to his full power—it wasn't just that he carried himself differently, that the laws of gravity that constrained a creature of his size without a power core no longer applied, but the air around him as well, like the very earth beneath him seemed to float a little.

"N-Nikola," she stammered, stepping in front of Ampersand. Why had Sol taken her pulse emitter? Why the *fuck* had he done that? And where the *fuck was he*? "Nikola, I—"

[*Dear one, please forgive me.*]

Cora blinked in confusion; this hadn't come from the mechanized voice in her ear but spoken Pequod-phonemic translated by her view-finder. Why would Ampersand ask her for forgiveness in Pequod-phonemic? So Nikola would hear him, as well?

Then she realized; she was not the *dear one* he was addressing.

[*I have failed you, dear one. I abandoned you when you most needed my care. I beg your forgiveness.*]

Ampersand brushed her aside, putting his body between her and Nikola.

[*When I turned you over to the custody of the humans, I was unable to care for you. I was not well. I was not capable. But that has not been true for some time. I should have intervened sooner. I should have developed a plan for your care and removed you from their custody. Had I done so, none of this would have happened.*]

Ampersand stood up straight, centering himself and crossing his hands in front of him in a gesture that a human might mistake as polite. He bowed slightly, but kept his head up straight, not taking his eyes off Nikola.

[*I should not have left you in the custody of the humans. They were well intentioned, but they do not have the means to help you. Despite the pain you have caused, I am still your caretaker, and you are still mine.*]

Cora had been staring at Ampersand so desperately that she hadn't realized that Nikola's laser focus had shifted to her, and she grabbed on to Ampersand's arm for stability. The focus of his eyes seemed to coalesce like the center of a galaxy.

[Do you have the means?]

[*I have the desire; therefore, I have the means.*]

At last, that demonic laser focus moved off Cora and onto his real target.

[Why do you have the desire now where you had none when you surrendered me to the humans?]

[*Things have changed.*]

[Yes, things have changed.]

He raised his hands slightly in what Cora read as an intimidation gesture, and he bowed his head, the ridge over his eyes only intensifying the effect.

[You were a broken thing, ready to follow me into death when last we spoke. And now things have changed. If your negotiations with me fail, you would fight me to the death rather than surrender willingly. What, I wonder, has changed you?]

At this, he shifted his focus again to Cora.

[I KNOW THAT THIS IS YOUR DOING, LITTLE COUSIN.]

"Please, don't hurt him," she blurted, pushing Ampersand's arm out of the way and stepping in front of him. As she did, she felt her legs start to buckle, and this time, she didn't fight it, falling to her knees and clasping her hands in front of her. "Nikola, I don't know what to do, I don't know what I can say . . . We are at your mercy. You don't have to do this—"

[CALM YOURSELF, LITTLE ONE,] said Nikola, this time speaking directly into her earpiece. His focus softened, and again he looked at Ampersand. [YOU HAVE NOTHING TO FEAR FROM ME.]

She felt a pair of hands wrapping around her shoulders, pulling her to her feet and back away from Nikola.

[YOU BELIEVE I INTEND TO FINISH WHAT I STARTED. YOU BELIEVE I BEGRUDGE YOU FOR SAVING HIS LIFE.] He kept his gaze on hers, but it softened, and the air around Nikola seemed like it had thinned back to normal. He looked at Ampersand.

[I WOULD ASK IF YOU REGRET HER DOING SO, BELOVED, BUT THE ANSWER IS OBVIOUS. INDEED, YOU ARE CHANGED. I WOULD NOT ASK YOU TO DIE WITH ME WHEN THAT IS NOT WHAT YOU WANT.]

[*One day, dear one, but not now.*]

Nikola took a step toward them, then another. The air around her thickened as she felt Ampersand's defenses rise, and Nikola stopped before he got too close. He looked again at Ampersand, folding his hands in front of him almost in mimicry.

[IF YOU TRULY HAVE THE DESIRE, YOU WILL SHOW ME.]

[*Yes.*]

[YOU WILL LET ME KNOW YOU.]

[*If you submit to me, yes.*]

She felt a shift in both of them, as if Ampersand had grown taller and Nikola was diminishing. In effect, he was making himself smaller, lowering his body to the ground and folding his arms against his side like a bird, bowing his head and closing his eyes. Now it was Ampersand who had the eyes with the bright, laser focus.

[*You will become my conservatee, and I will be your caretaker. I think, perhaps, that should be the arrangement for the rest of our lives. But you must do as I say, and only as I say.*]

[FROM THE MOMENT I FOLDED SPACE, FROM THE MOMENT I ARRIVED ON THIS EARTH, THAT IS THE ONLY THING I HAVE DESIRED FROM YOU, BELOVED.]

Then it was as if the silence might swallow them, a silence so deafening her ears started to ring. It was only now that she realized how unnatural it was—no sound of birds, of insects, of even the wind in the trees. Nikola opened his eyes and looked up at them and rose to his full height. He looked at Cora, even took a step toward her, but again, she felt the air thicken around her, around both of them. An unmistakable claim—*She is not for you.*

[MY POOR LITTLE COUSIN,] said Nikola, again speaking to her directly. [I HOPE ONE DAY I MAY EARN YOUR FORGIVENESS.]

Nikola took a step back, again diminishing himself as he looked at Ampersand, and spoke in Pequod-phonemic. [I HAVE A GIFT FOR YOU. A GIFT FOR BOTH OF YOU.]

"A gift?" said Cora, grasping Ampersand's forearm harder.

[REVENGE.]

The air grew thick, *extremely* thick. The only time she'd felt something like it was the one time Nikola had shown off to the three Obelus Similars in Death Valley. Cora looked again at Nikola, who now wore a mad, cat-stalking-a-toy expression. The trees in the valley swayed unnaturally, like they were being pulled on strings. Then they flattened like they'd been mowed down by the force of a nuclear bomb. This destroyed several acres of forest and reached all the way to what looked like a dried-up inlet, the force of Nikola's telekinesis parting the trees down the center like a comb parting hair and then ripping them all out of the ground. It was only then that Cora saw where Semipalatinsk had been hiding, because they were being dragged ingloriously out of their holes underground toward the inlet.

This was the first time she had seen the whole group, and it only struck her now what even as few as "hundreds" looked like—a huge mass of bodies, genuinely an infestation. Up on the hill, less than half a kilometer away, she watched the way they spilled out, bodies piled upon bodies like rats escaping a flood, dragged along on their backs and stomachs by an unseen force.

In the space of less than a minute, Nikola had all of them strung out on the dried-up lake bed, which itself looked like it couldn't be more than a few years old, perhaps the result of a dam somewhere upstream. They even looked like rats, their ropelike tails thrashing helplessly in the mud and sand, their slate-gray skin suits the color of wet fur, but they sounded like locusts. Lion-size locusts and all the attendant horror that entailed.

"This isn't all of them," remarked Nikola, surveying his handi-work. "Several dozen of the juveniles are missing."

Cora felt the air around her thicken further, and all three of them rose into it like they were in an abduction beam, gently gliding down to the edge of the tree line below and landing softly like angels. The sight of the pod all laid out on their backs reminded her of photographs she had seen taken by exterminators—*This farm was infested with hundreds of rats, but don't worry, we got them all.* They were quieting now, and a few of the adults scattered throughout seemed to have stopped moving altogether, their features hanging slack like they were dead.

Ampersand surveyed them, calm, collected, then Cora nearly jumped out of her skin when he blasted something in the physeterine-common language so loud she nearly had to cover her ears. She wasn't getting a translation in her viewfinder, but even without it, she could guess what he was saying:

Which one of you did it?

All of them, adult and juvenile alike, were splayed on their backs like they were on the operating table. There was a repetition to whatever he was saying to them, the same pattern of phonemes over and over, and she felt the air grow even thicker. Then one of the juveniles responded.

"What are they saying?" said Cora, almost as much to herself as to anyone.

"The juvenile is claiming that they were ambushed by our caste-peer Esperas. They say, 'The diplocrat-Oligarch amyg-daline claimed peaceful intent, but had a Similar lying in ambush.' They claim they had no choice but to defend them-selves."

Before Nikola had even finished his translation, Ampersand had blasted something again in that loud, clicking, booming language, like what a cicada might sound like if they were the size of a minivan. This time, her viewfinder did pick up the translation.

[*Who among you are the cannibals?*]

At this, most of them fell silent.

Ampersand waited about a minute before repeating the question, and the second time, it was met with an even completer silence. Even the juveniles seemed to have stopped fighting the invisible force holding them supine on the ground. Ampersand raised his hands to his midsection, forming a triangle with his fingers and thumbs. The earth in front of him gave way, rose in the air, the dirt falling away from it until it was nothing but sand, *molten* sand.

He drew more and more grains of sand from the ground, liquefying them as he did so intensely that she could feel the heat from it even ten feet away. Soon the mass in front of him was the size of a basketball, molten glass reddened by heat and darkened by the carbonized residual material inside it. Then he drew a rod out of the mass like a single string out of a ball of yarn and broke it. Then another, then another, each about two feet long, slightly larger in diameter than a drinking straw. Again and again he did this, in short order moving so quickly he felt like an assembly-line machine. Within a few minutes, he had hundreds of these blackened glass biopsy rods, one for each of them.

And she felt *rage*, rage like she'd never felt from the other side of the wall. If they wouldn't admit who the cannibal was, it was the only way. Really, wasn't this the humane choice? The alternative would be to slaughter and dissect them all. He wanted *revenge*, and she shared that desire. She wanted him to find the one who had hurt her, tear open the giant rat's skin like old, rotted clothing, do to them what they had done to her. Soon, he'd completed his assembly line, and then all at once he lifted them into the air and into adult and juvenile alike stabbed the glass tubes right through their midsections.

At this, the silence broke as many of them cried out in pain. A few dozen, who Cora was now convinced had poisoned themselves like the two porters with Brako had, didn't react. With one telekinetic tug, he ripped all the rods out of them at once, now dripping with blood. She almost sneered at their cries of pain; the disease they'd infected Paris with would cause that pain a thousandfold to anyone who caught it. It was no better than they deserved.

Then he began his examination. It was as he did this she realized that unlike times before when it had felt obvious to her which feelings were coming from him, this felt like they were of one mind. That in a way, she had been right, the high-language experiment had made it so her mind was no longer fully hers. She tried to come back into herself but was so overwhelmed with disgust and hate that she couldn't even remember what pity felt like. Looking at them was disgusting in the way that the crunched-up remains of a stomped-upon cockroach were disgusting; it was gross, but you did not pity the roach.

Rod by rod, at the rate of perhaps about one every five seconds, Ampersand went through them. As he did, the crying and writhing slowed but did not stop, and that burning anger and determination from the other side of the wall did not cool. Then he stopped on one of the tubes, giving it extra-special attention, and this one made his eyes brighten like wildfire. He spoke in physeterine-common, and her overlay translated:

[*At least one of you are cannibals.*]

He raised a hand and pulled one of them out of the crowd, kicking and screaming and covered in mud, a small stream of red blood trickling down its front. He dragged it along its back, stopping it just short of his feet and standing over the wretched thing. Then its stomach began ripping open by itself, its limbs pinned to the ground as it screamed, like a live frog being dissected.

Ampersand looked at the juvenile beneath him, vivisected and crying and wretched, and again a plume of loathing flared in her chest she found hard to tamp down, hard to compartmentalize, to say, *This is not mine.* She looked at all of them, the *liars*, the *cannibals*, and was suddenly hit by the smell of ammonia. She imagined Ampersand ripping open all of them, watching each and every one of them, adult and child alike, bleed out pitifully and then burn to dust, and felt the static in the air of his power, of him about to do that very thing.

"Ampersand, *no!*"

Cora positioned herself between Ampersand and the entire pod, right into his line of sight. "Not like this."

"*They are cannibals.*"

"This is a *child.*" She looked at the juvenile on the ground. A kid, not much younger than her infuriating edgelord brother. She could absolutely see a scenario where Felix, in a bid to impress Nils, did something terrible and unforgivable just to prove that he could, that he wasn't a boy but a *man.* "Killing them won't bring the dead back."

Ampersand didn't move, but the air lost some of its thickness. "*They have no legal personhood in any country, and even if they did, how could any human law bring justice to wholesale attempted genocide? They will never face any justice but what we administer."*

She looked down at the one on the ground, the dissected frog. The way Ampersand had cut them open drew almost no blood, and grotesque as it was, they could probably stay like that and survive for a long time—hours, maybe even days. That was probably the intent. Even if they were some kid who saw something gruesome and decided to get in on it, they still did it. They still participated in a murder.

"They hurt me, too. And after what they tried to do, after what they did to Paris, I agree, they have to face some sort of . . ." *Punishment* wasn't the right word. "Consequences. But killing them, killing *any* of them, it isn't going to undo anything."

"*It will protect us from them.*"

Her first impulse responded, yes, that was correct. Burn them all, right here. Technically, it wasn't even against the law, because they weren't legally people anywhere on Earth. At worst, it might be classified as cruelty to animals. And after what the Americans had done to their resources, what was the logical progression for *them* to do but to treat all of humanity as hostile, as well? The damage had been done; the bell could not be unrung. They had already declared war on human civilization before humanity even knew what was going on, and the threat they represented could be eliminated right here and now. She was almost ashamed of how long she humored this mindset, of how much of her psyche was no longer fully hers. Even stranger that this didn't upset her.

"They have as much right to live as we do," she said. "And they're only *transient* because . . ." She chose her words carefully, not wanting to say, *Because of your people.* "Because of what the Superorganism did to them."

Ampersand spoke in physeterine-common as loudly as he had before, and a wave washed over the pod.

[*It was Nikola, not I, who was captive. I will allow Nikola to decide their fate.*]

Some of the juveniles, already crying, made a pitiful wailing sound. She looked at Nikola and drew away behind Ampersand like she was a child hiding behind her mother's skirts. Nikola's eyes brightened, the focus broadening until it looked like the center of the galaxy. He stepped forward, almost gleeful that he'd been granted permission to unleash the godlike power he'd just been aching to unfurl.

He looked down at the juvenile still prostrate before Ampersand, and the ground vibrated, the rocks on the ground almost dancing. She looked again at the pitiful crowd and saw a few reaching out for one another, most of them with their eyes closed. They weren't even pleading a case, just closing their eyes and waiting for the end of the world. Then Nikola said something in physeterine-common, and there was a reaction. Not a hopeful one, but some of them stopped speaking, others still opened their eyes. The words translated on her view screen:

[**Whoever was the xenovirologist that designed the human plague, show yourself.**]

One of them moved, struggling to stand up. At first, Cora mistook their difficulty in standing for telekinetic pressure until she saw that they only had one leg. They rose on three limbs, using their tail for balance and leaning on their forelimbs like a gorilla, and said something in physeterine-common. Presumably, "I did."

Nikola's eyes again popped with that bright madness. He reached up his right hand, and the one-legged physeterine jerked forward, flying over the rest of the pod until they stopped a few feet in the air in front of Nikola, who was so tall that even this massive creature could hover a few feet off the ground and still meet his eyeline. Nikola regarded them in that gleeful, sadistic way for several seconds.

[**Did you design the plague you intended to use to cull the human population?**]

The one-legged physeterine didn't answer immediately, either from unwillingness or inability, she wasn't sure. Then:

[I did.]

[**Are you capable of designing a cure?**]

They tilted their head toward the rest of the pod, as if they were weighing that there was anything they could say or do that might lead to any outcome for their extended family besides death.

[There are fail-safes.]

Nikola regarded the xenovirologist, keeping them suspended in the air like a pig on an invisible meat hook, then looked down at the juvenile, supine on the ground and guts exposed. He moved a finger as though tracing an invisible line, and the injury *seared* closed. The juvenile wailed in agony as Nikola cauterized the wound, glowing hot like metal. Then, aside from the fluid coming out of their breathing holes, they lay still.

"I NEED THE XENOVIROLOGIST TO DO SOME WORK FOR ME. I IMAGINE THEY WOULD BE DISINCLINED TO COOPERATE IF THEIR ENTIRE POD HAS BEEN TURNED TO ASH. WE WILL SPARE THE LIVES OF THE SURVIVORS, FOR NOW."

Ampersand spoke in a less booming but still quite loud physeterine-common:

[*I will remand them to the custody of the natives.*]

From the reaction in the crowd, they clearly thought this was a death sentence, and Cora wondered if it actually was. They were in China, which would find some way to turn this into propaganda regardless of how the pod was treated, and remanding them to the Americans would be nothing if not a lateral move. It wasn't that she thought that the Chinese would be crueler than the Americans (for propagandistic reasons, the opposite was likely true), but she was concerned about how Julian might respond.

"Wait," she said. "I have a request."

Both looked at her, but it was Nikola who responded. "ANYTHING YOU ASK OF ME, IF IT IS WITHIN MY POWER AND I AM GRANTED PERMISSION BY OUR BELOVED, I WILL DO IT."

"Can we move them to a different country?"

"WHAT COUNTRY WOULD YOU PREFER, LITTLE COUSIN?"

She racked her brain. *Which is the least evil country?* Which, among the least evil countries she could think of off the top of her head, would actually have the resources to receive them? "New Zealand?"

"It is as you wish, little cousin," said Nikola. The semiautonomous plating that surrounded the one-legged physeterine became invisible, and she could feel the wake of the air as it took them wherever Nikola had programmed it to go. "But first, I have another matter to attend." His own plating slid over him like an oil spill as he crouched to the ground and disappeared.

Cora looked up at Ampersand, grabbing him by the forearm. "Paris—"

"*She will be cared for, my love.*"

Cora turned and looked at the pod, all still terrified, confused, and in agony for the wounds in their stomachs. "They're all bleeding internally."

He hesitated, and she sensed his annoyance. Then he lifted his fingers into a triangle shape, and most of them cried out in pain.

"*They will live.*"

Cora released a breath, now unsure if they had done the right thing. Yes, it was true that they had just as much a right to live as any other *person*, but that was true in any war. And now, the pod had lost everything. They didn't even have a vessel they could use to escape this rock. They were stuck here, and they would always begrudge Ampersand that. They did not owe anyone forgiveness just because their lives had been spared.

Then Cora remembered, she hadn't heard from Sol since he'd told her he was in the Philippines, near the site where their vessel had crashed. She fumbled to pull out the phone she'd been using earlier. "Shit, there's no reception here. I need to make a phone call."

"*To whom, dear one?*"

"I need to contact Sol; he was in the Philippines near their vessel's crash site, but I haven't spoken to him since before I got there."

"*He will not answer.*"

She stopped scrolling through her contacts. "Why not?" she asked. "Where is he?"

· 55 ·

Paris looked down into the bay as some of the local motorboats entered the harbor. Fishing boats, she assumed, or perhaps boats for tourists. They were so unlike the yacht-like shape of American boats, two pontoons held in place by long sticks jutting out of either side of these vessels. A few of the captains had already made it to the beach and were dragging their boats ashore, close enough that she could even hear them shouting at one another. A bunch of skinny, fit little guys who looked in good enough shape to probably make it up this hill in ten minutes, twenty max. That meant she may not have time to wait for Cora.

A sharp pain hit her in the gut, and she leaned forward, putting a hand over the edge of the cliff face, imagined the rest of her body following. The cliffs here were so steep, it really would take minimal effort on her part. No great leap necessary; a tumble would do. She had done some coverage of the last Ebola virus outbreak in the Congo in 2007. She knew what death by hemorrhagic fever entailed. Fever so terrible one could die from the shock alone, and if that didn't kill you, your arteries bursting inside you one by one probably would.

"I AM GLAD TO FIND YOU, DEAR GENTLE CREATURE. WE HAVE AN AGREEMENT TO FULFILL."

Paris pulled her hand back and turned to face him. There he was, her conscripted angel of death, standing in the shadow of the trees. Black as ebony, hands like spiders, the crest on his head reminiscent of horns, he certainly looked the part.

"You have your power back," she said weakly.

"AND YOU HAVE GIVEN IT TO ME," he said, moving toward her. She could feel the power radiating off him. He moved so differently now. "YOU ARE FRIGHTENED."

She let out an incredulous cough and looked out into the horizon and was surprised to feel a sense of peace. If anyone had to find her first, it was a good thing it was Nikola. Even so, she found it difficult to spit out the words to form a final request—*Make it quick, but please leave a body so my family will have something to bury.*

"YOU HAVE NOTHING TO FEAR FROM ME."

He was practically standing over her now, and she struggled to look up at him. "Did you kill them?"

"WHOM DO YOU MEAN, DEAR GENTLE CREATURE?"

"The physeterines. Did you kill them?"

He cocked his head like a dog in slow motion. "MY BELOVED HAS SUBDUED THEM."

"Are you going to kill them?"

"WE HAVE NO PLANS TO DO SO AT THE MOMENT."

"I can only hope you'll show us the same mercy," she said, and hunched over into a short coughing fit. "Nikola, do you think maybe there's some way I could see my family before I go? My sister and grandmother in Puerto Rico? Some way that won't infect them?"

"BEFORE YOU GO WHERE, DEAR GENTLE CREATURE?"

"Before I die."

"I IMAGINE YOU CAN SEE THEM AS MANY TIMES AS YOU WANT BEFORE YOU DIE, BUT YOU SHOULDN'T SEE THEM WHILE YOU'RE CONTAGIOUS."

She snapped her head back up to look at him. "You said you can't cure it."

"I CAN'T CURE IT, BUT I AM NOT A XENOVIROLOGIST."

"You don't happen to know any, do you?" she said, forcing a smile, despite the fact that she was pretty sure he wouldn't understand gallows humor.

"YES, I DO."

Her forced smile froze in place and then faded.

"THAT IS PART OF THE REASON I SPARED THE SEMIPALATINSK POD. NEITHER I NOR MY BELOVED COULD ENGINEER A CURE IN TIME TO SAVE YOU, BUT THE ONE WHO DESIGNED THE VIRUS ALREADY HAS."

The bargaining phase of grief she'd beaten into submission hours ago came roaring back. "Nik . . ."

Nikola lowered himself to the ground next to her, loafing inches from the edge of the cliff like a cat in the afternoon sun. "I NEVER AGREED TO TAKE YOUR LIFE FROM YOU. I AGREED TO SPARE YOU A GRUESOME DEATH, AND THAT AGREEMENT I INTEND TO UPHOLD."

"You're serious," she whispered. "You aren't here to kill me."

"I HAVE GONE TO A VERY GREAT DEAL OF TROUBLE KEEPING YOU ALIVE, DEAR GENTLE CREATURE. I WOULD BE PUT OUT TO SEE THAT GO TO WASTE."

Her feelings slowly caught up with her thoughts as she realized what this meant. She had spent the last two hours coming to terms with her very imminent death, but now? But *now*? Not an angel of death but an angel of mercy, so nonchalant in the fact that he was here not to kill her but to save her. The dam broke, and in the space of two breaths, she went from frozen in time to sobbing.

"DEAR GENTLE CREATURE," said Nikola, lifting up a hand like he meant to grab her, but he wasn't sure how to or where. "WHY ARE YOU CRYING?"

She tried to answer, but whatever systems allowed for human speech had been shorted by waves of emotion manifesting as heaving sobs. She grabbed him by the end of his long forefingers, opened her mouth to answer, and then broke down again, bowing her head until her forehead almost touched the ground. She felt a hand fall on her like a cage.

"DEAR LITTLE ONE, I DO NOT KNOW HOW LONG IT WILL TAKE, BUT WE HAVE THE MEANS TO CURE YOU. BE AT PEACE. YOU DON'T HAVE ANYTHING TO FEAR."

"Why?" she finally managed, sitting up to meet his gaze and scooting away from the edge of the cliff. "Why did you save me?"

"BECAUSE I WANTED TO."

"*Why?*" She coughed. "You owe me that much."

"WHAT IS IT THAT YOU WANT ME TO SAY?"

"The *truth*, Nikola. Tell me why you did it. Tell me the truth."

For a moment, he just looked at her as an entomologist might look at a newly discovered species of butterfly. Then he moved his body between hers and the edge of the cliff. "DEAR GENTLE CREATURE, THERE

IS NO ONE SINGLE TRUTH. WHICH ONE IS IT THAT YOU WANT ME TO
SPEAK? DO YOU WANT ME TO TELL YOU THAT YOUR SURVIVAL BET-
TER ENSURED MY OWN? OR DO YOU WANT ME TO TELL YOU THAT I
BELIEVE YOUR WORK IS A BENEFIT TO YOUR CIVILIZATION, REGARD-
LESS OF YOUR CIVILIZATION'S DIRE LONG-TERM PROSPECTS? OR DO
YOU WANT ME TO TELL YOU THAT YOU ARE THE ONLY HUMAN WHO
HAD ANY INTEREST IN MY WISHES OR RESPECTED MY AUTONOMY,
AND I WOULD BE DISPLEASED TO BE DEPRIVED OF THAT?"

Then it seemed like he finally figured out what he wanted to do with
his other hand, as he placed it around her body and drew her closer to
him until her wet, streaming eyes were mere inches from his.

"OR DO YOU WANT ME TO TELL YOU THAT I HAVE GROWN TO
CHERISH YOU, AND IT PAINS ME TO SEE YOU HURTING AND THAT I
DESIRE TO CARE FOR YOU? YOU HAVE ALWAYS BEEN KIND TO ME.
ALL SOCIAL CREATURES DEVELOP BENEVOLENT ATTACHMENTS IN
RESPONSE TO CERTAIN STIMULI, SUCH AS NURTURING OR KINDNESS,
WHICH WE DEFINE AS 'LOVE.' AMYGDALINES ARE NO DIFFERENT. THIS
IS A PARTIAL LIST OF TRUTHS TO ANSWER YOUR QUESTION 'WHY.'
DOES THAT SATISFY YOU?"

Paris froze, mouth hanging open dumbly. It wasn't that she didn't
suspect it, nor that she thought he meant it in the same, romantic way
that an English-speaking human might use the word, but she never in a
million years would have expected him to admit it.

"Yes," she said, dazed. "Thank you."

"I CAN'T KNOW HOW YOU EXPERIENCE LOVE, AND LIKEWISE YOU
FOR ME. HOWEVER, WE CAN GO BY ACTIONS. IF, BY YOUR DEFINI-
TION, LOVE IS PATIENT, LOVE IS KIND, LOVE IS SELFLESS, YOU HAVE
SHOWN ALL TO ME. MY DESIRE IS TO BE SELFISH. AND SELFISHLY, I
WOULD KEEP YOU FOR MY OWN."

The relief she had begun to entertain evaporated. "What do you
mean?"

"YOUR CIVILIZATION HAS A CAPACITY FOR BOTTOMLESS CRUELTY,
ESPECIALLY TO ONE SUCH AS YOU—YOUR OCCUPATION, YOUR GEN-
DER, YOUR GENOTYPE, YOUR PHENOTYPE, YOUR POLITICAL VIEWS,
YOUR ADVOCACY—ALL THESE THINGS PUT YOU AT GREATER RISK OF
VIOLENCE. I WOULD KEEP YOU AWAY FROM THE VIOLENCE OF YOUR

KIND, SAFE FROM ANYONE AND ANYTHING. I WOULD NEVER ALLOW
THE SAME THING THAT HAPPENED TO YOUR MENTOR TO HAPPEN TO
YOU."

Of course there would be some horrible catch to this. Of course he
wouldn't just cure her, then let her go to fly free, little butterfly. She would
be cured, but only at great cost. He would never let her go. She buried her
face in her hands and cried.

"Nikola, please, I . . . I just want to go home."

"THEN I WILL TAKE YOU HOME, WHEN YOU ARE NO LONGER CON-
TAGIOUS."

She pulled her face out of her hands, still feeling every inch the butterfly caught in a net. "You said you were going to keep me."

"I WOULD NOT KEEP YOU AGAINST YOUR WISHES. THERE IS A
PART OF ME THAT WOULD LIKE TO GIVE YOU NO CHOICE IN THE MAT-
TER, BUT HOW COULD I ESCAPE FROM BEING SOMEONE ELSE'S PRIS-
ONER ONLY TO MAKE YOU MY OWN? THAT WOULD MAKE US BOTH
UNHAPPY."

"You mean . . . you'll let me go?"

"I WOULD KEEP YOU, IF YOU WOULD CONSENT TO IT. BUT IF YOU
WOULDN'T, THEN I WILL TAKE YOU WHEREVER YOU WISH TO GO
WHEN YOU ARE NO LONGER CONTAGIOUS."

Paris wiped her face, surprised to find her feelings now changed.
If he had forced her into captivity, that would be one thing, but didn't
being the princess in the dragon-guarded tower confer some benefits
in an inherently dangerous, cruel world? A world where its inhabitants
were at all times hanging on to life by a thread that was all too easily cut?

"There may come a day when it might make sense for me to take you
up on your offer, but not now, Nik. Not now."

"AS YOU SAID, LOVE IS SELFLESS. WHEN YOU ARE CURED, I WILL
RETURN YOU TO YOUR FAMILY."

She swallowed a thick coat of slime in her throat. "When can I see
Cora again?"

"WHEN YOU ARE NO LONGER CONTAGIOUS."

She nodded. She was so tired. "I'm trying to make my civilization
better. I believe it can be better. Many other people and I, we're trying
to make it better with what tiny bit of power we have. I understand,

though, why you want to keep me away from it. After what happened to Kaveh . . . I understand."

"WE ARE ALL STILL BEHOLDEN TO EMOTIONAL REALITIES THAT LIE OUTSIDE OUR UNDERSTANDING OR CONTROL. I BEG YOUR FORGIVENESS FOR STATING THAT HUMANS ARE INCAPABLE OF LOVE OR THAT I HAD NONE FOR YOUR MENTOR. WE BOTH KNOW THAT IS UNTRUE."

"Even though he was just an 'insect,'" she said with a weak smile.

"IF WE ARE USING INSECTS AS A METAPHOR FOR INSIGNIFICANCE, HOW GREATLY DO OUR TWO KINDS DIFFER? VERY LITTLE, I WOULD ARGUE. IF HUMANS ARE 'INSECTS,' THEN SO ARE WE. PERHAPS I AM LONGER-LIVED AND MORE DIFFICULT TO KILL, BUT EQUALLY MORTAL, EQUALLY SMALL, EQUALLY INSIGNIFICANT. WE ARE ALL MOTES OF DUST IN A COLD, CRUEL UNIVERSE. THERE IS NO SHAME IN FINDING CONNECTION IN THAT COMMONALITY."

"No," she breathed, her weak smile fading as another wave of emotion crept up on her. "No, not at all. I . . . Of course I forgive you."

She broke again, weeping but not in incoherent sobs this time, and leaned her forehead into his muzzle. "I'm just so glad you're . . ." She stopped just short of saying *okay*, as she feared that might come with a correction about how he wasn't *okay*, would never be *okay*. Instead, she stated the equally true, "I'm just so glad you're here."

"I AM GLAD I HAVE FOUND A WAY TO HELP YOU WITHOUT KILLING YOU."

She cry-laughed and looked at him, cupping his giant head like she might a child's. "After we fulfill our agreement, where will you go?"

"I DO NOT DOUBT THE COMMITMENT TO MY REHABILITATION BY THE HUMAN EMPLOYEES OF BELLA TERRA, EVEN IF I'M UNSURE OF THEIR METHODS. BUT I DO NOT BELIEVE IT WISE TO REMIT MYSELF TO THE CUSTODY OF ANY INSTITUTION WITHIN THE UNITED STATES, ALL THINGS CONSIDERED."

"That makes sense." By now, it was all she could do to sit upright. She raised her hand up to the area below his eyes, barely even able to accomplish that much, letting gravity sink her palm into it.

"I WONDER, ARE WE STILL IN AGREEMENT THAT I SHOULD HAVE THE RIGHT TO CHOOSE WHEN AND HOW I DIE?"

"You should have the right, if you're of sound mind by the standards of your own people."

"THEN WE ARE ALSO IN AGREEMENT THAT I AM NOT OF SOUND MIND AND SHOULD ONLY MAKE SUCH A DECISION WHEN I AM. THERE-FORE, I HAVE ENTERED AN AGREEMENT WITH MY BELOVED. HE WILL ACT AS MY CONSERVATOR. I WILL DO AS HE WISHES."

She blinked, her eyelids feeling like they were weighted down with cinder blocks. It took her a moment to register what he'd said. "Do as he wishes? Like what?"

"ANYTHING I AM ASKED."

She struggled to look at him. "You mean, you have to do anything he says? Regardless of whether you want to do it or not?"

"YES," he said. "ANYTHING AND EVERYTHING."

December 15, 2009

Remarks by President Julian on Modernizing America's Nuclear Arsenal in the Face of Extraterrestrial Threats

THE WHITE HOUSE

11:52 A.M. EST

THE PRESIDENT: My fellow Americans,

As president, I must make decisions that are neither easy nor free from controversy, as is the case with the announcement I am making today. It was a difficult decision, but a necessary one. Today, I am announcing that in the interest of national and global security, the United States will be embarking on a new initiative to build and modernize our nuclear arsenal.

We are no longer living under the Sword of Damocles that was the Cold War; now, we have a new sword hanging over our heads, one that is not held by human hands. One that possesses power and technology about which we know very little.

The new nuclear weapons we will be building are not aimed at starting a new arms race against our fellow humans but rather to ensure that our current stockpile is up to date and capable of deterring hostile actions against our country from any enemy, human or otherwise. We are not seeking to increase the number of nuclear weapons we possess but rather to build a reliable and modern deterrent that can ensure the security of our nation. The United States remains committed to international agreements and treaties related to nuclear disarmament.

I want to emphasize that the decision to rebuild and modernize our nuclear arsenal was not taken lightly. We will continue to work toward a world free of nuclear weapons, but until that goal is achieved, the United States must ensure that we have a strong and modern nuclear deterrent to meet a wholly unprecedented threat when it finally arrives. Thank you, and God bless America.

· 5 6 ·

The Atlantic Press Awards weren't the most prestigious of the year, but it was still Paris's first time attending and an honor to be invited at all considering she had only just gotten back into the journalism game (before being kidnapped by aliens, anyway). She had skipped the modest little red carpet area, despite being the second-most in-demand interview of the evening. Now safely inside the lobby, glass of red wine in hand Portia Black–style, she waited.

She'd taken out her box braids, letting her natural hair frame her head like a 4c halo, and tonight, she was sporting a cream-colored, knee-length pencil dress. One of her many regrets was not reaching out to Cora before this evening, if not to ask if they could come to the awards together than just to talk. But she had only been home for less than thirty-six hours, and after the ceremony, she was fulfilling a promise to Renée and her grandmother in Puerto Rico—Abuela was too sick to travel, and if the last two years had taught her anything, the story could wait, her family could not. And so, tonight would be her last opportunity to see Cora before she left.

She had seen Cora briefly when she woke up at Kings County Hospital in Brooklyn with half of the Jamaican side of her family standing over her and the other half filtering in over the following day once they found out she was awake. She'd debated whether to tell the doctors the truth before ultimately deciding it was in her best interest, but in hindsight, she wasn't so sure. There wasn't any of the virus left in her system, but telling the truth meant she had to stay in the hospital for about five days longer than she might have otherwise and got a visit from pretty much every official in the health department all the way up to the U.S. surgeon general. Cora had been among the first to visit her, and they'd exchanged brief "I'm glad you're okay"–type words, but she'd taken the hint and left Paris alone with her family.

For the Atlantic Press Awards, Cora decided not only that she was going to be fashionably late but that she would humor the small red carpet. She was one of the last to arrive, uncharacteristically confident in her posture and movement as she spotted Paris.

"Hey."

"Hey."

Cora had dyed her hair a dirty blond that might be close to her natural shade and had it styled long and wavy like a 1940s movie starlet. She wore a black dress, her eyes smoky and her lips a perfectly lined, deep bloodred. She was so stunning one might miss the strange, sad, wistful expression on her face, a melancholy Rita Hayworth.

"You look amazing," said Paris.

"You do, too. I like your hair."

"It's my 'I didn't have time to get my hair done' hair."

"It suits you, though."

"That dress is killer," said Paris.

"Kaveh bought this for me to wear to the Pulitzer luncheon. If I was ever going to wear it, tonight would be the night."

Paris looked at her, and going by Cora's expression, she surmised that she might not be ready to have the "so what becomes of us?" conversation. Paris was beginning to fear they never would.

Cora looked over Paris's shoulder and sighed. "Oh boy."

"Fancy seeing you two again," said a voice from behind her. Paris turned, and there was Nils Ortega.

"Hello to you, too," said Cora.

Nils's eyes hopped back and forth between the two of them. "You both have a lot to be proud of." He looked at Paris. "Everyone thought you were dead. The U.S. intelligence apparatus thought it. I thought it. Everyone but Cora. When she didn't know what else to do, she and a CIA agent who considered me his mortal enemy came to my apartment, talked me into giving them sensitive foreign intelligence, because Cora was going to turn over every stone on Earth to find you."

Cora looked at the floor shyly but didn't say anything to contradict him, and a swell of emotion rose in Paris's chest. Paris had known on some level that this had to be the case, but no one had told her what shape Cora's actions had taken, that in her desperation, she'd gone to Nils of all people. And Nils had actually helped her.

"I never thanked you for your help," said Cora to Nils. "It ultimately led us right to some things even the Belarusians hadn't found. I know it didn't seem obvious, but if not for that intel, I wouldn't have found out where Paris was."

"Well, maybe this won't be the last time we collaborate."

"Maybe."

"Do you have any idea how they got to New Zealand?" he asked as if he suspected her of being involved. The pod had been discovered north-west of Christchurch just in time for the situation to turn into a siege; true to Nikola's word, most of them were still alive (although about fifty of the juveniles had disappeared), but despite everything, they were not ready to surrender.

"Not a clue," said Cora. "I just hope the Kiwis can rise to the challenge."

"I'm sorry to hear about Agent Kaplan," said Nils.

"Who'd have ever thought you'd say that?" Cora laughed.

"Kaplan," said Paris. "Was that the CIA guy?" That must have been the man she'd seen with Cora in those live feeds of the abandoned green-houses.

"Yeah," said Cora.

"What happened to him?"

Her smile faded. "Helicopter crash."

"Oh," said Paris. "I'm so sorry."

"Without getting into the gritty details, he finally decided to be a hero. But . . ." She looked at Paris, her eyes becoming glassy. "If not for him, I wouldn't have found you."

She looked at Cora, then at Nils, not knowing what to say. "I'd . . . like to know more about him."

"He was—" Cora started, but was cut off.

"Ladies and gentlemen," said a voice over the speaker. "The ceremony will begin in five minutes. If you would please find your seats . . ."

"I have to go backstage now," said Cora. "The in memoriam segment comes around the halfway point."

"You'll do great," said Nils.

"Thank you," said Cora. She looked at Paris, and despite the confidence Cora was carrying herself with, it was striking how at peace she seemed with Nils. Perhaps time really did heal all wounds. "I'll see you soon."

. . . . .

Paris looked at her program as the lights fell. They'd just gone to commercial, and up next was the in memoriam for Kaveh. Nils sat a few tables over, talking with a couple of his *New York Times* buddies, the face of serenity. The countdown from break began, the music rolled, and then the host, one of the newer late-night talk show hosts by the name of Dave Arroyo, walked onstage to gentle applause and stopped at the podium.

"Investigative journalism is not without its occupational hazards," said Arroyo. "Anyone who devotes their life to investigative journalism not only reveals truths that may want to stay hidden but accepts that theirs is arguably the most dangerous form of journalism one can engage in. Every year, investigative journalists lose their lives in pursuit of those truths. Tonight, we honor such a journalist."

Kaveh's image faded in on the big screen behind him. They hadn't gone with a headshot but something more candid. The image not of a professional putting on a front but a guy having fun at the beach, laughing at someone off-screen.

"To speak in his memory, we are honored to hear about Kaveh's life from a perspective we haven't heard before. Her first time speaking in public, please welcome Ms. Cora Sabino."

As the audience clapped politely, Arroyo exited stage right while Cora entered stage left. At first, she masked her nervousness well, until she got to the podium and saw the words in front of her, then the mask slipped. She looked at his image and swallowed so hard the mic picked it up.

"Right now, if you know me for anything, it's probably for being the subject of a photograph that has become a flash point in our cultural dialogue." Her voice shook with the timbre of a person who was not practiced at this. The image behind her faded from the picture of Kaveh to the infamous photograph of her protecting Jude and Nikola in downtown Los Angeles.

She turned to the audience, looking relieved when the image faded back to Kaveh. She pursed her red lips, took a deep breath, and dove in. "When I was first asked to do this dedication, I wasn't sure if I should accept for a number of reasons, not least of which that I didn't know Kaveh for very long—I only knew him for about three months before he died. Moreover, I didn't know if I could do him justice. He was a genius, not just in the literal IQ-based, high-SAT-score sense"—this elicited a gentle, sympathetic laugh from the audience—"but in a subjective, artistic sense. His greatest gift was his way with words. He was the most gifted person with words I've ever met.

"But then I realized that it wasn't my place to try to pay tribute to him by rising to his oratory level; quite frankly, I don't think anyone could. Rather, the best way I could pay tribute to him was by speaking his truth. Journalists don't just tell the truth, they frame the truth. They tell a story with it. A successful investigative journalist must also be a gifted storyteller. They take the truth and turn it into a narrative.

"And it was this gift, not just his way with words but his gift as a storyteller, that made him great. Even in death, he changed the world with his skill as a storyteller. A simple, factual retelling of his relationship with Nikola Sassanian wouldn't have made such an impact; it had to be told with nuance, sensitivity. It had to grip the reader."

The image then faded from Kaveh's face to the cover of the May 2008 issue of *The New Yorker*. "In the end, it was this piece for which he would become most famous," she continued. "But that of course wasn't the only truth he ever told or elevated. Kaveh first rose to prominence through his yearslong investigation that culminated in an exposé of abuses perpetrated by the CIA, with which he collaborated with my father, Nils Ortega. This would ultimately lead to sweeping reforms in U.S. intelligence gathering. He also spent years following naturalized American citizens wrongly imprisoned on charges of terrorism, many of whom were also from his native Iran, which led to his second bestseller and brought public attention to the fact that this was happening at all."

The photo then faded to another picture of Kaveh, but this one was in black and white, much more somber. "The very first time I met Kaveh, the only thing he knew about me was that I was on speaking terms with one of the Fremda group—which at that time no one outside the

U.S. government had seen—and that my only prerogative was to protect the one for whom I'd been conscripted as interpreter, Jude Atheatos. He knew nothing about Jude or his intentions for humanity. The first time I talked to Kaveh, I had a panic attack that resulted in me fainting and getting a minor head injury, but his first priority wasn't himself or defending the world from whatever nefarious hypothetical Jude might do but checking me for a concussion. His first instinct was to make sure I, a person he knew nothing about, was okay. That instinct would follow him for the rest of our relationship."

Cora swallowed again, and this time, it almost looked painful. "There was another, even more serious incident that's particularly difficult for me to talk about. After the incident at Pershing Square that made me instantly famous, my mental state deteriorated further, and Kaveh was the only person in my life who was trying to help me. Even so, I began to self-harm and even contemplated suicide. One of these incidents of self-harm was particularly violent and ended with me in the hospital."

Paris was confused as to where this was going or why Cora thought this belonged at a memorial for Kaveh that was going out on live TV. Out of the corner of her eyes, she saw Nils sit up, suddenly very interested.

"In this case, Kaveh withheld the truth and lied both to the doctors and the police to keep me from being involuntarily committed. Because of Kaveh's quick thinking, he protected me from all the scrutiny that would have come with this incident being made public. At the time, I was hanging on by a thread."

Paris looked at Nils again and was taken aback by his expression. He looked like he was watching his house burn down.

"Kaveh was able to keep that information from being made public," Cora continued. "But he wasn't able to prevent the police report from falling into the hands of then congressional candidate Jano Miranda, who had many close ties with the police in Orange County. And Jano Miranda, who was a fierce ideological enemy of Kaveh, wasted no time passing that police report to my father, Nils Ortega."

Paris gasped, and the audience erupted into quiet, confused murmurs. All eyes turned to Nils, whose face had turned to steel, his jaw clamped shut, his blue eyes shooting daggers.

"Now I imagine most fathers," said Cora, looking directly at Nils, any trace of nervousness or unsureness in her voice or form now evaporated, "upon seeing a police report wherein their former colleague was suspected by the police of domestic violence, would be moved to protect their daughter. Their daughter, after all, is the subject of the most famous photograph in the world. She has no job, no money, and more crucial, she is fourteen years the junior of said colleague who is suspected by the police of brutalizing her. One would think that this father would be moved to protect his daughter, but that's not what Nils Ortega did."

Nils's expression had cooled, no longer the expression of someone beholding a disaster but now a locked door with the key thrown away.

"Within hours, Nils was in contact with Kaveh," said Cora, cold as ice, "letting him know that he had the police report. Within days, he was blackmailing Kaveh, telling him that this police report would be, in his words, 'pretty damning' if it were to be made public, both for Kaveh and for me. As he so often did, he told Kaveh he would keep this information to himself if Kaveh agreed to give Nils classified information he'd obtained from his time spent with Nikola Sassanian. Ultimately, Kaveh did give Nils what he asked for."

Cora's cold expression took on a hint of a satisfied smile. "Kaveh told Nils that four CIA agents had been killed by the ETI code-named Obelus at Bedford, Virginia, in October of 2007, and that those killings had been covered up. Nils immediately relayed that information to then presidential candidate Todd Julian, who, in exchange, offered Nils Ortega amnesty from any potential charges of espionage if he was elected president. While Nils would never publicly endorse Julian, he would spend the months leading up to the election engaging in cyber campaigns promoting Julian's ideology and spreading lies about his competitor."

She looked directly at Nils. "All these exchanges are documented. These documents are now publicly available on *The New Yorker*'s website."

Half the audience was whispering in their bewilderment, some ladies at her table insisting to one another that this *had* to be staged. This *had* to be a hoax. Paris felt like an owl for how wide her eyes had grown and felt strangely proud of this girl's audacity. She had planned this. She talked that way to Nils's face and she'd planned this.

"All these men possessed a truth," she said, addressing the audience as a whole, and they quieted down. No one was looking at Nils; all eyes were on her. "Todd Julian used this truth to discredit not only me but everyone who advocated against the Third Option, as if the American government's decision to cover up the murder of government officials had *anything* to do with the debate about alien personhood. It didn't then, and it doesn't now. Todd Julian used this truth to advocate for a discriminatory, illogical ideology. Todd Julian used it for political gain.

"Nils Ortega used this truth as a transaction, exchanging it to a powerful man for the promise that he would never have to face consequences for the government secrets he helped expose, for the espionage of which he is quite guilty. Nils Ortega used this power to protect himself and to forge new, more powerful alliances. Nils Ortega used it for personal gain.

"Kaveh Mazandarani used this truth to protect someone he loved. He knew that my father was unscrupulous, that he did not want intel out of concern for the public good but for how he could use it to his own personal advantage. I think even Kaveh would tell you that what he did was morally wrong, but there was a reason why he did it; he did it to protect me."

At this, her coldness melted, and a tremor entered her voice. "Kaveh never told me that my father had blackmailed him into sharing classified information with him. And Kaveh had no idea that I had anything to do with the incident at Bedford. I never told him. He found out when Todd Julian revealed it to the rest of the world during the Senate hearing in which I testified last year."

She pursed her lips and paused, looking down at her notes as though she'd lost her place. "Kaveh overcame so much in his life. His family was nearly killed in their escape from their home country of Iran. He had to learn to survive in this foreign place. He had to endure the suicide of his brother. He struggled with substance abuse for most of his life. But he was always working on himself. He learned from his mistakes. He overcame his addiction. In his last piece, he wrote about the possibility for humanity to evolve into something better, because he was the embodiment of that possibility. If he could better himself as he did, learn from his mistakes, perhaps there was hope for everyone." She swallowed hard, the muscles in her neck growing tense with emotion. "He was the best of us.

"The lesson we can take from his work and his life is that while the truth is not subjective, it always comes in the context of a story. So my question in the delegation of truths that are mine to give or to keep my for myself is not 'What is the truth you are trying to share?' but rather, 'What story are you trying to tell?'"

Cora gave Nils one last curt look before exiting the stage. At first, no one moved, no one initiated the rote, mechanical exercise of applauding after a speech. She was well off the stage before anyone did start an uncomfortable, confused applause, and it took just as long for Paris to get to her feet.

She hurried to the other side of the venue and saw that Cora wasn't heading backstage but toward the exit. This was her opportunity. As the door closed behind Cora, Paris jogged after her, clumsy in her high heels. She didn't know what she'd say, figuring that whatever needed to be said would come to her when the moment came. But when she opened the door and looked into the night, Cora was already gone.

57

Sol Kaplan couldn't see himself in the mirror, but he knew he looked like an injured Tom in traction right before, in an indignant rage, he shook off his body cast and neck brace and got right back to chasing Jerry, to the delight of millions. The cartoons always needed to include that part. Currently, the damage was: a cracked skull, legs broken in four places, pelvis shattered, arms broken in six places, four cracked ribs, one cracked clavicle, a couple of fingers and toes thrown in for good measure, and the coup de grâce, spine severed in four places. After a few operations, and a few more on the way, two of those severances might be salvageable-ish. But nothing was going to save him from the reality that even in the best of circumstances where all of his bones mended optimally, he was now a paraplegic.

He turned on the TV and was met with the triumphant face of the person he second least in the world wanted to see triumphant (after Nils Ortega)—Todd Julian giving roughly the fortieth speech this week crowing over the victory of his new defense bill. The millions of people out of work would have to bootstrap their way out of the depression, but don't worry, at least we'd have an arsenal of new, shiny nukes to greet the alien envoy.

The Atlantic Press Awards were airing on C-SPAN, as was the memorial service for Mazandarani, and he considered watching it for a millisecond before thinking better of it. Being in traction made one feel powerless enough, but to watch that situation unfold might just be too much for him to maintain his charming sense of humor. Plus, he didn't want to see Nils Ortega. Ortega was probably having a pretty good night, as he didn't even know Sol was alive. *Missing* in CIA lingo always meant "dead." So, he just watched TV. *Flip This House* had come and gone a couple of times and now had moved on to *Flip That House*, which was totally different.

He felt the shadow of someone entering the room but physically wasn't able to turn to look to see who it was until she came into view. There were many people in the world who would love to finish him off, and what an easy time of it they would have; just close the door behind them, borrow a pillow, and that would be that. And as he watched her round his hospital bed, her expression so full of compassion for his sorry state, he couldn't help but think that she had every right to be one of those people.

"So," he said, surprising himself with how slow and gummy trying to speak at all was. The clunky foam neck brace didn't help. "You did it?"

Cora nodded. "He is fucked."

Sol tried to swallow, tried to make his mouth less dry, but it was a struggle. "In respectable society, anyway."

She nodded, hugging herself as she did, more at peace than triumphant. She'd obviously just come from the event, still in her black dress and her styled hair, no longer a flat-black bathroom dye-job but a professional, multihued dark blond that fell in large curls over her shoulders.

"I know it mustn't have been easy for you," she said. "Giving me that evidence about Kaveh."

"Well, I never would have discovered it if someone hadn't slipped me that hard drive they 'found.'" He tried to do finger quotes, but only managed to do it in his left arm, which, while broken, was not in traction.

"We turned that hard drive inside out but couldn't find anything useful," she said. "It was a Hail Mary, but I figured your army of hacker creeps might know how to look somewhere we didn't."

"My army of hacker creeps was able to dig up metadata that an alien missed," he said.

"Well, you know, he's a biologist, not a hacker."

He thought back to the night they had gone to Nils's apartment, the night she'd had that breakdown over the way Mazandarani had died, her role in his death. Her little show of hysterics had fooled Nils, had even fooled him. He didn't doubt that her guilt over Mazandarani's death was sincere, but it never occurred to him that she might have been in control of the situation the whole time.

"I still don't see how you managed to take it without Nils noticing," he said. "He was keeping an eye on the bathroom door the whole time you were in there. Did you sneak in after we left?"

"Let's just say I have access to certain alien tech that even you don't know about." She sat down on the bed next to him carefully, so no part of her body was touching his. "You could have kept those emails to yourself forever, and I never would have known what Kaveh did for me. What Nils did to him. So I'm grateful to you."

He made a failed attempt at a shrug. What could he say? He could have taken it to his grave and nearly did. But much as he hated Mazandarani, the guy really had loved her, and she deserved to know.

The moment he'd pushed the button on that pulse emitter, he'd known the crash wasn't survivable. But about a week later, he'd regained consciousness here at Bellevue in full Tom-and-Jerry traction regalia. His mother and sister, Miriam, were there, as well as his elementary school–aged niece and nephew, Alona and Ariel. They had already made big plans while he was still in a coma to make Miriam's house accessible for him, and Alona and Ariel were already taking courses online on how to help him recuperate. Every day, his mother showed up at the hospital to frame this tragedy about how *she* was the real victim here for being put through this worry, and every day, he thought, *Yeah, I probably deserve this.*

More than once, his mother betrayed that she was *glad* he was in traction—in part a punishment for having been so very distant from them for the last twenty-odd years, but mostly because it would prevent him from doing the sort of things that would lead him to *being* in traction in the first place. After all, this was quite a way to find out little Solly Kaplan had actually been a covert CIA operative for the last twenty years. All of them praised God for this "miracle" and told him that as soon as he was able, he needed to go back to synagogue and reconnect with the rabbi and their community. He did plan on it as soon as he was able (if for no other reason than he would soon have no choice), but he knew it wasn't a miracle that saved him, at least in the ecclesiastical sense.

And it certainly wasn't human medicine.

"Why did he do it?" he asked.

"Why did who do what?"

"Why did he save me?"

Her expression softened. "I don't know. Probably because he thought I'd want it."

"You would?" he slurred. "Even after I . . . Even after—"

"Just because you're kind of an asshole doesn't mean I want you *dead*."

"Are you why he decides who lives and who dies?"

"Now that I think about it, he's never saved a human life without my explicit request for him to do so, until . . ."

"Until what?"

She smirked the same smirk he used to always give her. "Until you."

"What's special about me?"

"I'm not sure. I think he saved you on a whim."

"But a whim based on what he thought you would want."

She shrugged.

"You remember what I said in Minsk?" He tried to smile and failed. "What power you could wield."

"I wouldn't," she laughed dismissively. "There is no great man that's going to right this ship, and even if there were, it wouldn't be me."

"Why not you?" he said without jest. "Out of everyone on this planet who spends their life clawing for power, the Putins and the Julians of the world. Why them and not you?"

She chuckled silently, like if he'd asked some charming non-consequence question like if she was planning on seeing that Wells girl again. "Soft power, I suppose. The power of influence."

"I hope you use it more wisely than we have."

"Who's 'we'?"

"The agency. The U.S. All of us." He strained to move his eyes, look around the room.

"I think these meds might be making you a little loopy." She looked at the forest of IVs that surrounded him. "Does the morphine they've got you on count against a drug test?"

"Doesn't matter. I'm resigning as soon as I'm able to hold a pen and paper."

She seemed relieved. "I mean, in some ways, it's a shame. The CIA needs slightly fewer evil people to make it slightly less evil."

"I don't think I was making the agency better. I think it was making me worse. It's ... it was never ... When a system is founded on something so broken ... I'm not saying the agency has done *zero* good, but ..."

"At least you were able to use that system for something good once."

"I'm sorry."

She shook her head and smiled. "It's not a big deal for Jude. He doesn't even use a fraction—"

"No, I'm *sorry*," he stressed.

Her smile disappeared.

"I'm sorry for the way I treated you. Even as I was doing it, I knew what I was doing, and you didn't deserve it. I did it to get back at them, your—Nils, and Mazan—and Kaveh. And I don't know why, you ... I didn't ... I didn't want to hurt you. I did care about you. You're one of the only real friends I've ever had."

He was actually finding her hard to read. The only word he could use to describe her expression was one of pity.

"Please, say something," he whispered.

"I'm glad you're okay."

He tried to smile and again failed. She didn't owe him anything. He knew that. "'Okay' is a very generous way to describe this."

"So what are you going to do with your new life?"

"I don't know." He took a breath as deep as his body would allow, which wasn't very. "I'll never walk again." He'd known it for a few days, but this was the first time he'd said it out loud.

She looked at the floor, still implacable, then touched his unbroken hand with the kind of gentleness that only came from someone who had experienced the type of pain he was in. "You will." When he looked at her for an elaboration, she smiled serenely. Then she leaned in toward him, placing her cheek next to his, and whispered into his ear, "I'll put in a request."

His throat hardened, tears started forming, and his training told him to keep them right in the bottle where he'd been storing them for decades. But then he wondered, *Why?* Why, of all times, of all situations, was this the one to hold back tears? Why, of all people, was she the person to hide them from? So he let them fall. It was the first time he'd cried since he was a little boy. In a soft, fluid motion, she moved her lips to his forehead and gave him a long, soft kiss. He almost wished the painkillers weren't so potent, so he could feel it.

"Be good," she said.

He opened his mouth, but nothing came out. He was ripped open, stripped bare, confronted with the living embodiment of every person he'd used his power to hurt instead of help, and she was looking at him with a forgiveness he did not deserve. And he loved her. Not in a way that wanted or expected anything from her, not in a way that he wanted to make her his. Not even in a way that wanted her love in return. He simply loved her.

So he said nothing.

She lifted her hand and gently placed it on his cheek, grazing her thumb over his cheekbone. "See you around, Sol."

And then she left.

58

When Cora opened her eyes in the mountains near the village of Kita-kata, Fukushima Prefecture, Japan, it was about 10:00 A.M. local time. Her hair, expertly styled, had been flattened from the journey, and somehow, her lipstick had even managed to smear quite a bit. It would be nice, she thought, to use the *onsen* on the patio, but it would take some time to get that filled. Tomorrow, she figured, despite the fact that given her trans-hemisphere travel it was already tomorrow.

She'd missed so much school this semester that she was unable to pass all but one of her classes, but given the extenuating circumstances, the school allowed her to drop them rather than fail her. They'd given her the option to try again in the spring, although she hadn't yet decided if she would take it. She liked Columbia; she liked her friends there. It made her feel normal. But did it make sense to fall back into a routine, to entrench herself into other people's lives, if at the end of the day it would always end with a painful conversation like the one she'd had with Paris? *There is no saving this civilization, and I have to go soon.*

She washed some rice and set her rice cooker. Once that was going, she took a shower, washed her face, and partially blew her hair dry—she'd let it grow out so much that at this length and thickness, it took forever to dry on its own. Just as she turned the hair dryer off, her phone rang. At first, she was inclined to ignore it, even hesitated to answer when she saw who it was from. But no, this was a call she had to take.

"Hi, Olive."

"That was *insane*," said Olive like she was describing a WWE match.

"I'm . . . surprised you watched!" said Cora. In truth, she had been afraid Olive wouldn't speak to her. Not three months ago, she was still referring to Nils as "Dad." "You understood what was happening?"

"Mom told me. She was standing up and cheering when you called him out. She said he'd done all sorts of illegal and bad things, but the public didn't know about that. Did you tell her you were going to do that?"

"No, I didn't."

"Well, after what he did to you and to Kaveh, I can't believe he thought he'd get away with it! You pwned him. Totally pwned him."

Cora laughed, unsure if Olive was too young or too old to be saying *pwned*. "So does this mean you're not going to be a journalist when you grow up, after all?"

"No," she said with a surprising sureness. "Mom told me about the things Nils used to do, the way he'd trick people into thinking he was a good journalist, but he wasn't. She says there aren't enough good journalists, but we need them. So if I don't grow up and be a good journalist, how are there ever going to be any good journalists?"

"Yeah," said Cora, eyes growing hot at the thought of Paris, who despite it all still wanted to save the world by being a "good journalist." "Yeah, you're absolutely right."

"Maybe I'll go to Columbia, too."

"Maybe," said Cora, wiping her eyes. "But only if you don't get into any more fights with Simi Parquette."

A loud, indignant eight-year-old huff. "Fine."

"And besides, NYU is the better school for journalism, anyway."

They said their goodbyes and hung up. Cora didn't know how to explain to her sister just how bad things were going to be for her generation, that she wasn't yet old enough to understand where this ship was headed. Still, things were never going to get better if the next generation didn't think it possible for things to get better in the first place.

After spooning some of the rice into a bowl, she sliced up a mango and a few apples. She slipped into a camisole and some pajama shorts, figuring a light nap was in order. But before she could do that, she had to check on the situation that had temporarily taken up residence in their house. The physeterine juvenile was hunched in their nest of pillows in the office upstairs, tail wrapped around their right leg as it often was when they were anxious, but this time accompanied by the anklet

Ampersand had affixed to them. Just as when last she'd seen them, their eyes were glued to the news monitoring the situation down in New Zealand.

"Do you understand what's happening?"

Without looking at her, the juvenile coded some instructions into their translation tablet, positioned it so she could read it, then spoke in Semipalatinsk-creole:

[**I understand.**]

It had taken some doing to convince Ampersand that keeping them inside that containment cell was inhumane, no matter what an improvement it was to the situation down in New Zealand, which was pretty grim, far worse than she'd imagined it would be. Ampersand's compromise was that the juvenile could be moved upstairs into the room labeled on the house's floor plan as "office," as it did not have a window, even allowing them some mobility (even though they never took advantage of that freedom), using the anklet to monitor their form of house arrest.

"I brought you some food," she said, putting the rice and fruit down near them, but not too close. They always ate it eventually, but never when she was looking. "Canada's going to debate adding physeterines to their ETI personhood law in parliament next week. That's a pretty good option for you."

Perhaps it was the relatively large number of physeterines, the nature of their introduction to humanity, or simply the way they looked, but the international community was much less eager to extend full personhood to physeterines than they had been to amygdalines. The Japanese were conspicuously slow on the uptake. It really was one thing to accept the good PR for how they had handled the *Jūdo-san* crisis; opening the door for the possibility of physeterines begging asylum was another matter.

[**Where would I go in Canada?**]

"Same as all refugees do. Turn yourself in at a port of entry. They take it from there."

The juvenile's flat-screen showed a feed of the military encampment surrounding the caves the physeterines had holed up in and were now in a standoff. Yet another thing she'd failed to consider—the South Island of New Zealand was lousy with caves. She was surprised that so much of the twenty-four-hour news cycle was still so focused on it, considering there had been nary a peep from inside their underground fortress since it had been discovered a couple of weeks ago. "You can always go down there and be with them."

[**My people are under siege.**]

"The entire world is watching. The Kiwis aren't going to hurt them, even if your people come out guns blazing. New Zealand won't want an alien Waco being broadcast in real time." She said this more to herself than the juvenile, as she knew the juvenile had no idea what she meant by *Waco*.

[**I cannot ever be with them.**]

"Sooner or later, they're going to have to surrender, or they're going to starve."

[**I can never be with them again. This is my fault.**]

She furrowed her brow, kneeling next to them. "You think they'll see it that way?"

[**It was my idea to abduct you without telling my parents. My actions forced the evacuation. My actions led the Similar-Oligarch to hunt them down. Many poisoned themselves because the Similar-Oligarch captured them. How many of my parents are dead because of me? It is my fault. I can never be with them again.**]

Cora rose to her feet, crossing her arms in front of her. "You know you can't stay here."

She didn't wait for a response, closing the door behind her and leaving them alone with their twenty-four-hour news cycle and only a crude translation tablet to make sense of it. They really had tried to do what they thought was right for all parties, including humans and even amygdalines to some extent, and it could have been so much worse. But all the same, she wanted the juvenile gone. She had no desire to adopt or protect this one the way she had Ampersand.

"*Come to me, dear one.*"

She went down the long spiral staircase to his lair; the lights were dim and warm as he preferred, and it was even warmer down here than it was upstairs. His forelimbs weren't tucked under his body but lying in a circle in front of him like he was holding an invisible basket.

"*Come to me, dear one,*" he said again.

She sat down in the space he indicated, folding her limbs as he wrapped his around her gently. She'd dropped her bomb on the other side of the world, and now here both of them were, protected in their fallout shelter. They no longer needed to be protected from Nikola or Brako. Although rogue physeterines were now a concern, they weren't the biggest.

"Have you heard from Esperas?" she asked.

"*No, dear one. I do not believe he wants to be found.*"

She nodded, closed her eyes, and leaned her cheek against the side of his head. The unease she used to feel about Ampersand, especially after the first high-language success, was now gone. She was now the only human in history who had shared a consciousness with another person. And where before it would make her nervous, or giddy, or excited when he asked her to be close to him like this, that reaction was gone from her now, too. Now, it just felt natural and correct. Sliding in next to him was like sliding into a perfectly fitting house slipper at the end of the day.

"Do you want to try again soon?" she asked, leaning on the crest on his head. It was completely relaxed now in a way that it never was in the outside world.

"*I am ready, if you are.*"

"Will you want . . . something like last time?"

"*In what way?*"

"I mean like . . . the 'safe' memory, the one with Paris?"

"*We operated in extremes only out of necessity. I think it would be wise to explore less emotionally extreme memories and experiences before revisiting intense ones.*"

"Less extreme . . . both pleasure and pain?"

"*I believe that would be wise.*"

"So you want to ease into it."

"*I believe that would be wise.*"

Though this did elicit some nerves in her, that terror of being truly *seen* was now gone. There was something about the experience that removed even the potentiality for shame; even as he was going through one of her lived experiences in such vivid detail, he was also coming to understand the context. One day, perhaps, they might be able to go the other way, and she might know what it was like to be, well, him.

"*In a very short span of time, it was the most intense pleasure I've ever experienced, followed by the most intense pain. I could never imagine a body capable of enduring such pain, let alone surviving it, and I know that is far from the worst pain you have ever experienced.*"

Having shared that memory with him had sharpened it, and now just thinking about it, she could practically feel it, and she had to stop herself from checking to see if the skin on her back was still intact. It had become the sharpest, clearest memory in her head, and she physically recoiled from it.

"*I know I am only beginning to come into an understanding as to what existence is like for you, but even with such a limited understanding, know this.*" His grasp around her body tightened, slowly, fluidly, like tree roots growing around a stone. "*I will never allow you to suffer like that again.*"

She started to tell him, "I love you," but didn't feel compelled to, nor did she particularly need to hear it from him, either. Those words meant nothing to him because that was not how he expressed love. And there was a part of her, a part that was no longer human, that was relieved.

But the part that was human was still there and felt incomplete. Still wanted to be around other humans, to share things with them. To read and hear their words, to empathize with their losses, to see their faces light up with excitement when they introduced her to a new anime they could watch together, or went on walks with them in some Brooklyn neighborhood that most people overlooked.

"Ampersand, really, what are the odds of us succeeding if we leave Earth and try to save the species somewhere else?"

"*Remote.*"

"Remote?"

"*Extremely remote.*"

"And the odds of the Superorganism leaving human civilization alone?"

"*Extremely remote.*"

"Hopeless, you might say . . ."

"*In terms of probabilities, yes.*"

Her posture relaxed until her face was buried in his neck, and she felt him close his eyes and lean toward her. She thought of Paris at the awards ceremony in her cream-colored dress, perfectly tailored to her form, her hair crowning her head in an almost perfect sphere. How she'd wanted to talk to her about everything but didn't know if she could summon the courage to do so even if she hadn't been about to drop the bomb about Nils. Paris could change the world like Kaveh did without having to give her life to do it, but wouldn't she need all the help she could get?

"Do we have to go?" Cora asked, voice small. "If the odds of us effecting change either way are so remote, do we have to go?"

"*If I am here when the Superorganism arrives, they will take me. Even if the Superorganism allows this civilization to continue for another generation, or several, they will take me.*"

"I won't let them take you," she said, sitting up straight. "But if you even think of leaving Earth without me, or especially without telling me, I'll never forgive you."

"*I wouldn't disrespect you like that, my love. Our decision will be mutual.*"

She nodded and again relaxed against his head, felt the strange texture of his skin on her cheek. "Holy apostle Judas Thaddeus. Pray for me in my hour of need, bring help where help is almost despaired." Ampersand said nothing, only watched her as if waiting for an explanation. "Prayer to your namesake," she said. "The patron saint of hopeless causes."

"*Regardless, it is not my kind who is threatened with extinction, it is yours.*"

She sat up again, gazing at nothing as his words soaked in. It would be stupid *not* to leave Earth. It would be like staying put on a beach despite knowing a tsunami was on its way. But no, that wasn't a perfect metaphor, was it? After all, a person sitting on a beach despite an

offshore earthquake already having happened could not alter the outcome of the tsunami, but this wasn't so simple. Earth's odds of surviving true First Contact were "*remote*," but not impossible. They could
not control that a wave was coming, but they might be able to alter its
course. What had Sol said to her not one hour ago?

*Out of everyone on this planet who spends their life clawing for power,
the Putins and the Julians of the world. Why them and not you?*

"Why them and not us?" she whispered.

"*To whom do you refer, dear one?*"

Two years ago, Obelus had warned her that Ampersand would eventually feel compelled to dominate Earth if he stayed long enough, and
she had taken it for granted that that was an outcome to be avoided at
all costs. But now, for the life of her, she could not remember why she
had thought that. Ampersand who was bred to this purpose, who did
not crave power for power's sake but because he knew he was the most
capable, who actually *understood* what the human superorganism was
up against—who better than him to be in control? The Julians and the
Putins of the world were only growing in power, and they were the reason the Pequod Superorganism was all but guaranteed to bring an end
to civilization on Earth.

"Militarists are taking over the world," she said airily, and turned to
look at him. "Why them and not us?"

"*An intriguing question, my love. I have been contemplating the same.*"

ABOUT THE AUTHOR

Emily St. James

LINDSAY ELLIS is a *New York Times* bestselling author, Hugo Award finalist, and video essayist who creates online content about media, narrative, literature, and film theory. After earning her bachelor's degree in cinema studies from New York University's Tisch School of the Arts, she earned her MFA in film and television production, with a focus on documentary and screenwriting, from University of Southern California's School of Cinematic Arts. She lives in Long Beach, California. Her debut novel, *Axiom's End*, was an instant *New York Times* bestseller.